A VAMPIRE'S HEART

ELLOWYN FOUND 1

KAYLEIGH SKY

ALSO BY KAYLEIGH SKY

Backbone

Pretty Human

Doll Baby

Trinkets

Angel Dork

Jesus Kid

No Luck

This book is a work of fiction. Any references to historical events, real people, or real places are used fictitiously. Other names, characters, places, and events are products of the author's imagination, and any resemblance to actual events or places or persons, living or dead, is entirely coincidental.

Published 2018.

For information, address Kiss Drunk Books in writing at 712 Bancroft Road, Ste 277, Walnut Creek, CA 94598.

ISBN: 978-1-7329134-0-0 (ebook)

ISBN: 978-1-7329134-1-7 (paper)

Editorial services: Susan Selva

Cover: Tiferet Designs / tiferetdesign.com

THE ELLOWYN ROYAL FAMILIES
In order of rank

Dinallah
Nezzaram
Orla
Gennarah
Lotis
Senera
Wrythin

CAST OF CHARACTERS
In alphabetical order

Bettina, vampire, the Senera's cook and mother figure to Jessa

Brillen Acalliona, vampire, the murder victim

Fritt, vampire, the Senera's butler, bane of Mal's life

Isaac, human, works as a blood donor for Comity House, a friend of Jessa and also his donor

Jessamine "Jessa" Senera, half human, half vampire, a prince and also a "drainer" who can only survive on real blood instead of the synthetic product most other vampires drink

Malia "Mal" Senera, vampire, a princess, sexy, intense, and protective of her little brother, Jessa

Mateo, human, a blood donor for Comity House, implicated in the murder of a vampire

Moss Goran, vampire, Zev's cousin and confidant

Otto Jones, human, a detective with the Comity police, angry and embittered, seeking the murderer of his sister, Maisie

Prydwen "Wen" Wrythin, vampire, owner of Comity House and social climber, betrothed to Jessa in order to improve his family's royal ranking

Rune Senera, vampire, a prince and head of the Senera family, challenged his father Qudim in order to end the war with the humans and abdicated his position as the future King

Solomon Frenn, vampire, artist, and owner of True Heart Consignments

Upwood Prosper, vampire, a detective and Otto's partner

Uriah, vampire, protects Rune in his travels, former enforcer for Qudim, and cousin of the Seneras

Zeveriah "Zev" Dinallah, King of the Vampires, accepted Rune's abdication

1

THE RUN-IN

THE SECOND BLOOM was a dumb-ass name for a bar, but Otto liked the dark interior and the usually quiet customers.

Tonight, of all nights, he didn't want conversation.

"No fucking reason to bother anymore," Otto muttered as he sped past the pink neon sign and swung his car around the block.

With any luck his heart would explode and do away with his shit life. It threatened to anyway, not that he gave a damn, because it wasn't like it mattered. Until he remembered. *You aren't done yet, asshole.*

After he pulled to the curb, he locked up and headed down a short alleyway to a private parking lot for the nearby businesses. A single light fixture attached to the building at the end of the alley lit his way.

At first, the only sound was his footsteps until a chuckle reached his ears, and he tensed at the mean-ass sound of it. The slow drum of his heartbeat eased some of the pressure inside as he crept to the end of the alley. The parking lot wasn't large, mostly for people who worked at the businesses on the block. In the center of the space at the edge of illumination from a street lamp, three guys surrounded another guy, oblivious to Otto. One of the guys smacked the one they surrounded on the shoulder and rocked him back a step. Their target wore jeans and a hoody, arms wrapped around a satchel he held in front of him.

"Say you're sorry," said the ringleader.

"Sorry," came a mumbled reply.

"Faggot."

Humans. Only humans gave a fuck about that kind of thing anymore. Vamps didn't give a damn who they screwed, and they called the shots now no matter how it looked on the outside.

Another slam on the shoulder knocked the guy back again while one of the other guys grabbed onto his bag and jerked it out of his grip. It smacked the damp pavement, and the guys laughed until Otto strode forward and drew their attention.

Three gazes swung his way.

He yanked his badge out of his jacket pocket. A few millimeters over and he'd have grabbed his gun. So close. He didn't trust himself anymore, and these assholes didn't know how close they'd come to something a lot worse than a pissed-off cop about to shoo them away.

"Fuck you doin'?" he growled.

"Nothing," said one.

"Nothing? Looks like fuckin' assault to me, assholes."

"Officer—"

"Detective. Get the fuck outta here."

Not only did Otto not want the temptation of taking his rage out on the kind of people he hated most, he wanted a drink, not a trip to the station and an hour of paperwork. He was good with sending their asses scattering.

"Go!"

They bolted between the cars and fled toward the busy street.

Christ, no fucking balls. That was the trouble with bullies. They gave no satisfaction the minute anybody bit back.

He flipped the cover closed on his badge and slipped it back into his pocket.

The other guy knelt on the pavement outside the rim of the light. Otto's shadow drowned him in darkness. With a frantic jerkiness he swept a pile of... *romances?*... toward the mouth of his bag.

The image of a guy's naked torso and a woman's body held tight in the curve of a bulging arm decorated one of the front flaps. *His Saving Grace.*

Romances.

The guy wiped the covers off on his jeans before he crammed them back into his bag. His hands shook, and Otto frowned. Was that nail polish? Yeah, it was. And whatever the color, it was dark and chipped. The guy had short, nibbled-down nails. Not much to decorate. Every bit of tension seeped out of Otto's body, and a weird pain stabbed him in the chest and stole his breath instead. He swallowed a gasp at the shock of it and yanked back the hand he'd stretched to the frantic figure stuffing books into his bag.

Tenderness swamped him.

Maisie.

This bewildering rush of emotion had to be a flashback to Maisie, the most unromantic person Otto had ever known, and her collection of romantic novels. *"Find me a guy like this,"* she'd *laughed, tapping the bare-chested hottie on the cover, "and I'll give up my wicked ways."*

Too late.

Well, this guy didn't need his help anymore, and Otto was a long way from hero material anyway.

"Maybe you shouldn't be out by yourself," he snapped.

"Sorry... I—"

The guy threw a glance upward and Otto caught a glimpse of dark eyes and nostrils pinched thin in the cold. But it was cool out, not cold, so maybe a skinny nose was normal for him.

The guy lurched up with his bag. "I'm going."

Well, he wasn't a kid, not with that voice. It had a good weight to it, though he was light on his feet. Otto stared as he bolted out of sight down the alley.

Glowering at the energies raging inside him now, Otto squeezed the back of his neck and continued across the parking lot. He entered the bar through its back door and spotted a pair of vampires sitting at the counter.

Fuck my life.

Vampires everywhere. Even at work. Especially at work. His boss's voice jangled in his head. *"Otto. Come over here and meet your new partner. Upwood Prosper."*

Maybe if he drank himself blind, he'd wake up in the morning and discover today was one big cosmic joke and Upwood Prosper was still only a lousy memory he'd never have to deal with again.

Previously an enforcer in one of the underground cities, Prosper had been among the first vampire hires to a human police force—and the asshole who'd botched the investigation into the murder of Otto's sister. After the case went cold and his father died, Otto had moved almost seventy miles away, never expecting he'd have to deal with Prosper again. A million years of never setting eyes on the bastard sounded good to Otto, but no, the vamp had to go and apply for a detective opening in Otto's new town, and now... Now he was Otto's partner.

A second drink warmed his belly but brought none of the fuzziness he wanted. Too much adrenaline from the encounter in the parking lot.

Romances.

The guy was a walking target. Was that why they'd picked him to bully?

Otto hated bullies. And hated he actually was one a lot of the time, but his resolve to be better always dissolved at—

The vampires at the other end of the counter laughed.

Jesus fucking Christ. They sounded human. That was the kind of thing that held Otto up—twisted his insides into a knot only booze could loosen. He hated vampires and the way they congregated at every café and coffee shop. The pair at the end of the counter played a game with a handful of colored stones. They were weird with their games, like kids. One flashed its fangs, the glistening curves shadowed with tattoos Otto was too far away to see in detail. The creepy things grew back like lizards' tails. Otto guessed that made sense though. Each fang had a vein in it that pulled blood into a hollow chamber where it mixed with an enzyme that catalyzed the breakdown of proteins. The enzyme was fragile in the open air, so they had to bite to survive. *Nothing personal.*

Until Otto was thirteen, the world had been normal. Then a fracking accident by Nova Energies sparked a flurry of earthquakes along a web of underground faults and the vampires fled their collapsing cities.

They were the things of myths and nightmares.

Murderers.

Otto pushed his empty glass across the bar, still with no relief from the sharp edges inside him. As afraid as he'd been of humans, that little romance lover in the parking lot was probably terrified of vampires.

So?

Why the hell did Otto's thoughts keep returning to him?

Better than thinking about vampires.

He picked up his fresh glass and took a swallow.

Nothing. Nothing but a fire in his belly.

He oughta go home, but he wasn't going to. He oughta eat his gun, but he wasn't going to do that either. Not until he found Maisie's murderer.

Not until he made the bastard pay.

2

THE MURDER

THE WHORE BIT HIS LIP, heart pounding a little faster at the sight of the empty field across the street. He hugged the edge of the building, staying away from the spill of light from the street lamp. Ghostly buildings, still and silent, surrounded him. He'd fucked and fed a lot of guys in darkened alleyways, but he was afraid this time. His stomach was a knot of nerves and hunger, and it was the hunger that drove him here. All he had to do was get through the next half hour and find the nearest restaurant. He didn't care what kind of food, he'd eat anything right now, but he really, really wanted a burger. A green chili cheeseburger. His mouth watered at the thought. With French fries. And maybe a beer, though a Coke would be good too. But that burger...

His stomach twisted.

Maybe the guy wouldn't show up. He edged closer to the curb, out in the open now, but still no one approached him, no one called out. His throat tightened, and tears stung his eyes. He was too old to cry about this, and he'd gone too long to give up. Sooner or later they'd find him, but he was goddamned if he'd go easy.

He stepped onto the street. The touch of cool fingers against his neck shot terror through him. He whirled around, back pedaling. A vampire raised his hands, palms out. "I didn't mean to scare you."

"You fucking snuck up on me in the middle of the night. Jesus."

The vampire chuckled. "I love the taste of adrenaline."

Sicko.

But he wasn't about to say that and chase the guy away. "I thought you changed your mind," he muttered.

"No. Not at all." The guy approached, one hand still up, until he was near enough to slide an arm around him and steer him to the field. "Come on. Let's enjoy the night."

A half hour. A green chili cheeseburger. It would be over soon.

He let out a nervous laugh when the vampire took his hand.

"Are you afraid of me?" the guy asked.

"No. Of course not."

But he was. He was slipping into dangerous places, chased by hunger and fear. But he told himself he didn't need to be. The guy he was meeting had a donor card though this was a private transaction, and he wasn't about to turn down twice his usual fee. Maybe that was the thing that scared him. He'd do it for pocket change.

"Why this place?" he asked.

They were in the middle of the field now. The dark hulk of a warehouse stood behind them, commercial businesses all around. All dark and still. The sounds of life were so close. Would anyone hear him if he screamed?

The vampire pulled him into a hug and held him close to his chest.

"I like to be out in the open," said the vampire. "It's such a treat."

He shivered at the tingly scrape of fangs over his jugular. Feeding was... orgasmic in itself. The melting of bones in rapturous warmth. And he got paid. One more day free and alive. But a longing in him—a longing for a love he'd long ago lost—clouded his mind with grief for a moment. Until the vampire's chuckle dragged him back. Remembering himself, he pushed his stiffening cock into the guy's palm. The whisper in his ear came from miles away.

"Tell me... Do you feed Jessamine?"

A sudden unease stirred the hairs on the back of his neck. *Who?* Shit. He had no idea if he was supposed to know the guy. The name was familiar, but... "Who?"

"The prince. Jessamine. I believe he is a client?"

Was he? "The prince? I... No."

Cool air brushed his crotch. He gazed down at the open fly. The vampire pulled him out of his pants. A car passed in the distance. All so normal.

"Who?" asked the vampire.

A tongue swiped his neck. A nibble of teeth. Fingers stroked, and a breath warmed his skin. His limbs dragged at him, and he slumped against the body holding him.

"What?"

"Who feeds Jessamine?"

"I don't..." He racked his brain, rummaging through his memory. A name floated up to him. "Isaac," he whispered.

The pain of the fangs sinking into his neck shot fire into him. Through the bliss, fear rose. Too close. Too close to his jugular. He jerked while his hips bucked of their own accord.

The vampire hummed.

Darkness swept over him, clouding his mind, but a voice clamored in his head. *This isn't right. Run! Run!*

The city lights flashed and dimmed. He sank, falling...

Crashing onto the ground. Adrenaline spiked through him,

and he rolled away and staggered up into a billowing fog. As he ran, he gasped and sawed at the air. The ground resisted him, pitted and soft. He fell, crawled, and sprang to his feet again. At the parking lot, he stumbled and glanced back in a panic, but nobody pursued him. Nothing was there at all. Only the dark.

The vampire was gone.

Turning away again, he ran toward the city lights.

3

THE SCENE

A COP PULLED the blanket off the body, and Otto stared into the dead vamp's cloudy gaze. A glimpse of a tattoo tugged at him, dragged his stare down a bloodless face to a broken infinity sign, and Maisie's cynical grin floated into his memory.

Hell if he cared about solving this crime. What was another dead vampire to him?

Except he was here with a sledgehammer pounding against the inside of his skull. God, he wanted a drink. The snap of a camera beside him drove nails into his brain. He'd gotten, what? Two hours sleep.

"Almost done," came a woman's voice. Soft, as though the winces he hid at every syllable she spoke weren't so hidden after all.

He glanced at her and nodded.

The body lay in a lot the size of a football field that bordered the gray hulk of the warehouse behind him. Tall weeds stood straight in the hazy light. A crazy zigzag path cut from the body across the field to the corner of the parking lot where it met the sidewalk. Weird. If it'd been made by the killer, why zigzag unless somebody had been chasing him. Or her. Otto let his gaze drift across the uniforms to a small crowd hovering on the street. A tall vampire with his hair in a tight bun stood talking to a guy in running shorts and a T-shirt. Otto's stomach clenched, pushing acid into his throat. Fucking vamp was the reason he'd drunk himself stupid, hoping to escape the memories of Maisie that kept swamping back.

He strode to the patrol sergeant standing by a ramp that led into the warehouse.

"Any luck?" Otto asked.

"Not yet."

Otto's gaze rose to the cameras above the corrugated door at the top of the ramp. One pointed forward down the ramp, the other two angled to the sides. With any luck they'd get something on the film because Otto wasn't getting any kind of vibe from the scene. And that was weird too. Usually there was something, something that hit a chord inside him.

"What kind of warehouse is this anyway?"

Hamilton's was the name on the sign above the front door.

"Glass."

Probably a good business considering the vamps's inexplicable fondness for the stuff. Glass jewelry, bowls, vases, artwork. They had a thing for drinking Synelix out of elaborately decorated glassware. Though Otto shouldn't complain. It was the fake blood that brought the peace, and some of them actually liked the damn stuff. *Ghouls.*

"Hey!"

Otto spun. Across the field, Upwood Prosper bolted after the guy in running shorts. There was no chance of escaping a vampire. Prosper routed him after a few steps. He probably didn't break a sweat doing it. Probably didn't spend the night in his cups trying to banish Otto from his thoughts. Trying to forget the murder of his sister and the cop who'd investigated it. Otto hadn't been a cop nine years ago. It had been Prosper's job to find her killer, yet he hadn't. Was Maisie's murder even important to him? Or only one of dozens that had crossed his desk? If Prosper remembered her and Otto—and he had to—he gave no clue.

"Keep me posted," Otto said and headed across the field, skirting the beaten down path.

A cool lick of wind reminded him of the clouds hovering on the horizon, waiting to wash away the evidence of whatever had happened here.

The guy Prosper had corralled held up his hands, palms out. "I thought we were done."

Prosper glowered down at him. "What part of 'don't go far,' didn't you understand?"

"I thought you meant out of town. Look, I'm sorry, but I have to get to work, and I didn't see anything anyway. I was just passing by. I always run this way."

"Did you make the path?" Otto asked, stepping sideways and gesturing at the tromped-down ribbon.

"No. I use the sidewalk."

Otto's gaze dropped to his shoes. Clean enough, though the path was grassy not muddy, but there were no grass stains either. He nodded. "You can go." Prosper's head snapped around. "We'll let you know if we need anything else."

The guy darted off.

"The fuck," muttered Prosper.

Otto's head throbbed, and the words in his mouth burned like the acid in his belly. "How much energy you gonna spend chasing ghosts this time."

Prosper tipped his head back and a smile stretched across his face in slow motion. "This time?"

"You heard me."

Otto headed back to the body.

"Gonna make this as tough as you can, huh? Not sure what you have against me."

Surely he was baiting Otto. Nobody was that stupid. No way he forgot about Maisie that easily. Now it was Otto who had to find her killer, and he didn't plan to fucking rest until he did. Find him and peel his skin off in the blazing sun. If the sun ever blazed anywhere anymore. Though the sky was a clear blue, purple clouds piled on the faraway horizon, and that weird mist floated at the other end of the field. A gray ribbon of fog, rising and sinking as though caught on a current.

The yellow blanket covered the corpse again.

Otto ignored Prosper. A few of the local businesses had opened, and employees and customers stood on the sidewalks. A couple cops had gone to talk to them. Otto would follow up with his own questions later. It annoyed people to have to go over it again, but tough fuck, because Otto put a lot of stock on his gut reactions and getting a feel for a scene. That was probably the only reason he still had his job. His imagination leaped from scattered clues to the face of a killer with not much to go on. Nine times out of ten he was right. This time though? This time he was getting jack from the scene, but he circled the block anyway, noting the vehicles, the business names on the doors, the whish of an occasional car, the curious faces. Something might return to him.

He made his circuit twice before he approached the body again. This time the blanket lay at the vampire's side. Prosper's dark gaze held him tight. "You see this?" he asked.

The thing Prosper meant was the broken infinity sign. Up close, the tattoo was unmistakable. Only a group of vampires called drainers wore them. They were required too, actually. "Yeah," he said.

"Hate crime?"

"Something to think about."

Drainers made Otto's skin crawl. Just being a vampire was bad enough, but drainers were vamps whose bodies rejected Synelix. Mixing vampire enzymes into a glass of human blood didn't work either. They had to bite. Without fresh blood they killed in a frenzy of hunger and drained their victims dry. Though it wasn't their fault, Otto cared no more about the reason for it than he cared why other vampires hated drainers too. But they did, and drainers didn't usually go out alone. They got their blood from donor centers, and it was a legitimate job to feed them. Supposedly, it paid well. Humans who failed to get in at a center, sold it on the streets. Blood whores were illegal, but prostitution had always been illegal, and not much ever stopped it.

"Wonder why he was alone," Prosper said. "It was almost an invite."

"No sign of a struggle."

"Maybe he wanted it," Prosper said.

From the look of him dead, you'd hardly know he was a vampire, let alone a drainer. Otto didn't want to think maybe this was the drainer who'd killed Maisie and had finally gotten his comeuppance. That would mean there was nobody left to hunt, nobody to make pay. Or worse, it would mean Otto would never know if this had been the guy.

He crouched down. The tattoo look washed out, like he'd had it for years, but drainers hadn't started to be marked until eleven years ago. A faint line crossed the mark like a scratch. He stood and cast a glance around until he spotted the woman with the camera who'd been taking pictures earlier. "Hey, Dina, come on over here, will you?"

She approached with a quizzical frown, clipping her pager to her belt as she walked. "Whadda you need?"

"You get this?"

He pointed at the vamp's neck.

Her frown turned into a bit of a scowl. "The tat?"

"The scratch."

"Not sure that's a scratch, but yeah, I got it. Got it all. You guys are free to do your thing."

Prosper rummaged through the vamp's jacket. It had been lying about two feet from the body, lain out in the weeds as though the guy had put it there.

Prosper held out his hand. "You got a bag?"

Otto pulled a freezer-sized baggie out of his pocket and held it open. Prosper dropped a key card into it.

"You know where that is?" he asked.

The key belonged to the Sheraton. *Why was he alone? Or was he?* "It's a couple blocks away," Otto said. "Within walking distance."

Prosper glanced at the empty parking lot. All the police vehicles were on the street. "You think that's what he did?" he asked. "Walked?"

"Or flew."

"Funny."

Prosper dropped a glossy brown and yellow stone in the bag and waved a flyer at Otto. "This is from the Sheraton," he said. "Some kind of jewelry convention."

Otto picked out the stone. "What's this?"

"Tiger's eye."

"I know that. It's got something written on it."

Plain surfaces were anathema to vampires, blank canvasses begging for design.

Otto stiffened as Prosper leaned in. "It's a letter. Means resurrection."

"What's it for?"

Prosper shrugged. "Could be for anything. Some people keep them for good luck."

People. What a fucking laugh. Creatures or demons, but not people. A drainer sure wasn't. A drainer was... well, that. A drain.

"Anything else?"

"Nope."

Prosper looked toward the horizon. Vampires weren't as pale as myth suggested, though they were still pretty damn pale, and they'd never lived in total darkness. *"They use bioluminescence,"* a lecturer at the police academy had once said. *"Think glow sticks. You'll find they are much like us."* The color of Prosper's eyes was a shade lighter than mud. He was probably good looking if Otto wanted to look at him that way, vampires usually were. He flashed Otto a grin. "Gonna rain. Let's go sit in my car and go over this."

"It won't rain for a while yet." The strange wisp of mist lifted in a curve like a wing. "I'm not sittin' in your car. Meet me at the Starbuck's by headquarters."

Otto focused one last time on the corpse in the weeds. There was no sign of struggle, but the dead vamp didn't look peaceful either. One leg had folded under the other, arms thrown to the side. No rings on his fingers, but his nails were grimy as though he'd dug into the weedy dirt. Otto flashed on another pair of hands, chipped polish on the nails, scooping tattered romance novels into a bag. Had the guy painted his nails for somebody in particular? The memory of a strange pain lanced through his chest again. He massaged the flesh over his heart—what he had of one—his mind filling with the image of a thin nose and a wild stare.

Romances.

Who had time for that?

Not Otto.

He looked up to see Prosper duck into his car. Otto had come from home and parked on the street a block away. As he watched Prosper reverse, he noticed the mist again, but now it floated into the sky and broke apart.

4

COFFEE BREAK

VAMPIRES WERE HUMAN, or so Otto was told. He chose not to believe it. The fuckers had fangs.

They all had dark hair, with some variation in shades, and light skin. No wings, though ridiculous of all, they claimed to be the children of fallen angels. Contrary to myth, they had no special powers but were stronger, lived slightly longer, and at dusk, at the right angle, they faded from sight. Dimming, it was called. They had lived underground for thousands of years in cities carved from rock, fishing the cave lakes, foraging for mushrooms, crabs, and ferns. They'd hunted too because they had never been far from the surface of the earth, and some had lived in the human world. The myths were true, but more romance than reality.

Romance.

What kind of guy read romances? And why the hell was Otto still thinking of him? Christ, he needed somebody to fuck. Tonight, the minute he got rid of Prosper, who was probably dillydallying right now to show Otto he couldn't order him around.

Whatever.

Otto tipped his chair back against the short wall behind him and sipped his coffee. The coffee shop was busy, all the tables outside taken, a line snaking out the door. The view around him gave no hint it wasn't pleasant here, normal. Pedestrians made their way down the sidewalk, and a handful of cars passed by. A slight tremor rolled underneath him, and he closed his eyes for a moment.

The earthquakes, usually small thankfully, were commonplace now, and sometimes Otto wondered if the earth wasn't destined to shatter and shoot into space. Other times he didn't think it hardly mattered.

The war with the vampires had lasted six years before a scientist from a company called SynTech Solutions developed Synelix and the vampire who was now king somehow got ahold of it. Otto didn't know the true story of how the vampire king got it or what happened to the scientist who'd created it, but one of the vampire royals had used it to negotiate peace. Though it was hardly a peace to Otto. Vampires ruled but pretended they didn't. Their cities had fallen, but they had been preying on humans for centuries. They were hardly innocent.

The clack of a set of keys dropping to the table broke into his thoughts. "Back in a sec," said Prosper.

Otto let the front legs of his chair drop to the ground and finished his cool coffee. A minute later, Prosper dragged out the chair across from him and sat down. "Drove by the hotel," he said.

"What for?"

"Just to check it out."

Otto stared, feeling his ire rise hot and painful. "You break the case with your dogged detective work?"

"Very fucking funny. What the hell is wrong with you, Jones?"

Why the hell didn't they sound alien, otherworldly, something not exactly like everybody else? "Let's make a plan and stick with it," he said.

"Fine. The manager of the Sheraton said the convention is a five-day event, going on three days already. Gave me this." He unfolded a piece of paper and shoved it across the table. "That was taken on the first day, at a meet and greet." Prosper tapped a figure in the flyer with a long square finger. "That's our guy. Name's Brillen Acalliona. A wholesaler from the Eastern District."

"Who are the others?" asked Otto.

The flyer was poor quality, something they'd probably done on site. Acalliona stood in the center of a group of other vampires, smiling with the loose good cheer that usually went with a lot of alcohol. Otto swallowed, throat burning. "They don't seem to mind him."

"I think he was hiding it. That sweater covers him up," said Prosper. "The manager had no fuckin' idea."

"That's not legal." The point of a tattoo on the neck was its visibility.

Prosper shrugged. "Neither's murder."

"True."

"With a five-day convention I'm thinking he'd need to feed somewhere."

"Maybe he got what was coming to him," said Otto.

He glanced into his empty coffee cup, pushed back in his chair, and ignoring Prosper's stare, headed into the coffee shop. The gloom was like a breath, cooling his burning eyes. Wood paneling lined the walls, the floor was a dull terra cotta, and the thick glass of the windows blocked the light. Otto was tempted to walk out the other door and leave Prosper behind him. But he was on thin ice with his job as it was, and the echo of his lieutenant's voice droned in his ears as he stepped up to order another coffee.

"*Can you at least pretend you're not coming off a bender, Otto? Look. I don't wanna lose you. Nobody else has your track record, but do me a favor. Quit this job if you don't want it anymore. Don't make me do it.*"

Did he want it? He glanced around at humans and vampires sitting together at impossibly small tables. Machines whined as milk frothed. Everything was fucking normal as though a goddamn drainer hadn't murdered his sister and a vampire hadn't been assigned to work with him. The same vampire who'd never had the least bit of interest in the murder of a blood whore.

"Five dollars, please."

Otto paid for his coffee.

He needed his job. The likelihood Brillen Acalliona had drained his sister was slim. He wasn't from their district or from Heritage where Otto and Maisie had come from. Her killer was probably still out there. Uncaught because Upwood Prosper had dragged his feet harassing Maisie's deadbeat friends instead of the fucking vampires who'd paid for her. "*It's a dangerous lifestyle,*" Prosper had told Otto's father.

"*My daughter's no goddamn whore, demon.*"

But she had been. Otto had known it, though their dad hadn't known much beyond his next drink.

At the nudge of somebody behind him, Otto made his way outside again. The glare of the sun hit him in the eyes. But still the rain threatened, and the street rumbled underneath him. He sat down.

"Comity House is about a mile north of the Sheraton," he said.

"So let's go."

Otto shook his head. "No. We're doing this right."

"What the fuck does that mean?"

"Honey. Do you know what honey is?"

Prosper rolled his eyes. "Yes, I know what honey is. What of it?"

"You catch more flies with it."

Prosper got a look as though he'd swallowed sour blood. "I hadn't planned to knock their door down."

"The owner is named Prydwen Wrythin."

"Wrythin. He's royal. Low though."

"Still royal."

Prosper shrugged and swirled his coffee in his cup. "Name only. But like I said, I wasn't planning on kicking his door down. I'm here to do a job. You want to make that difficult, I can accommodate you."

"We give him the courtesy of making an appointment."

A bark of a laugh erupted from Prosper's chest. "Courtesy. A pimp is only one step up from a whore."

"That's what I mean. Good will, Prosper. We use honey. Somebody drained the drainer, and it wasn't a human. We're looking for a vampire."

A thin smile crossed Prosper's face. "That means you need me."

"I need you to stay out of my way."

"You aren't pushing me off of this case."

"We have a convention full of people who might have seen something." Otto tapped the flyer. "We should interview these people and the staff. Get a list of conferences in other districts and other drainer murders."

"The drainer part might not mean a thing. If he hid it, maybe nobody knew. Just got lucky."

Fucker. There was no sensible reason for that comment to bother Otto because he didn't like drainers any better than the next person. Blowing off this guy's case was as easy for Otto as Prosper blowing off Maisie's murder, and maybe that was it, maybe he wasn't ready to extinguish that last part of him that still gave a damn about a stranger's life. Even a drainer's. Something about this murder didn't sit easily with him. Something telling him it wasn't simple bad luck that had put Acalliona at the wrong place at the wrong time.

"I want to see if he had a car or rented one. Canvas the neighborhood again. If he walked there, maybe somebody saw him."

"In a commercial district? In the middle of the night? Not likely."

"Where was his donor card?"

"Hotel safe maybe?" Prosper shrugged. "Something to check."

"You check it."

Prosper grinned. His white teeth flashed, and somewhere behind his sharp canines, sharper fangs hid. "Trying to get rid of me?"

"Splitting up is more efficient."

"You aren't going to Comity House without me."

"I'll go back to the scene. If the manager shows up, I'll check on the security footage. In the meantime, you find out whatever you can at the Sheraton, and we'll meet up tomorrow at the blood center."

"I don't trust you, Jones."

"Like I give a fuck, Prosper."

Prosper's laugh followed him as Otto headed to his car. Part of him wanted to return to the scene, but he doubted the chaos had died down enough yet not to stab into his brain like knives. Another part of him wanted a drink. Something cheap and strong to burn out the niggle of dread in his gut.

You better not.

He snorted as he slid behind the wheel.

Yeah, right.

5

FEEDING

JESSA SPRAWLED on his belly on Isaac's bed in Comity House, held onto Isaac's arm, and bit. The gush of blood into his mouth cooled the raging heat inside him. He gulped at first then slowed to let Isaac's blood coat his tongue, savoring it.

"Swallow," Isaac murmured.

He stroked Jessa's back slow and easy, and Jessa obeyed. What choice did he have? Being a drainer shamed him, that's why he hated to feed and resisted his hunger as long as he could, but his memory of being sick—of almost dying, actually—was still as sharp-edged as terror.

After a moment, he pulled his fangs out of Isaac's wrist and flopped onto his back with a gasp.

"Jessa! What the hell? Are you okay?"

Isaac perched over him, gazing down with panicky eyes.

Strange. Yet, Isaac had been acting strange since Jessa arrived here. A frown formed on his face, but he made himself smile. "Just not hungry, I guess."

"Liar. You never feed enough." Isaac gave a wink that clashed with the worry on his face and said, "Unless you've found somebody else to slake your thirst. Is he pretty?" Isaac asked, a smile dancing on his lips.

"Goof."

Jessa visited Isaac once a week, though many drainers fed two or three times that much.

"I mean it though, Jessa. What's wrong?"

Isaac's question stumped him. He was wrong—a failure as a vampire and a human. Yet, if he said it out loud... It was as if the wall of denial protecting him would crumble like the underground cities. If the Upheaval hadn't happened... Well, he'd be like every other vampire. Nobody would have to be afraid of him the way he was afraid he might have once drained somebody in a mad frenzy he'd wiped out of his memory... and his family had lied to him about it. Maybe he was a murderer.

"I wish I could drink Synelix."

Isaac sighed. "I guess I'm a dick because I'm happy you can't myself. You're my only real friend, Jessa."

Jessa leaned over until their foreheads touched. "Rune says nothing is chance."

Jessa wasn't sure he believed that though. Thinking anything was within his power didn't mesh with thinking nothing was and making the best of it.

And making the best of it was what Jessa did. He'd gotten some good things out of his life so far.

When he'd fallen ill the first time, Mal had put him in a room in the castle they lived in that had a view of the gardens and the mountain. The room had clearly belonged to a young girl once—all white and gold and frilly—light filled and airy as a cloud. Mal had bought him a store's worth of stuffed animals. He seldom had the energy to get out of bed, but the toys had kept him company. And then he'd found the books piled on the built-in bookshelves in the closet. Romances and detective novels. He'd burrowed back in bed with his newfound treasures, his heart stuttering over the heroes on the covers. Strong and brave and beautiful. Too bad he wasn't beautiful.

He bit his lip. "I want to be normal though."

"You are. You have to drink blood. That's normal for you."

"Not draining people."

Only rogue vampires drained people on purpose. The stories of "turning" humans were myths. Only murderers did that.

"Be patient, Jessa. Somebody's going to come up with something better than Synelix any day now." He smiled. "And I'll be out of a job."

Jessa frowned again. A strange tone tugged at Isaac's voice, stretching it as thin as glass. Jessa half expected it to shatter. Something was wrong.

"Are you okay, Isaac?"

"Why wouldn't I be? You're the one not eating."

Jessa scooted back into the corner of Isaac's bed and leaned against the wall. "In a minute," he said. "We have time."

Isaac lay on his side, propped on his elbow, and dropped his arm into Jessa's lap. "Fifteen minutes. I have to meet a new client."

Jessa sighed but didn't pick up Isaac's arm right away. A wisp of longing stirred inside him. What would it be like to drink from somebody he was madly in love with? The thought scared and excited him, but it was a silly waste of time to imagine because it was never going to happen. Feeding from a fated love was as rare as finding a blue rose. And hoping for it was like hoping for a gorgeous hunk to jump off the cover of one of his romances. Or for somebody like the guy who rescued him in the parking lot the other day.

And that reminded him. "I have something for you."

Isaac groaned as he scrambled off the bed. "Jessa."

"Just a minute." He grabbed his bag from where he'd dropped it on the floor when he came in. "I got these for you."

Isaac approached and wrapped his arms around Jessa's waist, looking over his shoulder as Jessa rummaged in the bag. "On your illicit book run?"

Jessa snorted. "It's stupid for Uriah to have to drive me places when I should be able to go out on my own. I'm just like everybody else."

"Yeah, but drainers are an easy target for people who don't want peace between us. Just give it time. Everybody will get used to each other."

"I hope so. Anyway, I found these. I almost got caught, but it was worth it."

Isaac let him go and took the mysteries Jessa passed to him, saying the titles out loud. "*A Taste of Death. The Snowman. Tripwire. Double Indemnity.* This one's real old."

Jessa dropped his bag again. "Is that okay?"

Isaac kissed his cheek. "It's amazing."

When he pulled away, he grinned, and Jessa's heart swelled. It was so easy to make Isaac happy. Sometimes it scared him how easy it was because it reminded him of how little Isaac had.

"You are amazing," Isaac added, and Jessa blushed.

While Isaac made room on his little bookshelf, Jessa gazed out the window. Comity wasn't much of a city. Most buildings were shorter than they were tall and sprawled all the way around the base of the mountain. But Comity House was on several acres planted with lush gardens that made Jessa feel at home when he visited here. He loved flowers and fashioned floral themes into most of the jewelry he made, though he was seldom allowed to work. Certainly not without one of his cousins in attendance.

"I feel like the air right before a storm," he said. "You can feel the pressure building and building until you want it to burst. I wish they'd find a cure, but like you said, you'd be out of a job if they did. Everybody here would be, so why would they bother?" He moved his fingers to his neck, hovering over the mark there as though it had a magnetic pull to it. "We're profitable."

Isaac came up behind him. "I'm not going to say people aren't that cold, but you can't give up, because it's an allergy, and people grow out of allergies all the time."

"I'm twenty-three."

"That's young."

"Older than you."

Isaac didn't reply, so Jessa gazed at his reflection in the glass. He was young and homely with a skinny nose and a thin upper lip. His bottom lip was full, and the two looked weird together. His hair was a bizarre mix of colors, not dark like every other vampire, his eyes more amber than brown. He was fast and limber, but not as strong as most vampires. And he drank blood, so he didn't even make a good human.

"Come on," said Isaac. "Drink some more."

Giving in now, Jessa returned to the bed, propping himself on Isaac's pillows. Isaac lay beside him, and Jessa cupped his elbow and the back of his wrist in his hands. The slide of his fangs coming out sent a frisson of pleasure through his body. He tugged Isaac's arm closer and sank his teeth into a long blue vein. The blood drenched his tongue, and his stomach rolled, but he drank anyway, pulling in long swallows. After a moment, he lifted away again and said, "Not too long."

"I won't let you," Isaac murmured.

The same enzyme that broke down the blood Jessa took in was present in his saliva and was supposed to boost Isaac's recovery and improve his immune system, but Jessa was half human and worried he'd fail in this way too. He sucked slowly, and a bitter flavor burned his tongue. Weird. Jessa's heart accelerated, and he took only a few more swallows before pulling away again. Isaac smiled and got up, but Jessa knew what that taste was now.

Fear.

Isaac tasted like fear.

6

FOG

CHUCK, the warehouse manager, was a tall guy with thinning hair, a barrel chest, and watery blue eyes. Otto followed him around the perimeter of the building while the guy pointed out the randomly spaced cameras. Not that Otto gave a fuck about any but the ones on the corner of the delivery ramp, but trailing the voluble manager in the early drizzle was a dozen steps up from Prosper's grating presence.

"Now not all of 'em work. Deterrent," the manager added, glancing back.

"You've had break-ins before?" Otto asked.

"Oh yeah. We have specialty glass in here. Orders from Prince Rune. I have very particular clients on top of my retail trade."

"The prince, huh?"

Chuck nodded. "Prince Rune often sources his own glass, and I do the purchasing and arrange for shipping. Not great amounts. All art quality though."

"For what?"

"I'm guessing art," Chuck said with a laugh.

Right. Ha, ha.

They circled back around to the steps leading to a single glass door. Chuck held it open. "After you."

"The film feeds to...?"

"A memory chip. They're all self contained, but again, they don't all work. Reception is spotty, as I'm sure you realize. Some of the cameras are in dead areas, but nobody but us needs to know that. Even the ones that work go in and out, but whatever I can do to help, just let me know, of course. I can't get over somebody being killed right outside my front door, so to speak. A vampire too. They aren't that easy to kill."

Easy enough for another vampire. Not so easy for humans.

"Looks like another vamp got this one," said Otto.

A tiny reception area led into a narrow hallway with dingy gray walls and cobwebs in the corners. The top of Chuck's head flirted with the ceiling. Otto was tall too and eyed the acoustic tiles warily.

Around the corner, a few doors lined the hallway. Chuck entered the last one, and Otto followed him into a spare office with a row of small, square windows set high in a wall. The light that drained in was pale and soft.

Chuck pulled out a chair. "Make yourself comfortable."

A computer monitor and DVR sat on a desk in a corner of the room. Bookshelves lined with fat red and green binders covered the other walls.

Otto sat. "What do I do here?"

Chuck tapped the keyboard. "It's all set for you. Click the arrow to start. You can fast forward and reverse, whatever you need. And this..." He pulled a box that looked like a speaker away from the wall, "is an intercom. Just press this button here and talk if you need me. I'll be here all day."

Otto nodded. "Thanks."

A moment later, alone, he stared at a screen that might as well be a still life for all that anything moved on it. The camera had caught a sliver of the parking lot and a long trapezoid of darkness that had to be the field. The lights had created a luminous gray gleam along the edge of the pavement. The timer at the bottom of the screen jumped in ten second increments. Otto fast-forwarded. Noises outside came in dull through the thick walls. The early morning coolness grew stuffy. The manager had made a copy of the recording, so Otto had no real reason to sit here, except it wasn't the station, wasn't someplace where he had to interact while his hangover eased. The blur on the screen didn't help, and he was antsy as fuck.

His hookup the night before had done nothing to dispel his pent-up energies. The guy's long dark hair had been too much like a vampire's probably, the skin showing between his ink, vampire pale, his nips pierced. When Otto had tugged on one of the metal bars with his lips, the guy had thrust his chest at him, practically chipping a tooth.

"Oh, sorry," the guy had gasped. "They're sensitive."

Otto's weren't, and he'd never seen the appeal of playing with them, but he knew some guys liked it, so he was willing to suck on their nips if they wanted him to, though his hookup was just as happy when Otto's focus had drifted to his shiny red cock. He'd stroked it while the guy rolled his hot ass until Otto let loose in the condom inside him and the guy collapsed with a laugh and said, "Fuck, that was nice."

It only took Otto a few minutes to thank him and get him the fuck out of his house, still as wired as when they'd arrived.

Now he pinched the bridge of his nose and stared at the screen. According to the coroner, death had probably occurred between midnight and four in the morning. The body had been discovered at five thirty. Time of death was difficult to establish with vampires. They were hardly undead, but they had an ability to recuperate from injuries mortal in a human. That had probably contributed to the myths surrounding vampires, but it also contributed to the uncertainties surrounding death. But Brillen Acalliona had been drained, and if that's what had killed him, there was no recuperating from that. So a four-hour period was likely.

Restarting the film at eleven, Otto sat with his elbows on the desk, fingertips rolling circles at his temples. The same shadows filled the monitor. The timer jumped—11:00:10, 11:00:20, 11:00:30... He forwarded it by fifteen minutes, watched for a few minutes more, then forwarded it by another fifteen minutes until a thickening of the darkness occurred at twelve forty-five. Otto straightened, reversed the film by three minutes, then restarted it. He wasn't sure what he'd seen. The picture jumped from an empty parking lot and field to an oblong a shade darker than the night. A second later the oblong took on a grayish cast. Ambient light shone around something that had moved in front of it. Otto squinted as though he might force a view of the black night.

What was it? And why here?

Because it was near the Sheraton. Within walking distance. But if Brillen was in that field, he wasn't alone. The shape in the dark was too big.

For three minutes and fifty-three seconds nothing happened. Then the film jumped ahead and the shape in the field shrank and expanded. They were moving but staying close together. Otto struggled to pick out their separate shapes. A fuzziness surrounded them.

A minute passed.

Then the movement grew jerky, and Otto leaned closer to the screen. This was the murder, but... He wasn't sure and strained to see, but the bigger figure, the one he thought was Brillen was... *absorbing?*... covering up the other figure. The amorphous blob wavered back and forth until—

Fog?

Otto stopped the film and leaned in close. That only made his vision worse. The snowy dots lost all shape. But that was fog. It was a dove gray color, opaque in places, transparent where the night penetrated like a physical thing. It gave the fog a mottled look. Otto drew back and started the film again. The fog enveloped the figures, hunkering low to the ground, growing lighter, darker.

It blew away. So suddenly Otto jumped. One of the figures ran, and the fog reformed over the other. A few steps took the escapee out of the camera range, but Otto knew he was following the beaten down path through the weeds, heading for the street.

Was that what it had been like for Maisie?

A desperate hope rose in Otto that the guy had gotten away. Nobody appeared to pursue him. After a few minutes the fog floated up, drifting as lightly as the mist he'd seen here the morning before.

What the hell?

Was the fog a coincidence? A weird but natural phenomenon?

If the camera had caught a body in the field, it wasn't visible to Otto, but he knew it was there. Fog didn't kill, and in the pit of Otto's gut that was the only certainty about this murder he could grab onto yet. He was as sure as he was of his own lost soul that whoever had run away from there wasn't the killer either.

So what the fuck was going on?

7

CHASED

OTHER THAN A TOWHEE hopping across the veranda, nobody was in sight. The kitchen was empty too, so there was no Bettina to spy on him through the patio door.

Slipping outside, Jessa ran for the garage. Rune's car was closest to the garage door and also the one Jessa most loved to drive. It had taken forever begging and pleading before Uriah had broken down and taught him. Now he jumped behind the wheel and pulled his knit cap over his head. The driveway split, leading in one direction to the front of the castle and in the other down the valley to a neighboring town now called Garnet. That wasn't where Jessa wanted to go, but it was better than pulling out in full view of the castle.

A few minutes later he flew along a narrow ribbon of pavement that wound through the foothills into Comity. It took his face hurting to realize he was smiling like a maniac as he drove. He wasn't a prisoner. He always had Uriah or one of his cousins to take him places. It was just that... Well, this time he was out alone.

On my own.

The wind tossed a few strands of hair that had worked out

from under his cap. The day was young with clean, puffy clouds in the pale blue sky. Rain was on its way, but it wasn't here now, and he was strong.

Like everybody else if he didn't think about the tattoo on his neck.

And that's what he wanted—to not think about the way he was different. He was pretty sure those bastards the other night had seen his tattoo, though all they'd seemed to care about was how he'd crossed in front of them in the parking lot and made them stop. His mind had been on his books and getting back to Comity House before Uriah arrived to fetch him home. Isaac would keep his secret, but if Uriah ever found out Jessa had gone out by himself, he'd tell Rune and—

Well, Jessa would be grounded for a thousand years.

So, yeah. At twenty-three, he needed his freedom. *And sex.*

Oh, yeah.

Jessa chewed his lower lip and thought of the big guy who'd saved him. He wished he'd gotten a good look at him, but with the light shining from behind the guy, he hadn't.

Imagining him made Jessa's belly hot and his balls heavy. He wanted something to grind himself against. Something hot and smooth like the dip inside the big guy's hip.

Jessa groaned.

The guy probably had dark eyes like a full vampire, burning and entrancing.

Shit.

He wriggled on his seat. He needed to stop thinking about this before he drove Rune's car off the road.

When he reached Garnet, he got onto the freeway and headed into Comity, trying to focus on Mal's birthday present. Money wasn't exactly an object, but Mal had no reservations about buying herself whatever she wanted. She loved her pleasures. Jessa loved flowers and jewelry and sex. At least he thought he loved sex.

Stop thinking about that.

But it was hard. The more he tried not to think about it, the more he imagined the big guy's hand on his dick, squeezing and pulling until Jessa stood on his toes, trapped by those burning eyes, spurting helplessly into those sticky fingers.

"Oh damn," he muttered.

He ached now. *Idiot.*

Luckily, there was nobody at the co-op. The city sprawled in front of him, the earlier clouds broken apart, the shine of the sun bright and cold.

The co-op was in a commercial section that was slowly limping back to life, but half the space was still unrented. The streets had been made for more cars than anyone drove now, but there was still light traffic as people took care of errands on their lunch hours. He parked in the service alley behind his building and used his key to get inside. In addition to a storage area, kitchen, and bathroom, there was a large space on the street side that was divided into sixteen stalls. Jessa didn't actually rent his stall because the Seneras owned the building—for him—but he made enough money from the sale of his jewelry to pay for it if he wanted to.

He headed through the quiet room to the last stall in the corner by the window.

His space was cluttered with plastic tubs and containers for his beads and crystals, jars and tubes of glue and paint, and spools of various grades and types of wire. Stuck to the walls was a collage of pictures he'd taken of the flowers he designed his jewelry around. His pieces sold well, and scaling up if he wanted to made sense, but like Rune, he created for the love of it. He already knew he needed acceptance and didn't want to add in the pressure of hoping strangers would like him enough to become his customers. The thought of it bent his shoulders with an invisible weight, so he made things when he wanted to, but today was about Mal.

At his worktable, he set down his bag and pulled out a collection of round copper medallions and several glass cabochons. His plan was to paint a sprig of wildflowers and make a necklace with the cabochon and a matching bracelet and earrings out of his best glass beads. The painting would be something small and intricate like the scrimshaw so many vampires had tattooed on their teeth.

After he'd gone through his tools and fetched the right sized brush and a hole-punch for the paper, he propped the photo of a sprig of yellow sweet clover under the window. As he painted, he thought of his own plant—at least, he thought of it as his own. He'd never seen another flower like it and had found no references to it. Rune had told him they were finding new species of plants all the time. His flower was yellow too with orange dots on it, a delicate cross between a sunflower and an orchid, except it grew on a vine and had tiny, serrated leaves. It was a little flower and hard to see. Jessa called it the Gold Star.

After he finished his artwork, he set it on the windowsill, grabbed his camera, and headed outside to take pictures of the wildflowers in the field while he waited for the painting to dry.

The yellow tape fluttering in the breeze didn't register until he started across the street. His stomach did a little flip. Well, that was strange. Had there been an accident? Or maybe a mugging? This wasn't the greatest neighborhood—one of the reasons he wasn't supposed to be out on his own. He was a drainer, and without trying, he tempted humans and vampires alike to hurt him.

As though *he* had been the cause of the war.

He paused when he came on the tape and looked around. Though the coffee shop on the corner was open, nobody sat at the tables outside or approached on any of the sidewalks, so he took a breath and stepped over the tape. Pastels and occasional splashes of jewel tones dappled the field with color. Lacy white crowns of wild carrot grew with sprigs of baby blue-eyes and buttercups. He took a couple shots before bending down to comb the weeds. He didn't expect to find his flower, yet there it was. The spark of orange caught his eye and he gasped in surprise. It was just beginning to bloom, a few stray blossoms on one tendril. He straightened, changed the focus on his lens, and bent down again.

"HEY!"

Jerking back, Jessa stared. Somebody was coming across the field at him. A big guy and moving fast. *Fuck.* Did the guy want to hurt him? Jessa's tattoo wasn't visible, not from this far away. He stumbled over a clump of dirt.

"Stay where you are! Police!"

Jessa spun, leaped over the yellow tape, and raced back down the street. The ricochet of the slanting sun on the plate glass windows half-blinded him, and he blinked, eyes smarting in the light as he zigzagged like an idiot, torn between going back for Mal's necklace and making a run straight for his car.

Rune's car.

Getting caught wasn't an option. Not pissing off the humans had been pounded into him from the first day they'd discovered he was a drainer.

Don't go out alone.
Don't make a fuss.
Don't argue.
Don't disobey.
Don't disappoint.

The last was the worst. Jessa's family trusted him. Veering away from the co-op at the last second, he made a beeline for the alley.

"POLICE! I'm ordering you to stop!"

The gravelly voice woke heat in Jessa's belly. He hadn't gotten much of a look at the cop's face, just the dark, short hair, but he imagined the guy was gorgeous and tough. He wasn't so interested he planned to stop and get a close-up though.

He grabbed onto the corner of a building, propelled himself into the service alley, jumped into his car, and got it going right as the cop came careening into the alley behind him. Slamming his car into reverse, Jessa gunned it out of the alley onto the street, where he shifted into drive and took off. He was already turning onto a cross street when the big guy trotted onto the pavement and stopped, dropping his hands to his knees.

Shaking, he gripped the steering wheel and took the back streets out of town. His lungs didn't want to take in any air, and he was dizzy by the time the trees hung over him again.

Luckily, Jessa was pretty forgettable, and the cop wasn't likely to know who he was. They hadn't gotten close to each other, and hopefully, Jessa had gotten far enough away the cop hadn't gotten a good look at Jessa's license plate either. Was he really as gorgeous as Jessa imagined—wanted him to be?

Were his hands rough? His skin hot?

A shiver ran down Jessa's spine and heat bloomed in his belly again. His attraction bewildered him in a way because he still fantasized about the guy in the parking lot. Vampires were gorgeous. Hot guys surrounded Jessa every day, so why was he fixated on these two?

Maybe it wasn't anything more than sex. He was long overdue. Isaac had had sex, and Isaac was twenty-two. Not that Jessa wanted to have sex for money. No, he wanted the kind of sex that would shatter his brain, fling him spiraling into unforgettable bliss, and give him the expression of ecstasy all the heroines on his book covers wore on their faces. Kiss-plump lips and dreamy eyes.

Was that even real, or a fantasy of romance novels like fated love?

Abadi, the first wife of Jessa's father, Qudim, had come to him through an arranged marriage. They hadn't loved each other and neither had been faithful. Jessa dreaded a loveless marriage. He wanted passion, but he understood duty. The story of Qudim's marriage to Jessa's mother, Dawn, warmed him to his soul. That was fated. They'd been fated to meet and marry, and when Qudim lost her, he lost his sanity.

Both Abadi and Dawn had died in the Upheaval. Before that, Abadi had attempted to murder Dawn and had been banished with most of her family. Jessa had been born of a love some people said only existed in myths. Maybe that's why he loved romances and happy ever afters so much.

True love was rare.

A treasure worth obsessing over.

A treasure that would never be his.

You have enough.

He was royal, and when he scaled the rise in the road as it curved toward the garage, the castle rose before him, its stone pale and bright in the sunlight.

The massive edifice was older than the Upheaval but only by a few years. It wasn't a real castle, only made to look like one, and had turrets on the corners and a pair of curved stairs in front that led to each side of a half circle portico. Trees covered him again then opened back up to a lawn and garden that extended to the faraway tree line. The mountain in the background rose craggy and green.

After Jessa returned the car to the garage, he peeked out the side door, waiting for somebody to accost him and haul him before Rune, but nobody did, so he hurried out and headed to his greenhouse.

The building wasn't large, but Jessa grew most of the

annuals they planted around the estate and a few perennials. He tossed his car keys on the table by the door and grabbed a hat off a hook. After cranking open a few windows, he pulled a cart away from the wall, loaded the bottom rack with bags of soil and set flats of pansies, stock, and violas on top.

The day passed as he loved it—with his hands in the dirt, doing something productive. Now, new flowers bloomed in all the planters that circled the castle.

Happy and sweaty, he returned his cart to the greenhouse, not entirely surprised to see Uriah waiting for him. Uriah's usual job was taking care of Rune, though Rune didn't really need muscle. It was just that his work took him into dangerous places sometimes, so Uriah, one of their distant cousins, was never far from his side.

With a sigh, Jessa pushed his cart back into its place against the wall then flashed Uriah a smile. "What's up, Uri?"

A slow smile crept onto Uriah's face. "What's up?"

Jessa shrugged. "Yeah. Does Rune want me?"

"No. But I'm to escort you inside."

Jessa hung his hat up. "I'm not done."

"Prince."

That was all Uriah had to say. Uriah wouldn't hurt him, and he had no fear of Mal or Rune either. They loved him, though probably too much. Jessa had no control over his illness, but it made him guilty anyway for the way it flowed into everybody else's life. Marrying would set his family free by turning him into somebody else's problem. Jessa knew his duty and would do it, but a part of him—the part that believed in true love—kept putting it off. Guilt ate into him for that one too, so he obeyed. He was complacent and amenable and cheerful—most of the time.

"Fine," he grumbled, grabbed his keys, and stormed outside.

Uriah appeared at his side a second later and kept pace with him. They entered the castle through a small door under the back steps and through the kitchen to a flight of stairs to the second story and Jessa's room where he stripped, washed the sweat off his body, and picked a new romance from his stash. A few hours later, Bettina brought him a bowl of soup and a plate of cheese and bread on a tray.

At some point, he fell asleep. He wasn't sure what woke him. The light was already on, so it wasn't that. He rolled over and squinted at Mal, who stood in the doorway with her arms crossed under her breasts, chin dipped down, eyeing him along her nose the way Uriah did. But Mal's smile danced on her face with dimples that played peek-a-boo on her cheeks. Her smile was like a viper's though. Fangs lurked underneath it.

With a sigh, she let her arms fall and crossed the floor. "What am I going to do with you, blossom?"

"Don't call me that."

She wrapped her arm around the pencil post at the foot of his bed and leaned her cheek against the pale wood. "It's an endearment."

"Well, I'm not a blossom. You are though."

Mal's smile broadened. Her skirt hugged her hips, black like the shimmery spaghetti-strap top she wore. She stood in thigh-high, six-inch-heeled boots. Long black braids spilled from a silver tie on the top of her head. Jessa's braids were always a mess, and definitely not that glossy black. Not like a vampire's at all.

"Flattery will not get you out of this room, my darling. You were bad."

"I'm grown, Mal. I want to work. I have a business to run."

She cocked her head, black eyes glittering. "I wasn't aware the co-op was open on Mondays. And besides, you know it's dangerous to go out alone."

"Lots of drainers go out."

"I doubt that, Jessa, and not one of them is a prince."

Being royal doubly flawed him somehow. He wasn't sure how that worked, other than being a colossal letdown to everybody.

"Take me out with you."

"Out where? I just got in, and I'm going to bed."

A quick glance to his window showed him the first hint of color in the sky. "Tonight."

She yawned behind her hand. Mal was like the vampires of myth. She tolerated the day, but she didn't love it.

"I have papers to grade."

"Did you meet anybody?" he asked.

"No." She released the post of his bed and returned to the door. "My fair princess continues to elude me."

"Is it because of me?" he murmured.

The days of the Seneras ruling the vampires had died with Qudim and the war, but Jessa was afraid their fall from importance had really been because of him. Before the Upheaval, he'd been normal. Drainers hadn't even existed. To Jessa, they were a constant reminder of the things vampires had lost, especially the right to drink blood as they had for thousands of years. But the Seneras had lost everything, and the thought it was Jessa being a drainer that had compounded their ruin stuck to him like his tattoo. Though maybe having a drainer in the family was a cosmic punishment for Rune turning on Qudim. But for Jessa, it always came down to him. His father had once told him the Seneras had special powers, but even with those powers, they had fallen to the second lowest family. That Mal and Rune had found somebody willing to marry Jessa bordered on the miraculous.

"Silly," she murmured back.

"I'm serious though, Mal. I really want to go out. Anywhere. I won't be a bother."

She dipped her chin again with her viperish smile. "I like to dance."

"I can dance," he lied.

Her smile widened. "We'll see."

After she'd gone, he got off the bed and stepped onto his balcony. The damp air stung. It was light enough now to reveal the shadows below and a pale wisp of mist in the trees.

Jessa shivered.

The mist was always there. Always watching.

COMITY HOUSE

TEN YEARS ago—ten years after the Upheaval and eleven months after Synelix distribution reached every city—the first bodies began to appear. The victims were all human and all completely drained.

The Ellowyn king dispatched his soldiers to maintain order and allowed the human police to investigate. His concession to the humans earned him enemies among the vampires who had not agreed to the peace in the first place.

The killers, when caught, refused to believe they had drained anyone, though they'd done little to hide it. Rounded up and held in custody, it wasn't until they attacked each other, and close to a thousand of them died of malnutrition, before anybody realized they had starved to death on Synelix. Only blood sated their hunger.

To appease the riotous humans, the King agreed to the marking of drainers. Other vampires hated drainers as a symbol of Ellowyn capitulation. Humans feared them. But with blood, warm and fresh from a vein, drainers posed no danger. Donor centers opened. Drainers were a minority, but even so, Comity and the towns around it were home to more than thirty thousand drainers and a dozen donor centers. One center, Comity House, catered to the wealthy and the royal family.

The collection of three-story buildings, all of them topped with giant antennae and satellite dishes, was something between a private hospital and the pricey hotel it had once been. The exterior was a pinkish stone, single story up front with a three-story atrium behind it and two sets of buildings on either side.

Otto parked in front of the entrance and strode to the steps, ignoring Prosper, who waited for him in the shade of an awning. Otto pushed past the doors into a room with a long wooden counter on one wall, chairs, couches, and tables dotting a... black rug.

Leave it to vamps to decorate the place like a fucking crypt.

"I'll be right with you."

The disembodied voice floated into the gloom. Heavy drapes in dark jewel tones covered the windows, yet the air was sweet with the scent of the flowers that decorated every flat surface. It was like a florist's shop in the bowels of hell.

"Booming business," Otto muttered.

"I think so," Prosper answered. "Over three thousand clients and one hundred and fifty donors. Minimum number running through here's gonna be about three hundred a day. There's five wings attached to this main one."

Otto glowered at him, but Prosper stood gazing at a mosaic of the sun on the ceiling spreading from a central chandelier.

"And you know this because?"

"I asked. Anything come up on that license plate yet?"

"No. I talked to a few people in the area. Not one business stays open after six p.m., and nobody admits to being there after hours."

"What's your theory with the video?"

"I don't have one. It's too early."

He'd requested a photographic enhancement of the scene, but he wasn't holding his breath on that.

In the next instant, Prosper dropped his gaze and dipped his chin at a vampire who appeared out of the shadows behind the counter. Now Otto noticed the open door there. The vamp's bronze-colored dress clung to her. Her hair was loose, its black-ness broken by a single white streak.

She dipped her chin. "I am Anya Tiliths. Detectives Jones and Prosper?"

Prosper nodded.

"We're here to see Prydwen Wyrthin," said Otto.

A smile flickered on Anya's lips. "Of course. We were expecting you. Come with me, please."

She led them out of the lobby into an atrium that took Otto's breath away. A golden glow streamed through a tinted skylight, and the space was warm and lush with plants. Here, the murmur of voices floated in the air, rustles coming from the foliage. Water babbled.

By the time they'd followed the winding pathways to the other side of the atrium, several vampires had materialized only to slip away again, and a lone human had trotted by, slight and fair, her hair as light as the sun. Otto swiveled his head as he walked, watching until she disappeared too.

Young.

A lot younger than Maisie had been. Were they all young?

Sex during a blood exchange was illegal. Age, beauty—none of that ought to matter. Maisie had been a common blood whore, but she'd also been twenty-nine when she was killed.

Too old for a place like this?

"Detective?"

Otto startled out of his thoughts, unaware he'd stopped in his tracks.

Anya gestured to an arched doorway. "Through here, please."

Now they circled a sapphire blue pool surrounded by palms. A naked girl swam. Two naked boys lay on their bellies on the damp cement surround.

No sex, my ass.

From here they crossed a game room to a staircase covered in burgundy carpet. The same burgundy carpet covered the hallway upstairs. Voices murmured in hidden places here too. Anya led them away from the voices and followed a curve in the hall that opened a few steps later onto the lobby below. Silver laced the glass in the skylight. Money all over the place. You'd hardly know vamps had lived under rocks until recently. They loved luxury so much.

As though sensing Otto's thoughts, Prosper grinned at him.

"Gentlemen?" Anya gestured at an open door. "Through here, please."

Otto stepped in ahead of Prosper and entered the room where a handsome, short-haired vampire stood behind his desk. "Prydwen Wrythin?" Otto asked.

The vampire dipped his chin. "Detective—?"

"Jones."

"Prosper," said Prosper, coming up beside him.

His chin fell lower than was typical. Then Otto remembered. Wrythin was royal. From the lowest family, but still royal. Odd though he wore his hair so short. Otto wasn't sure he'd seen hair that short on a vamp before.

"Please," said Wrythin. "Let's sit by the window. It's a lovely day."

The love these night crawlers had for the sun still boggled Otto's mind, though long, full-on sun exposure usually had most vamps running for shade. In fact, not much sunlight found its way past the white awning over the window.

They took their seats in leather club chairs, which surrounded the low coffee table. Otto faced a statue of a naked man standing on a pedestal beside the window. The glass it was made of was a stunning gold and purple color. Whether the figure was human or vampire wasn't clear.

"So, Mr. Wrythin," said Prosper. "Do you know a Brillen Acalliona?"

"Call me Wen, please, and no, not personally." Wen smoothed his tie. "I recognize his name though. A petitioner."

"A petitioner?" Otto asked.

Prydwen nodded. "A would-be client. Not local, but somebody who might want to use our services. They typically come with references."

"So a drainer?"

"I presume. He had a card."

Otto rolled the word presume around in his head for a moment while Prosper asked, "When you say, would-be, does that mean you didn't serve him?"

"Correct."

"Do you ever have non-drainers petition you?" Otto asked.

For an instant neither Prosper nor Wen moved. A quick glance passed between them. Wen smoothed his tie again. "No. That's illegal."

Wen smiled at Otto, but Otto was aware of his attention on Prosper. His smile was brittle and didn't make it all the way to his cold vampire eyes, but it told Otto Wen didn't trust Prosper any more than he did Otto. He had also lied.

"When did you see Mr. Acalliona?" Prosper asked.

"Day before yesterday, I believe. What is this about, by the way? I'm only able to talk to you because Mr. Acalliona isn't a client of mine."

"Wasn't," Prosper said.

Wen frowned. "Excuse me?"

"He's dead," said Otto. "Past tense."

"Oh, my God." Wen placed a hand on his chest. "I had no idea."

Prosper flashed them both a glimpse at his incisors. At least he didn't drop them, Otto thought.

"Anyway," said Prosper. "Back to the would-be. Mr. Acalliona had a valid donor card. Why wouldn't you serve him?"

"I offered to run his card. It only takes a couple of days, but he declined. Usually people make advanced arrangements."

"What do you mean by running the card? A security check?"

"Yes. I use a firm my attorney recommended. They make phone calls where they can... ask questions of associates."

While Prosper talked, Otto's attention drifted back to the statue. Though made of glass, smooth and glossy, it exuded warmth and pliability, as though the color had been painted on a living body. He imagined warm skin that would melt his fingers if he reached to caress it. The face was indistinct, but its beauty shone anyway. The figure rested mid thigh on a pedestal. One arm curled behind its head, the other stretching up as if reaching for the sun hidden by the awning.

When Otto turned away, he caught Wen's eyes on him, hot and angry.

Surprised, he frowned. He'd been following the conversation enough to say, "We'll need to see the paperwork."

"Our files are confidential."

"He wasn't a client," Prosper said.

Wen sighed and rubbed his forehead. "I suppose that's true."

He rose and pushed a button on the intercom on his desk. "Anya, will you bring Mr. Acalliona's application to me?"

He turned back.

"Run us through the process," Otto said. "Pretend I'm a prospective client. What do we do first?"

"You'd be here. I'd interview you." Wen returned to his seat, glancing at the statue before meeting Otto's gaze. "You'd have to demonstrate financial means. As I mentioned earlier, most of our clients are referrals."

"Okay," said Prosper. "We're referred. Knock, knock."

If possible, Wen's eyes grew darker, and Prosper flashed him a smile, clearly enjoying the rise of Wen's ire.

"We have five dormitories. Each one has donors and staff and operates independently. Anya or another greeter would meet you and bring you to me," said Wen. "You'd complete an application and review our gallery."

"Gallery?"

"Our donors."

Otto smiled. "Oh, I like that. I get to pick whoever I want?"

"Yes."

"Can the donor refuse?"

Prosper snorted at him. "This is a job. You don't get to refuse."

Wen's lips parted just as a knock came on the door and Anya entered. He extended a hand, and she brought him a file folder. When the door closed, he passed the folder to Prosper and turned back to Otto. "They can refuse. They don't."

"Why not?"

Now it was Wen's turn to smile. The tips of his fangs showed behind his incisors. "I'm told we're charming to humans."

Otto forced his jaw to relax. "Okay. So I've seen the gallery and picked someone. Did Mr. Acalliona get to that point?"

Wen's expression turned sour. "He did. He chose Isaac."

"We'll want to talk to Isaac," said Prosper.

"I never approved him."

"So does that mean they never met?"

"They met. This isn't a taco truck. I don't expect you to understand, but feeding from another being is extremely intimate, sometimes painfully so."

"But there's no sex."

"Absolutely none. We abide by your laws on that matter and enforce it to the letter."

A raspy laugh stuck halfway up Otto's throat. He guessed the nubile creatures at the pool were just eye candy.

"And none of your donors work it for a little side money?"

Wen frowned. "Excuse me?"

"Blood whores," said Prosper, sliding Mr. Acalliona's application into the file folder. "We'll need a copy of this."

"Are any of your employees blood whores?" Otto asked.

"They may have been at one time. I wouldn't hold that against them. The Upheaval created hardships for your kind too."

Nothing in Wen's voice told Otto he gave a good goddamn about human hardships, but flouting the law probably wasn't good for business, and this was a profitable business by the look of things, though he doubted drainers were the only clientele. But that was a crime for a different investigation.

Otto's gaze skated to the statue for a moment before he let it settle on Prydwen again. "We'd like to talk to Isaac."

Prydwen sighed and returned to his intercom. "Anya? Is Isaac available?"

"No, sir. Not today."

"Arrange something for tomorrow or the day after."

"Yes, sir."

"Thank you."

Wen turned back without taking his chair. "I assume you heard that. Is there anything else?"

"Just the copy," said Prosper.

"Anya can help you. I'll walk you down."

Prosper went out the door, and Otto stood. When he reached Wen, he turned back to the statue by the window. The tightening on Wen's face was a whisper, but Otto noticed it.

"Where'd you get that?"

"A local artist. A client's brother."

The burning in Wen's eyes drew Otto in like a lure. He pulled away from it with a grin that brought a scowl onto Wen's face.

"'Appreciate your cooperation," Otto said.

Wen nodded, and Otto followed Prosper downstairs. He was across the lobby when Anya appeared in the doorway behind the counter and motioned to Prosper.

"A phone call. You can take it in here."

Otto remembered the antennae and satellite dishes on the roof. The kids here lived a quality life the outside world had yanked out from under everybody else. Even Otto had to sit on his front porch to talk on his phone. He had reception on two TV channels on a good day. He remembered the necklace Maisie had worn. Her new dress. As though she'd come into money.

Prosper turned to him, and Otto said, "Meet you outside."

Clouds and a sharp, glary light met him beyond the doors. By the time he slid halfway into his car, Prosper was coming down the steps. He sat sideways, arm slung over his steering wheel, and tensed as the ground moved underneath him. Prosper paused, meeting Otto's gaze. Slowly, Otto stood again. Prosper was already pale. It wasn't like he had much more color to lose, but he also looked sick.

"What?" Otto asked, trying not to shiver as his skin crawled.

"The license plate." Prosper cleared his throat. "GL8SS?"

"Yeah."

"It belongs to Prince Rune."

Otto shook his head. That wasn't the guy he'd seen. He let his eyes blur, floating back to a minute and a half that had seared itself into his brain. A guy in a knit cap. Otto had never gotten close enough to see him, but he'd been light on his feet, limber and fast. Why would he be driving a vampire's car?

"I guess we talk to your prince," Otto said.

Prosper made a face. "What for? It's a dead end."

Otto's head snapped back up and his eyes narrowed. "Nobody's above the law."

Prosper's flat expression told Otto otherwise, but damned if he'd let anybody get away with murder, even the murder of a lowlife drainer.

He slid back behind the wheel and gazed over his shoulder at Prosper before he started his engine.

"We talk to him."

9

A PHONE CALL

AFTER MAKING sure the cops had set off for their cars, Wen rushed through the central atrium to the gardens behind the building. His tension eased when the area was vacant. He strolled into the sun, wincing at the light but wanting the warmth that sunk into him. A few early blooming roses and cherry blossoms scented the air. The draw of the curved bench by the fountain was only natural, he supposed. It was Jessa's favorite place to sit and wait for Isaac. He thought of Jessa's peculiar confession that he felt close to his mother here. Wen doubted Jessa remembered much of his early years beyond the chaos of crumbling rock and panic. Where those tender feelings came from Wen didn't know, but he was willing to indulge Jessa's romanticism to keep his ambition on course.

The white stone bench was warm, the breeze across the fountain cool.

Wen bent his head over his phone, shielding his eyes. He had a landline that usually worked, but he wanted privacy, so he punched in a number on his satellite phone and hoped Jessa wouldn't be the one to answer, as he, strangely, liked to do. But no, it was the prince himself who picked up, which was also strange.

What is wrong with these royals?

Wen's head filled with memories of home and the reverence that had flowed to every royal family, though the Seneras had always acted like commoners. Qudim and his fated love. *For pity's sake.* Not that Wen wanted to return to Celestine, despite his attachment to the old ways. Here he had a chance to rise, and he intended to.

But Rune's voice, though it said nothing out of the ordinary, sent a chill through him anyway.

"Yes?"

"It's Wen, sir."

"What do you want?"

"A client that came to me yesterday was killed. Murdered. I just talked to the detectives assigned to investigate it."

Rune was the high prince. Wen knew the chiefs of police in the district reported to him, but Rune, of course, shared nothing with Wen, so what news Rune bothered to keep up on, Wen had no idea.

"Why do I need to hear this from you?"

He cringed at the impatience in Rune's voice, and his chin dipped automatically. "He was a drainer. My client."

"And?"

"I'm worried about Jessa."

Silence followed. No clouds covered the sun, but the air suddenly chilled.

"Why would this concern Jessamine?"

In some strange way, Rune's use of Jessa's full name put Wen in his place, as though only family had the privilege of using Jessa's nickname.

"What if it concerns him?" Wen asked, laying weight on the what.

"How could it?"

"He's a prince."

"This is not news, Wen."

"I don't like coincidences."

"Similarities, you mean."

"Who would want to kill a drainer?"

"I can think of any number of reasons, none of them connected to your center or to Jessamine. Even Ellowyn are prejudiced. In any event, I have another job I might have to take. If so, I'll be out of town again, but I'll apprise Malia of this development. It'll be up to her to keep Jessamine in line. He's innocent, you know?"

The sudden softening of Rune's voice startled Wen.

"I won't let him wander unescorted when he's mine."

The minute the words left his mouth, Wen regretted them. The softness vanished from Rune's voice. "Jessamine will always be ours. You forget yourself, Prydwen."

"I'm sorry, sir. I'm... I'm worried."

"You did your duty."

The call cut off with a ringing in his ear. Wen sat frozen for a few minutes, hoping the sun would warm him again. Losing Jessa wasn't acceptable. Marrying him wouldn't be much of a step up, but he'd belong to a family higher in rank than his. And Jessa was dutiful though taxing on Wen's nerves. His devotion to those silly romances he packed with him everywhere was an embarrassment. Not to mention Wen didn't appreciate the inklings of inadequacy that crept up on him whenever Jessa blathered on about fated love.

With a shiver, Wen stuffed his phone into his jacket pocket and returned to his office, but when his gaze fell on the statue by the window, his thoughts returned to the cop, Otto Jones. He swallowed the bitterness that rose into his mouth.

10

AUTOPSY

"WELL, THIS IS SHAPING UP STRANGE," Prosper mumbled over a candy bar he'd gotten from a vending machine.

Otto's stomach churned, but he glowered from under his brows to hide it.

Light blazed in the stark white hallway, the tang of chemicals and things he didn't want to think about floating on the air, and a draft as chilly as the blast from a sub-zero refrigerator blew out of the vents in the walls, but Prosper chewed on a chocolate bar as though dead people didn't lie beyond the swinging doors at the end of the hall. Well, why would it matter to Prosper? He was a fucking vampire. He drank blood.

And ate chocolate in a room with a gutted body and the stench nightmares were made of only minutes earlier.

Ate chocolate while steadfastly ignoring the past he shared with Otto.

Back then Otto had dogged Prosper's every step until Maisie's case turned cold and forgotten. Prosper hadn't cared a murderer walked the streets. All he'd cared about was rousting her skeezy friends and the vamps who'd sullied their blood by drinking from blood whores.

As Otto strode down the hallway toward the elevator, Prosper's steps a whisper behind him—light as a vampire's—the walls blurred, and a vision of Maisie appeared. She stood in his kitchen again, wearing one of his T-shirts and drinking his coffee, strong as mud, the way she'd liked it.

He slipped into the memory, the world forgotten for a moment...

"Where'd you get that?" he asked, staring in bewilderment at a necklace that had to be hundreds of dollars above her means.

He was staking everything on getting into the police academy. They sure as hell had no hope of relying on their father.

She set her cup down, lifting the pendant in front of her. "What do you think it'll get me?"

"In trouble."

He loved her laugh. It was sweet and girlish, but she was tough and heartless.

"It was a gift," she said.

A payment, he knew. And it had gotten her killed. The necklace hadn't been with her body. Somebody had stolen it and left her dead in an alley.

Now, ten years later, somebody else was dead, drained of blood, but everything Otto had thought he knew about this murder was blown to smithereens. Coming back to the present in the sterile hallway, he hit the button by the elevator with his thumb.

Paper crumpled behind him. Prosper leaned sideways and dropped his candy wrapper in the trashcan.

"So we're looking at the murder of a true Ellowyn," Prosper said. "I guess that changes things."

Otto snarled at him. "Changes nothin'. Who the fuck would pretend to be a drainer?"

Prosper's face turned wary, but he gave a grim smile. "Somebody who wanted human blood?"

"But he didn't get it, did he? Wrythin refused him."

A fake tattoo. Who would want to brand himself as a drainer if he wasn't one? And, of course, Prosper would care about this now. For the same reason he'd never cared about Maisie or made any effort to solve her murder. To Prosper, drinking human blood was the mark of an Ellowyn. Yet, the *need* for humans was thought to be a weakness. With Synelix, vampires didn't need blood anymore. Keeping humans around for a few drainers stuck in many a vampire craw.

But a murdered vampire with a fake tattoo was a crime Prosper would apply himself to. The murder of a blood whore only Otto had loved had never been worth Prosper's time.

"One of you killed him," Otto snapped, stepping into the elevator as the door slid open.

Prosper followed him but stood at a distance. So what if Otto scared the shit out of vampires too?

"If it was just one person," said Prosper.

"Vamps and humans working together?"

"We do."

Otto snorted. "We're never going to solve this. A fake drainer drained. No defensive wounds and only one small scratch on the neck. No car. No close associates. A list of clients from every district with no known personal contacts. An unidentifiable witness. A prince lurking at the scene, and a donor center that rightfully refused him service."

The elevator door opened and Otto exited. They were outside before Prosper spoke. "This was personal."

Otto paused on the sidewalk. "What are you talking about? There was no evidence anybody was pissed at him. No defensive wounds. He was practically clean."

Prosper shrugged. "Maybe not pissed, but it was insulting as fuck to drain him. Why shame a guy like that?"

Otto went cold. Strips of clouds dimmed the sky and striped the pavement with shadows. "My sister was drained."

For a moment Prosper's eyes went blank. Then he shrugged again. A quick twitch as though he had no reason to linger on the subject. "Humans don't count."

Something burst in Otto's eyes like a ricochet of light off the sidewalk. It pierced his brain, too damn dry to deal with his memories. He needed a drink. He needed the world to go back the way it was when he was thirteen and vampires only appeared on Halloween. This was a world his parents had created. Or their parents, busily draining the earth of its last stores of gas. But not him. Or Maisie.

The world around him burst into white flames, and a heavy grunt thudded in his ears.

Prosper stumbled backward, tripping over the lip of a square of pavement. He waved his arms to catch himself and glared at Otto. "What the fuck?"

"Humans. Don't. Count?"

"I didn't mean it that way." He pointed at Otto. "Stay back, and don't fucking hit me again."

"You piece of shit."

"Whatever. Fuckin' human."

"Keep out of my way."

Prosper shook his head and jabbed his finger at Otto again. "Like hell. You stay away from the Senera family without me. I'm your ticket in, bub, and don't you forget it. Get your head back in this ballgame. You've got issues I don't give a fuck about. Leave it to a goddamn human to get all huffy over vampires. And by the way, we are Ellowyn. With our own world before you humans destroyed it. You were losing the goddamn war, remember? We allowed you to live."

The truth of that statement raced like lightning fire through Otto's body and incinerated everything it touched. His memories. His hope. The kid he'd been with his bike and drum set in the garage. His wary, lustful dreams of a cock that wasn't his in his grip. After the Upheaval, hunger had taken over his life. He'd rummaged every day for food and water. And the minute the sun went down... vampires. They'd hunted in the dark. They were stronger and faster, and they'd won. Now any point to the world was gone. Any point to him.

"Fuck. You."

"Oh." Prosper shook his head with a chuckle. "Good comeback. Why don't you call it a day and go drown your sorrows. Pretty much all you're good for."

Rocked by that, Otto said nothing and let Prosper go. The sun waned, and the shadows deepened as he stood there, bleeding out inside.

Yeah. A drink.

But he didn't need it, did he? He was stronger than that. Strong enough to go home and make a pot of coffee and sit down at his kitchen table with a notebook and list everything he knew about this case and listen to the clock tick and the cars pull into the driveways of the houses where his neighbors lived with their families.

I'll find something in the notes. A crack, a hint of something strange, something that leads the way.

But nothing would lead the way because there was no way anymore.

He got into his car. Maybe he'd make it home without stopping for a drink.

Maybe.

11

ELLO'S LAIR

OTTO MADE it home where he drank a couple shots before he set out for Ello's Lair. The club occupied an old Days Inn stripped of its interior walls to create a single space. It sat half a mile from a busy shopping center between a tire store and a hair salon. It wasn't much to look at during the day—tinted windows in a single story grayish exterior. The roof was flat. The only door in front was metal and painted a slightly darker gray than the exterior.

Otto parked across the street in front of a Safeway and leaned against the car, arms crossed over his chest while he stared at the activity near the club. He'd never been in it before. No reason to. Everybody going in was a vamp. Long loose hair, braided, or knotted. Skimpy skirts, spiked heels, bare chests. Otto drank to get from one minute to the next. He never celebrated, never relaxed and watched the show, never danced. But Ello's Lair was a dance club.

Every second Thursday of the month—which this was—was Jazz Night.

Malia Senera, sister of Prince Rune, was a regular attendee

at Jazz Night. The band performing was called Xylochord, and this was their first appearance at Ello's Lair.

Otto had no idea what he expected, if anything, but if she showed up maybe he'd get a feel for her before he met the family the next day. Prosper wanted to walk away from Rune, and Otto wasn't far behind him. The possibility it was a vampire prince who'd drained Brillen Acalliona was remote, but Otto was also sure that wasn't who'd run from him either.

But seeing Princess Malia might give him an edge, and he'd take it before walking into their home territory.

When the line in front of the club disappeared, Otto crossed the street, flashed his badge at the muscle at the door, and strolled inside.

A red haze suffused the air washing over the bodies packed on the dance floor. The stage for the band in front of the bar was empty. The club was sectioned into thirds with the bar and stage in the center, flanked by a dance floor on both ends, though the one farthest from the entrance was smaller and half hidden behind an arched doorway.

Watchful vampire eyes tracked him to the bar. He took a stool. One of the vamps on the other side of the counter stared at him.

"Jack. No ice."

The guy nodded.

A moment later, Otto took a swallow of his drink and looked around. The red light flowed from light to dark, deepening the shadows that surrounded the walls. Over the few windows red drapes hung from ceiling to floor. Urn-shaped lamps glowed gold on the tables and counter. Otto wasn't sure how they did it, but the noise was strangely muffled around the bar. When he'd passed the dance floor, the music had been loud and throbbing.

He finished his drink and ordered another. He was halfway

through when she arrived with a handful of vampires in tow. Tall, in thigh-high boots with needle-thin heels that had to be six inches. All around her, heads turned. She wore black leather shorts and a filmy red blouse over a black camisole. Her dark hair fell in a single long braid over her shoulder. As she strode onto the dance floor, dancers reached to touch her arms and shoulders. Fleeting touches. She grinned in response, flashing a dimple in her cheek. The vampires who accompanied her stayed close. She pulled one of them near her and laid both arms across his shoulders.

Otto froze with his glass halfway to his lips, his gaze on the guy dancing with her.

Not a vampire. His hair was too light and not a wisp of menace wafted off him. A human.

Otto drank, a long swallow that burned his throat.

The guy swayed with his boots stuck to the floor. They were mid calf over skin-tight leather. His shirt was a plain pinstriped button-down that looked bizarrely sexy over the leather. But the guy danced for shit. The princess slapped him on the shoulder. His long hair, tied back by a few braids, was a mix of indeterminate color in the red light.

Otto finished his drink.

Another song began, and the human loosened up. He still wasn't any good, but he made a couple moves that were limber as fuck. Otto grimaced at the images that sprang into his head. How bendy was this guy?

"Another?"

He turned to the bartender, who gestured to his empty glass. Otto pointed toward the dance floor. "Who is that?"

"The princess."

"The guy with her."

The vampire shrugged. "Never seen him before."

Otto slapped two twenties on the bar. "Find out."

The vampire shrugged but pocketed Otto's money. A minute later he set a new drink down. Otto picked it up.

Now the guy was dancing with one of the vampires who'd accompanied the princess. He didn't dance any better, and they were both laughing. The princess approached the bar. She was several yards away, and Otto froze when she turned her head and stared at him. The moment didn't last long before she looked away again. Beautiful but ferocious. Otto preferred soft. Malleable.

Bendy.

He gazed back at the dance floor but lost sight of the human. The princess disappeared too. He sipped his drink, watching the band set up.

It wasn't until the band started playing that he spotted them again, this time the whole entourage, sitting around a table in one of the booths. It wasn't long until the princess met Otto's stare again, this time with a slight smile and a tip of her head. Otto returned her smile with a grin. She laughed, and the guy beside her leaned in. She said something to him, and he looked at Otto. Even from across the room, the dazed look on his face was apparent. It was a fairly average face with a thin nose and—

Otto frowned.

Familiar.

"Hey." Otto turned, and the bartender swapped his drink for a fresh one and said, "That's the second prince. Jessamine."

Jessamine.

That's who it had been. The one in the field. Otto focused on him again. The princess was leaning in close, speaking into her brother's ear. He nodded and she pushed him. Now he stood, and two of the vampires rose and followed him. He approached the bar not far from Otto, darting quick glances his way. Otto stared back, watching the color rise in the prince's cheeks. A crossling.

Otto had heard of another prince but had thought he was disabled and housebound. This guy looked like touching his toes bending backwards was child's play.

Otto took a swallow of his drink.

Fun to see.

Not that this guy did it for Otto. He didn't tick off any boxes. But he was shy looking and that always set off Otto's hero complex. He got another glimpse through the braids that had come loose from the guy's tie.

Disabled how? Mentally, maybe? Was he a serial killer who now and again escaped the castle?

The eye peering between the braids flittered away again.

One of the vamps with the prince bent down and straightened a moment later, scowling at Otto. He skulked down the length of the counter and loomed over Otto on his stool. Flashes of red from the lights pooled in his black eyes. The creature's scowl cut lines in his face.

"The prince wants a dance."

Otto glanced around him. The prince was staring at his drink. A drink with an umbrella in it. And then he wrapped his hand around the glass. He wore nail polish, maybe red, maybe black, it was hard to tell. Otto stared and flashed on a figure crouched in a parking lot, cramming romances into a backpack.

No. That had been another thin-nosed guy with polish on his nails. Had to have been. It was the only possible explanation because coincidences like that never happened except in...

Movies.

Romances.

Otto recalled a thin nose, a startled stare. He looked into the dark eyes watching him. "Is he mute or something?"

The vampire glowered. "Be honored."

"Fuck that," he muttered, but he got up, feeling the whoosh of whiskey to his brain, stepped around the vampire, and approached the prince. When the guy jolted upright and stared into his eyes, Otto's heart squeezed tight and stole his breath. *What the fuck?*

Up close, near the whiter light behind the bar, the mix of gold, honey brown, and red in the guy's hair stood out. His eyes were a close match.

No, not pretty at all.

Mesmerizing.

Otto shook himself. "Dance?"

The guy didn't move, didn't speak. Otto held out his hand. The prince looked down at it, slowly reached out and took it, and Otto tugged him toward the smaller dance floor past the alcove. Only a few couples danced in here, and the music was soft and faraway. The light was low and gold and no drapes covered the windows. Headlights winked on the glass.

Otto pulled the prince in close and got a giddy laugh. The vamp chaperones stood on either side of the door. Otto focused on the prince.

"Put your arms around my neck, and we can talk," he said.

The prince breathed out. Everything about him, his hair, skin, breath, was floral and woodsy.

"What's your name?" the prince asked.

As he'd been earlier, he seemed stuck to the floor, though this time he was rigid too.

"It's Otto. Just sway." They barely stirred the air, but Otto didn't mind. The prince's heat relaxed him. After a moment, he chuckled. "Is yours a secret?"

"Is my what a secret?"

"Your name."

"Oh." He cackled this time. "It's Jessa, short for Jessamine, which means jasmine."

Otto didn't know what the fuck his own name meant. Was that a vampire name?

"It's French," Jessa added as though Otto had asked his question out loud.

"It doesn't do you justice."

Jessa blinked. "Oh."

By now, the princess had joined them. She reclined against the wall with her companions on either side of her, watching them. Odd. So maybe there was something wrong with the guy if they had to keep such a close eye on him. But Otto was about a hundred percent sure she'd sent the prince to him. Jessa had appeared attracted to him, but too shy to ever do this on his own.

"I have jasmine in my front yard," Otto said. "It's too heavy handed. It doesn't sneak up on you at all."

The guy's eyes glazed.

Otto had no idea what he was doing. Trying to get close? Trying to get a feel? This was the guy he was looking for, the one who'd run. But he didn't need to do this, didn't need to feel glued to him.

"Why'd you ask me to dance?" Otto asked.

The guy stammered at first. "I-I-I... You're human."

"So are you."

"Half," he whispered, and Otto inhaled the sweet breath that came his way and fingered some of the hair falling over Jessa's shoulder.

"It's red."

"My mother."

It was soft as silk. Otto brushed it off Jessa's shoulder and froze as ice rushed through his veins. He tore his gaze away from the tattoo half hidden by Jessa's choker and stared into his stricken eyes.

"You're a drainer."

"Yes," Jessa whispered.

Otto had no time to say anything more. The princess and her vampires surrounded them. Otto let go and stepped back.

She wrapped her arm around Jessa's neck, towering in her heels, fangs grazing her blood red lip as she smiled. "Too close, Mr....?"

"Jones."

"I'm sorry to interrupt, Mr. Jones."

"Right. Well, it is a school night, isn't it?"

Her smile didn't quite falter, but he'd surprised her by knowing her job. It wasn't a secret, but her eyes darkened anyway.

"It seems you know me, but I don't know you."

Otto smiled. "You will."

Then he turned to Jessa, but anything flippant he wanted to say died on his tongue, and all he managed to get out was "Sweet dreams, baby prince."

A growl chased after him, but it was only alpha posturing by one of the vamps, and he ignored it. He pushed through the throngs on the dance floor, the notes of a melancholy sax following him outside.

The nearby lights pierced his brain but flickered and went out by the time he reached his car. He looked back. The door to the club opened briefly, still lit inside. They had their own power source.

Otto got into his car and drove to another bar a couple blocks away. He wanted to drink and not think about a baby prince with freckles on his vampire skin and a thin upper lip that didn't match the plump bottom one.

He wanted to forget he'd have to see him again in just a few hours and pretend a potential murderer hadn't already burrowed underneath his skin.

12

COPS FOR GUESTS

BETTINA SANG as she sliced strawberries for the tea. The sound mesmerized Jessa. He didn't remember any of the words. Only the servants spoke Celes anymore. Jessa must have spoken it before the Upheaval, but now he only knew a few words.

The sound was sibilant and secretive like a whisper.

After adding the strawberries to the tea, Bettina wiped her hands off and turned her gaze on Jessa.

He sat at the long wooden table, the stone beneath him cool against his bare feet.

"Malia is waiting," she said.

Only Bettina and Fritt called Mal by her real name and only because she hated it.

"Nobody's here yet," Jessa muttered.

Bettina shrugged. "Anger the prince as you wish."

Actually, that wasn't Jessa's wish at all. He'd thought Rune would explode when he'd learned Jessa had not only taken his car to the co-op but had run from the police in it. The purple Rune's face had turned had been alarming. Also, alarming was being grabbed by the throat, yanked into the air, and slammed into a wall.

"I might just throw you in the pit, Jessamine."

Jessa had quailed at the threat though he was pretty sure Rune wouldn't do that. Rune and Mal had always loved him, no matter that Jessa's mother had been human and they were full vampires. The fingers around his neck hadn't dug in, and Rune's forearm, pressed against his chest, had held him up. He hadn't really been afraid, but Rune's reaction had clued him into how badly he'd fucked up. Nevertheless, he'd complained, "I wasn't doing anything wrong."

"That's not the point," Rune had growled. "I am responsible for you."

And afraid for him. But it wasn't like Jessa's life didn't go cock up every time he turned around anyway. His heart hurt when he thought of Rune and Mal tied to him forever. He didn't want that life for them, and he knew what he had to do. With a sigh, he pushed his chair back.

"Can I have some tea?"

"Let it steep."

He stuffed his hands in the pockets of his shorts and went outside. It was mid morning, and the sun was bright and high. He hugged the edge of the castle, keeping to the shade. Brightly colored umbrellas surrounded the pool where Mal sat in a swimsuit and wrap-around skirt. Jessa dragged a chaise lounge close to the sun and flopped down on it. His chest was bare, his hair pulled into a knot on the top of his head.

Mal set her book on the table beside her. "Remember what we discussed. Let us do the talking."

"I'm going to defend myself if it comes to it."

"You behaved indefensibly."

Shame heated his skin, but it was mixed with a dose of outrage too. "Look. I know I panicked, but that's because of you two. I can take care of myself, Mal, and I have a right to."

She waved him off with a glower. "That's not the point."

"You sound like Rune."

"That's better than sounding like a petulant child."

"I'm not a child."

"You aren't using your experience to evaluate this situation either."

"What does that mean?"

Mal sighed. "You aren't just a drainer, Jessa. You're a Senera. We have to stick together. We have enemies who would like nothing better than to find a weakness."

She tugged the string of her wrap-around where it tied at her neck, and Jessa resisted reaching for his own neck. *You're a drainer,* Otto had whispered.

Had that been horror in Otto's eyes?

"And I'm the weakness," Jessa said bitterly.

Mal dropped her hand. "I didn't say that."

"This—" Jessa swung his arm into the sun, gesturing to the castle and gardens and mountains, "—is my prison."

"Oh, for God's sake. Don't be so melodramatic. I took you out to the club."

"You broke into my dance."

Mal pursed her lips. "I changed my mind about him. I thought it might be fun for you to dance with a stranger, but something... I don't know. I just didn't trust him."

Jessa had burned like a fire for him, and it had taken every ounce of his being not to fling himself into the guy's arms. *Mine.*

But that was stupid. Romance novel stupid. He chewed on a nail, his stomach jumping with nerves as Fritt approached from the patio with the two cops following him. Oh no, that... that couldn't be.

Fritt stopped before Mal who bobbed the foot of the leg she had crossed over the other, her elbow on the table, cheek resting on her fingertips. She looked so unflappable, so unimpressed with everything around her. Jessa longed to copy her and stop worrying himself into a snit.

Fritt dipped his chin. "Princess Malia and Prince Jessamine, in your hospitality will you welcome Detectives Prosper and Jones?"

"Of course," said Mal. Her gaze lingered on Otto, lips twisting into a smirk. "Well, well," she murmured.

Jessa held his breath, focusing on making no movement at all, nothing to draw anyone's attention his way. But then Otto stared at him, smirking too. "Prince."

Jessa swallowed.

The other detective, a vampire, inched into the shade and dipped his chin low. "My honor," he said.

"Ours," said Malia, and Jessa echoed her.

A scowl crossed Otto's face, brow furrowing as he glanced around. "Where is Prince Rune?"

"On his way," said Fritt, who turned and strode back to the castle.

Rune was with Wen. Wen had a reserved temperament that was like cool water to Rune's. But Rune's temper was false and only mirrored his mother's, whose furies were legendary. Rune was artistic and passionate, but the violence in his belly never rose to his heart, which was why Jessa wasn't afraid of him. But it was good Wen was here to balance Rune's mood.

For a moment the silence stretched. Jessa dipped his chin down, watching them from under his brows. The vampire cop shifted his weight from foot to foot and cleared his throat. Otto smirked at Mal again.

"You lied," he said.

Light danced in Mal's eyes. "Oh?"

"It wasn't a school night," he said. "It's spring break."

She grinned. "So it is, but I didn't lie. You made the observation. I simply failed to correct you."

"It'll go much better if we're open and honest."

"Better than what?" she asked.

But Otto didn't reply. A servant appeared, carrying the pitcher of strawberry tea and several glasses. She set the tray on the table under the umbrella and Mal smiled at her. "That's all, Saria. Thank you."

"Tea?" asked Mal.

"No," said Otto.

Prosper cleared his throat. "Do you have any other family here today?"

"No. Only Prydwen. I suppose we can think of him as family."

The cops shared a look, then Otto turned his frown on Mal. "Prydwen Wrythin?"

"Jessamine's swain."

Oh shit. Sweat broke out under Jessa's arms. Of all the things to bring up. *Don't tell him.* But she was going to, it was as clear as the calm blue water in the pool. Her smile widened, and Jessa's stomach lurched. Wouldn't it serve her right if he hurled all over the patio?

Otto's brow furrowed. "Swain?"

"Fiancé," she said.

Goddamnit.

Otto's gaze shifted to Jessa.

I don't love him, he wanted to bleat. *It's arranged!*

But why in God's name did he want to do that? He had nothing to explain. He was engaged. He was beyond lucky Wen had agreed to the arrangement. And Otto—as though reading Jessa's thoughts—dropped his gaze to Jessa's neck.

Beyond lucky.

"You tried to hide that," Otto said.

Jessa frowned and shot Mal a look, trying to decipher Otto's words. "Hide Wen?"

"Your mark."

"Everyone knows," said the vampire cop. He'd shifted farther under the umbrella, away from Otto, who now stood alone.

"Who is everybody?" Otto asked, directing his comment to his companion. "Not you."

"Our business is no one else's concern," said Mal.

"That's not the point," said Otto. "The law is the law."

"You saw it," said Mal. "It was visible."

Otto's gaze returned to Jessa, slipping down his chest and belly. Jessa jumped up, poured a glass of tea and took it back to his chair. The cold from the drink spread relief through his body.

"What do you want with me?" he asked Otto. "I wasn't sure who you were the other day."

"Wait for Rune," Mal said.

Jessa shook his head at that. "I don't have anything to hide."

"None of us do," said a voice from behind them.

Every head snapped to Rune. He had a way of appearing out of nowhere. Wen was several yards back.

The vampire detective bent at the waist. "Your Royal Highness."

"Who are you?" asked Rune.

"Upwood Prosper. This is my partner, Otto Jones."

Otto and Prosper stood with their backs to him, but Jessa imagined them gaping. Rune was gorgeous. His hair fell to his shoulders with a bit of a wave and a few light brown strands in the umber mix. But it was the darkness of his eyes and the tortured depth of them that set him apart. He was a romantic character in every way. Jessa had sketched and painted him a dozen times and never came close to capturing his essence.

When Rune stepped under the umbrella and took the chair on the other side of Mal, Otto and Prosper turned again.

Wen took the chair behind Rune, and Uriah, who had followed them, came to stand beside Jessa's chaise lounge. Rune concentrated on Otto. Jessa wasn't sure why, but he ignored Prosper.

"I spoke with your lieutenant a few minutes ago. You want to know why Jessa ran when you accosted him? He's a drainer. Of course, he'd run. We taught him to assume the worst and ask questions later."

"I identified myself. Your precautions don't extend to running from the police," said Otto.

"They do, actually."

"I wasn't running from you," said Jessa. "I wasn't doing anything wrong, and I didn't want to involve my family. And besides, anybody can say they're the police."

Jessa doubted his face had gone as dark as Otto's, but it chafed at him to explain doing an ordinary thing on an ordinary day. Especially in front of Wen, probably adding to his stockpile of all the reasons Jessa would never be allowed his freedom. Wen already scoffed at Jessa's co-op jewelry-making business. *Hobby.* It wasn't like Jessa was gifted in any way. Not like Rune.

"It's not safe for drainers," said Rune. "You know that. You're investigating the murder of one."

"No. Brillen Acalliona was not a drainer."

Jessa swung his leg over his chaise lounge and sat straight on the side while Mal's eyebrows rose and Rune's frown deepened.

"I don't understand," Rune said.

"The tattoo was fake," said Prosper.

Mal's glass clacked the glass table when she set it down. "Who would fake being a drainer?"

"Are you sure?" asked Prydwen after a glance between Mal and Rune. "That's a terrible accusation. That means he was attempting to drink illegally."

"If that was his motive," said Otto.

"But what else could it be? What benefit could come from pretending to be a drainer? They are abhorred."

Abhorred... abhorred...

The echo reverberated like a shudder through Jessa's body until Uriah's fingers closed on his shoulder and squeezed. Mal winked at him, and Rune glowered at Otto.

"Abhorring them is the kind of idiocy Jessa ran from. I'd like to know what you know."

"Not much," said Otto.

Rune swiveled in his chair and looked back at Wen. "He came to you, yes? Acalliona?"

Prydwen nodded. "I was... uncertain of him."

"Why?" asked Otto. "You didn't mention that the other day. I thought your investigations are routine."

"Only if I approve of the references. Merely being a client is not a good enough reference."

"There were no references listed on the application," said the vampire cop.

"No. We are discreet."

"Who was the reference?" Otto asked.

"A donor."

"One of your donors recommended him? Isn't there a protocol against that?"

"None of my donors is a blood whore if that's what you're implying. I don't control what they do outside of the house, but they know the rules. This particular donor worked for a time in a different center in the Basin District."

"Who is the donor?"

"Mateo Lopez."

"We have an appointment to see Isaac. Can this Mateo be available too?"

Wen scrunched his face and gave the same look he got when his Synelix came chilled. He always took it as a personal affront when that happened but would never complain or send it back. Sometimes Jessa was sure Wen thought of him the same way.

"I'm afraid that won't be possible," Wen said. "At least not now."

"And why is that?" asked Detective Prosper.

"I don't know where he is. He hasn't been back to the house in a few days. I'll probably have to let him go."

Wen wouldn't do that, Jessa knew. To Wen's credit, he had a good reputation with the donors. Some centers practically locked them in and paid them little. Wen allowed them to come and go and provided luxuries they'd probably never enjoy anywhere else. Wen's one rule was that they didn't displease a client. The rest of their time was their own.

"Did you report him missing?" Otto asked.

"I don't know that he is missing," Wen said.

Detective Prosper said nothing, but Otto glared at Wen. "Did you at least attempt to contact him?"

Wen stood, and Rune held up a hand, directing his words to Otto. "You were invited here. I could easily have brought Jessa into town to answer your questions, but I travel a great deal, and I dislike being away from my family, so I invited you here. You are guests in my home."

"This is a criminal investigation."

"And my district."

Jessa held his breath, his gaze riveted on Otto's face. Anger played under the surface of his skin, and his eyes narrowed.

Jessa jumped up. "Our family was together the night of the murder. I ran because I didn't know who you were. You can arrest me, but you won't find the murderer here, and badgering Wen won't help you either. We didn't hurt anybody or kill anybody and we don't know anything."

Otto approached him, and Jessa's head swam at his proximity. *Mine.*

No. Not yours.

Otto wasn't as good looking as some of the heroes on Jessa's book covers, but that was partly because of the deep crease across his forehead and his perpetual scowl. But he was big and gruff the way Jessa liked. His shorn hair was dark and his eyes a light blue. Lighter than the sky. Lighter than the water in the pool. Jessa licked his lips, sweat trickling down the side of his face.

Uriah stretched his arm across Jessa's shoulder, palm out. "Close enough."

A grimace that was probably supposed to be a smile lifted Otto's lips. "You're telling me the truth." Jessa blinked. "But people always know something," Otto added. "Always."

"I don't."

"Do you know Mateo?"

"I met him."

"Fed from him?"

"That's personal," Wen complained. "You're making an unfounded leap from Mateo's disappearance to Mateo knowing anything at all."

Otto's eyes on Jessa's warmed for an instant, Jessa would swear it, then he turned to Wen.

Rune stood now too.

"I don't believe in coincidences, Mr. Wrythin," Otto said.

"Donors come and go. Some of them develop relationships. Some of them become sensitive to the bites. That can happen when the parties are not mated."

"Mated?"

"Fated," said Rune.

Otto chuckled. "You believe in that?"

"My father did. And Qudim was ruthlessly unromantic."

A strange look crossed Otto's face before Wen said "The point is, a donor can leave for any reason."

"We'll need Mateo's address."

"I don't have it. Most of my donors come off the street. I provide living accommodations and wages in exchange for a service, that's all. I don't follow after them."

"That's cold," murmured Mal.

"I run a good business."

"Why do they leave?" asked Otto.

"I have no idea. Isaac might know. They were friends."

"Isaac doesn't know anything," Jessa blurted, clamping down too late on his tongue to bite the words back.

But he had Otto's attention again.

"How do you know that?"

"We talked about it."

"About the murder?"

Jessa nodded. "When we thought the victim was a drainer."

"You feed from Isaac?"

He nodded again.

"We'll talk to him," said Otto. "What were you doing at the murder site?"

Jessa stammered, the change in subject discombobulating him.

"His shop is in the co-op on C Street," said Rune.

"The field isn't on C Street," said Otto.

Jessa's face warmed. "I was looking for my flower."

Rune sighed. "Oh, that." Otto turned to him. "It's one of the new species," Rune explained. "At least Jessa thinks so."

"I call it the Gold Star," said Jessa.

A bewildered look filled Otto's eyes, and he shook his head. "And this flower grows at the murder site?"

"Around here too," said Mal. "Jessa painted it if you want a look."

"It grows on a vine," Jessa said, drawing Otto's attention back to him. "It's yellow with orange dots and has five pointed petals. You have to look for it because it only grows with other grasses and flowers and attaches to the ground like ivy or strawberries. Wild strawberries are hard to see too."

Jessa bit his lip to shut himself up.

"I assume you can cross Jessa off your suspect list," said Rune. "He's not the least bit violent."

Otto nodded. "We're done for now."

Jessa forced a smile and tried to swallow his disappointment. After giving him a pat on the shoulder, Uriah led Otto and his partner away. Fated love wasn't real no matter what Qudim thought, and Otto wasn't the guy in the parking lot. He was cold but redolent as sun-warmed stones.

Sleepy summertime.

But it didn't match the heat in Jessa's belly. His gaze stayed glued to every one of Otto's steps until he lost sight of him.

13

CRACKING UP

AFTER ANOTHER MURDER call dragged Otto out of bed, he tried to forget Jessamine Senera.

The victim in Otto's new case was a human found in a car that had flipped upside down in a canal. What at first had appeared to be a simple accident clearly wasn't when the victim was extricated from his car and found to have a bullet hole in his forehead.

A few days later, Otto and Prosper's boss instructed Prosper to divide his time between the new investigation and Acalliona's. Rumor had it the King had an interest in Acalliona's murder. Apparently, he didn't particularly care about the murder of a human.

"Why not both of us?" asked Otto, scowling from where he sat at his desk with a third coffee that did nothing to stop the banging in his head.

Their boss grimaced and smoothed the front of his suit jacket. He only wore a suit on official business. Where was he going? The Chamber of Commerce? The mayor's office? A local coven meeting?

"The drainer's case is an ice cube. I want you to spend your time where it counts."

Well, Prosper wouldn't spend his time doing anything, Otto figured, and over the next weeks, Prosper did nothing to prove him wrong. When Otto asked about the interview with the donor, Isaac, Prosper shrugged. "I haven't been able to pin him down. The kid's a fave."

He sneered over the last words.

A few days later, a sudden lead in the murder of the "swimmer" as he'd been dubbed, led to a confrontation with a busboy at a local bar and grill Otto often went to. It turned out the busboy had gotten together with a woman customer who'd offered him herself and fifteen hundred dollars to pop her husband. Why the guy thought dumping the car in the canal was good cover was beyond Otto. He worried more about the strange queasy guilt that had worked its way into his gut. Had he sat beside the wife, shit-faced or getting there, while she'd made her plans?

He wanted to puke.

What had he missed? What had he missed in the drainer's murder? Had that gut instinct that had helped him for so long just shriveled up and died? None of the pieces of the Acalliona murder floating in his head connected in a way that made sense to him. Was his gift for solving murders, the only real talent he had, gone? The next day he set up an interview with Isaac.

"Waste a time," said Prosper.

Otto slid his phone into his pocket, grabbed his keys out of his desk drawer and said, "Feel free to wait it out in your car."

Prosper chuckled but strode into Comity House at Otto's side, though he griped at Otto's sour look.

"Come on, don't be pissed at me for the way things are going. Not my fault the fucking killer is sitting on his ass making pretty bead necklaces."

Otto stopped dead in the middle of the lobby. "You don't know that."

Prosper sneered. "True. Maybe he's braiding his hair."

"Like I said, wait in your damn car."

He resumed his path to the counter, and Prosper kept pace. "You think it's this Isaac kid?"

"I want to talk to the guy on the tape."

"Okay, suppose it isn't the prince. Could be both these kids. They're whores. They could've combined forces. Lured twice as many guys. Robbed them and ran. This time got out of control."

"Your imagination has gotten more colorful over the years."

"What does that mean?"

"Isaac isn't the one who's missing."

"Maybe he killed Mateo to make it look like him. No honor among thieves, right?"

"How 'bout we just talk to the kid."

The memory of Jessa's face framed by braids, the beads around his wrists, the freckles on his bare calves, hovered close to the surface of Otto's awareness. Jessa came to him every night in his dreams. At every lull during the day.

Why?

Otto had no trouble hooking up with good-looking people. Why was this pinched-nose guy with the chipped nail polish invading his thoughts? It was nothing to do with fate. Jessa had been the guy in the parking lot surrounded by bullies, Otto was sure. They hadn't touched or talked. Not really. Just one quick look into a startled pair of eyes. Startled and... hopeful?

Yes.

And tender. Otto thought back to the interview at the castle and the fear on Jessa's face at the mention of Isaac. He was willing to bet Isaac was far more than a donor. A lover? Fire erupted in his belly and rose into his throat. He swallowed it down. And what about Prydwen? Did Prydwen know about

Jessa's lover and not care? Or did he care? Had Acalliona tied in somehow?

He told himself the burn in his gut was probably booze from the night before. It sure as hell wasn't jealousy. Not over a crossling prince he didn't even know.

He snorted at the thought, coughing into his hand when Anya, who'd emerged to escort them to Isaac, glanced at him curiously. "Okay?"

"Yeah, fine," he said. "Allergies, I think."

"Oh, you wouldn't be the first," said Anya. "Vampires seem to have better resistance, but among our clientele, allergies can be a problem."

"Isn't that the source of their problem?" said Prosper, his face stiff with disgust as though drainers cavorted with their donors right in front of him.

Anya shrugged, expressionless. If she had an opinion about the drainers who came here she wasn't giving it away. No doubt Prydwen paid her well. He appeared to rely on her. Was Prydwen faithful? *Swain.* How fucking poetic. Otto tried to picture Prydwen in tights like a suitor from the Middle Ages, but the image broke apart and in its place appeared the naked guy in the statue upstairs. Was that Jessa? Or just a likeness? The figure was lean and supple.

Bendy.

"Are there any other crosslings here?" Prosper asked.

Anya slowed, half turning to look back at him as they strolled through a lodge-like room stuffed with furniture. A handful of youngsters curled on the couches and chairs, studiously ignoring Otto and Prosper, noses in their books. None over thirty. Again, Otto's thoughts went to Jessa and Isaac, and this time his stomach twisted itself into a bitter knot.

"You know... Inbred," Prosper added when Anya didn't answer.

"I don't think that's what inbred means, but in any case, I accept copies of their donor cards and file their applications. I don't investigate them."

"But Prydwen does."

"Yes," she agreed. "You'd do better to direct your question to him."

She continued across the room and down the length of a long hall with a wall of windows that looked onto the garden. She entered what looked like a waiting room. In addition to a circle of squat club chairs, there was a round coffee table strewn with books and a kitchenette in the corner. Anya pointed to the kitchenette. "Make yourselves comfortable. We have coffee, tea, or hot chocolate if you'd like. Isaac is right outside. I'll send him in."

She disappeared through a door in the wall of glass. A moment later, the greenery moved, and a boy with dark tousled hair stepped from between a pair of tropical-looking bushes and entered the room. He shut the door behind him. "I'm Isaac."

"Sit," said Prosper, pointing at the chairs.

His resistance was obvious, but apparently, the kid thought better of pushing Prosper's buttons and dropped onto one of the cushy chairs, sinking low. His position forced him to look up, and he wasn't getting out of that chair without a struggle. Surprising Otto, and from the look on his face, Prosper too, Isaac took the initiative and launched into his alibi. "I was with a client the night Mr. Acalliona was killed. After my client left, I went to the kitchen to get something to eat. Then I watched a movie with two other kids and went to bed. That was about three thirty. I couldn't sneak out of here, kill a guy—a vampire—and sneak back before morning."

Prosper cast a shadow over the kid, a glower on his face. Still pissed at Otto, probably. Sweat beaded the sides of Isaac's nose, his breath quiet. Nervous.

"It's not that far away," Otto murmured.

"I could run it in a half hour, I guess. I can't kill a vamp though. I'm not that strong. No human is."

Prosper laughed, appreciative, but his glower stayed. "You guys did your best."

"I'm the one sellin' my blood," said Isaac. "I'm not feelin' sorry for you."

Prosper's eyes narrowed. "You all stick together. Which means your alibi is for shit."

Fear flashed in Isaac's eyes, and Otto cast a warning stare at Prosper. "Let's hear him out."

"What for?"

"That's why we're here."

"I'm not stupid," said Isaac. "You think I know something. I already told you I don't, so I don't trust either of you."

"We always know something," Otto said, dragging a chair closer to Isaac's. Of all the people Isaac should be scared of, Otto probably topped the list. Usually he didn't give a shit what people thought, but he was curious about Isaac because, wary of him though he was, Otto didn't scare him.

"Look, kid, I'm not interviewing for a job. You don't have to trust me. The question is, do I trust you? You have a lot of reason to want me to."

Isaac flushed and dug his fingers into the arm of the chair. "I didn't do anything. If that matters."

"It does," said Otto, ignoring Prosper's chuff.

Isaac pulled his gaze off Prosper as if he had to drag his eyes away. He focused on Otto and chewed his lip. "I met Mr. Acalliona. Right here."

"In this room?"

Prosper sounded doubtful, and this time Otto agreed with him. Comity House was all about being upscale. Luxurious accommodations. The room was comfortable, but not much nicer than what you'd find in an office building.

"Mr. Wrythin hadn't approved him yet. He wasn't a client."

"But they aren't, are they? Before you agree."

Isaac shook his head. "Mostly that's true, but not always. Sometimes they're already clients and just want somebody new. I guess we don't all taste the same."

The twist in Otto's gut drove bile into his mouth. Isaac's comment was bad enough, but the look of dejection on his face was worse. Jesus, what was the kid thinking? That selling his blood wasn't just a cold, old-fashioned cash transaction? No emotions required? Vampires had the morals of alley cats. But was Isaac looking for something else? Was he in love with Jessa?

"Who is Mateo?"

Isaac's head shot up, and he dug his fingers into the chair again. "You know who if you're asking. A donor."

"Your friend?"

"I work with him."

"I bet," said Prosper. "Together at the same time, right?"

Isaac threw him a glare. "Asshole."

Prosper stepped closer. "What the fuck?"

"You can't intimidate me. I haven't done anything wrong."

The kid wasn't stupid, he didn't sound like a gutter rat, and Otto saw his point, but Prosper was antagonizing him for a reason, so Otto went along with it, though he spoke through gritted teeth. "Answer him."

Now it was Otto Isaac burned with his glare. "No. No sex. No kinky feed fests. I do my job, and I try to make it as easy as possible. You think people like having to rely on us?"

People. Otto resisted shaking his head. Not people. Vampires.

"You're lucky we fuckin' do," Prosper snarled.

"You don't like me," Isaac said, struggling to the edge of his chair, neck strung out and tense, biting out his words. "I don't care. Pin it on me. I don't care."

The sorrow in his voice struck a cord with Otto. It floated under the grating attitude like the wistfulness in Maisie's cynical laugh. But she had regretted nothing, at least not anything she'd admit to. She sold her blood and her body. She bought things. Stole things. She adjusted to the way things were after the Upheaval. He doubted she hated vampires, because hating them wouldn't change anything. *"The world's always been crap,"* she'd said. *"That's on us."* She was beautiful like Isaac, and beauty came with a price.

"Nobody's pinning anything on you," Otto said.

"We don't fucking have to," said Prosper. "You're it, plain as moonlight. Wha' did you two cook up? You stick around here to misdirect us while Mateo holes up with the money? Or the jewels?"

Isaac gaped at him. "Jewels?"

"Acalliona was a jeweler."

"Well, I didn't know that." Isaac looked at Otto. "Look. All I did was meet with him. In this room. I said no, and Mr. Wrythin said he'd run his card. That's all."

"How many friends do you have here?" Prosper asked.

"Nobody helped me."

"That's not what I fuckin' asked."

Prosper towered over him now. Otto stood and stepped closer. "Back off."

Christ, this was the same shit Prosper had done with Maisie, wasting time and effort on the wrong people.

Prosper's face twisted. "The whore's lying."

Otto had no time to jump in before Isaac grunted, "You asshole," and thrashed in his chair. He lurched halfway to his feet before Prosper clamped a hand on top of his head and pushed him back down. "FUCKING SIT!"

Goddamn vampires.

The room vanished before Otto's eyes and a haze reddened the scene in front of him like a bloody mist.

His growl rose. "Let him alone."

Prosper pointed with his free hand. "Fuck off."

But Otto was on him, twisting Prosper's collar in a knot in his fist, dragging him from Isaac. Prosper kept his grip though, and a strangled cry spilled through Isaac's gritted teeth. Prosper shook him. "Admit it. You bastards murdered one of us."

His fist tangled in Isaac's hair and the kid's cry rose into a wail. Something broke in Otto's head and let loose the long-hidden horror of Maisie's death. She would never have gone down without a fight either, and the images that had played in his head for years before he'd smashed them back into the dark flashed through the red haze in his eyes. Maisie freeing herself. Maisie finding a broken bottle and stabbing the bastard in the heart. Maisie dashing into a crowd and running away. Maisie escaping. Torturous, traitorous, taunting images because Maisie didn't get away. She did go. He'd lost her.

How his gun got into his hand was a mystery to him.

Prosper bent Isaac's head back. Panic flared in the kid's eyes, and Otto jabbed his gun into Prosper's temple.

Something thumped.

Isaac. The kid dropped to the ground and scrambled backward. Prosper froze, only his gaze shifting sideways, looking at Otto.

"You fuck," Prosper whispered.

The door flew open, footsteps thudding on the tiled floor outside. Otto's ears rang, and an ache began behind his forehead, but his arm was steady.

"This," Prosper bit out in a hiss, "is career suicide."

"Or yours."

"I'm not moving," Prosper said quietly.

After a moment, or an hour, muffled sounds came from the doorway.

Isaac again?

"Stay back, please."

Anya.

A strange nervousness raced through Otto's veins, and he stepped back. Prosper glared but said nothing.

"Please leave." Anya stood inside the door with Isaac behind her. She pointed toward the garden. "You can go that way. Just follow the path. It'll take you to the street."

With that, she turned and led Isaac away, closing the door behind them.

Prosper lifted his lips, hooked fangs long and gleaming in his grin. "You are so screwed."

14

ROOFTOP DINNER

SHADOWS STOLE INTO THE ROOM, but Jessa didn't switch on a light. He brushed a finger along the spines of his books, hovering over *Samantha's Surrender*. He'd forgotten the image on the cover, but he had no doubt if he pulled it out, the hero would look like Otto. Never Wen.

He moved.

Doll Baby.

Two guys.

He was tempted but didn't want to put himself in a position of longing for a hero who wasn't anything like Wen.

The Ticking Time Warp. A futuristic murder mystery. He took it off the shelf and set it on the edge of the tub.

Here, a golden light suffused the space. Even the fixtures were gold. Whatever little girl had lived here had clearly been spoiled. Maybe she still was. Wherever she was. She was happy though, one of the survivors of the Upheaval, Jessa was sure.

She had to be.

Shucking his clothes, he got into the tub and sank into the hot water. A long sigh escaped his throat. The scent of flowers from his bath oil permeated the air. Soon he'd be sitting down to dinner with Wen. He wanted to make their date nice. Be nice.

With a sigh, he picked up his book. Sonofabitch. The guy on the cover looked like Otto.

One hand took on a life of its own and dropped beneath the surface of the silky, slightly oily water. Jessa bit his lip and slipped his fingertips from the base of his cock to the tip. It wasn't right to do this though, because his brain kept skittering away from Wen. It was Otto in his instant fantasy. Otto, standing in front of a black futuristic car with palm trees and an emerald sky behind him. He wore a leather jacket over a white T-shirt and black slacks. A gun hung from his fingertips. *Ticking Time Warp.*

Jessa was a ticking time bomb. He thought he might explode. He squeezed his dick. *Picture Wen.*

He pictured Otto in his jeans and brown sports jacket standing beside the pool. His frown had appeared confused sometimes, though he'd probably never been looking at Jessa and wondering why he longed for somebody he had no right to. He'd been trying to solve a crime, wading through clues.

Jessa dropped the book onto the rug beside the tub and lifted a knee, spreading his legs. His fingers tightened, his strokes long and slow, and his teeth worried his lip. His heat built in the warm water, spreading through him like lava.

So good.

But not... Otto's fingers.

Was it wrong to do this? To fantasize about somebody who didn't know him? Who had a job to do? Who wasn't Wen?

His dick shrank.

Shit.

Sighing, he let his palm rest on his stomach. They'd never cross paths, no need to. He tried to imagine a need, a way for the investigation to circle back to him. Was there one? The only connection to him he knew about was Comity House. Maybe the murdered vamp had picked Wen's center because it was closest to his hotel. Not because Wen sold blood. The thought of that made Jessa shudder. Comity House was reputable. Wen was above reproach. He deserved Jessa's loyalty.

Did Otto have another lead now? Was he on a stakeout?

Jessa's cock fattened again at the thought of Otto skulking around in a dangerous neighborhood.

Weirdo.

But the possibility excited him. He stroked faster and imagined sitting with Otto in his car in the middle of the night, watching some rundown house or an apartment building with a concierge downtown. Or a tent in a razed section of town with the orange glow of a candle seeping into the dark.

Was the vampire cop with him?

What would Jessa do in Otto's place? Was he smart enough to put the pieces of evidence together like a puzzle?

A big gray muddle yawned in front of him.

Maybe mysteries were made of threads instead of puzzle pieces. Tangled, knotted threads he'd never pull apart.

But it didn't matter anyway. He wasn't going to fall in love with Otto, and he wasn't going to solve any murders. He had Wen.

The shriveling of his cock sent a rush of despair through him, and a groan slipped from his lips.

Stop it. Get a grip. Wen is good to you.

Jessa was lucky.

He grabbed the side of the tub, dragged himself out, and stood. After drying himself off, he braided his hair, got dressed, and set his book on his nightstand.

He was fitting his earrings into his ears when Bettina appeared.

"Stop fussing. Your swain is here."

Jessa wanted badly to go out to dinner. But ever since the murder he was stuck in the castle. Rune would loosen his leash, but not Wen. *It's not safe. Wait until they catch the murderer.*

What if they never did? What if it had nothing to do with drainers?

"Do I look okay?"

Bettina blew out a sigh, but her lips twitched with a smile. "You'd catch my eye."

But would he catch Wen's? He wasn't sure how visible to Wen he really was. Maybe looks didn't matter, but Jessa was doing his best tonight. It was Wen he was marrying.

He followed Bettina from his room and headed to the roof. The air here cut through his filmy shirt but closer to the dining table warmth from the heat lamps wafted over him.

Having dinner on the roof was his idea. Wen stood staring into the distance but turned as Jessa approached. Bewilderment filled his eyes, but he kissed Jessa's cheek and pulled a chair out for him. Jessa struggled to picture Otto doing that. He'd probably assume Jessa didn't need help pulling out a chair.

Stop thinking about Otto.

He sat and smiled at Wen, whose bewilderment intensified for a moment.

"You look lovely tonight, Jessa. I'm sorry you went to all this trouble for just us."

Jessa deflated. Well, it had almost been a compliment.

"It was no trouble," he murmured.

Wen took the chair across from him, and as though on cue, Fritt appeared, pushing over a cart with their meal. There was silence as Fritt prepared the table and wheeled the cart away.

"Looks delicious," Wen commented, picking up his knife and fork.

They ate for a few minutes while the lights strung around the rooftop terrace danced in the breeze. Wispy clouds drifted ghost-like across the sky. Jessa watched one, a shiver running through him. *Was it watching him back?*

"Is something the matter?"

He dropped his gaze back to Wen. "Just admiring everything. It's romantic up here."

He took a swallow of his wine. He wanted to be romantic. Maybe, if he put his all into Wen, his heart would swell. Maybe it was a simple matter of willpower. He wouldn't look at the cover on his book tonight. He'd only think of Wen.

Taking a breath, he reached for Wen's hand. Startled, Wen straightened, drawing away for a moment until he twisted his wrist and took Jessa's hand in his.

"This is romantic," said Wen. "It was thoughtful of you to set it up. And the meal is fabulous. I don't know of any place outside Celestine that beats Bettina's cookery skills."

"Were there restaurants in Celestine?"

"Naturally. Restaurants, shops, theaters. Celestine was a modern city."

Jessa had seen pictures, of course, but only of a few relics still standing in the wreckage of what had once been their world.

"Do you miss it?"

Wen squeezed his fingers and let go. "No. Condemning ourselves to the darkness was a ridiculous thing to do. We have every right to be here."

"We can't go back though. We have no choice."

Wen smiled. "Are you saying we get along with humans because we have to?"

"I don't believe that. I think we get along because we're not different. I've just never heard you agree with me."

Wen picked up his wine glass and took a swallow.

"It's not a matter of agreeing with you. I don't know how it came about that we lived underground, nor do I care. I'm not convinced humans are like us, but I accept them. I'm not glad there's been so much pain. Some of my friends believe in the prophecy theory of our rise. No harm in it, I guess. They believe in the treasure. Perhaps there is one. I don't discount the possibility. I just believe in hard work more."

Jessa scoffed. "Rune says the treasure is a fairytale."

Prydwen's smile stretched wide and genuine this time. "So were we. Now go on..." He pointed at Jessa's plate with his fork. "Eat."

Jessa returned to his steak. It was drenched in mushrooms and a red wine sauce. Mushrooms layered his potatoes and dotted his peas and glazed carrots.

"Do you need to feed again?" Prydwen asked a moment later.

"I guess."

"You don't drink enough. Isaac told me."

Jessa frowned. "I don't like to talk about it."

"I wonder if that's what the treasure is," Wen mused. "Our freedom from humans."

"You are free. You have Synelix."

Wen sighed. "Yes. I was tired of the dark and tired of war. I'm happy with my life now and being able to provide for you."

"I could make my business into something profitable, Wen."

"Of course you could. Where did that come from?"

Jessa shrugged, pulling his wine closer to him. "You all treat me like I'm glass."

"You were ill."

"A long time ago. Isaac's whole family died."

"And we take care of Isaac. Which reminds me. You won't be bothered by the human detective anymore."

For a frozen moment Jessa thought Wen knew all his deepest, darkest fantasies about Otto and the struggle to banish him from his thoughts. Not to mention, Wen's voice had an ominous weight to it. Jessa's heart pounded. Would he know if something bad had happened to Otto? *Mine.*

He worked so hard not to listen to that voice. They weren't fated. It wasn't possible. He was bound to Wen.

"Did... did something happen?"

"Apparently there was some altercation involving Isaac."

"Is he—?"

"Unharmed. No thanks to Detective Jones." Wen stared into Jessa's eyes. "You won't have to endure either one of them again."

"Are they fired?"

"I understand Detective Prosper is still employed. I might have to hire protection. I won't have my employees mauled."

"Mauled? Why didn't you tell me about this?" Jessa took his napkin off his lap and dropped it on the table, pushing back in his chair.

Wen looked confused. "I am telling you about it."

"Would you have if it didn't accidently come up?"

"I don't understand you. You went to all the trouble of setting up a romantic dinner and you wanted me to talk business?"

"Isaac isn't business. I have a right to know about him."

Wen pulled his mouth into a thin line. "What right do you have?"

Jessa went cold. The gusts from the heat lamps hit his skin like blasts of dry ice. Terror of losing Isaac froze his belly. What if Wen wanted him to feed from someone else?

He licked his stiff lips. "I feed from him. You know that's a personal thing, Wen."

Wen's jaw tightened. He poured more wine in his glass and nodded toward Jessa's. Jessa pushed it over. "I don't want to sound cold, Jessa, but it's best to keep a careful distance with your chosen donor. That's part of what the centers are for. I don't think feeding needs to be an unpleasant experience, but, if you're getting too close to Isaac..."

"Wen. Something's going on."

Wen set the wine bottle back in the tub. "What do you mean?"

"I..." His life had been tolerable until the murder and Otto and... suddenly it wasn't anymore. Suddenly, Otto jumped off every cover of his books and Jessa imagined himself in a real-life murder mystery. Suddenly, seeing Isaac in his tiny room at Comity House wasn't enough. He wanted to go places with him and do fun things, though he hardly knew what fun things existed to do. "I was bedridden for seven years."

Wen frowned. "I'm confused."

So was Jessa. "I... I have a feeling about things. All the time I spent alone... I can't explain it. I just know I didn't pick the day I went to the co-op by accident."

Wen's eyes rolled. "You sound like the prince and his no-coincidences theory."

"Why was Brillen Acalliona murdered? Did he know something?"

"I have no idea. Money is the usual reason."

"Like a treasure?"

Wen laughed, and it sounded genuine, not the polite chuckle he offered to others. "You do have too much time on your hands."

"It's not a game."

"Well, it's not an Adi 'el Lumi conspiracy either. Most things like this are fairly straightforward. As I said, money is the usual motive."

"I thought the Adi 'el Lumi was a myth."

"It is. Like teleportation. I've never seen an Ellowyn glamor anyone either. What's gotten into you? I can't change your circumstances, but if you want something to do, maybe it's time for you to make a commitment."

The air that had been so cold a moment ago heated like a fire, and the lights tossed in the edges of his vision. Jessa's filmy top clung to his sweaty skin. "That isn't what I meant. At least not yet," he added hastily. "Rune is almost never home, and I don't want to leave Mal alone."

"The princess is quite capable. Really, Jessa..." Wen drained his wine in a single swallow. "I'd be pleased if you thought more of your commitment to me than to your family."

"I do think of our commitment."

Wen's pain hurt him. Especially since Jessa's fantasies were out of control. Longing for Otto was wrong. He sighed and pushed his hair off his forehead. His family wanted this marriage for him and the relief of knowing he had a supply of blood for the rest of his life. They'd given him everything, and he owed them the peace of mind of knowing he was cared for. Otto...? Otto was a hero on a book cover.

"I will commit, Wen. Just... I just need a little more time."

Wen stood. "Fine, Jessa. As you wish."

"Wen—"

"I'm going home. I have an early morning." He bent and pressed his lips to Jessa's head. "I am loyal and patient. Your well being is my first concern."

Why didn't he say love? And why did the face that filled Jessa's imagination still belong to a bitter-eyed cop?

15

CLANDESTINE

A LONE BEAM of sun snuck in through the crack in Otto's curtains and stole across the room until it found his face.

"Bastard," he muttered though he doubted the sun took much offense.

His head pounded, and he stank of sweat.

Getting up was probably a good idea, but coming up with a good reason to was another story. At least not this early—he had no job to go to and like hell was he talking to a shrink—but later...

He cracked his eyes open.

The sunbeam shifted, reaching for the wall behind him. Fuzzy gray cracks spread across the ceiling. When he was feeling particularly energetic he'd make a mental list of the items he'd need to repair the damage until the realization it was bound to crack again in the next earthquake sapped his interest. Now he was used to the filigree design and tracing it while he lay there contemplating his crap-ass existence oddly mesmerized him.

Except for today.

Today, he just felt like shit.

With a groan, he rolled off the side of his bed and staggered up. After a cold shower, he made a pot of coffee and opened the cupboard over the fridge. Without thinking, he reached for the bottle there but froze before touching it. A tremor shook his fingers, and his mouth went dry. Why not one? A slosh in the cup to banish the pain behind his eyes? He swallowed, slammed the door, and took his cup onto his porch. Wispy clouds dimmed the sun, but it was still light, and the breeze was soft. Before sitting on the top step, he snatched the paper off the walkway and flipped it open. April 23.

Jesus, what had he been doing for the past three days?

Drinking.

But where? His memory was a fuzzy gray hole in the dark. Not that it mattered. He had no fucking job anymore. No way to hunt Maisie's murderer. Though guilt jabbed him at that thought because the truth was he hadn't been hunting her murderer for years. He'd been pissing away his life in whatever bar struck his fancy at the time. And doing his job. But now he had no job. And he knew damn well Prosper would let the Acalliona case go cold as ice. Which was Otto's doing.

He dropped the paper on the porch and took a swallow of his coffee. The liquid boiled in his gut, and pain bloomed in his head again. He shifted his position and leaned back against the porch post.

How are you getting out of this mess?

His job wasn't coming back, he was pretty sure of that. If he broke down and agreed to the shrink maybe, but the truth was, he'd lived in rage and hate for so long he wasn't sure how not to anymore.

Was he anybody beside Maisie's brother? Her final mourner? An uneasy feeling even that had no meaning anymore broke him out in a sweat.

Concentrate.

He needed to look ahead and forget the past for a while.

He took another swallow of coffee and checked off the things he knew.

One, he didn't trust Prydwen Wrythin for shit. He was a vampire. Not to mention, a dead fish.

Two, Brillen Acalliona had been living a life Otto related to —empty. He'd been fifty-seven, a successful businessman who'd employed between twenty and twenty-five people at any given time. He was quiet, seldom seen by his neighbors, and belonged to a now defunct merchant guild. No family, no friends, yet always friendly with business associates. He travelled to several conventions, plus Gem Fest in Pacific Grove each year. He appeared to have no hobbies, unless painting on a fake tattoo and drinking human blood counted as a hobby. Had he been addicted to it?

Otto stared into his cup. An oily shine glimmered on the surface like the rainbows he'd found in puddles when he was a kid. He'd played outside every opportunity he'd gotten when his mom was dying. Not long after—

Vampires.

Like the thin-nosed, freckle-faced vampire that begged to be thrown down on a bed and ravished to within an inch of his life. Nothing Otto imagined Prydwen doing. Nothing Otto was going to do, for fuck's sake.

With a grunt, he struggled to his feet and staggered when the ground shuddered underneath him. He steadied himself with a hand on the post beside him, went inside, and set his cup in the sink. After he found his keys on the dresser, he located his jacket on the floor of the hall closet. For fuck's sake. He picked it up and shrugged it on, still standing in the doorway, gaze settling on a shoe box on the shelf over his head. Family photos. The thing had sat there unseen for years, a part of the woodwork. He had no idea why it would register now, but it superimposed on an image of patio furniture, a crystal blue pool, and a grinning vampire. What the hell kind of connection was that?

None.

No connection.

What he needed was some of his old instinct to kick in, but he was getting fuck all. He headed outside, got into his car, and drove to Denny's.

After pancakes and more coffee, he headed off again, a weird panic spiraling in his gut when he realized he had nowhere to go and nothing to do.

He followed the flow of light traffic past the shopping center where the Captain's Chest, one of his favorite bars, hid away in the back corner, small and dark inside. But he passed the shopping center, swung around at the next signal light and drove to the Hamilton warehouse.

The yellow tape was gone.

Climbing out of his car, Otto looked at the camera and followed its trajectory into the field. Why here? Was it Acalliona's choice or Mateo's? Acalliona's probably. It was too close to the Sheraton to be coincidence.

He stared at the shops on the other side of the field. The coffee shop was open, and somebody exited a chiropractor's office and strode away down the block. Otto watched until the guy disappeared and the area was quiet again except for the fluttering of the tall grass in the field. Flowers bloomed, sparse and multi-colored.

Gold Star.

Jessa's eyes had lit like fireworks.

Otto strode into the field, wading through the weeds. Most of the flowers were white with occasional spots of yellow and lavender. He stooped when he reached the approximate spot where he'd seen Jessa when he'd given chase and found a tiny flower with five orange-spotted yellow petals. Parting the weeds, he found a few more.

Bent down as he was, the blood pounded at the front of his head. Wincing, he straightened and looked around. Most of the commercial space here was empty. He left the field and crossed to C Street. One car stood against the curb at the far end. On the other side, a shattered building grinned like a snaggletoothed vampire. War and the Upheaval marked the world with the sign of failure like a drainer's ink.

But here the pale sun lay on the street like a cleansing glow, and the bridal shop beside him had a newly painted sign on the door and shadows moving on the other side of the glass front. Across the street was a purple door with B & B in gold lettering. Bangles and Beauties Co-op was written in the same gold lettering on the bottom corner of the window. The glass was tinted, but a few shadows moved behind it. A narrow walkway cut through the row of businesses to a service alley in back. A few garbage bins stood against the wall of the next block of buildings. Otto followed the alley back to the cross street alongside the field. At night there'd be any number of places to hide and no one to see.

Where would a scared kid run?

Otto returned to his car and pulled back onto the street.

Mateo's employee records made no mention of family or a former address, but Mateo wouldn't be the only one to lose his family in the Upheaval. Was it possible he was hiding in Comity House? Was Prydwen lying? Would Isaac lie? Otto would, to protect a friend. If he had any friends, but he didn't. He had an obsession that waned with every year Maisie was gone. She'd hate him for the shadow of a life he was living. She'd had the lowest opinion of people of anybody he'd ever known, but she'd loved them too. She never backed away from friendship. Which was why that idiot Prosper had spent weeks combing through the dozens of people who'd loved her, looking for a hidden enemy instead of the drainer who'd killed her. Though in his more rational moments, Otto admitted he might have done the same.

"Somebody always knows something."

But Prosper hadn't found the right somebody and a murderer walked free.

Who was the right somebody this time?

Otto parked on a corner near Comity House and settled back in his seat. Maybe the stars would align and Mateo would saunter up the street. Maybe he wasn't involved in the murder at all and was nothing more than a flighty kid who'd picked an inopportune time to disappear.

As he sat there, the sun slid low, and another temblor rocked through his car. He gripped his steering wheel, waiting it out. After another hour, darkness fell, and lights winked on. This had been a good year for power so far, only two brownouts. In the early years, he'd lived by his Coleman lantern.

A few blocks from Comity House, lights spilled through the open doors of a bowling alley and cars packed the parking lot. He found a spot in a distant corner, shut off his engine, and headed inside.

The place drew families, and oddly, kids looking to hook up. He pushed through the bodies in the lobby, head already pounding from the clack of balls and pins and people shouting over the racket. By the time he made it to the lounge, his shirt clung to his sweaty skin. He got his drink and sat at a small table in the corner. It was blissfully quieter in here. A few other patrons sat around him, but there was ample space. He watched people walking by the door until Isaac appeared, hands in the pockets of his jacket, shoulders rolled high as he crossed the room and sat at Otto's table.

"Want something to drink?" Otto asked.

Isaac shook his head. "I just wanted to say thanks for sticking up for me. I'm sorry you lost your job."

Otto shrugged. "It's not exactly lost."

Circling the drain though, and he wasn't going to do anything to stop it. No shrink for him. He didn't care how fucking mandatory it was.

He pulled his glass over but didn't pick it up.

"No clue where Mateo is?"

A glower settled on Isaac's face, and he pushed his hands deeper into his pockets. "I told you."

Otto nodded. "Right. What about where he came from? Family?"

"I don't know. He never talked about anybody."

"Ever moonlight too?"

Isaac didn't ask what Otto meant by moonlighting and didn't seem offended, though he said, "I'm not a whore."

"Know anybody at Comity House who is?"

"No. It's against the rules."

"Right," Otto murmured again. He picked up his glass. Got it halfway to his lips this time before he set it back down. "Any suspicions?"

Isaac snorted and looked away. "I don't spy on people, and I don't care either. I pretty much keep to myself."

"Why's that?"

Isaac sneered. "So I don't get caught up in things like this."

"Why are you here, Isaac? You don't owe me anything."

Isaac was silent. He stared at the tinted windows that looked onto the bowling alley with a strained expression, as though looking for somebody he knew he wasn't going to find. Finally, he looked back.

"Jessa's scared of something. Sometimes I think it's Mr. Wrythin, but I can't be sure. I can't really come out and ask him. I just let him know he can talk to me if he wants to."

"Is it typical for a donor and feeder to become friends?"

Isaac's grimace had a sour look to it. "It's not encouraged. I like Jessa though."

"How old are you, Isaac?"

"Twenty-two. I've been a donor for four years, over two with Jessa."

Otto had no idea what that was like, letting somebody feed off him. It was surreal. He'd clung to his job and his home. The normalcy of work and his neighborhood. But Isaac didn't have that. Maybe that made him more resilient. Or more susceptible to the smallest amount of affection. It hadn't been Otto who'd set this meeting up, but the postcard that had appeared in his mailbox hadn't particularly surprised him. He was easy enough to find. He didn't hide.

"What are we doing here, kid?"

A slow seep of air whistled past Isaac's lips. "I think somebody's following him."

"Why do you think that?"

"I told you. He's scared."

"Lots of reasons for that."

"I figured you might help."

"You figured wrong. I don't have a job anymore."

"Is that what it takes? You have to get a paycheck? Something in return? Do you want something?"

"What are you offering?"

For a moment, Isaac said nothing. He stared, but his eyes were distant.

"Me."

Otto's stomach churned. He wanted his drink but didn't want to show the shake in his fingers. He was an asshole, for sure, making Isaac whore himself out. He told himself he wanted to see how far Isaac would go for a friend, but maybe he really only wanted to spread his pain over everyone else. He clenched his teeth until his stomach settled.

"I don't know if I can do much of anything."

A light shone through the shadow over Isaac's eyes. "Will you try?"

"I'll try."

Isaac nodded, swallowed. "So how do we do this?"

"You go home and let me do my job."

The smile that tugged at Isaac's lips when he realized Otto wasn't going to make him pay up compensated for a lot of crap in the world.

"Thanks."

"We'll see whether I earn it."

He waited until Isaac was gone before he reached for his glass and brought it all the way to his lips this time. Its fumes filled his head and made his mouth water.

I figured you might help.

Why? Why had the dumb kid figured that?

A cheer rose in the bowling alley and somebody near the door of the lounge clapped their hands.

He swallowed and set the glass back down. His last time dry had lasted four months. He'd had a reason for quitting, but he'd forgotten what it was now. He'd forgotten most of last month. Most of last year. Nothing special had marked a single day of his life for the last ten years. Thinking he had any kind of special murder-solving talent anymore was a damn joke. He was empty as fuck. Had he saved lives? Or had he just stumbled and blundered through his cases the way Prosper had with Maisie? He'd been hanging onto his job by a thread for months.

He got up and went home.

The next day, after a stop at Denny's again, he drove to the mountain. The Upheaval had thrust it high above the earth's crust, and it was now a good three hundred feet higher than it had once been. Still rocky, dotted with canyons and meadows and pines above the oaks and alders and cottonwoods. Back in the day there'd been a coal, then glass-quality sand mine in the foothills. After it closed, the area had become part of a regional park and now was Senera property. It was useless, much of it still caved in, but vampires loved anything to do with glass and many of the old shafts had been excavated though never brought back into use. Maybe the Seneras hoped to reopen it one day after the earth settled down. Supposedly, the Seneras had a difficult relationship with the Dinallahs, the first of the seven royal families. Maybe a source of private wealth wouldn't hurt their standing.

Side roads branched off into the foothills, but Otto took the one up the mountainside. Patches of mustard still glowed in the spring sun.

He'd never been this way before the interview with the family. The peacefulness of the countryside probably belied the watchful eyes on him. Where the road turned to drop down into Senera Valley, the shoulder widened into a dusty, tree-studded field. Otto swung his vehicle onto the dirt and parked in the shade. A Steller's jay yelled, and a handful of leaves fell on his hood. He rolled down his window, listened to the buzzing of insects, and gazed down on the valley.

What a place to live. You'd hardly notice anything awful had happened to the world. That castle full of vampires had once belonged to humans, and now the bastards nested in it like a real family.

Otto half expected Jessa to suddenly materialize and hunt flowers in the meadow. What a coddled little vamp. Otto had lived with a dad who'd checked out. Put his badge in a drawer and never took it out again. Up until he'd dropped his badge on his lieutenant's desk, Otto had thought they were nothing alike.

God.

He dropped his head and scrubbed at his face. When he opened his eyes a moment later, a car appeared on the road, heading away from the castle. It blurred in the fading light, silver and sleek, but large and comfortable too, not made for speed. Five minutes later, it disappeared as it began the climb to Otto's lookout. Then it passed. Wen and Isaac. Isaac's mouth was moving, his face turned slightly toward Wen.

After a few minutes, Otto followed.

The next day, he sat outside Comity House, but nothing happened. He didn't drink. He read the newspaper in the evening and went to bed. The next day he did the same thing. There was no reason to do this day after day other than a promise.

But the promise was enough, and he didn't stop.

16

SECRET LIFE

CLOUDS COVERED the sky and a drizzle hung in the air. Wen's tires rolling across the gravel whistled. Isaac waved through the rear window, and Jessa waved back. An ache in his belly told him he was still hungry, but he didn't want to take too much. No matter what Isaac said about Jessa not hurting him, Jessa doubted his saliva was as regenerative as a full vampire's. Sometimes, he'd feed from Mateo to give Isaac a respite, but now Mateo was gone. And Jessa hadn't much liked him anyway.

When the car was halfway across the meadow, he turned and went back inside. His footsteps thundered on the tile. Usually, he bypassed this part of the castle. The huge reception area and the dining room behind it were too formal, though Rune had softened its angularity with giant hanging tapestries.

Ducking into a narrow hallway that led back to the kitchen and the servants's stairs, Jessa headed down into the basement. Cold seeped from the thick stone walls. Here his footsteps fell without a sound on the heavy rug-covered floors. At the end of the hall, a wood door stood open. Jessa paused on the threshold. Rune faced away from him, gazing at a glass figurine on a table.

The figure was the size of a child but from its position on the table Rune had to look up at it. It twisted torturously like a creature writhing under impossible forces. The glass was red and gold.

Naked from the waist up, Rune's exposed back was its own piece of art, tattooed down the spine with the symbols of the Revelatory Passion. The Lessons of the Fall they were called. Love, sacrifice, forgiveness, God, resurrection, hell, heaven, and broken. Jessa wore the symbol for broken on his neck. *It's the same symbol for God," Rune had told him once. "Just an imperfect one."*

Without Rune and Mal, who would Jessa be?

"You're beautiful," he said.

Rune turned, his pale skin shiny in the heat. "Not like you, blossom. What are you doing?"

"I'm bored."

"You're spoiled."

"I couldn't be."

"Come here."

He followed Rune to a massive table piled high with giant sheets of paper. Some were detailed, computerized maps, others only loose hand-drawn sketches. Rune rifled through several, dragging some aside until he said, "This one," and pulled out a sheet he pushed toward Jessa. The map meant nothing to him, mostly a large body of water surrounded by marks meant to be mountains and valleys, areas of occupations, and a key for distances and measurements. "This," said Rune, tapping the body of water, "is an inland sea, and this island in the middle of it was once, what is now left, of Chicago. A major city. Now it's an island, lifted on a ridge of rock, the rest underwater like Atlantis." Rune's face grew soft and wistful. "I love the cities that have slipped underwater. I can explore them for hours. They seem preserved somehow.

Even the dead, trapped in their cars and homes, feel almost alive."

Jessa shivered. How close was he to being trapped alive? Coddled into forgetting the life going on out of reach?

He forced a laugh. "Well, that's cheerful. What are you trying to tell me?"

"It only feels like nothing changes, Jessa."

"Because it doesn't. This is my life forever. I'm a drainer."

Rune frowned as he circled the table, eyeing his maps. "That isn't a bad thing, and it isn't your fault. None of us asked for this."

"I like the above world," Jessa murmured, glancing back at the glass figurine.

Hearing himself say the words surprised him. He'd caught surprise in Rune's dark eyes too, before he'd turned away.

"Wen likes it too," Rune said.

Of course. A stab of annoyance struck him and the words, "I'm not anything like him," tumbled against his lips, almost spilling out. If they were alike, he might be happy about that, but as it was, he wanted to run away from anything about Wen and drainers. Only the taste of Isaac's blood in his mouth held him rooted to the ground, because he had no choice.

"Show me how to blow glass."

Rune smiled. This wasn't Jessa's first request, nor his first lesson, but Rune always humored him. He crossed the room and held out two foot-long dowels. "Take these. One in each hand. Point them end to end and spin them with your fingers. That's right. Keep them level."

"Why can't I just blow glass?"

"You can. Glass is beautiful no matter what shape it takes. Creation... that is an act of will."

"The world is sloppy and messy and random."

"Not a bit," Rune murmured with a smile.

An ache grew in Jessa's fingers and wrists, and his gaze fixed on the turning dowels as he held the ends point to point.

"We might be risen like the Adi 'el Lumi say. This might be our heaven."

Rune laughed. "I hope not."

"Who are the Adi 'el Lumi?"

"No one. They don't exist. Maybe once. What brings them up?"

"I think they're real."

"Nobody has talked about them in years. They're like angels. Nobody believes in angels anymore."

"We're angels."

Rune smiled. "Well, you are."

Jessa shook out his wrists and offered Rune the sticks back. "Why would somebody pretend to be a drainer?"

Rune frowned and turned away. He set the dowels back on the table beside the figurine and leaned against the table's edge, arms folded across his chest. His head tipped to the side and eyed Jessa silently for a moment. "I don't know," he said finally. "But I can guess."

"That's what humans are afraid of. That we have no control."

"That's what you're afraid of, Jessa, and as long as you feed, you do."

"I hate this."

"Jessa." Barely a second passed, but Rune was suddenly in front of him, arms wrapped around him, holding him tight to his chest. "I won't let anything happen to you."

"I'm not worried about me."

Rune loosened his hold and leaned away. "Who?"

"Isaac. Maybe even Wen."

Rune was quiet for several long seconds. Then a half smile graced his face. "You mentioned Wen last."

Jessa flushed. "I think Isaac's in more danger."

Rune nodded and squeezed Jessa's shoulders before releasing him. "I have to finish up here. Go on though. I'll make sure nothing happens to your Isaac."

But Rune didn't return to his glass. He went to his maps spread across the giant table, a look of absorption on his face.

17

THE SUMMONS

THE BANGING on his door thudded into the darkness of Otto's dream. He swam through memories of shaking earth and falling sky and thrust his blankets away in a panic. When the banging came again, he staggered into the hallway, hit a switch, and flooded the entryway with light. Blinking, he opened the front door.

"Detective Jones?"

"Mister," he muttered, rubbing his eyes with fingertip and thumb. Hell those were vampires on his front porch. He looked again. *Yep.* "What do you want?"

"King Dinallah requests your attendance."

He worked his eyes into a squint, trying to focus. Three vamps. Two males waiting at the steps, the female at his door. "Attendance at what?"

"The manor."

"That's hours from here. Days if the roads aren't passable."

"We're driving."

"I'm not going."

The woman smiled. "It is a request, but... not."

"I don't work for Dinallah."

Her smile broadened. "Today you do."

The two vamps behind her moved slightly to either side and advanced a step. Jesus Christ. "I need a shower."

He slammed the door. By the time he emerged from his bedroom again, they were standing in his living room. He strode past them down the steps to the waiting car.

Dinallah Manor had been built before the Upheaval at the base of the Santa Lucia Mountains. Otto might usually resist a request he had no obligation to honor, but the manor was close to Pacific Grove where the gem festival Acalliona attended each year was held. It was a weak link, but the intersection of Acalliona, the festival, and Dinallah was a curious one, and Otto had a strong suspicion of coincidences.

Plus, it wasn't like he had anything else to do.

Relaxing into the corner of his seat and door, he closed his eyes and didn't open them until the sun climbed into the sky and they stopped for food. At one point they got off the main highway and wound through fog and thick eucalyptus groves.

Dinallah Manor was a stunning house of sharp angles and broad planes of glass. More fog softened the mountains behind it, and the lights inside spilled golden puddles into the courtyard where the car pulled to a stop. The roofline was flat, one main house and two wings that flanked the courtyard. Italian cypresses in clay pots framed the entryway. Everything here was grace and elegance. It had none of the strange morbidity of Senera Castle. Climbing out of the car, Otto followed the female vampire across the terra-cotta pavers. The entry door opened, a tall thin vamp waiting a step inside.

"Justin will take you to King Dinallah," said the woman. "Have a pleasant visit."

Otto shook his head in astonishment but followed the butler or guard or whatever he was.

The same simple elegance outside met him inside. It wasn't

until they reached the end of the long foyer and turned into one of the wings that the dark vampire decor he was used to appeared. Still, it wasn't as gloomy as usual. The gray light came through tiny windows set high in the outer wall. Tapestries hung on another wall, most of them depicting a city carved out of white rock. The rugs on the floor were blood red.

"In here, please," said Justin, pushing open a heavy wooden door.

The half of the room he entered was empty of furnishings except for a narrow table under one window. The other half was homey, with a cluster of coffee tables and upholstered sofas around the incongruent addition of a throne. The thing wasn't particularly ostentatious. It was wood, with a tall, carved back, heavy, wide arms, and a cushy upholstered seat.

As Otto crossed the room, he noticed the scenes depicted on the fabric on the sofas—more of the hidden cities.

He halted in front of the throne and gazed at a vampire, who smiled at him.

"Detective Jones?"

"I'm not a detective anymore."

"Hm. Debatable. I am Zeveriah Dinallah," said the creature. "Zev, usually."

His voice was deep and warm, his smile amused. Otto had trouble guessing the age of most vampires, but he'd heard enough about the Ellowyn king to know he was near forty. His eyes were warm, dark embers, but Otto didn't trust the amused twist to his lips. The bastard had to be ruthless. He'd turned on Qudim Senera and conquered the world.

Made peace.

Otto cleared his throat, masking his snort at his own thoughts. *Peace, my ass.*

Capitulation was more like it because the vamp sitting on

his wooden throne, face half hidden by the fall of his wavy hair, ruled them all.

"What do you want?" Otto asked.

The vamp beside the throne, who hadn't moved until now, scooted to the edge of his seat, while Dinallah raised an eyebrow and gestured to his companion. "My cousin. Moss Goran."

"Still don't know what you want."

Silence met him. Nothing emerged from the vampires, but a soft click from the door behind him sent a shiver up Otto's spine. A moment later the squeak of wheels grew louder until a dining cart slid into Otto's side vision.

The tall vampire who'd let Otto in transferred the dishes from the cart to the coffee table between the throne and the sofa, poured three drinks from a decanter, and wheeled the cart away.

Dinallah picked up one of the tall glasses. The heavy amber ring he wore shone golden in the light. "I'll be specific. I want you to sit and relax. That is a command," he added with a broader smile.

Otto gritted his teeth but sat and took a glass.

He stared at it until Dinallah said, "It's a juice made from moon lace."

"What's moon lace?"

"A fern. It's sweet. A favorite with children."

Guessing it wasn't alcoholic, Otto took a cautious sip. Nectary. A mix of licorice and melon.

"Help yourself to some food."

Otto's glare returned. "I'm tired," he said. "Not sure why you couldn't just send a message. Or make a fucking phone call."

Dinallah sat back, bracing his glass on the arm of his throne. "I like to look into the eyes."

"Only works on non-psychopaths," Otto said.

The vampire laughed. "Are you a psychopath?"

"I guess that depends on who you ask."

Dinallah cocked his head. "I'm asking you."

Otto set his glass on the table. "I'm just tired like I said."

"You aren't afraid of me," Dinallah observed.

"Maybe I have nothing to lose."

"Can I give you something?"

For the first time, Otto shifted his gaze to the silent Moss. He sat with his elbow on the arm of his chair, the side of his face resting on his fingertips. The King had been sitting that way only a moment before. They were very alike. Mild expressions, a simmering fire. One spoke while the other watched.

"Trouble with your offer," said Otto, looking back at the King, "is I don't know what I want."

In a way, that was true. He despaired that finding Maisie's murderer would only leave him with a deeper loneliness.

"In that case," said Dinallah. "Let me start with what I want."

"Go on."

"I kept tabs on the Acalliona murder because I was told he was a drainer. I hate bigots. They slither under the rocks of both our worlds, and I want them thrown into the blazing sun." He spat his last words, his lip curled over the tip of a fang. Otto was surprised at the venom in his voice, though why he didn't know. No matter how strong the pull to run his fingers through that dark hair, Otto wasn't fooled. This was a creature that had crushed his enemies, and somewhere beneath the manor was a chamber where the covens met. As fun as laying Dinallah underneath him would be, that tender mouth hid fangs and a bloodthirsty hunger.

"I can't help you," said Otto. "I was fired."

Dinallah lowered his chin, burning Otto with his dark gaze. "Would you?"

Hell no.

But that wasn't true anymore. Not since his promise to Isaac. Jessa was a vampire. Was Otto really worried about him though? And why did the little bastard keep creeping into his head?

He returned to his original question. "What do you want?"

"Cooperation," murmured Moss.

"I'm here," said Otto.

"I've had you reinstated, though you won't be working directly for the police department anymore. You'll have every resource you need, and you can call on your colleagues at any time."

"Help with what?"

"I want you to solve the murder."

Otto picked up his glass and took a sip of his juice, wishing for something stronger than fern. Fern, for fuck's sake.

"Look. A lot of murders are never solved. Cops nowadays don't have half the tools at our disposal even my dad had. Without reliable computers, a murder that isn't—" He made air quotes—"a smoking gun case has a good chance of never being solved. Those are the facts we have to work with."

"Are you willing to work with them?"

"Why?"

"Prince Jessamine is worried about his donor Isaac."

Otto kept his face still. "I don't believe Isaac is involved."

"That's good to hear, but Prince Rune has requested protection for Jessamine. I remember Jessa. My family was very close to the Seneras once. The Ellowyn oftentimes have complicated connections. Dawn, Jessa's mother, was human. She chose to abandon your world to live with her fated love."

The sorrow that passed through the King's eyes disappeared quickly, but Otto's scalp prickled with an odd alarm. The vamp was hiding something. Something personal. Something that had nothing to do with a murdered vampire.

"Abadi was Rune and Mal's mother," Zeveriah continued. "Her family the Nezzarams were banished to a distant district after the war where they are free to live as they wish but not to leave. They would destroy Ellowyn or human for their own gain. Abadi attempted to kill Dawn, though she and Qudim had separated many years before. Brillen Acalliona was distantly related to the Nezzarams on his mother's side."

It wasn't until that last sentence that Otto had any idea why Dinallah was telling him what he was. Otto drew in a breath. "That's... tangled."

Dinallah smiled. "I agree."

"Abadi is dead too?"

The King nodded. "Qudim stayed in Celestine to save as many people as he could. He was bigger than life in many ways. A good King once. Rune led the family out. Abadi was with her family and died in Majallena. The Seneras made it out, and Rune returned for Qudim. While he was gone, a building collapsed on Dawn, killing her and burying Jessa with her."

"Jesus," Otto murmured.

"I'm told he remembers nothing of that. He was hurt. Perhaps the shock took his memories. Malia dug him out, and by the time Rune returned with Qudim... Well, there was nothing they could do. Less than ten years later, Jessa fell ill. It didn't occur to anybody he might be a drainer because he didn't bite anybody or even try to. His human biology compensated to some degree. Eventually, his illness was linked to Synelix, but his recovery was quite slow."

"Why are you telling me this?"

"To explain why his brother and sister are so protective. I

doubt Rune thinks Jessa is in any danger, but I understand why he doesn't want to take a chance. People hate, and Jessa is one of those they have chosen to hate. I don't know why Jessa is worried about Isaac, but he is, so I want you to work on the Acalliona murder with him."

Otto snorted a laugh. "Jessa? The guy makes jewelry for a living."

The King's eyebrows rose. "Wasn't Acalliona a jeweler?"

Otto sighed. "I work best on my own."

"You've always had a partner, and the Ellowyn will trust Jessa even if they don't like him. They won't trust you."

"He's safe in the castle."

"Rune and Mal aren't jail keepers."

Otto chuckled this time and scrubbed his face. Tiredness crashed over him, and the hazy light made his eyes ache. He was back in his dream from the morning, helpless as he spiraled into a nightmare. Too close. He didn't want to get that close to Jessa. But he'd promised Isaac and...

He let his hands fall to his knees. "I'll need access."

"You'll have it. You'll have your badge. All the resources you need. I also have a lead you don't know about. Another drainer was murdered two years ago. The murder was unsolved, but there was a suspect."

Otto straightened, his tiredness backing off. "Oh?"

Moss startled him by breaking in. "An Ellowyn named Solomon Frenn owns an art gallery in Windon. You know the town?"

Otto nodded. "It's nearby."

"Frenn was released," said the King. "No evidence."

"At all?" asked Otto. "Something had to bring him to someone's attention."

"Hate brought him to someone's attention," said Moss. "Solomon Frenn makes no pretense of his hatred of humans and drainers. The victim belonged to a family Frenn wanted banned from the local council—a lower family anyway—because they were one of the first to turn on Qudim."

Otto stared at Dinallah. "You turned on Qudim too."

A stiff smiled lifted the vampire's lips and a strange glow burned in his eyes. "I gave him a way out. Solomon Frenn would see me dead too. Though loyal to Qudim, he was also Abadi's lover. The Nezzarrams waged war against Qudim for threatening to execute Abadi after she tried to kill Dawn. My family fought alongside him. Qudim was ruthless, but he allowed Abadi to live, and the war ended. The hatred did not."

Otto rubbed an ache in his temple. *For fuck's sake.*

"Solomon reviles Synelix, drainers, and humans, though I'm not sure in what order," Moss said. "He publicly cursed the family of the drainer and was the first suspect for her murder, but he had an alibi."

"What was it?"

"A meeting of local business owners."

"Including humans?" asked Otto.

"No."

"What's the name of the group?"

The King raised his eyebrows and looked at Moss. "Comosoro Leaders," said Moss.

"Okay."

Dinallah looked back at him. "You'll help?"

Maybe it was that word—help. It dropped the King's demand to a plea and Otto... was a sucker.

Every time.

But he'd have a freedom he'd never have with the cops, though he technically still was one. And now he had a name. A possibility. A step closer to Maisie's murderer. Solomon Frenn.

A way to keep his promise to Maisie. To Isaac. He shut off

any thought of Jessa though, because underneath his exhaustion something warm stirred every time he let his guard down.

He nodded. "Okay. I'm in."

And a dull echo deep inside him reverberated like the clang of a steel door slamming shut.

18

STRANGE MOTIVE

ZEV STOOD at the window and stared into the courtyard where the detective ducked into the back seat of the waiting car. He'd find the killer before...

Before it was too late.

It's already too late.

Zev's heart froze like a stone in his chest, icy as winter. His mind flew back to the last winter of the war and a soggy backyard where he'd hunkered in the dark, gaze sharp, hunting the heat flare of the human he'd waited for.

Asa.

A face appeared in the windowpane in front of him, alive and flushed, so close his numb fingers rose, seeking the creature's warmth. But it was just Moss, because Asa was long ago dead.

Yet...

I felt him.

A remembered terror—one that wasn't his but had dragged him out of a dark sleep on the night of Acalliona's murder—swept over him again, and he shivered.

"Are you cold?"

Moss came up behind him.

"No. The fog is burning off."

"Just in time for the sun to set." A soft chuckle rumbled in Moss's voice.

"The witching hour," he murmured.

"Relax," Moss said. "You've honored your promise to Rune."

Always and more than that.

Resting his fingertips against the leaded glass, he watched a strip of fog drift away as the car carrying the human cop pulled through the gates and disappeared.

IN FOR A PENNY

THE FAINTEST of blues edged the skyline and the streets were quiet. This was the time Otto usually crawled home from whatever bar he'd gone to that night. His father had settled on a favorite place to drink and that's where Otto and Maisie could always find him, whereas Otto went from bar to bar because he didn't want to be anything like his father, a cop who'd given up.

Otto had a second chance.

Don't blow it.

The voice of the female vampire followed him up the walkway.

"Good night, Detective."

"Good night," he said.

Inside he fell onto his bed and dreamed he had fallen into a crack in the earth.

THE MESSENGER

JESSA HID his detective novel in the inside pocket of his jacket like the gun his PI hero carried. This book was called *Frolics in Frisco*, and Jessa loved the reckless PI, Jackson Stork. He was big—*like Otto*. Dark-skinned and pale-eyed. Biracial—a crossling—*like me*.

Now all he had to do was sneak away from Mal's birthday party and get back to his book. He'd left off at the part where somebody had just sent a dozen dead roses to Gloria Tilson. Was it her stalker? Jessa was pretty sure it wasn't the killer. The killer was cold and methodical, and a dozen dead roses was pretty dramatic. Something a spurned lover would do.

He gazed across the veranda. A few couples wandered off into the woods. Others still sat at the table in the dining hall behind him, talking and eating and drinking. He looked back at Mal. She wore a shimmering red dress that clung to every pale curve. Brightly wrapped gifts were piled on the credenza against the far wall. The table was laden with meats that seeped blood, potatoes crusted in salt, and mushrooms. Mushrooms in pates and strudels and soups. Mushrooms in condiments pickled and spiced. Mushrooms stuffed and wrapped and candied. A few dishes were made with Jessa in mind. Carrot soup. Roasted asparagus. Salmon in a dill sauce. Tonight though...

Tonight he'd eaten meat. Blood red. Usually he only ate it because Wen liked it. He needed Isaac, but he didn't want Isaac coming to him. He thought he'd explode if he didn't get away from the castle. He wanted to drink coffee at a coffee shop and eat a banana muffin. Or go to a movie, which he never got to do. Or go dancing again. Or play cards with Isaac in the common room with the giant palms rustling around them. Anything but spend another day at home.

Even the gardens chafed him.

He slipped outside, heading for the veranda steps. A glitter of stars splashed the sky, and underneath, lanterns glowed like golden fireflies. An orchestra played, and a few couples danced on the lower patio. Jessa circled the fire pit toward a maze of boxwood bushes, but a low voice stopped him before he'd gone more than a few feet. "Prince."

The address wasn't directed toward him, but he looked back anyway and spotted Rune on the far side of the fire. Rune separated from the others standing with him and joined Uriah, who gestured toward the castle and said, "A courier wishes to speak to you. I put him in the library. My apologies he wouldn't speak to me."

"From whom?"

"Dinallah."

"I see."

Jessa's pulse kicked up. Anything excited him nowadays. Rune smiled when his gaze met Jessa's. "Enjoying yourself, blossom?"

"I wish you two would quit calling me that."

"It's an endearment."

"You sound like Mal."

Rune threw an arm around him, dragging him away from the path that led to the maze. "You weren't trying to run off, were you?"

"Of course not."

Rune sighed. "Not that I blame you. But sometimes we have to put on a good show, so stick close by."

At the veranda steps, he let Jessa go and disappeared inside. Jessa followed him as far as the entrance hall. A form took shape in the shadowy passage from the kitchen and appeared at his side. Wen smiled at him and took a sip of his champagne. "Where did you get off to? I was looking for you."

"The gardens. Well, almost the gardens. A messenger arrived for Rune. I wonder what it's about."

Wen frowned into the entrance hall as though the study door now held curious revelations for him. He was casually dressed for Wen—gray slacks and an untucked short-sleeved shirt, cream with pale blue stripes. In Wen, the line between human and vampire was as thin as a wisp of fog. But Wen was a social climber, and vampire blood counted for him.

Blood Jessa didn't have.

"I'll find out," said Wen.

Well, that was no fun. Jessa wanted to be the one to find out. He pictured himself hiding in Rune's armoire like Jackson Stork, spying into the study through the keyhole. Not that he had any chance of getting in there now.

He chewed his lip, side-eyeing Wen's stare.

"What are you getting up to?" Wen asked.

"Nothing."

"Just let me handle it."

Why?

But he bit the word back. It wouldn't do any good to remind Wen that he wasn't a damsel in distress. Wen had visited him too many times in his sick room, bound to him when Jessa was twelve and already devouring the stash of romances forgotten in the closet. At twenty-six, Wen had just begun construction on Comity House. He'd been patiently waiting for Jessa for eleven years now. Guilt stabbed Jessa in the belly, and he tasted blood on his bitten lip.

Wen frowned. "Why are you so tense?"

"It's a courier from the King."

Wen rolled his eyes. "Melodrama for no reason most likely."

"Or something important."

It plainly irritated Wen when Jessa disagreed with him, and his frown deepened. "Leave it to me."

"Maybe it's a secret job."

Wen chuckled. "A secret job? You are imaginative. Mapmakers don't usually operate in secret."

Jessa shrugged. "It's mysterious though. Maybe he won't tell you."

Wen's brows drew together at that, outright irritation flashing in his eyes now. "You must not think much of my status in the family."

"That's not true. Nobody talks to me either."

That was probably the wrong thing to say, putting Wen on the same level as Jessa, and the distaste in Wen's eyes at the comparison chilled him.

"Excuse me," he said.

"Where are you going?"

"To get a drink. I'll be right back."

Jessa skipped the champagne and went for a brandy. The aroma rising from the swirling liquid as he walked soothed him. He'd gone too long without feeding. His nerves frayed. His thoughts fogged. The world hardened and froze. He ached for the soft skin of Isaac's wrist against his lips. It never occurred to him to feed from the neck, though he knew some vampires did it. On the days Isaac came from another client, the telltale puncture marks sometimes lingered on his skin. Jessa hated feeding then, though logically he knew Isaac wasn't being hurt. Wen would never risk the health of his donors by over-scheduling them. He'd hired a doctor to take care of them after all.

But those marks... They stirred something in Jessa, something that made him shudder yet tingle low in the belly at the same time.

He swallowed a burning gulp of brandy and returned to the hall. Now it was empty, though light spilled from Rune's study. Prydwen entered, and Rune turned before following. His gaze met Jessa's, and a wistful smile pulled at his lips before he retreated inside. He pulled the door closed behind him but didn't shut it all the way.

Jessa approached. Was it left open for him?

He didn't enter. He didn't knock. He leaned against the wall and stared at the tapestry facing him across the hall. Angels fell from the clouds, wings in tatters, flames belching from the earth below.

Inside his study, Rune chuckled. "You want to help?"

"If I can."

Jessa imagined Wen's stiff glower. He disliked his position and sought any opportunity to make himself useful. Wen needed people to count on him and admire him, and bestowing favors made that happen.

"You can help," said Rune, "by hearing me out and accepting my decision. I don't want to leave home with this murder unsolved, but I have a job I can't keep putting off. I have thought hard about the way we treat Jessamine and have decided some things need to change."

"What things?"

"I have received instructions from Dinallah about him."

"About Jessa? I don't understand. Jessa's—"

"Yours? Some day. But you aren't married, and right now he's my concern."

"That's unfair."

A long silence followed. Finally, Rune spoke again. "I think a lot about the randomness of the last days. The way one building crumbled and another stood. How a child could die beside a child who lived. No rhyme or reason. I've done everything I can to keep Jessamine safe but imprisoning him is possibly the cruelest."

"What? How is it? Jessa isn't normal."

"Who is to say that, Wen? Are you sure it isn't we who are abnormal? In any case, Jessamine is Qudim's son, and I wouldn't forget that. I want him to remember it. I won't be here forever."

"Bah," said Wen. "You are young."

"None of us has a crystal ball. I want you to humor me on this. Jessa deserves better than for us to coddle him."

"I do my best to be an asset to your family and to our people, but I think I have some rights in decisions regarding Jessa."

Rune's chuckle was a rough rasp as though dragged over rock. "This isn't about what we want. The King wants Jessamine to help the human detective in his investigation of Acalliona's murder."

"That's ridiculous. I forbid it. Jessa has nothing to offer."

The scrape of a chair sent Jessa's heart pounding, and his muscles went tight and ready to bolt before he stilled himself and relaxed against the wall again. He was Jackson Stork. Confident and fearless. He pulled in a breath and slowly released it.

Otto.

He was going to see Otto again. Hunger spread through him, an ache in his fangs. He needed to feed. To be strong for what was coming.

The memory of Isaac's slightly bitter blood bloomed in the back of his throat. What did Isaac know? What was he hiding?

Jessa had swallowed Isaac's fear, an acrid burn that flowed through his veins now, and he wanted to help Isaac.

To be like Jackson.

Jackson's clients were always beautiful women in peril. Women Jackson fell for but always had to let go. He saved them and went on his way. The perfect hero. So far, Jessa had found six of the eleven book series. He had to read them all. He owed Isaac to know what he was doing. Jessa loved him, and Isaac's blood had given him a real life again. Nobody else's had eased Jessa's exhaustion much at all. Maybe he wouldn't even be alive without Isaac.

Jessa wasn't sure why Rune was allowing this, but he didn't care why either. He just didn't want Wen stopping him, and he edged closer to the door.

When Rune spoke again, the rumble of threat in his throat stirred Jessa's memories of Qudim. "Nothing to offer? That was a telling comment, Prydwen. You would do well to think before you speak again."

"Forgive me. It didn't come out the way I wanted it to. Concern for Jessa overrode my manners, but I object on record."

"Why exactly?"

"Drainers aren't safe."

"No one is, Wen. We're all at risk. That's life. I was wrong to wrap him up like glass. Jessa can help. Ellowyn will accept him. He knows us and can help solve a crime. And doing that will keep him safe."

Edging closer to the study, Jessa leaned the side of his head against the wall and stared at the wedge of floor visible through the parted door.

"I don't want that filthy human near him."

Jessa cringed at the sound of Wen's hiss. It was pure vampire. Ancient and dark. But the one that followed was the sound of chaos and destruction. "I don't care what you want,"

Rune whispered, his voice a wisp of menace gliding through the dark. "I care about my family. You are not that."

"I—"

"Shut up. I want you to know this about me, Wen. I don't hate humans. Jessamine is half human."

"I didn't—"

"I loved Dawn."

"Of course."

"No. No, of course. I'm peaceable. I gave up almost everything for peace. I brought my family low for peace, but not lower than yours. I'm letting Jessa do this because I think he can. I'm watching you now, Wen, and I will flay anyone alive who harms me or mine, drain him, and spit his blood upon the stones. Now go!"

This time Jessa fled to the gardens outside where the air chilled his sweaty skin. Puffing faint plumes of vapor in front of him, he crunched along a gravel walkway that circled around to the front the castle where the lights spilled gold on the driveway. He weaved through the cars parked along the shoulder and strode down a grassy slope to a stone patio around an oak tree surrounded by a wooden bench. Here, the mountainside dropped away, and the lights of Comity winked in the dark.

Jessa patted the book still hiding in his jacket pocket. He needed to finish it and read a few more. Would investigating a real murder case be like his books? Best to stay away from romances for a while. He needed to keep his head clear of his fantasies about Otto.

Mine.

No. Wen was his.

Wen forgets half of who you are.

But it didn't matter. At least not for now. Wen wouldn't let him do anything like this once they were married. It would be back to making jewelry and living in his books. But for a reason he didn't understand Rune had given him this opportunity at a real life. A chance to help Isaac and forget he was just a drainer.

The lights below winked like flares drawing him on, and his grin stretched wide on his face.

I'm coming down there.

Wen be damned, Jessa intended to solve a murder.

21

AMBIVALENCE

SO FAR, no trio of vampires had reappeared at Otto's door to knock some sense into him. So far, Otto had dodged his promises and let the Acalliona case freeze colder than his useless heart.

Four days watching snatches of TV before his signal cut off. Four nights driving aimlessly until every night found him sitting outside of Comity House, wondering which window belonged to Isaac.

Wondering what the hell had turned his blood into sludge. He'd done nothing since the vamps had let him out by his front door.

Not true.

Okay, he'd gotten his badge, pager, and gun back, and maybe that was the problem. The surreptitious stares and sneers of guys who didn't need a vampire king to fix things for them.

He'd been out, and now he was back in, and what if he fucked it up?

Four days of doing nothing. Of wallowing and feeling sorry for himself and never once thinking of Maisie or...

Jessa.

Four days until he ran out of coffee.

Well, fuck.

So far, he'd stayed sober. But tonight...

Tonight, he grabbed his keys and jacket and headed out again.

At midnight the only thing open near his house was Denny's, a minimart, and the Captain's Chest. Otto circled the block three times before parking his car at the curb and storming toward the bar. The sooner he got a drink in him, the sooner he'd have no more reason to try not to drink. Staying sober didn't give him any more balls than being drunk. The thing he needed to do was figure out a murder that got more tangled with every new clue and looked less like a tryst with a blood whore gone wrong. Too much rode on Otto getting this right.

Like a prince.

A freckled, friendly—*fanged*—prince.

He slammed open the door of the bar, grunting at a sudden resistance, and pushed harder.

"Goddamnit!"

A figure staggered away from the entrance, swiped a hand down its face, and barreled toward Otto with a glare. Fortunately, the guy was about as drunk as Otto planned to be before the night was over and got all of two clumsy steps in before Otto flashed his badge in the guy's red face and said, "Fuck. You."

Blustering, the guy bellowed, "You coulda broke my nose."

"Whatever," Otto muttered.

At least his badge had come in handy for something. It wasn't exactly worth the price of clashing with Prosper again though. "An' here I thought you had no friends," Prosper had jibed.

Otto's laugh had torn at his clenched throat. "You got off easy. You want the case, take it."

"After you," Prosper sneered. "Same as sloppy seconds."

"Funny."

Four days of thinking even somebody as incompetent as Prosper might be better at the job than Otto.

Four days until he figured out this case meant something to him. That it was his last fucking chance to be better than the asshole who'd let his sister's killer go free.

He sat at the end of the bar and set his glare on the wary bartender watching him.

"Jack Daniel's neat."

He got a nod and a moment later his drink on a napkin. The stuff was beautiful, a lovely amber... like a prince's hair. Golden and red and honey brown. He pinched a corner of the napkin and pulled the glass over. His mouth kept watering, but he knew it would burn like hellfire going down. Bowels of the earth burn. But then it would flare in his gut like a heater kicking on on a cold wet winter morning. The kind of morning that made him want to burrow back under the covers.

Fuck facing the day.

What for? What good was he?

All he had to do was drink that damn thing, and it wouldn't matter anymore. The pain inside would burn away.

Count 'em. How many people will lose if you fuck this up?

Isaac. Jessa. Mateo. Were they in danger?

Was Otto? From himself for sure. From the tumbling of his resistance to his own doubts when he was sober. Drunk, he never wondered if he should have confronted Maisie about the necklace she'd worn and pushed for a confession when she'd lied and said she hadn't stolen it. If she hadn't been wearing it...

Well, maybe she wouldn't have died if she'd had nothing worth killing her for.

But he'd never know.

He peeled his drink off the square napkin. The whiskey sloshed as glossy and thick as sugar water. He lifted the glass to his nose and breathed. The burn in his airways was sharp and bitter. He took another breath, parted his lips and—

His pager went off.

After the first few seconds of shock, he laughed. Timing like this, it just didn't happen. Except it had. He set the glass down and twisted the device attached to his belt until the number on the display became visible. It went to the front desk at the station. He stared at his drink. A swallow? A sip?

A second tone came through. He pushed his glass away, took a five-dollar bill from his wallet, and set it on the counter.

The bartender eyed him on his way out. "Nice day, officer."

He flashed the guy a grin. "Detective."

With a quick glance at the traffic on the street, Otto dashed to his car and snatched his phone from its cradle. He punched in the number displaying on his pager. A voice answered, "Comity Police, Fraser."

"This is Jones. I got a page."

"Yeah. Call came in about ten minutes ago. Break in at the Comity House Donor Center. Team 2B responding."

"Any casualties?"

"None reported."

"Thanks. I'm on my way." But the minute he cut off the call, he hesitated, called back, and said, "Tell them to wait for me. I'll be there in thirty."

"Will do."

Cutting off the call, he punched in another number and a woman answered after two rings. "Prince Senera's residence."

"My name is Otto Jones. I'm a detective with the Comity Police, calling for Jessa Senera."

The woman made a humming sound. "It's after midnight, Detective."

"You're a vampire."

"We sleep, Detective. Hold on, please."

Apparently, they did sleep. A few minutes later, a groggy voice as warm and sweet as honey, said, "Yes? Is this the police?"

"Detective Jones. We've met."

"Um... I remember."

"I can't explain much right now, but King Dinallah suggested I get your input on the case I'm working on and—"

"Like hell."

Voice sticking in his throat, Otto pulled the phone from his ear and stared at it. Then he coughed and said, "Excuse me?"

"I'm supposed to work *with* you, not give you input. Like a partner."

"Partner," Otto echoed.

"You know. Equals."

Hardly, you little—But he gritted his teeth, took a breath, and said, "That's why I'm calling you. If you want me to pick you up, be ready in fifteen minutes."

He disconnected. Fangs. They all had fucking fangs.

22

BREAK-IN

IN CELESTINE, Uriah had been an enforcer. When Jessa asked him how he had gotten confessions out of people, he'd said, "You don't want to know."

Well, yes, Jessa did want to know. Or maybe not. Clearly, vampire police work was different than the human variety.

In the car on the way to Comity House, he stole glances at Otto, noting the heavy browed scowl on his face. Probably pissed off Jessa was with him, but too bad. Jessa had read his detective novels and had tried to get information from Uriah. He aimed to carry his weight.

"What do you know about the robbery?" he asked.

"That it happened."

Bastard.

Jessa gritted his teeth. He hated people thinking he was nothing but a... a drain. He wasn't going to have many more opportunities like this because sooner or later he'd have to marry Wen. Make jewelry. Not that he didn't like doing that, but his business was nothing more than a hobby in everybody else's eyes. The chance to do something important mattered to him. A memory to hold onto when all the rest of his life was romances and beads.

"Nobody was hurt?"

"I wasn't told of anyone."

Jessa stole another sideways glance. Otto shifted his grip on the steering wheel, turning his wrist up, the tendons popping into relief in the glow of the street lamps. The bone was thick and strong. Jessa inhaled, seeking the scent of Otto's blood. His mouth watered, lips tingling for the feel of Otto's warm skin. Damn, he needed Isaac. He swallowed and looked away.

Soon Comity House came into view, lights on in too many windows, spilling over the open lobby doors.

Otto stopped the car by the steps, and Jessa jumped out.

"Jess!"

Jess.

Jessa liked the sound of that, but he didn't stop.

The movement of shadows inside formed into cops. One held up her palm. "Excuse me. Who are you?"

"Prince Jessamine Senera," he said, barreling past her. Inside the lobby, he rounded the corner of the counter and stepped into the back office. "Anya."

She looked up from the file cabinet. "Jessa. What are you doing here?"

"Helping Detective Jones."

She blinked, which for Anya was akin to a gasp of surprise. "Well, the police have already looked around and asked questions, but Wen is in the Palmdale Room if you want to see him. I'm looking for the inventory for his office."

"His office? Was anything stolen?"

A ghost of a smile crossed her lips. "That's what I'm trying to find out, Jessa."

"Okay. I'll go look for Wen."

He turned away and caught a glower from Otto, who waited for him in the middle of the lobby. "Stop running off."

Jessa ignored him and headed for the Palmdale Room.

"Tell me something," said Otto, coming up beside him. "Do clients have free access here?"

Jessa slowed his steps. Candles made the only light and shadows played against the walls and plant life. "I don't know." He hadn't thought about it. "I do. I think some places are just for the donors though."

"Are the donors restricted from any place?"

"I doubt it. Or maybe just from the offices. This is home."

"Luxury living for some," Otto mumbled.

"Wen takes good care of them."

Maybe Wen wasn't the love of Jessa's life, but he didn't abuse people either.

"I wonder why anybody would leave."

Jessa pushed aside a palm frond as they skirted a pool surrounded in rock and ferns. The low lights and shadows playing along the pool's edge offered a dozen hiding places. Jessa shivered, and the hairs on the back of his neck stood up.

"A lot of reasons. Being comfortable isn't everything."

"It's pretty nice," Otto said.

Maybe it was. Jessa chafed at the thought of doing nothing for the rest of his life. Of Wen not understanding and resenting Jessa for being ungrateful. Especially when Otto's heat was melting him from behind and making him sweat. What if Otto smelled him? Oh God. A torrid wave rushed over him when Otto brushed past him into the Palmdale Room.

Mine.

Jessa swayed, then his wooziness fled at the sight of Isaac sitting on a couch with a blanket over his shoulders. He rushed over, relieved at the smile that popped onto Isaac's battered face.

"You're hurt."

"I'm okay."

Jessa dropped onto the couch beside him before taking a look around the room and freezing for a moment on Wen's hard-eyed stare. Otto broke away from two cops by the door and headed over.

"Need a doctor?"

"I saw one," Isaac said, lifting a bag of melting ice from the couch beside him. His eye and cheek flushed angry red and purple.

"Did the robbers attack you?" Jessa asked.

Isaac squinted through his puffy eye. "Kind of."

"Wait a minute," said Otto, stepping sideways. He dragged over an ottoman, sat down, and rested his elbows on his spread knees.

Wen sat on the arm of the couch, looming over them. Other than the cops by the door, they were alone. The Palmdale was a recreation room with scattered furniture and shelves jammed with books. Jigsaw puzzles half done and a few games in progress on the tables steeped the room in lonely desolation.

Wen sighed, and when Jessa glanced at him, he was rubbing his face. "I don't think there's much we can offer," he said after he dropped his hand.

"You never know," said Otto.

Jessa wondered if he should take Wen's hand but suspected Wen would only pull away if he did. Wen didn't like overt displays of affection.

Jessa turned to Isaac and slung an arm across his shoulders. "I'm sorry."

"I've never been robbed before," Wen said. "I don't keep anything of value here. No cash."

Otto eyed him with a small frown. "You've got art. That statue."

"Yes," Wen mused. "That's worth something. But it's still there."

"Well," said Otto. "Crooks can be dumbasses sometimes."

Jessa smiled, liking Otto's tone. He sounded like Jackson Stork.

"I surprised them," Isaac said.

Otto patted his knee. "Start at the beginning. Don't leave anything out, even if you already told it to somebody else."

"My office is in shambles," Wen interjected.

"I'll get to it," said Otto, returning his gaze to Isaac. "Go on."

"I was getting something to eat after my client left."

"When was this?"

"Around midnight. Her appointment was at eleven."

"Is that unusual? That late?"

"Not for her."

"What's her name?"

"That's confidential," said Wen.

"Not anymore. Very little is confidential in a murder investigation."

"Murder? This was a robbery."

"I doubt it."

Jessa ping-ponged between Otto and Wen. Wen scowled but didn't comment back.

"Anyway," said Isaac. "I went to the kitchen to make a sandwich. Nobody else was up that I saw. I was putting stuff back in the fridge, and I didn't see them come in. The door is big and hid me, but when I shut it, suddenly they were there. I didn't have time to call out before they rushed me. One of them knocked me down, and I hit my face, but when I got up, I was by the door where the fire alarm is. I pulled it and they ran."

"Good thinking," said Otto.

"Would they have killed me?"

His voice fell, and Jessa hugged him tighter. "I'm going to go get you some juice. I'll be right back."

He jumped up and rushed out. The nearest kitchen was probably the one Isaac had been attacked in, at the bottom of the stairs nearest his room.

Jessa brushed past the palms, again feeling the heaviness of the shadows. A soft voice floated on the air, but he didn't see anybody. Nobody was in the kitchen now either. He stepped carefully across the floor. *Did they dust for fingerprints?*

The space didn't look any worse for wear. Isaac's sandwich still sat on the countertop. Which was metal. Perfect for fingerprints. Maybe they wore gloves. No blood anywhere. No broken glasses or dishes. The back door was shut now.

"Huh."

Jessa spun around. "Jesus."

Otto grinned. "Scare you?"

"No." *Yes.*

Otto chuckled. "What are you doing?"

"Getting juice."

He opened the refrigerator door and peeked over the top. Otto gazed back into the hallway with a frown. Jessa returned his attention to the fridge and grabbed a bottle of grape juice. By the time he poured a glass, Otto had circled the kitchen.

"What are you doing?" Jessa asked.

Otto set his hands on his hips. His face was scruffy, a little puffy under the eyes. "No cameras anywhere."

Jessa's heart jumped at the thought of secret, prying eyes, which was silly. Everyone knew he was a drainer, so what if the camera got a shot of him? He'd never thought about the lack of surveillance before, but his panic would probably be the first reaction for many other drainers too.

Guilt hit him again, because Wen had thought about that.

About what it was like to be on display. The whole center had been arranged for privacy.

"This is a safe place," he said. "Or at least it was."

Otto's gruff face softened. "Go on. Take Isaac his juice. We can't do anything else."

"Will they get away?"

"Probably."

"Why?"

Otto leaned against the counter and crossed his arms over his chest. "Well, if they took something and try and sell it, we might get lucky and catch them. Maybe they have a record. Isaac can take a look at some mug shots. If he recognizes someone, we'll have something to go on, but he didn't get a good look."

"What about fingerprints?"

"In here? We don't have the resources. Too many people pass through. We'd have to take prints from everyone who lives here, every client, every worker, every friend. That's not gonna happen, and even if we got something it'd be shaky evidence. Who's to say they weren't here for some other reason? Deliveries. Maintenance. Moral support for a drainer friend. Most of our records were lost in the server crashes, so we have to have a real likelihood of success. It would take forever to even go through local records. It pays off sometimes, but with the amount of people going through here?" Otto shook his head and pushed off the counter. "And if this is just a burglary, it's nothing to do with Acalliona anyway."

"If."

"If," Otto agreed.

Jessa went ahead of him with the glass of grape juice. Wen was gone, but Isaac lay curled up against the arm of the couch. As Jessa approached, he sat up with a smile. "Hey."

"Here you go."

Isaac took a sip and gazed at Otto, who waited by the door. "Do you think this is connected to Mr. Acalliona's murder?"

"Could be," said Otto. "Might not be. No use speculating without more evidence."

Which Otto had said they'd probably never get.

Jessa leaned into Isaac. "Come live with me."

It wasn't the first time he'd asked, and the way Isaac's eyes shut down told him it probably wouldn't be the last time. "This is my job," Isaac said.

Being Jessa's blood whore wasn't, he didn't say, but Jessa heard it anyway. With a sigh, he stood. "Be back soon, okay?"

Isaac smiled now. "I'll be here."

Otto turned out the door, and Jessa followed him.

Most of the lights were off now, but outside, a faint blue color softened the night sky.

Jessa strode to the passenger side of Otto's car but didn't get in. He waited until Otto met his gaze and said, "Isaac's my friend, and I'm a part of this. I don't have to know everything to help. I'm a quick learner, and a drainer's just as good as anybody else, so don't ignore me. You don't really have a choice anyway."

He thought the last part might make Otto mad, especially since he'd taken the time to tell Jessa about fingerprinting, but instead, he laughed and opened his door.

"Oh, I have a choice, Jess. I can toss the whole thing." But then he winked at him. "Ever been to Windon?"

Windon. It sounded familiar, but the answer was easy because he never went anywhere outside of Comity.

"No. What's there?"

"An art consignment store."

Hiding his smile, Jessa climbed in the car and buckled up.

23

A SECRET MEETING

AT THE BOTTOM of the hillside were the ruins of an amphitheater. Rows of chairs and the supports from the stage were buried in weeds and wildflowers. Jessa liked to take photographs here. The prince was a strange creature to Wen, a contradictory mix of stubborn human and ethereal Ellowyn. Wen didn't mind his duty to Jessa though. He wasn't the type to fall in love. His mind meant more to him than passion. But Jessa was his. He'd put effort into him, bent his will to Rune's rule to climb a step higher among his people. At some point he would need children. He imagined Jessa would want that too. The strange passions of the crossling would find an outlet in the eager minds of their children. Surrogate children who would be Seneras, related to the rest of the Wrythin family through marriage.

It was what Wen had worked for. It was what he deserved, and he'd let no vile human take it from him.

He crept down the hillside into the bowl of earth that had once held the amphitheater and sat on a wedge of concrete in the shade thrown by part of the roof over the old stage. He thought he was alone until a voice said, "Why so close to the Seneras?"

"We're a half hour away at least. Nobody comes here."

The vampire he spoke to was older. He looked like a human in his prime. Beefy, settled. His head was shaved, a loose shirt over the beginnings of a gut, but for all he looked like a human in his mid-fifties, Wen had no illusions that going against him was a good idea. Fortunately, he had no desire to. He lowered his chin though the vampire was not royal and not from any of the seven families. But he was proud, and he was of true blood, and that was all that was needed for Wen's respect.

The vampire extended a hand and clasped Wen's arm at the elbow.

"Any closer to solving the murder of our brother?"

"No," said Wen. "But King Dinallah is involved."

"Dinallah? What does Dinallah care about a lowly drainer?"

"Pity he wasn't really a drainer," said Wen.

The vampire rolled his eyes. "We are a ludicrous people trying to live at peace with humans. The old ways were simpler. Now we still hide while the weak drink human blood in the open. This killing is like a knot inside me. I wouldn't shed a tear for a real drainer, but Brillen was one of us."

Wen had no idea who Brillen was, only that he'd had the proper recommendations.

"So why am I here?" the vampire asked.

"We were robbed last night. Somebody broke in. The detective who was fired is now back on the case."

"Cops are useless. I doubt I'd do much complaining if they actually did their job for once."

"This one wants to. And he's doing it with Jessa as his helper. On the King's command," he added.

The vampire turned to him, making a face of surprise mixed strangely with indifference. Even to this vampire, Wen's family was lowly. They shared a love of race, but nothing else. Jessa wouldn't matter to him. Still, the vampire looked curious. "I thought he was a simpleton."

Wen bristled. "Not at all. A drainer."

"A crossling."

"Qudim was a sire to respect."

"True."

"The detective has Dinallah's ear, and Dinallah has ordered Jessa to help him. To ease the way into our homes."

"You want the murder solved, don't you? Not all vampires will talk to a human. Not even a human cop."

"Jessa is mine."

The vampire laughed. "Now that I can respect and understand. Old fashioned jealousy."

Wen took a breath, surprised at the heat that simmered inside him. He didn't love Jessa, but he felt... affection.

"Jessa is... fond of romances and flowers... Too many years bedridden, relying on his imagination for company."

"As you yourself said, Qudim was a sire to respect. I wouldn't underestimate his son."

"I don't. It's the human I don't trust. They are low, and this one was fired from his job after attacking one of us. I don't like him."

"You don't fool me, Wen. I see how you burn. You want your place in the Senera family, and the human threatens you."

"I don't want Jessa corrupted."

"Better to find out if he's corruptible now, no?"

The hiss that erupted from Wen's mouth surprised them both. "You shame me."

The vampire's laugh was a soft, sibilant whisper. "Love."

"Not love."

"Yet still, you want me to murder the human."

"I leave it to you."

The vampire's laugh deepened. "Of course. I take the risk. Willingly," he added. "And soon."

Wen frowned. "Why not now?"

"I like to understand things. Puzzles especially. Complicated processes. I think it best we don't upset the apple cart as the humans say. I want to see where this detective takes his suspicions. You'll have your reward soon enough. We all will. The time for us to rise is soon."

Wen had no hope of that. He wasn't religious or delusional. Their cities were gone, and he'd never wanted to be a part of them anyway. Drainers drank from humans, condemned to die without them. Wen had a place in this world, but he wanted power too. When Qudim had fallen, the Seneras had dropped in rank, but not below the Wrythins as Rune had bluntly reminded him. That slap in the face still burned.

The vampire stood, and Wen followed him up the hillside. An old road wound to a broken parking lot below. From there an old highway cut through the hills. They stood at the top of the road and gazed down on the sprawl of Comity. The sun glittered on glass and a sprinkle of lakes. The areas crushed in the Upheaval and not rebuilt had grown green over the years. On the far side of the city was another ridge of hills and on the other side of that was the ocean.

"What is your detective doing today?" the vampire asked.

"Investigating the jewelry connection, I imagine."

"Keep close to your Jessa. Show an interest in his life."

"I always do."

"You are a good lover, Wen. I'd bleed the little drainer dry myself."

The heat in Wen's body cooled to a hoarfrost that seared his throat. His tongue froze, and his lungs seized. But it didn't matter. The vampire clapped him on the back and flashed his fangs as though he hadn't just threatened to murder Wen's betrothed and said, "Soon the treasure will be ours."

Wen managed a nod and stood fast, holding his breath until the vampire strode off, his loose shirt flapping in the breeze.

24

UNDERCOVER

IT WAS STILL dark and only a couple of tables were taken. Otto waited until the server set down two mugs and filled them with coffee. Then he took a swallow from his and said, "Let me see what you've got."

Jessa opened a fabric shoulder bag sitting on the seat beside him. They sat in a booth at the Denny's by Otto's house, waiting on their breakfasts. While he watched Jessa set several rolls of cloth on the table, Otto sipped his coffee, letting it banish the fog in his brain. The aromas of bacon and toast got his stomach waking up.

Jessa's hair was alluringly tangled with a few thin braids near his face. Ginger whiskers sprouted along his jaw. He blinked and smiled when he met Otto's gaze.

"These are my bracelets," he said, unfolding one of the cloth rolls on the table. "And my necklaces," he added, unrolling another bag.

He was decked out with his own jewelry too this time. Three hoop earrings in one ear, two in the other, three bracelets, and a necklace with an amulet that reminded Otto of Maisie's.

Like a cloud over the sun, his mood darkened.

He pulled the bracelets over, rolling the beads under a finger. A few were strung together, some wired. Some of the beads were glass, some metal. They varied in spacing and color, each one unique. The ones on Jessa's arm made a pleasant clacking sound whenever he moved his arm.

"It's all costume jewelry. I like people to be able to afford it."

"It'll do," said Otto, gazing down at the necklaces now. "It's just to get us in the door."

"Can't you just make him answer your questions?"

Otto glanced up with a grim smile. "I can't make him not lie."

The plan was to present Jessa to Solomon Frenn as a jewelry maker looking for a retail outlet. It didn't matter to Otto that Solomon only sold estate sale items and high-end art. Otto didn't want the guy on the offensive. He was a citizen who'd never been charged with a crime, but most likely was sensitive about it. Otto wanted a feel for the guy without the walls that went up whenever cops asked questions.

"Won't he lie anyway?"

"Yep. But he might not be as careful. Plus, I don't know what I want to know yet, so this gives me some flexibility. Where'd you learn to do this?"

Jessa grinned. "Books. I love books."

Otto chuckled, lifting one of the necklaces to the light now beginning to seep through the window. It was too faint to help much, but the tiny painting under its glass cabochon was easier to see. These were far more than costume jewelry. Otto picked up another necklace. This one was a tiny still life of green pears and yellow roses.

"These are good. Really good."

"Thanks. My mom was an artist."

"Well, you definitely got her talent."

"It's a vampire thing."

Otto picked up another necklace. This one was simpler. A golden flower painted on sepia paper. But it was the most beautiful one of the pieces, he thought. He liked its simplicity. The one Jessa wore was beautiful too but heavy. Some kind of design decorated the inside of the amber stone. It wasn't gaudy, but vampire tastes ran to the ornate.

"It's a human thing," said Otto. "Your mom's talent."

A faint color spread into Jessa's cheeks while he rolled his cloth bags up. As soon as he returned them to his shoulder bag, their breakfasts arrived.

Jessa had a thing for fruit... and mushrooms. He dove into his omelet and fruit bowl while Otto worked on his pancakes and scrambled eggs with a side of bacon.

"Any questions?" Otto asked.

Jessa shook his head. "You're my boyfriend, and we're trying to find a place to sell my jewelry."

"And why Solomon's place?"

"Because we've tried others, and either they don't want to do business with a human, or they don't want to do business with a drainer."

"Good. The rest we're playing by ear."

He stuffed a strip of bacon in his mouth while Jessa ate a strawberry only slightly redder than his lips. His nose didn't look quite as pinched as usual, his amber eyes like jewels. Weird. Otto wasn't sure when the vamp had started to look so damn appealing. Especially that tangle of hair.

After Jessa had gotten into Otto's car that morning, he'd rolled himself into a ball, feet on the dashboard, chin on his chest, and dozed off. Nothing about his position had looked comfortable, but it had taken Otto back in time to the house he'd lived in with Maisie and his dad after the Upheaval. The one he'd grown up in was rubble and the new one was in a lousy neighborhood, but at least it still stood. He'd found a porn magazine under the mattress in his bedroom, the lack of originality of the hiding place making him laugh out loud. But that had brought Maisie peeking in, and when she'd seen the magazine, she'd darted over and snatched it out of his hands.

"Let me see that."

"Give it back, Maisie, geez."

His embarrassment had been at the level of self-combust, but Maisie had simply made herself comfortable against his pillows and leafed through the magazine. The thing had to have been decades old. Eventually, he'd edged closer, peering at the flying pages. Mostly women alone, a few women with men, and—

A guy.

By himself on a straight-backed chair, shirt open, pants undone, bent into an impossible curve, the head of his own cock in his mouth. Otto's breath had wheezed in his throat.

"Is that real?"

Maisie had tipped her head from one side to the other. "Yeah. I think so."

Looking back, Otto realized she'd probably only been about fifteen then. In his memory, maybe because she was older, she'd always been all-knowing, adventurous, and wise.

A moment later, she'd dropped the magazine on the bed and rapped his shoulder with a grin. "Have fun."

Of course, he tried it. And failed to get his chin much past his sternum. But the idea of watching a guy do it was the thing that had stayed with him.

Now, chomping on another piece of bacon, he tried not to think of Jessa bowed like a pretzel with his dick in his mouth. He told himself it was pretty damn sleazy to fantasize about a guy while he was innocently stuffing himself full of fruit.

"I thought vamps didn't like fruit."

Jessa frowned. "Um... We're human too."

Otto stared at him for a moment as though the words had hit a stone wall and stopped somewhere in space before gradually continuing on. He cleared his throat. "Right. I forgot."

Human, my ass.

But that's what the scientists said. Essentially no different at all. The fangs were extra teeth even humans sometimes developed. In vampires they were specialized, an adaptation that had guaranteed their survival.

When Jessa pushed his plate away, Otto pushed his thoughts—and his fantasies—to the background too.

And again—as the morning light fell on Jessa's face—Otto was struck by his prettiness. Exactly when had that happened?

He grabbed the tab on the end of the table and said, "I'll take care of this and meet you in the car."

Jessa headed out, and Otto waited at the register. Outside the sun rose higher, shining pale pink through the layers of clouds.

In the car, Jessa sat curled up again, shoulder bag on his lap. His eyes were half-lidded, and he looked peaceful and trusting, striking Otto with the unwelcome realization he had the safety of a drainer vampire prince in his hands. A jolt of unease hit him, and he squeezed the steering wheel and concentrated on the drive.

An hour later, Jessa straightened and said, "What's that?"

Otto glanced to the side of the freeway. "Peewee golf."

Jessa swung his head around, a frown puckering the skin over his eyes. "What's peewee golf?"

Otto chuckled. "Do you know what golf is?"

"Wen said there used to be a golf course behind Comity House. That it was a very popular pastime, but that it took hours to play and used a lot of water for some reason."

Otto barked out a laugh. "Well, usually the water was recycled. But yeah... hours. Hours smackin' around a little ball on what they call a "green," which is lawn. The idea is to hit a ball with a piece of equipment and try to sink it into a little cup. The peewee version is for kids, so it's smaller, and they have to get their ball past different, fun obstacles. Adults like it too though."

"Vampires like board games and cards."

"I know."

They sat around like old men in the park playing chess, except they liked coffee, so they usually congregated at coffee shops and Synelix bars, flashing their painted nails and fangs.

He glanced sideways, catching sight of Jessa's necklace again. The etching inside looked like some of the tattoo designs vampires liked. "What is that inside your necklace?"

Jessa startled and reached for his amulet. "It's a letter from an alphabet called the Letters of the Revelatory Passion. Pictograms, I guess, for things like heaven or sacrifice. There are seven of them, one for each family and each birth period, like your horoscopes."

"Oh yeah? So what's yours, your family's and yours?"

Jessa's fingers fell back to his lap. "Our sign is sacrifice. *Emmolith* in Ellowyn. Mine is love."

When he fell silent after that, Otto asked, "What is that in Ellowyn?"

"*Lith*. The literal meaning of *Emmolith* is destruction for love."

Jesus.

"That's bleak."

"People say love is a ferocious thing."

People? Didn't he love Wen?

"What do you think?"

"I think it's like *Joal*. Salvation." Jessa twisted in his seat and faced Otto, the frown back on his face. "What about you? What is the sign of your birth?"

"Ares."

"The Ram. You're like Rune. When is your birthday?"

"Was. April 4."

Jessa's stare was as hot as the sun used to be—as pleasurable on his skin as lying by a pool in summer.

He smiled as he eased his car onto the split in the highway. "I know what you're thinking. I'm thirty-three."

"I'm twenty-three."

"Mal and Rune are a lot older," Otto said.

"Doddering," Jessa said with a laugh that made Otto struggle to focus on the investigation again. He hadn't crossed Mal or Rune off his list of suspects yet. "Mal just turned thirty-five and Rune is thirty-eight. My mom was with my dad for six years before I was born. I was a surprise."

"A happy one."

Jessa smiled. "I hope so."

"I had a sister." He looked sideways in time to see Jessa's face turn sad at the past tense. "Three years apart. One good thing about the Upheaval was us getting close. Before that we fought all the time."

He fell silent then, waiting for Jessa to fill in the empty space.

"I was always close to my family. I don't remember Celestine. I barely remember my mom, but I know Abadi wanted us dead. Mal and Rune stayed with Qudim and took care of me. I almost died a couple times."

"How did you find out you were a drainer?"

Jessa didn't speak for a moment, and Otto glanced sideways again. Jessa stared out the windshield as the green hills and the fruit stands whipped by.

"I got sick. Vampires don't usually get human diseases, but I'm half human, so we thought I had the flu or something and it would probably go away, but it got worse. I was dizzy. My heart pounded in my chest. I had fevers and trouble walking. White gums." He laughed suddenly. "Mal bought me a whole store's worth of stuffed animals. Anyway, when I didn't get better, we found a human doctor, who said I had a type of anemia most likely triggered by the Synelix." He rubbed the tattoo on his neck.

"You didn't realize before?"

Jessa gazed over, his expression musing. "I wasn't hungry. I didn't improve that much with human blood either. I had enough energy to read and get around the castle a little, but not much more, not even with blood transfusions. My doctor said my immune system was still over-reacting to the original exposure to Synelix, so when I was sixteen I had a splenectomy, and that helped too, but it wasn't until Isaac that I felt good again."

"You feed from others though, don't you?"

"Sometimes, and I'm okay when I do now. I just don't like it."

"Why not?"

Jessa shrugged. "I don't know. I like Isaac. Feeding from him feels like... talking. I don't feel like I'm taking anything."

Otto was quiet for a moment, chewing on his impulse to say something nice. The entire morning so far had progressed like a bizarre date, and Otto didn't date. Otto picked up guys, fucked them, and shut the door on their asses. But right now, seeing the way Jessa hugged his shoulder bag made him melt inside. For fuck's sake.

He needed to steer the conversation to Mal and Rune. Mostly Rune, who had the jewelry connection with Brillen and maybe a revenge connection because of his mother's family, but when he opened his mouth, he said, "You don't take anything, Jessa. It's an exchange and not your fault. You didn't ask for any of this. Hell, neither did I. I was a kid when everything went cock up. You got a raw deal."

Jessa sighed. "Mal and Rune got a raw deal, but I'm going to fix it."

"How?"

"By marrying Wen."

For some reason Otto flashed on the statue in Wen's office. Was it some kind of down payment? A promise to deliver Jessa and get the kid off their hands?

"Don't you love him?"

Jessa whipped his head around, a panicky look in his eyes. "I —" And then he deflated, shoulders sinking, before he took a breath and smiled. "I will, I'm sure. It's a practical arrangement between our families. I admire Wen for everything he's done for drainers and the way he treats his donors."

Otto stuck on the same old question about Mateo Lopez he kept asking himself. *Then why leave?*

When they reached the next exit, he turned off and headed into Windon. Groves of oaks, eucalyptuses, and sycamores shaded the place, and shops and eateries appeared alongside the road. Beside him, Jessa fidgeted.

"You okay?" Otto asked.

"I'm nervous. I'm a drainer, and what if..."

"Not a damn thing he can do about you being a drainer. I won't leave you for a second. The worst he can do is refuse your merchandise, and that'll be okay. I want to see his reaction to you. And here's the thing about the lying, Jess. Go into this for real and you'll believe it. The jewelry is yours, right? You want him to sell it. If he agrees, you're not lying. Your middle name really is Daniel, so you're Designs by Danny. Not a lie. He doesn't know me from Adam, so I'm just your boyfriend/manager, Otto. Otto Caruso."

"Caruso?"

"My mom's maiden name, so not a lie. You'll be fine. Just remember you don't owe this guy jack. Just from what I know already, I can tell he's a dirt bag. You aren't. That gives you an edge."

Jessa's face flamed red. "Thank you," he muttered.

Otto chuckled. "Your freckles stick out when you blush."

Jessa snorted. "Thanks for that too."

Otto parked against the curb and joined Jessa on the sidewalk. Some of the structures they passed were old houses that must have been here since the town was built. Some had turrets and gingerbread details, some wrought-iron fences and overgrown gardens, hunched on snippets of property that had probably been acres once.

True Heart Consignments was one of several shops in a building that had been fashioned without any conformity to its surroundings. The front was beige stucco and plate-glass windows with a flat roofline. Awnings over the front drowned the interior in shadow. Old and musty, the large square space contained a counter against the back wall and two glass display cases near one end of the counter partitioning off a corner of the room.

Some of the glasswork hung from the ceiling on suspension wires, and Otto had to resist the impulse to duck.

Beside him, Jessa hugged his shoulder bag.

"Relax, Jess," he whispered, surprised when Jessa straightened, took a breath, and shrugged his shoulders as though shaking something off.

"Danny," Jessa whispered back, right before he marched to the counter, leaving Otto gaping after him.

What the fuck?

Maybe the vamp was channeling Sam Spade. Catching up to him, Otto reached the counter where a human guy looked up from a sheet of paper he was crossing items off of. Behind him, a vampire stepped through a door.

"Yes," said the human.

He was a youngish guy, about Jessa's age, and cute in a wispy, pallid kind of way. His light hair was barely darker than his skin. His eyes an indiscriminate hazel, not quite blue, not quite green. But something off about him tripped Otto's alarm system.

"My name is Danny," said Jessa. "I called about selling some of my pieces. Are you Mr. Frenn?"

"No."

"You didn't say you were a drainer," said the vampire, stepping to the counter.

He towered over both Otto and Jessa. He was impressive as hell. Otto had never seen a bald vampire before, but this guy rocked the look. His dark eyes smoldered in their sockets, deep creases in his cheeks giving him a hard edge. Well, no mystery what Abadi had seen in him. If the guy snapped his fingers, a dozen people would probably drop to their knees, begging him for the time of day. He was the vampire of myth, and Otto didn't like one damn thing about him. That didn't make the guy a murderer, but Otto would put odds on it.

"We're here to talk business," said Otto into the silence, "not your personal issues."

The vampire laughed, his face lit with amusement, and said, "You I'll talk to."

Otto curled his arm around Jessa's neck and let his fingers brush Jessa's collarbone. "This is the talent."

The vampire eyed him, a smirk growing on his face. Jessa stood as stiff as the statue in Wen's office, heat radiating off him.

"My pieces are popular," Jessa said. "Who makes them isn't important."

"That's your opinion, and what do you need me for if your pieces are so popular?"

"I want to expand."

"What's your name?"

"Danny."

"Your full name."

"Just Danny."

The vampire shifted his gaze to Otto. "You his keeper?"

"That's me."

The vampire chuckled again. "See that piece there?"

Otto glanced back. A framed panel of pale blue glass hung from the ceiling. The glass was bubbled and dotted with inclusions that projected an impression of motion as though water flowed across the piece.

"The artist is Adini," said Frenn. "Like the Adini Treasure."

"That's a fairytale," said Jessa.

Frenn shrugged. "Perhaps."

"What is it?" asked Otto.

"Adini was paradise, the Garden of Eden, where jewels were as common as stones. Supposedly God collected them all after banishing Adam and Eve and hid them. Adini means treasure. That piece over there is worth thirteen thousand dollars. And it'll sell. All of Adini's pieces sell with no talking mouthpiece doing his work for him."

Otto shrugged. "Not a drainer, I'm guessing."

The vampire rocked his head in slight assent. "No. True, he isn't."

Otto brought his fingers up Jessa's neck in slow strokes. His skin was warm and soft, and Otto sweated as though the press of Jessa's body against his side was burning him up. He didn't dare look Jessa in the eye and kept his gaze fixed on the vampire. "I make sure Danny's safe. Consider me the deterrent."

The vampire grinned again. "Nice to meet you, Deterrent."

"Otto Caruso."

The vampire sighed. "Let me see what you got, drainer."

Otto eased away.

While Jessa laid his bags on the counter and began to unroll them, the human stood, refilled a plastic display case with a stack of brochures and disappeared through the back door.

An artist's depiction of Celestine City on the cover of the brochure piqued Otto's interest. "Mind if I take one of these?"

"Go ahead. World's most magnificent city and your kind laid waste to it."

"You got your licks in."

Another flash of admiration lit the vampire's eyes but darkened when he turned back to Jessa. He looked closely at the pieces though before murmuring, "Not bad, drainer, but I've seen better. I take forty-five percent."

"That's high."

"You're taking up space, and I don't turn over jewelry as fast as art. Take it or leave it."

"Forty."

The vampire's eyebrows rose. "What part of take it or leave it didn't you understand?"

"It's too high."

"You know where the door is."

A muscle bunched in Jessa's jaw, and he started rolling up his bags. Otto said nothing.

The vampire laughed again. "I'm feeling magnanimous today, little drainer. Come over here and look at this." He didn't wait and headed to the corner partitioned by the glass cases.

Jessa looked wide-eyed at Otto, and Otto nodded and mouthed, "Go on."

Inside the partition, Solomon Frenn stood by one of the waist-high display cases. As they approached, Solomon removed a set of keys from his pocket, separated one from the others and used it to open the case.

"Think you can outsell these?"

"You saw," Jessa said. "Of course, I can."

Another grin split the vampire's face.

You tell 'im, baby.

Jessa was playing this in perfect tune to Solomon's personality. The asshole probably ate kind people for snacks. He liked a little bite in return.

The shelf inside the case was lined with red felt and covered in necklaces and bracelets. Mostly, the ornate metal work vampires favored.

"You get human customers?" Otto asked.

"Windon's infested," Solomon remarked.

Asshole.

Jessa bent over a necklace of tiny glass beads fused into the shape of an infinity symbol. He straightened with a glower on his face. "Forty."

Solomon grinned. "Okay, drainer. You win. Just do better than the paste around your neck."

Jessa hissed, his fangs sliding down in a flash.

Otto startled. Apparently, the little vamp liked his necklace. Solomon's face had darkened but lit with another smile a moment later.

"Good show. That I can respect. Come back over here. We need to sign some papers."

Looking sick now, Jessa brushed by Otto and returned to the counter. Otto made a slow circle of the shop until Jessa passed by a few minutes later and said, "That's it."

Otto paused before they reached the door and approached a glass spiral in pink and red in the shape of a figure reaching for the ceiling. The artist was the Adini Solomon had mentioned. Once more Otto thought of the statue in Wen's office. "Beautiful," he said.

"Pure vampire," came Solomon's voice from behind him.

Under the laugh was a menace that followed Otto out the door.

25

GETTING TO KNOW YOU

STORMING DOWN THE STREET, Jessa got to the car before Otto. His whole body flamed. The day was mild, borderline cool, but sweat prickled his hairline.

Asshole.

But why had he gotten so mad over his necklace?

Because it hadn't been over his necklace. It had been over that slime ball Solomon looking down his nose at him.

He startled at the weight of Otto's arm around his shoulders again.

"C'mon. Let's get some lunch."

"The human was a feeder," he blurted. *Tattletale.* An absurd thought, but it pricked at him anyway.

Otto fixed a startled gaze on him. So close, the sweet blood scent tickled Jessa's nose again. He let Otto tug him along the sidewalk, sinking into the blue of Otto's eyes like a cool, refreshing pool. He was lost until Otto looked away, guiding him through the gate of a wrought-iron fence that surrounded the patio outside an old Victorian house. They sat at one of the tables, not speaking until they had their menus and waters.

Jessa wrapped his hair around the side of his neck, though

nobody looked his way. They chattered. Humans, a few vampires. Not mingling, but enjoying the same space, the same clear, cool day. Jessa's fingers brushed the front of his neck, following the ghostly caresses of Otto's fingers.

Otto took a swallow of water, his Adam's apple bobbing. The skin over it was bristly. Jessa imagined it was salty and rough enough to burn his tongue if he sucked on it. Would Otto let him do that? Jessa wanted to. He'd never kissed anybody like that. Not even Wen.

He gulped his water and set his glass down in time to Otto's clicking lightly on the table too.

"How do you know that?" Otto asked. "And what exactly do you mean, his feeder?"

Jessa repressed a shudder as his mind dredged up a memory of a vampire's bloody face raked raw by Qudim's fangs.

The recollection came from their early days in the castle. Back then they'd kept to the night when humans were weakest. Candles had burned, flickering strange shadows on the tapestried walls and Qudim's throne. Jessa had snuck down from his room and crouched on the stairs, peering through the standing bodies at the bloody vampire and the human who'd knelt beside him. A feeder.

"Kill," Qudim had rasped. "Kill it."

Jessa never knew what had happened after that. Mal had appeared, snatched him up, and carried him away.

"A vampire can drain someone to the brink and they will want more," Jessa said. "It's like a drug, but nobody can prove the feeder didn't want it. They look empty. I think it's like being dead. They come so close."

He ground his elbows into the table to drag himself out of his memory of the war and Qudim's ferocious grief. Humans had become his enemy, and Dawn was lost in his hate.

The human across the table frowned at Jessa with his brows

drawn low. The blue of his eyes darkened and his lips pulled thin. Was he angry? At Jessa? Jessa had no say about his blood-line or a love that had turned dark and vengeful. He'd never want to read about a romance like that.

Otto nodded and took a breath. "Okay. This is good. It fits with what we know about this guy. He hates humans, so he reduces them to food. The part that doesn't fit is why he hates drainers. They feed off humans too."

"Jealousy?"

Though to Jessa's way of seeing things nobody with any brains would be jealous of a drainer.

"Makes sense," said Otto. "Though that doesn't explain why all the rest of you hate drainers so much. Why aren't drainers considered pure?"

"We're different for one thing. I mean, look at us Ellowyn. Same hair color, same eye color. Pale skin. Nobody who's different fits in. Most vampires can drink Synelix. Why can't we? What's wrong with us?"

"Nothing."

"I mean that's probably their thinking. That and the fact Synelix ended the war. All the vampires who wanted to keep fighting probably think they surrendered for something that turned out to be defective. Maybe they don't think it's fair some of us can drink blood and the rest can't. I guess there are a lot of reasons, but I think it's mostly because drainers are different. Look at both our people. We hate each other."

Otto's lips parted, and his eyes narrowed. The quickening of Jessa's heart stole his breath. He waited for Otto to deny it, but instead, Otto said, "Look at your menu."

Jessa dropped his gaze. His heart actually hurt, but he took a breath and focused on the choice of dishes.

Not answering didn't mean Otto didn't like him.

His throat tingled, his memory returning to the heated

strokes of Otto's fingers, the weight of his arm on Jessa's shoulders... *the stares.*

Jessa had caught Otto's attention on him several times. Long, heated stares like the ones he read about in his romances. The hero and heroine locked in an imaginary embrace.

He chewed his lip, glancing up. Now Otto dropped his gaze.

"It all looks good," Otto murmured.

Jessa ordered the mushroom soup and lasagna. Otto got the steak sandwich and fries. Soon they had tea instead of water. Jessa squeezed lemon into his. When he looked up, Otto was staring at his chest this time. He motioned with his chin at Jessa's necklace. "What got you so worked up about that?"

Jessa's ears burned. "It was a present. Rune gave it to me after my operation. He found it on one of his jobs. It's not expensive, but it's not paste. The letter carved inside is *Remorra*. It means Hell." Jessa swallowed at the memory. "I liked it, and Rune said I could have it when I woke up. Bribing me to be okay, I guess. I don't know. Maybe Solomon thought it was cheap because it's an imitation of the royal necklaces."

Otto leaned against the table to look closer, and Jessa held it out to him. The soft whisper of Otto's breath brushed his skin. Otto raised his eyes, and Jessa's heart fluttered.

"Where are the real ones?" Otto asked.

"Gone."

"In the Upheaval?"

"Some. The others were lost a long time ago. Mal would know. She teaches a class on Ellowyn lineage. You should talk to her."

Otto nodded and sat back. "I'll add it to my list."

"You don't keep a list."

Otto tapped his temple. "It's in my head."

"Jackson Stork keeps a notebook he buys at the Dollar Store

along with those little half pencils, and every night he goes through all his clues and plans the next day."

Otto's forehead creased and his mouth opened, but then the server arrived with their food, and he stayed silent. After she'd made sure they had everything they needed, she left, and Otto frowned again. "Who is Jackson Stork?"

"A detective in one of my books."

"Oh."

"Are we going to tail Solomon?" Otto laughed, but Jessa really wanted to do that. Outside of interviewing a cast of potential suspects, tailing the bad guy was the most detective-like task Jessa's imagination conjured for him. That and going undercover, but he thought that was one he could check off his list now. He smirked at Otto's laughter. "Ha ha."

"Well, where would we tail him?"

"I don't know." Jessa shrugged. "Wherever he goes. I'm just trying to figure out how to do this."

"You're doing a pretty good job to be honest. You played Solomon just right."

Otto took a bite of his sandwich and Jessa ate some of his soup. As he chewed, Otto shifted on his chair and pulled a folded piece of paper from his pocket. He set it on the table and pushed it closer to Jessa. One of his fingers sported a ragged hangnail, and the skin underneath was pinker than the sun-browned top.

Jessa's mouth watered, the desire for blood and salt over-riding the flavor of his soup.

Stop.

But stopping his hunger was beyond him. He shoveled a forkful of lasagna into his mouth and pulled over the flyer.

His fingers trembled. He wanted Otto's finger. He wanted it in his mouth, teasing him with blood. He wanted Otto's hand between his legs, stroking him.

Stop.

What about Wen?

They weren't bonded yet. He didn't owe Wen his chastity, and he didn't begrudge Wen Anya.

He took another bite of lasagna and unfolded the flyer only to have his stomach plummet and his lasagna stick in his chest. He swallowed to get it down and drank some of his tea.

"Are you okay?"

Jessa nodded. "Yeah. The photos are..." *Real.* "I don't remember Celestine, but the photos give me a strange feeling." *Like I can't breathe. And it's dark. So dark.* "Rune likes this kind of thing. Not me."

"You don't have to go."

Like hell. Jackson Stork wouldn't pass up a possible lead. "When?"

An amused look crossed Otto's face. "This weekend."

"As us?"

The amusement broadened into a smile. "Us works."

Us.

Jessa pushed back his hair and let his lashes flutter against his cheeks for a moment. They all did that in romances. Batting their lashes. Sharing those long, hot stares.

He lifted his gaze. Otto's eyes had darkened, and his jaw bunched.

Oh, wow. He'd flirted.

And it wasn't a game.

Though Jessa had never imagined himself as someone anyone would lust over. Not even by Otto. *Mine.* Now he wasn't so sure they were fated, though he had thought so, but maybe he'd imagined it. He wanted this experience, and it was all coming together as though it was meant to be. The murder of a drainer. Otto rescuing him outside the bookstore—Jessa's heart was sure now that his hero had been Otto. Chasing him from the field by the co-op. The King's edict that Jessa help. But fated love? Well, it drove people insane.

People like Qudim.

And Jessa wasn't somebody anybody went crazy over. He was strong again, but his face was ordinary. Otto's was gruff with a faint glimmer of suspicion on it. He probably knew Jessa was trying to seduce him and didn't like it.

Jessa pushed his plate away.

"What are we going to do tomorrow?"

"Take a day off. Maybe you can make some more jewelry."

"Maybe."

"I liked the flower necklace you painted. Was that your Gold Star?"

Jessa smiled. "Yeah."

"I saw it."

The comment was off the cuff and stunned Jessa silent for a moment. Otto swiveled, sitting at a slant in his chair, arm across the back, gazing down the street toward the consignment store. How had Otto seen it? It was small and hidden and hard to see unless... He'd looked for it.

"Where?"

Otto glanced over. "At the murder site. I was checking out the scene again and took a look."

Jessa bit his lip because he tried to picture Wen wading through the weeds and came up with nothing. Wen was busy though. Wen wouldn't even think of it. They didn't share anything really. Certainly not a love of detective work.

Or romances.

"I was named after my mom's favorite flower."

"Jasmine."

He'd remembered.

Jessa nodded. "Is your mom gone too?"

"Cancer. My dad a few years ago."

"I'm sorry. And your sister?"

Just like that Otto's face went blank like a curtain coming down. "Her name was Maisie. She's been gone for about ten years now. I don't know anybody who didn't lose somebody. I don't even recognize some of the places I grew up."

He fell silent then, and Jessa drank his tea. A moment later Otto asked, "How was your meal?"

"Good."

"Have you known Wen long?"

The change of subject discombobulated Jessa for a moment, but he said, "For half my life almost."

"Are arranged marriages common?"

Jessa nodded. "Love marriages are rare."

Otto laughed. "Sure was with my parents."

"I'm sorry."

Otto shrugged. "No reason to be. They had a good run for a while."

"I want forever." The declaration spilled out and hung in the air like something physical Jessa wanted to stuff back inside him. He forced a smile that probably looked like a grimace. "Why are you a cop?"

Otto squinted at him but said, "My dad, I guess. He was a cop."

"Are you glad you got your job back?"

"Not particularly. I can live without the politics, but I've got my teeth in this case."

"You sound like Jackson Stork."

Otto laughed. "I'm gonna have to read one of these books of yours."

"You'll love 'em."

Otto nodded, his lips twisted in another amused smile. "Just as long as it's not a romance."

Jessa smiled back, trying to not be disappointed if Otto was warning him off his flirting campaign. But there was something in the twist of his lips and the look in his eye that was almost like a dare. And Jessa ached inside. The rest of his life would never be more than a comfortable friendship with Wen, and something of Qudim flared inside him. Something that burned with an eternal flame.

Mine.

26

A DARK EXHIBIT

OTTO PICKED Jessa up at Comity House, waiting for him in the lounge he'd passed through the first time he'd come here. Again, voices floated from hidden places. From where he sat, he gazed on an open space with a grand piano sitting unattended on the black and white tile floor. He frowned, wondering if they entertained here. Did they have galas, fundraisers for less fortunate drainers?

He's a feeder.

How many vampires fed from humans? Technically, it wasn't illegal if no money exchanged hands. Stories of the mythological vampire had vampires and humans falling in love all the time. Myths based on truth?

His gaze rose at a flicker of movement from above, and he got to his feet and stood, mesmerized. Most of Jessa's hair was in a knot on top of his head, but some of the loose strands had been woven into tiny braids that fell to his shoulders. Otto approached the stairs as Jessa descended with a smile, his eyes crinkling. His dark gray eyeliner intensified the gold in his autumn-brown eyes and a hint of glitter sparkled on his cheekbones. His hand closed on the wooden ball on the stair rail as he stepped down to the floor. Jessa was half an inch shy of Otto's height. Broad shoulders, big hands, but willowy like one of the leggy weeds in the castle meadows.

At the car, Otto opened Jessa's door and started around to the other side.

"So this is a photo exhibit," Jessa said. "What happened to the jewelry angle?"

Otto laughed. "Jewelry angle? I think somebody's been reading too many Jackson Stork novels. Nothing happened to it. We just don't have a reason to suspect jewelry played a part in this. It was Acalliona's occupation, and it brought him here, yeah, but maybe that's all."

"But Solomon Frenn?"

"Owns an art store and—"

"Is an artist," Jessa said.

"Is he?"

"It said on the door. Owner and artist."

Fuck, Otto hadn't noticed that.

"That piece hanging from the ceiling was his too, I'm pretty sure of it," Jessa added.

"You think he's that Adini guy?"

Jessa nodded. "I got a feeling from him."

"Strange if he is and doesn't want anybody to know."

"Those bits of material in the glass looked like beads, which people use in making jewelry too."

"Sharp eye."

"I watch Rune work."

Otto pulled onto the street and headed toward the freeway. "Is it profitable for him?"

"Oh, it would be. Rune has a reputation, but he doesn't sell any of it."

"Why not?"

"I think he's a purist. Me? If you want a necklace, I'm charging you. Fair price, but I'm still charging you."

Otto laughed. "Something about a paycheck."

As he drove, he twitched with a vague unease, as though Jessa was yanking apart a wall he'd spent a lifetime erecting stone by stone. He didn't for a minute buy the spiel vampires and humans were essentially the same species. Or that vampires were the children of the angels cast out of heaven. For fuck's sake. That one was easy to blow off. But now Jessa was saying they were all the same too, driven by the same boredom and desires.

Hardly.

How had Maisie endured getting so close to them?

And why was he?

"What are we looking for?" Jessa asked as he gazed at the flyer laying on the dashboard.

"I'm not sure. The sponsors interest me though. I'm wondering why a merchants guild would sponsor a photo exhibit."

"I don't know. Our jewelry is a link to our past. Maybe they see the photos that way too?"

"Could just be another venue, I guess. The flyer says there'll be jewelry modeled on original pieces for sale too."

"Where is Oak Valley anyway?"

"Smack in the middle of the Central Valley. It'll probably be warm."

"Oh, I like that," Jessa said, settling back in his seat. "I have my sunglasses."

He put them on and flashed Otto a quick glimpse of fangs. And instantly, Otto remembered there was nothing about Jessa that wasn't ultimately dangerous.

He focused on the freeway in front of him, but the creature

beside him tugged at his senses. He'd swear the fragrance wafting over from the passenger's seat wasn't cologne or aftershave. It wasn't exactly floral, wasn't exactly woodsy. It was what he imagined scented the air in the foothills after a spring rain. Fresh and rich and clean. He shot a quick glance to the side. Jessa's head rested against his seat, and he was still. Sleeping? Did feeding tire him out? What did the crazed hunger that drove drainers feel like? Otto's imagination balked at picturing Jessa as insatiable. Murderous. His brain stuttered at the thought. Jessa was only gentle.

He's a vampire, you idiot.

An hour later, Otto pulled into Oak Valley and took a tree-lined street to the Veteran's Memorial building. It supposedly looked much like it had before the Upheaval, though it had been retrofitted since because of the earthquakes. The building was a white single story with terracotta steps and three sets of glass doors behind three archways decorated with two blue and beige embossed medallions on either side. The medallions reminded Otto of a cameo that had belonged to his mother and that Maisie had sometimes worn.

Otto barely got his car door closed before Jessa hastened up the steps without him. Seeing a pair of vampires twist as they strolled past and follow Jessa's path, Otto set off at a trot, catching him before he got inside.

"Stay with me," he murmured.

Anger flashed in Jessa's eyes, but hurt welled underneath it, and Otto's heart clenched in sympathy. It was a fucked up world that made Jessa unsafe, that was true. But God, he didn't like these feelings, didn't like where Jessa was leading him without even trying. Taking a breath and remembering why he was here, he paid for their tickets and took a pamphlet with a map of the exhibit inside. The building had been added onto over the years and there were multiple rooms interlinked in a maze-like fashion.

"Where do we start?" Jessa whispered, gazing at a giant photo on the wall across from them.

The picture was of one of the underground cities, blurry but compelling, like a wreck on the freeway. Otto yielded to its pull. He nudged Jessa with his shoulder, and together they approached it. A plaque on the wall read *Amaryllis Covens*.

"Do you know the place?" Otto asked.

Jessa shook his head. "Only Celestine, and I don't even remember that."

Otto found a reference in his pamphlet. "Says it was named Amaryllis because of the red rock it was built out of. It's one of the last cities constructed and one of the smallest."

The photo reminded Otto of pictures he'd seen of cliff dwellings. Facades had been carved out of the rock, the dark rectangles of doors showing buildings in rows of three. Abandoned carts littered the street in front.

Jessa gasped and leaned closer. "Is that a dog?"

"Looks like it."

The animal was in the corner of the photo, half its body out of sight.

"Why doesn't somebody get it? The city looks stable."

"It's dead by now, Jessa. This picture was taken years ago. Come on. Let's keep looking."

Groups of visitors sauntered from photo to photo. Interspersed through the rooms were display cases of jewelry. Many of the photos depicted the attempts at excavation before the vampires had finally given up hope of returning to their homes. The episodic quakes were seldom strong and close to the surface, but fractures in the underlying rock made it too dangerous to stay underground. Some of the cities glittered as though made of starlight. For maybe the first time, pity welled inside him.

"That's ours," said Jessa.

He'd stopped by a stand with a glass case on top. Otto joined him. Inside was a stunning ring like the one he'd seen on King Zeveriah's finger.

"Dinallah wore one just like it."

"This must be a copy," Jessa said. "Our father wore the real one, the one the King has. It was supposed to be Rune's."

"And Dinallah took it? Why?"

"He won."

"But Rune agreed to step down."

Jessa nodded. "It wouldn't have been right for us to stay in power. Qudim could have stopped the war, but he said Synelix was an abomination and he'd never let us drink it. Rune sacrificed his honor to save us."

"How, Jessa?"

Otto knew he should know this, but all he knew was Qudim had fallen. How, he hadn't cared.

"Rune led him into a trap. There was no way out. I think he knew our father wouldn't surrender."

"I'm sorry, Jessa."

Jessa turned, his eyes warm and soft. "He did that for us."

Otto had a hard time accepting that anything good sprang from a vampire, but he nodded for Jessa's sake. The war was over, the world dragging itself out of the darkness, though he had a feeling not everyone was happy with that. He looked closer at the ring. "It really is beautiful."

Multicolored roses bloomed inside a large amber stone set in a gold filigree design of more roses.

"It's painted on the underside," said Jessa, "so it looks like the roses are inside it. Supposedly, the real ring is thousands of years old. Some people say it came from before the fall."

Otto managed not to roll his eyes. *That again. Fallen angels, my ass.*

They went on from room to room. Most of the photos came

from the excavations, and some showed the piles of gemstones that had drawn humans into the dark. The largest room was in the center of the building, its ceiling two stories high, window-less walls on all four sides. Otto caught his breath as he entered. There was only one photo. It had been blown up to cover most of the wall behind it. It was not black and white, though it appeared to be.

"Celestine," Jessa murmured.

It was only a small part of the city, a small part of the common plaza. Celestine architecture was reminiscent of the Corinthian style except the façades of the buildings were carved on the surface of the stone and the interiors of the buildings carved into the rock itself. The open space was cavernous, and the rock glistened. By the time the excavators had reached Celestine, the excavation program had been aban-doned, and only a few pictures of the Ellowyn's central city existed.

Otto read a few paragraphs in his pamphlet. The main building in the photo was the Celestine Library. The plaza had been a popular area, once busy with shops and cafés. Carts ran on tracks and a pulley system.

Otto looked up, and his heart raced. Where was Jessa? *Shit.* The amber-colored head bobbed in front of the crowd staring at the photo. He squeezed his way through. A few people saun-tered off. Other than the two vampires outside, everybody else Otto had seen was human. When he drew up at Jessa's side, he frowned at the pasty look on his face. Jessa's gaze looked frozen. He followed it.

"Jesus," he muttered. The last thing he expected was to see a face peering out of a dark doorway. This was no excavator. Its face was a ghostly blur, but it gave the impression of sinking back into the dark, avoiding the camera. "Are they still down there?"

Jessa stirred, and a shudder ran through him. "I don't know. What if they can't get out?"

"They could've gotten out," said Otto. "Somebody took the photo."

But that had been their home, and they didn't want to leave it. Had there been others? Were they alive anymore? He vaguely remembered reading about Chernobyl in history class and the peasants who'd refused to leave despite the killer levels of radiation. Change was an enemy they fought by digging their roots into the poisoned ground. A faint chill he didn't want to analyze ran through him.

"Come on," he said. "I want to look at some more of the jewelry before we go."

A sign led them down a hall lined with photos of Ellowyn tattoo designs. A door at the end opened to a cluster of booths set up in the back parking lot. Otto bought two iced teas and gave one to Jessa, who took it with a smile.

"Are you okay?" Otto asked. "I didn't think what it might be like for you seeing those photos."

"They don't mean anything to me. Bettina, our cook, loves to tell me about how things were though."

"You aren't sad about it. I would be."

Jessa took a swallow of his tea before answering. "I spent years wishing I could get out of bed. Years wishing Mal and Rune didn't have to take care of me. Wishing I didn't feel sick. Wishing my romances were real, that I wasn't a drainer, that my mom was alive." A smile crept onto his face. "Wishing I had adventures."

Knowing it was a lousy idea to get too close to him, Otto slung an arm over Jessa's shoulders and steered him to the row of booths.

"What kind of adventures?"

"Like this. On the hunt for a killer. Seeing new places.

Looking for clues and putting the puzzle together piece by piece."

Otto laughed. Strange how much Jessa made him laugh. His voice sounded rusty to him though, and he took a swallow of his tea. They paused at a booth where a vampire sat on a stool painting a plate with an intricate design. It looked like a scene from one of the cities. The brush had a tiny point and little of the original white surface showed on the plate now.

"Is having to wear the drainer sign whether you want it or not the reason you don't tattoo your teeth?" he asked.

Jessa blinked as though startled, then shook his head. "They're too thin. My bones are thinner too. Not brittle, but I won't ever be as strong as a full Ellowyn. My heartbeat is a little faster, my temperature a little warmer. Ellowyn aren't cold though. We have real blood. We're all AB negative, one of your blood types. We can get any human illness but we usually don't. Ellowyn and humans can reproduce." He grinned. "Luckily for me."

And me.

Much as he didn't want to, Otto liked the little vamp, and the realization sent a zip of panic through him. He liked his solitary life too. No bodies of those he failed to save joining the collection he'd already let down. Maisie, dead at a vampire's hand, and his father, drained of the will to resist as though they'd drunk his blood to the last drop.

His mouth went suddenly dry. He needed a drink. His gaze scanned the booths as he followed Jessa's pointing finger. "Let's look here."

A banner at a blood red booth read *Olnett's Collectibles.* Sitting on a folding chair inside was a human woman knitting a white and yellow blanket. She smiled vaguely when they came up and said, "Let me know if you see anything you like."

Bracelets lay on tables, necklaces hung on strings from the

ceiling, and earrings dangled from jewelry trees interspersed among the bracelets. All were made of glass of different colors fused into different shapes. Jessa was lost in the designs.

"Did you make all these?" Otto asked.

"Sure did."

Would a human be involved in Acalliona's murder? Not the actual killing, of course. Not that way. He looked at the literature on the front table. Her name was Mary Olnett, a mother and grandmother and owner of pug dogs. For fuck's sake, that was so normal the hairs on the back of his neck stood up. Long gone were the days of suburban hobbyists making a little cash on the side with their beads and wire art. Hardly collectibles, though Jessa looked smitten.

Otto tapped his elbow. "Come on. Let's keep looking."

He dug his fingers into his palm when they passed the booth for Oak Valley Ale & Cider.

"The Keepers of the Treasure," said Otto. "Any idea where that comes from?"

"No. Jewels. Jewelry. The gems and metals they use maybe?"

"They're one of the sponsors. It's a merchant guild."

"For jewelers?"

"Masons and guilds have pretty much died off up here," Otto commented.

"I don't know much of what it was like below. I could ask."

"Maybe." He smiled. "Let me think of the right questions."

"Well..." Jessa bumped him as they turned away from the booths, walking toward Otto's car. "Why would a bunch of people get together to kill a jeweler? That makes it a conspiracy. Why not one person for a personal reason?"

"Then why in Comity? Whoever was on the surveillance tape—Mateo, I'm still thinking—ran away from the parking lot. And if it was Mateo, he didn't kill Acalliona, and if it wasn't random, whoever did it knew where Acalliona was going to be. I'm not sure Isaac doesn't know anything about this. Sorry, but they were friends."

"Says who?"

"Wen."

Jessa frowned slightly, slowing as they reached Otto's car. "That's not true though."

"What? That they're friends?"

"Isaac isn't as tough as he acts. Mateo is. They aren't close, but I guess Wen might think they are."

"Is Wen good to them?"

"Not in a personal way. I don't think Wen is comfortable around humans." He smiled at Otto's stare and shrugged one shoulder. "I know. Anyway, Wen isn't cruel either. Nobody wants for anything in Comity House. Most donor centers don't provide housing, but Wen says the blood is stronger if they don't have to struggle so much. Vampires have always had human feeders. They treat them like pets. Sometimes they fall in love."

Otto unlocked Jessa's door. "Like your mother and father."

"Oh no." Jessa laughed. "That was true love. Qudim went insane when my mother was killed."

"Dinallah said she died in the Upheaval."

Jessa's face fell dark now. "Yes. Qudim stayed in Celestine after the first quake and sent us away. We got out, but Rune went back. Then there was another earthquake, and a building fell on my mom. Mal said she was the only gentle thing in Qudim's life. After that, all he wanted was to eradicate humans from the earth. I loved him though. He took me places. Mal says I look like my mom."

Otto gazed over the roof of the car. "I'm sorry, Jessa."

But Jessa shook his head. Otto was lost in the contrast of Jessa's stubble against his light skin and outlined eyes. The sun, winking through the clouds, brought out the gold in his hair. "I have people who love me. I'm not like Isaac. I don't know where Mateo is, and I don't think Isaac does either."

"I'm afraid," said Otto, "that if Mateo is still alive, he's in danger. We need to find him."

If there was still time.

27

PUMPING ISAAC

TWO DAYS LATER, Jessa returned with Otto to Comity House.

"Where are we taking him?" he asked.

"Denny's," said Otto.

Jessa scowled, though a hint of doubt had crept into Otto's voice as though even he knew his obsession with Denny's was a bit odd.

"You want to drive all the way back across town to go to Denny's?"

"Well, where else?" Otto asked.

"Pizza?"

It turned out they went to Scott's Spot, Isaac's favorite burger place. Isaac insisted he didn't know anything about Mateo—they were hardly more than coworkers—all the while shredding his napkin into tiny squares. When their food arrived, they ate without speaking. Outside, clouds took over the sky, and rain pattered the roof and street. When he finished his burger, Isaac murmured, "Sorry you bought me lunch for no reason."

Otto shrugged. "I don't mind. You're Jess's friend."

Isaac gave Otto a look similar to Jessa's, which showed surprise that Otto cared who Jessa's friends might be. It warmed Jessa's belly, and a tiny smirk lifted the corner of Isaac's mouth.

"I just can't figure out why nobody knows where this kid came from," Otto added. "It's one of the first questions on a job application. Where do you live?"

"I didn't live anywhere," Isaac said, running a finger through the condensation on his glass of Coke.

"Ever?"

Isaac lifted a brow, fixing his stare on Otto for a long time before looking at Jessa, then back at Otto. "I don't know where Mateo was before here, but I think he had family in Willits. At least once. A grandma, I think. Might not even be alive anymore."

A faint annoyance entered Otto's eyes, and Isaac dropped his gaze back to his glass.

"Nobody mentioned that before," Otto said.

"I just thought of it."

"Was the grandma his mom's or dad's mother?"

Isaac frowned. "His dad's, I think."

"So the last name would be Lopez?"

"Yeah. I guess so. They live near a school I remember him saying. But that's all I remember. I forgot about it until now."

The annoyance remained on Otto's face. "I'm not about to make any trouble for you."

"I know," Isaac said.

Jessa leaned closer to Otto, watching the way his pupils flared. "This is a break in the case, right?"

Otto guffawed, "Not quite," while Isaac snickered.

"Just remember, you didn't get it from me," Isaac said.

"Nope. Mum's the word."

They waited until the rain let up and headed back to Comity House. After dropping off Isaac, Otto drove Jessa home.

By the time they reached the castle, the clouds had blown away, and sunlight fell bright on the mountainside.

"Want to see the garden?" Jessa asked.

Otto parked the car in the driveway. He didn't quite meet Jessa's eyes but said, "Sure."

Nobody emerged to greet them, but the weight of curious gazes followed. Bettina and Fritt probably. Maybe Uriah. A surge of love for his family swept through Jessa's body in a warm wave. They had always been there to keep him safe. He waited for Otto to join him, his gaze filled with Otto's rolling shoulders. The solid shape of his thighs in his jeans. His ever-present glower. Jessa knew what he wanted, and it wasn't Wen. In the same way his family watched out for him, he needed to watch out for his family. He had to set them free someday. He had to marry Wen. Mal and Rune had put their lives on hold for too long. But first...

Until the investigation ended...

Jessa wanted Otto's hands on him. His lips. The heat of his burning gaze. He licked his lips, looking up when Otto reached him. "This way," he murmured.

Otto followed, crushing small stones underfoot. Jessa headed for a set of steps to a passageway that led under the castle and emerged by the side of the back veranda. Small sconces on the plastered walls lit the narrow space. The door to Rune's studio was closed, but a light gleamed along the threshold.

"Look at this," Jessa whispered, gesturing into a room midway down the hall.

The "dungeon" was the one place that reminded Jessa of an actual castle. The rest of it had a dollhouse quality to it, as though made to look like a castle, but the room Jessa gestured to didn't even have electricity. A lantern sat on a ledge inside the door and when he switched it on, shadows flew across the room to hunker in the corners. The walls were stone, the floor earthen. In the center was a rough-hewn hole in the ground. It was round enough for a dozen people to stand in comfortably but sank down thirty to forty feet.

"What the hell is that?" asked Otto, edging to the dark lip.

"The pit."

Otto twisted his head, gazing back at Jessa in the doorway. "Yes. A pit. Why is it here?"

"It's the dungeon where Qudim kept people."

"Excuse me?"

"Not humans. Ellowyn who defied him. As punishment. Mal and Rune used to threaten me with it if I disobeyed them."

"Did they put you in there?"

Jessa warmed all over in a confusing kind of way. Why did Otto's response please him? It wasn't horror on Otto's face. It was rage. Rage at Mal and Rune's supposed abuse infusing his face with a deepening red. Maybe Jessa's brother and sister were a bit ferocious looking, but Jessa was as safe as a baby in its cradle here.

"Of course not. I'm afraid of underground places."

Otto slowly deflated but still looked annoyed.

Jessa led him up another set of stairs near Rune's studio to the first floor and down a short hall that led outside. A few stray clouds, gray tinged and pearlescent, raced by to catch up with the others, hiding the sun as they passed. Flames leaped in the fire pits and warm air gusted against them as they crossed the veranda.

"Is your mother why you're so into flowers."

"I don't know. Nobody else in the family was, though Bettina loves her herbs. I like beautiful things. Don't you?"

"I guess that depends on the beautiful things," Otto said.

Jessa swallowed. What did that mean for him? He wasn't beautiful. Did he have a chance with Otto?

The gardens spread across the estate—rose, herb, water, and woodland. Jessa's favorite garden was in the middle of a maze of boxwoods. "Do all this yourself?" Otto asked.

"Just the herb garden and the one in the maze."

"In the maze, huh?" Otto grinned. "Is it like a prize you win if you can find your way out?"

"Not exactly. It's smack in the middle. C'mon."

The maze was one of the original features of the garden, and Jessa had loved to play here with Qudim when he was small. After a few twists and turns the boxwoods opened onto a large square of gravel and stone benches surrounded by trees and flowering bushes. "This is my tiny garden."

Otto frowned, looking bewildered. "I like it. It's pretty, but I don't get the name."

"All the flowers are tiny."

Woodland stars grew in clusters, wild thyme among the stones. Purple wood sorrel, pansies, violas, and forget-me-nots hugged the rim of a pond.

As he gazed around, Otto's expression went from perplexed to curious. His chest swelled, and Jessa breathed the sweet-scented air with him.

"This really matters to you?" Otto asked.

"Yes."

"Half the city is in ruins."

"Flowers grow there too. I have pictures."

Otto laughed. "You are a strange vampire, Jess."

Well, he was half human, so that made sense, but living in the upper world had made him more human. He wondered sometimes what he'd be like if Celestine had never fallen, and he'd never thought of himself as a drainer. Would his humanity have died in the dark?

"One more place," he said and turned away.

On the other side of the maze, a lawn sloped down the hillside. In the curve of the little valley behind the garage sat his greenhouse in the sunshine. When he opened the door, warm air gusted out.

He shivered and stepped inside. Otto followed him, his eyes narrowing. Jessa's stomach somersaulted at the thought of Otto rejecting him, and he turned away. Cold spread inside, burning like fire from his wrist. Bewildered, he looked down at the fingers wrapped around him and slowly raised his eyes to Otto's again. The heat licked higher and higher on his body until it spread all the way through him.

"This is my castle," he said.

28

RESISTING HIM

FUCK, he was an idiot. Otto had no business being here. Investigating the murder was his only job, that's all the King had asked for, and all he needed to concentrate on for Maisie's sake. But his head was stuck on her floral print dresses and her filigree flower earrings and tiny blossoms falling like sun on the ground.

Falling like you.

But no. No falling. Not for this silly kid destined to marry another vampire. Besides, Otto's dad was probably flipping over in his grave right now. Not to mention, Otto had never fucked a vampire before. Would Jessa be cooler? Would he wrap Otto's dick as hot as he liked?

Well, he wasn't going to find out because he wasn't going to go that far. As soon as he found the killer that was it. He'd go back to his life the way he liked it.

Plain house. Plain furniture. Plain life.

The occasional hook up.

Hot and fast.

The flush on Jessa's neck drew his attention to the tattoo. His pulse fluttered like a butterfly was trying to escape from inside him.

A drainer. A drainer for God's sake. But the word had no force. Otto drank in the pink of Jessa's parted lips, the pattern of his freckles, the heat of the arm trembling in his grip. His Adam's apple bobbed, and Otto inexplicably wanted to scrape his tongue across the vampire's ginger stubble. Sex wasn't a good idea. It was better to not know the guy he was with. And besides...

"Jess."

The vamp's pupils widened, eyes tightening at the corners in a slight wince. "What?"

"I can't do this."

Jessa pulled away, swiped his palms down his hips, and turned to the table beside him. "I wasn't doing anything."

He pulled over a small glass jar and looked inside.

"What is that?" Otto asked.

"Seeds."

"It's not you."

Otto wished to God it was. Wished he wasn't on fire inside and his idiot body didn't draw him closer and closer to an other-worldly scent that clung to Jessa with the stickiness of honey. He lifted his fingers, and the fragrance wafted from his skin where he had touched Jessa. *Mine.*

No. Vampire. A drainer, hiding his fangs behind his human teeth. He was the enemy, a distraction from the sole purpose of Otto's life. A life so lonely only whiskey blunted the edges of his grating existence. "It isn't you," he said again.

"I'm a drainer."

"That isn't it."

"Then what? Wen?"

Otto grabbed at that with a mix of relief and shame, because he didn't really care about Jessa's engagement, but it was there, the perfect excuse. "Jess, I—"

"I like it when you call me that."

Jessa stepped close again, the space he invaded vibrating at the intrusion like he'd set off a tripwire.

Run.

"Your name?"

"I'm twenty-three years old. I'm not my family's blossom. I like romances and makeup and jewelry and pretty things. But I'm not weak. I'm not—"

"No—"

"A drain."

"I know you aren't." Otto found himself stepping back, out of the way of Jessa's potent presence. "But you're not available either."

"Yes, I am."

That baffled Otto and sent panic racing through him. "Wen."

"We're both free until our acceptance ceremony. Wen is thirty-seven years old. He's not waiting alone for me."

But still... It was cheating, wasn't it?

"I guess I don't really understand that."

Jessa's face fell a little, and he gave a wistful smile.

"I used to drive myself crazy hoping Wen would fall in love with me. And to be fair, wishing I'd fall in love with him. But we didn't. We have a contract, and we do like each other. Arranged marriages have time between the contract and the acceptance. It's civilized and accepts the reality. Nobody's under the illusion love's involved. Well, except for me. I was. I guess that's why I love my romances, but I don't want it to all be a fantasy."

He stepped closer, and Otto backed into the wall.

Vampire.

Jessa's bloodline glowed in his eyes. His face loomed so close every stray freckle scattered across his cheeks jumped out. The bump on the bridge of his skinny nose. The flecks of gold in his eyes like specks of mica in a loamy riverbank.

Otto's throat seized, choking him.

"I want this. Just a kiss," Jessa whispered. "Just to see what it's like."

What it's like?

Otto pressed back in a panic but there was nowhere to go with the wall behind him. "What do you—"

"I'm a virgin."

Otto raised his palms. Of course he was. Tied to Wen and living on romances. Bed bound for most of his teens. But at twenty-three? At twenty-three, Otto had been fucking jaded over sex. It was a release that had nothing to do with his heart. It wasn't romantic. So why think of romance and false gold and...

Mine.

What the hell? Jess wasn't his. And the easiest way to make that clear was to fuck him and be done with it.

But all Jess wanted was a kiss.

"I don't want to hurt you."

Otto dropped a hand, reaching behind him, fumbling for the doorknob when Jessa flew at him. His weight knocked Otto back. Grunting in surprise, he wrapped his arms around Jessa's back, stunned at the crash of Jessa's mouth against his. Never so drunk as on blossoms and heat and the wine of Jessa's breath. Fruity and spicy. He buried his fingers in Jessa's long braided hair and invaded his mouth, dizzy with the moans and whimpers filling his head. *You can't... Run.* But he held tight. Jessa panted, the sounds he made spilling like a sweet drink down Otto's throat, warming his belly and blurring his brain. *Such soft lips.* Parted and wet with desperate kisses. The rasp of stubble like fingernails teasing the skin of his spine.

Otto shuddered and cupped a round ass cheek, digging his fingers in until Jessa rocked against him, suddenly a ravenous sex demon.

The switch knocked him stupid, but he clung to the thought

they shouldn't do this, that he was forgetting something that would come back to haunt him. Not Wen. Not the royal family. Not even Maisie. But something that—

"The case," he murmured against the brush of Jessa's lips.

The vampire was humming, eyes closed, a flush to his cheeks. His cock, hard as iron, rolled against Otto's thigh.

"Jess."

Jessa opened his eyes to smoldering slits.

Fuck.

"I won't jeopardize the case," Jessa whispered.

His lips were spit slick and pink, and it took a minute for his words to register in Otto's brain. In the meantime, he squeezed the ass still cupped in his palms. Hot as any human's.

He frowned through the fuzziness in his head. What was Jessa doing to him? He'd fucked hundreds of guys and never once lost control.

But with Jess...

He raised a hand and cupped the bristly jaw, running his thumb along Jessa's lip. He shook his head.

"You tempt me," he whispered.

"I hope so. I've been flirting with you for days."

Otto burst out laughing, and Jessa grinned.

"You're too cute."

"I don't want to be cute."

"I swear, Jess, at any other time." He caressed Jessa's lip one last time and let his hand fall. "But I can't."

Jessa's eyes closed briefly. Then he opened them and stepped back. He hit something with his heel, and Otto looked at the jar Jessa had been holding earlier, now lying on the ground. It had fallen without Otto's notice. Jessa picked it up and cupped it with both hands.

"What kind of seeds are those?"

"Four o'clocks."

"A flower?"

Jessa nodded. "On a bush. They're very old-fashioned. A human gardener gave them to me, and I planted them outside here."

"Are they pretty?"

"They're not blooming now. Not 'til summer, but you can see."

He gestured to the door, and Otto opened it and stepped outside. The air chilled him, though the sun was still out. A stab of grief hit him as though he'd let something go he'd never get back. He pushed away the memory of Maisie waving cheerfully as she'd breezed out his door for the last time. He should have stopped her. He shouldn't let the vamp get away from him.

Mine.

But he didn't stop him. He stuffed his hands in his pockets and reminded himself of his professional obligations while Jessa showed him the row of plain bushes alongside the greenhouse.

Maybe in the summer they were beautiful, but Otto wouldn't be here to see it.

29

VISITING THE FAMILY

THE FOG FELL OVER THEM, heavy and damp, and Otto flipped on his headlights.

Jessa shivered, close enough to a shudder to make Otto glance over.

"You okay? Need the heater on?"

"I'm fine. The fog's just kind of creepy."

"Pretty thick," Otto agreed.

They were heading to Willits, Mateo's hometown according to what Isaac had told them. It occurred to Otto that Isaac had only told them what he had because he didn't believe Mateo was anywhere near there, and neither did Otto. Most likely his family and friends would be close-mouthed, but Otto wanted a feel for the place because he hoped it would help put him in Mateo's headspace. Not that he had any confidence that would do much for him anymore, but it was all he had at this point.

After he switched on the defroster, he relaxed in his seat and focused on the murky road in front of him.

Less than an hour later the fog had evaporated, and the sky had turned a flat white color.

Otto got off the highway and pulled into the parking lot of

the Sunview Terrace Apartments a few minutes later. Years ago, the complex had probably been appealing to families, but time had painted the multicolored exterior with water stains and dreariness. The buildings were a mix of two and three-story units in faded yellow or blue.

Otto turned off the engine, and Jessa popped open his door and jumped out. Otto joined him on the walkway.

"Are we going to knock on doors?" Jessa asked.

"I hope not. I thought we'd check the mailboxes first."

According to Isaac, Mateo had lived with his grandmother, but none of the names on the wall of mailboxes that fronted the parking lot was Lopez. There was Rangel, Avila, and Estrada, but no Lopez.

Great.

"Okay, blossom. Guess we're knocking on doors."

Mateo hadn't lived here in three years, and although a few cars were parked in the driveway, they knocked on seven doors before the tenant answered and said they didn't really know any of their neighbors and didn't know that name.

Jessa stood behind him with his hair pulled tight across his neck.

After getting no answer at three more doors, Otto said, "Maybe they're at work. Let's finish this building, get something to eat, and try again in a couple hours."

Jessa opened his mouth, but before any words came out, he grabbed onto Otto's arm as the building shook. A pot on the railing tumbled off and crashed to the ground below. An instant later, a door opened two apartments down, and a guy poked his head out.

"What was that?"

"A pot," said Otto, looking over the railing to make sure nobody had been standing under it.

"Idiot place to put it."

As the door started to close again, Otto raised a palm and stepped over. "Just a sec. Have you got a minute to answer a question?"

Suspicion immediately filled the guy's eyes. He was about fifty and wore a blue shirt with a logo with an eagle on it over a T-shirt and a pair of dark gray slacks.

"Is that a uniform?" Otto asked. "I won't keep you long if you're heading out to work."

"I'm a security guard. I just got home."

Otto nodded and made himself look pleased. "Then maybe you can help. I'm with the Comity Police, working on a missing person case. Mateo Lopez? We received information that he used to live here with his grandmother, Estelle, but I don't see her name listed."

"That's because she's dead." The guy glanced behind him. "Just a minute."

He swung the door closed but didn't quite shut it. Otto glanced at Jessa, who widened his eyes. But then, as Otto was about to tap on the door, the guy returned.

"I left the stove on. I'm Estelle's nephew, by the way. Dan Estrada. Mateo's my cousin, but I haven't seen him in a long time. You're the second person who's come looking for him."

"Oh? Is he in trouble?"

"Not that I know of, but like I said, I haven't seen him in a long time. Probably the other guy has. Said he was a friend, but not the same age, though I'm guessing they were probably in the same line of work."

Interesting. What he did for a living was the kind of thing Otto would've thought Mateo would hide, but Maisie hadn't either now that he thought about it.

"It's important we find him. Do you have a few minutes?"

The guy sighed, glance flickering to Jessa.

"He's okay," Otto added. "He's with me."

The guy snorted. "I can handle you both." But when he retreated into the apartment, he left his door open.

After a quick smile at Jessa, Otto entered. Jessa followed quietly.

"Go ahead and sit down. I'm just finishing my coffee. You want some?"

"No, thank you."

Jessa shook his head, and the guy sat. "So whadda you want to know?"

"You said you haven't seen him in years. Not even for his grandmother's funeral?"

"Nope. Mateo found a way to make some easy money. I'm guessing his loyalty is with his own kind like the guy who came looking for him."

"But if he was looking for him, he didn't know where Mateo was either."

A quick flush of irritation crossed the guy's face. Then he shrugged. "So maybe he has no loyalty."

"Does Mateo have any friends here?"

"No. I doubt it. People come and go."

"What can you tell me about who was looking for him?"

The guy pursed his lips together, brows drawing down while he thought. "Early thirties, I'd say. Skinny and quiet... like you," he said with a sharp stare at Jessa, who pulled his hair tighter across his neck.

Otto edged closer to him.

"Did he say how he knew Mateo?"

"No. I didn't ask. I don't care. Mateo broke his grandmother's heart. He knew better than to come back. That's what I told this guy. I have no problem with vampires, but drainers?... Not their fault, I guess, but you can't trust them. It's too dangerous to. I wouldn't let Mateo stay here doing what he's doing. Or the other guy. I told him to go. He had marks on his neck like he'd just come from somebody. I didn't think those lasted."

He looked again at Jessa. "That's a vampire necklace you've got on, isn't it?"

Otto slipped his hand inside Jessa's elbow. "Thank you for your time."

The guy's eyes narrowed for a moment, then he nodded.

At the door, Otto paused. "Did you get the guy's name by chance?"

"I want to say Ash or Aiden, but I'm not real sure."

A moment later, he shut the door on them with a heavy thud.

Otto caught up to Jessa, already halfway down the stairs. He followed him to the walkway and gripped his elbow again, slowing him down.

"Hey, are you okay?"

Jessa wrinkled his slightly pinched nose. "Why wouldn't I be?"

"You don't have to do this."

Otto waited while Jessa took a deep breath and blew it out. "It's exciting."

"Exciting?"

Jessa nodded, and in the light trapped under the clouds gathering again, his eyes glittered.

"You weren't scared?" Otto asked.

"Of course not. Not with you there. I felt like the sidekick in one of my detective novels. It was fun."

Otto shook his head. "I need to be more careful with you around."

Jessa pulled his arm free. "I don't want you to be careful. I don't want to be protected all the time. I can take care of myself. I'm stronger than you, you know?"

"Wanna arm wrestle?"

Jessa laughed, the annoyance on his face blowing away. "I'm just saying I wasn't in any danger."

"I like making sure," Otto said, regretting his comment the minute he said it. It was too personal. It was Wen who should worry about Jessa, not him. But the color rising in Jessa's cheeks echoed the hot flush in Otto's body, and he didn't mind that at all.

Even though he told himself he should.

Even though getting in deep with Jessa was a bad idea.

30

SHOOK UP

ON THE WAY out of town they stopped at a minimart, got a couple of hot dogs, some snacks, and two Cokes, and continued on. Jessa munched on his potato chips, occasionally sucking on his fingers and driving Otto crazy with a sound he'd really rather hear coming from between his legs.

With a glare into the radiant light under the clouds, he rested his arm on top of the steering wheel and said, "Help me think."

"About what?" Jessa asked.

"What we know."

"Well... It starts with Brillen Acalliona."

"That's where we come in. The victim is the end or the middle. We're trying to work our way back from Acalliona's death."

"The convention brought him to Comity."

"Right. A jeweler's convention held in a hotel less than a mile from where he was killed. Attendees interviewed and checked out."

"Comity House."

"Which he went to because he was pretending to be a

drainer, but it didn't work. Is it related to the murder? Or an unconnected perversion? Blood whores exist for a reason. Acalliona's not the only one to drink from humans, but the tattoo... That's a twist. Why not pick up somebody on the street? He ended up with Mateo anyway."

"Maybe he didn't want a whore. Mateo was from Comity House."

"Okay. So Brillen comes to a convention out of town with a fake donor card. Where'd he get it? Somebody had to supply it. Or agree to make it. I'm guessing Acalliona's not the only one who likes their blood from legitimate sources. Still... it seems elaborate."

"If he thought he deserved better than somebody off the street, he'd go somewhere like Comity House."

"And Wen is on the up and up."

"Of course he is. He gave Mateo a job. Wen has a good reputation."

Otto shot Jessa a quick glance before returning his focus to the highway. Jessa defending Wen didn't surprise him. That was Jessa's nature and not the usual vampire-sticking-up-for-vampire bullshit. He believed in Wen—which gave Otto pause. It was hard for him to shake the feeling Wen was involved, but maybe he wasn't.

He gave Jessa another quick glance. "No offense, Jess."

"You don't have to like—"

The car rose, Otto's stomach lurching with it. Jessa gasped and grabbed for the dashboard. On the other side of the median, a pickup swerved in their direction, and the pavement rolled as though a wave had passed underneath it.

"Shit," Otto muttered, holding on tight to the steering wheel.

He pumped the brakes, though somewhere in the back of his mind a voice rose, telling him he shouldn't do that. A roar filled his ears. He relaxed his foot and steered away from the wall of cement at his side, scraping his door and fishtailing away into the center of the highway. The roar died, only his pounding heart drumming in his ears now. The car rocked to a stop, and he took a rattling breath.

"Holy shit. Are you okay?"

Jessa glanced over, blanched white, and nodded. "I think so."

Two cars had stopped behind them, but the pickup on the other side of the median continued on. Nobody within sight looked hurt, but the way ahead was impassable now, so there was no telling what the damage was farther on.

Jessa fixed a sick-looking gaze on the ruptured pavement. The edges were as jagged as somebody's exposed spine.

Repressing a shudder, Otto reached for his satellite phone.

"Can we get by?" Jessa asked.

"Yeah. We just need to back up and get over. The other side looks passable. Wait here. I want to check in and see what I can find out. Back in a sec."

The quiet outside the car was eerie after the thunderous roaring a few minutes ago. Heading back the way they'd come, Otto peered into first one car and then the other, checking on the occupants, who waved or nodded. Turning back, he stuck to the sunny areas, skirting the splotchy shadows under the pines. A few seconds later, an engine started behind him.

"Comity Dispatch."

"Detective Jones. I'm about fifteen minutes outside Willits. The highway ruptured in front of us. Any info on the damage between here and home?"

"The epicenter was Sac. Let me check on anything else I can tell you."

One of the cars behind him rolled backward, picking up speed as it went. It shrank in size and soon the other car followed it. The sun glinted off the windshield of the first car when it reversed through an opening in the median.

"No reports of casualties yet, but all local bridges are closed for inspection. No ETA on reopening."

"Okay. Thanks."

A moment later he slid back behind the wheel of his car. "We might have to stay the night. The bridges are closed for inspection."

"But my family. They're going to worry about me."

Otto handed over his phone. "Call."

Jessa climbed out and plastered his ass against the back window. Otto bit back a groan. *Damn.* All his efforts to remind himself Jessa was a vampire fell on his own deaf ears. Jessa didn't look like a vampire and didn't flash his fangs around like fashion accessories. No bitter humor glittered behind brutal eyes. Jessa was brutal's opposite. Suspicious but friendly. Spoiled but generous. Hyper-sexed, as the other day had proven, but untouched, and likely unloved. And he seemed resigned to it. But it was probably for the best because the last thing Otto needed was the complication of an affair with a bead-stringing vampire prince who wasn't allowed out by himself.

Now Otto—cynical, beat-up, quick-tempered, barely sober —was the worst choice for somebody like Jessa anyway.

So is Wen.

That's not your business.

But he hated the thought of Jessa wrapped up and set in a corner to be looked at by somebody like Wen. That bastard didn't appreciate him. Not like Otto could.

Mine.

No.

"Okay. Uriah says there's an inn near here. We should turn around and go back about a mile to a road that goes up into the hills. We can't miss it, Uriah says. It's for vampires."

"And me?"

Jessa grinned. "You're with me."

Great.

Otto started the car. "Everything okay at the castle?"

"Just a jolt."

"Good."

Otto reversed onto the shoulder, pulled back out and drove in the wrong direction until an opening in the median appeared and he turned off the highway and drove into the hills on a road that meandered through dense pockets of mixed forest. A drizzle fogged the windshield and when the inn appeared nearly an hour later, it jumped out of the grayness, a cabin-like two-story building of wood and glass. It wasn't large, and the parking lot was half full. "I hope they have room."

"Uriah called for us."

Otto pulled up beside the other cars and turned off the engine. He followed the movement of a guy in a yellow slicker climbing down an aluminum ladder from one of the balconies that dotted the second story. Jessa popped open his door, and Otto got out too.

They followed the guy in the slicker into the lobby. A few dimly lit lamps pushed back the gloom inside and turned the skin of the vampire behind the counter as luminous as candlelight. He dipped his chin, and the guy in the slicker said, "Well, everything looks good, so I'm just gonna collect my things and write up your invoice."

"Thank you."

"Anytime," the guy said, stepping away.

Jessa moved into his place and rested his fingertips on the counter. "Do you have reservations for Jessamine Senera?"

The vampire's chin bobbed low. "We are honored to have received a request for a room on your behalf, prince."

Otto leaned sideways to peer over Jessa's shoulder. "One room?"

The vamp fixed him with a stare. Otto would be hard-pressed to find any life in that stare. It was as black and empty as a grave in the gloomy room. But cheerful voices came from other parts of the inn, so maybe it was only Otto who thought a few lights might help the atmosphere.

"A room," said the vampire. "Per request. You may leave your clothes at the door for laundry if you'd like."

Great. Naked. That oughta work.

Jessa snatched the key. Forcing a smile, Otto traced his footsteps up the stairs and down a wood-paneled hall. The rugs on the floor were thick and quiet. Jessa opened the last door and stepped inside the room. Otto followed him.

"Wow," Jessa said. "This is gorgeous."

Gold and cream and rosy wood. A fire in the fireplace. The bed was large, framed by nightstands, and a coffee table and chairs sat in front of a pair of French doors to a balcony.

"Good to know there's no damage here," said Otto.

Jessa bounced on the side of the bed. "It's solid."

"I hope so."

He opened the French doors. Voices floated on the air. The glow of a heat lamp on the next-door balcony pushed back the drizzle. It wasn't entirely dark yet. The lights in the rooms were bright and spilled outside, pulling the trunks of the nearby trees from the gloom. Mist, as thick as a fog, hung in the space between the trunks. Otto stared at it, gray as smoke.

Jessa's voice at his ear shattered the stillness. "Let's go eat."

Otto blew out a breath. "Sure."

As he reached for the doors to pull them shut, he looked one more time into the trees.

The mist was gone.

31

A NIGHT AT THE INN

AFTER DINNER, they took a walk around the inn, their footfalls on the gravel loud in the dark. Jessa nestled closer to Otto, bumping his arm as they circled nearer the trees and the... mist.

Soft and pale like the breaths from their mouths.

The faint gray wisps clung to the trees like dark-loving vampires. But he was safe near the light.

"Are you cold?" Otto asked.

Jessa's lips parted, a no on the tip of his tongue, before he bit it back and said, "A little."

He let himself shiver. Hopefully, Otto wouldn't suggest going back inside. That would be Jessa's luck. A grand seduction was beyond him. He had the schemes from his romances to follow but... real life detoured and took odd turns he got lost on. Was it possible to tempt somebody who had already rejected him? He racked his mind for a story where that had happened but got nothing.

Instead, he flashed on perfect heroines who always knew what to say. Sassy heroines who shivered and melted in the heat of the hero's jacket a moment later.

But with Otto, they just kept walking. When they made

another circle of the inn, and Otto stopped, Jessa kept on for a few paces, lost in his thoughts before coming back to himself and turning.

"What?" he asked.

"It's all wrong," Otto said.

And vague though Otto's comment was, to Jessa it meant they were finally on the same wavelength. Otto didn't *want* to want Jessa, but he did anyway. This time, Jessa's shiver was more of a shudder, and he had trouble talking through numb lips.

But maybe he was supposed to be coy like the sassy heroine.

But he was tongue-tied instead. He had no talent for this. "I really want you." The words spilled out with a groan of despair that didn't sound sexy at all. It sounded... desperate.

And Otto chuckled. "Of all the fucking things."

"What?"

Otto shook his head. The silence tore at Jessa's nerves.

"I like you, vampire."

That wasn't what Jessa expected. "I like you too."

Otto smiled. Close. Close enough to touch Jessa's face, but he didn't. "I'll hurt you."

"No, you won't."

Because Jessa knew that. He wasn't a child. This wasn't love. They weren't fated... Were they?

Now Otto reached out and ran a finger along Jessa's jaw. "You have no idea."

Jessa swallowed. "Show me."

Otto frowned, and shadows hid in the marks of pain on his face. But still he stroked Jessa's jaw and sighed a ghostly breath before he took a step closer, sliding his arm around Jessa's shoulder and pulling him against the hot, solid wall of his chest. "Such a bad idea," he murmured into Jessa's ear.

"I know what I'm doing."

Otto chuckled. "You have no idea," he said again.

But this time he took Jessa's hand and led him inside.

Only a single family sat in the dining room now. The golden glowing lights led them up the stairs and down the cozy hallway. Jessa swept his gaze over the wood and the low ceilings and the homey warmth of the orange and green and yellow pattern on the rugs. He took it all in, embedding the images in his brain.

The swinging open of a door into a room about to change his life took Jessa's breath away.

Otto tugged gently on his hand, and Jessa followed him in.

They stood staring at each other, and Jessa's thoughts scattered like mist broken by the wind. The sensations in his body, untouched yet, overwhelmed him. Goosebumps and tremors. His heart raced, his lungs swelled. He inhaled Otto's scent and the damp air. Dust and furniture polish. Blood... a hint, tingling on his tongue, tantalizing like a memory half forgotten. His fangs pushed at his gums. His cock ached, pressing at his zipper. And his hole... *Oh God.* It twitched and itched as though it knew exactly what it wanted, though the thought of Otto's dick inside him sent panic and joy coursing through Jessa's veins.

Otto shut the door.

And Jessa jumped. Right into Otto's arms, knocking him back into the door with a grunt. When Otto straightened, still holding on, Jessa wrapped him in his arms and legs and buried his face in Otto's neck, burrowing into the warm blood scent. Otto's scent, sweet as liqueur. Sultry spice like cardamom and cloves.

"You aren't gonna bite me?"

"No," Jessa moaned.

He clung tighter, and Otto stroked his back, trailing fingers down his spine, finding the skin under his shirt with a flame-like touch. Jessa sucked in a breath.

"Shh."

Was he saying something? No. Moans spilled from his lips, fanning across Otto's skin like whispers.

He opened his eyes when the bed met his back, and Otto braced himself on his elbows and cupped Jessa's head with a hand, brushing away his hair with his thumb.

"Are you sure? You can't go back."

"I'm already gone." God, he sounded fourteen. How melodramatic. He swallowed. "Wen is good to me. I just want..." Qudim and Dawn's love. The undying passion and devotion of his parents before the darkness ruined it. "I don't want Wen to be all. And with us, we're free until marriage. I wouldn't cheat. That's not me."

Otto smiled, his thumb brushing in a soothing rhythm over Jessa's skin. "I don't have sex that counts. I'm not that brave. This is the deepest I've ever gone, but it's just for now."

"I'm bound," Jessa murmured. "I won't fight that."

But the fact he thought of it as a fight, as something he had to do, was like a fissure in the earth's crust, widening under an invisible pressure. What was love? He didn't know. Maybe he wouldn't love Otto. Maybe he'd take his pleasure like Mal and Rune as a joyful part of life. Maybe his heart didn't have to expand to the edges of the universe, though it was.

"Kiss me."

Otto smiled. "My pleasure, baby prince."

A faint breath touched Jessa's lips, and he opened to the kiss. Stubble rubbed his skin. He cupped Otto's shorn head and met him tongue to tongue. The weight that descended on him surrounded him in heat. Hard flesh pinned him, and he arched into it, rubbing his cock on Otto's hard thigh. He let his legs fall open.

Lust burst with the whomp of a bonfire igniting. The spread of heat through Jessa's body melted his bones. Otto plunged into his mouth, dug fingers into his skull, rocked against Jessa's cock and balls. *Skin.* Pushing into Otto's kiss, Jessa scrabbled at the back of Otto's shirt, yanking at it, fumbling for a touch of Otto's bare back. Soft, soft skin, iron rippling underneath, bunching as Otto rose onto his knees and pulled his shirt off over his head.

Jessa groaned. Loud and shameless. *Oh fuck. Fuck, fuck.* He dragged his nails through the hair on Otto's chest. It was dark and sexy as fuck, narrowing in a thin line that ran down to his crotch. Jessa's own hand had taught him the pleasure of desire. The ache. The restlessness. The crazy fantasies that saw him pinned down by a dark, faceless attacker who would give him everything he knew he shouldn't have. Crazy, mindless, biting passion. But this... He tugged at Otto's hair, dragging his fingers down the line to Otto's belly button. Solid muscle twitched under his touch. He lifted his eyes and sank into the hot gaze holding onto him.

"So beautiful," Otto whispered.

And Jessa nodded because, yes, Otto was beautiful.

He sat up and let Otto pull off his shirt and toss it onto the floor. Next, his shoes fell. Jessa unbuttoned his jeans and lay back when Otto gripped the waistband and pulled. Jessa bent his neck, watching the material slide over his fat dick, flattening it as Otto slowly revealed him. His mouth parted. Nudity meant nothing to vampires, but... He was naked. Naked inside and out.

"Yes," Otto said, a smile on his lips. "This. So fucking beautiful."

Pink. He was pink, growing rosy. His pubic hair was tinged with red, a little browner than the hair on his head. The scrape of fabric over the crown of his dick sent a shot of electricity up his spine. Fireworks exploded in his eyes. He let his head fall back on the bed. "What are you going to do?"

"Turn you inside out."

Yes!

His dick sprang up, his jeans ripping past his feet now. He

sat up again, legs spread, *like a blood whore*, hips twitching. A moan rumbled in his ear. His.

"Want this?" Otto asked, squeezing the ridge in his jeans.

"Yesss."

Could he come like this? His dick bobbed, animated by some instinct he had no control over. He fell back on his elbows, rocking, the motion strangely exhilarating.

"Know what I wanna see?" Otto asked, popping the button on his jeans.

"What?"

"Your hole."

"Oh God."

"You like that? Being exposed to me?"

A whiney "Yes," squeezed out of Jessa's throat.

"Pull your feet onto the edge of the bed. Show me that sweet hole."

Pants came from his mouth, but he obeyed, squirming back on the mattress. Something warm drizzled onto his belly. He peered at his dick, leaking a gossamer string of fluid.

"Taste it," Otto said.

Jessa gasped. "Me?"

"Don't you want to know what I'm going to be filling my mouth with?"

His eyes rolled to the back of his head. He was blind, but he wrapped his fingers around his cock, sliding his grip toward the head. He stroked his slit and shuddered.

"Go on."

Eyes on Otto again, he brought the finger to his mouth. How dirty. A slow smile lifted the corners of Otto's lips. "How flexible are you?"

He froze. "I... I don't..."

"No worry," Otto said. "Another time though, we'll see. Imagine if you could suck yourself off."

His chest heaved. "Can you?"

"Nope. You're our only hope. Now go on. Open your mouth. Put your finger in there and suck."

Jessa stared at the pearly gleam on his fingertip. He put his tongue out. The drop of precum swelled in his vision, growing heavy, threatening to fall. He stuck his finger in his mouth, and a salty tang spread on his tongue with a tingle. Odd. Weird, but not... bad.

Otto grinned. "Greedy."

He gaped, pulling his finger free. "You told me too."

"My turn."

Jessa stared with widening eyes as Otto shucked his jeans and his dark red cock sprang back against his belly. Oh God. All the hair, so dark and gorgeous, made Jessa want to spurt right there. He pulled his knees up and clenched his hole.

"Damn," Otto whispered.

He stroked Jessa's thighs and a tremble ran through Jessa's whole body. He gasped, alarm racing through him as Otto settled himself between his legs and closed his fingers around the grip Jessa had on his dick.

"Mine," he said.

Swallowing, Jessa nodded and removed his hand. The heat of Otto's palm was like none of his fantasies. It baked into his already hot dick, and he groaned as Otto leaned down, smiling, lips parting, tongue curled and ready to cradle Jessa's cock. Not in a million years did he think anybody would go down on him. Not Wen... No, no thoughts of Wen. He'd resigned himself. Resigned himself to companionship, safety, maybe affection. A good marriage that kept him close to Mal and Rune but freed them from the burden of caring for a drainer.

They worried about him. And worry was a terrible thing to live with.

The tip of Otto's tongue emerged, silky pink, hovering above

Jessa's slit. Jessa moaned again, bucked against the hand holding him down. Otto's other hand tipped Jessa's cock toward his mouth. His breath, hot as a stove, seared Jessa's flesh. But he didn't come closer, only hovered there, that tantalizing smile on his lips, light dancing in his eyes. Pressure built in Jessa's tense muscles. He strained to push his dick into Otto's mouth. More of that clear juice oozed from his slit. Sticky, tangy. His mouth watered.

"Suck me."

Otto laughed. "My pleasure."

And then he took Jessa deep into heat and slippery bliss. "Oh my angels... Oh my God... Oh... Oh."

The rumble of Otto's laugh vibrated into Jessa's flesh. He clawed at the bedclothes, and his fangs shot out, grazing his bottom lip. He opened his mouth and panted loudly. The throb in his balls and belly peaked into an ache inseparable from pain. His dick was on fire, laced with ribbons of pleasure as Otto's tongue swirled around him. He whimpered, pulling at the comforter in his fists.

"*Please...*"

Otto rose.

The air on his cock was like ice.

"Please what, babe."

"I don't know." Otto stroked him, fingers sliding easily on his slick skin. Somebody was touching him, giving him pleasure, enjoying him. "Do you like that?" he asked.

"You taste like honey. Skin's soft as velvet. So warm. I really hope you're as flexible as I think you are."

Jessa's laugh burst out in a series of windy gasps. "Who does that?"

"Hm. I've seen it. You taste so good. I want you to come in your mouth. Swallow your own jizz."

He breathed in gasps now. "I-I don't think so."

"Tastes good."

"I want—"

His voice failed him, but Otto knew what he wanted, and his eyes laughed. "What do you want, blossom?"

"I want to taste you."

Otto let go of his dick and crawled up him, dragging his palm along Jessa's ribs. "I like this," he murmured, stroking the hair on Jessa's chest. It wasn't much, the same light reddish brown as on his crotch, a light shadow across his breastbone. Otto circled Jessa's nipples with a fingertip, and Jessa's heart beat harder and harder, and his breathlessness made him dizzy. Afraid he'd pass out before he got what he wanted, he grabbed Otto's shoulders and twisted sideways. Otto fell onto his back with a chuckle.

"So that's how this is going to go."

"Yes," Jessa said. "My turn."

Otto stroked his hair, tugging at the strands. "Go at your own speed, Jess."

Jess.

He scooted down the bed until he came to Otto's dick. The color amazed him, the blood right there at the surface. Whiffs of cardamom and clove and... something earthy and intoxicating floated off Otto's skin. Jessa's head spun with every breath he took.

He bent low and brushed the hot skin with his cheek. Otto's cock jerked with a life of its own. The fingers in Jessa's hair stroked with a slow, gentle rhythm, soothing him.

He lapped Otto's cock from bottom to top and got a hiss for his reward.

"Good," Otto whispered.

Jessa took another swipe of the salty skin, and Otto trembled. His big muscles tensed, rock hard under Jessa's weight. A bead of fluid formed on the tip of Otto's cock. Jessa touched his tongue to it. It was like his, tangy and salty. He lapped again and got another shudder. The fat head without its foreskin was right out in the open. Jessa put it in his mouth, resting it on his tongue and sucking gently.

"Oh fuck. Yeah, like that."

Glowing with pride, Jessa sucked a little harder and swallowed. His mouth filled with musk. He moaned, and Otto pulled a little harder at his hair.

Fangs in, fangs in.

He sank down, swallowing and sucking until the tip of Otto's cock hit the back of his throat, and he pulled up, gagging, spit pouring out of his mouth. "Oh fuck. Sorry."

Otto laughed. "Holy fuck. You are pretty damn good at that."

"Really?"

"Oh yeah."

Jessa crawled up Otto's chest and rested on him, chin to chin. "I want to be good at it. I want to give you everything," he said, his voice growing throaty at the end. "I want you inside me."

Otto's eyes darkened to lapis lazuli. "Yeah?"

He drew his palm down Jessa's back, itching his sweaty skin with the feathery touch, cupping his bottom, his fingertips sliding along Jessa's crack. Jessa bent a knee, aching with desire, rolling his hips, pushing against the teasing press of a finger.

"So hot."

"Dying," Jessa agreed.

"You want it... right... here? Right in your pretty pink hole?"

"Yesss."

The touch was so light, so tantalizing, Jessa's channel itched deep in his core, aching for the scratch of a dick. He wriggled his ass. Otto tapped his hole and whispered, "I don't have any supplies."

Jessa's laugh was a giddy titter.

"Silly. This is an inn for vampires."

Otto frowned when Jessa struggled up and ran into the bathroom. The facility was small but clean and well appointed with a linen closet by the door and a medicine cabinet over the sink. He stopped for a moment, startled by the wild flush that appeared in the mirror. It spread into his neck from his chest, darkening his tattoo. His hair was a reddish brown tangle. He blinked at himself, then grinned, opened the medicine cabinet, and grabbed a handful of lube packets from the box on the bottom shelf.

Climbing back onto the bed, he dropped them at Otto's side, and Otto laughed.

"You have wildly overestimated my powers of recovery."

Jessa's cheeks heated again. "I didn't want to run out."

Otto sat up and leaned in. "I will fuck you until you beg me to stop."

"Oh..." Jessa panted and laughed. "Oh... Okay."

He lay back down, pressed into the mattress by Otto's body, draped half on, half off of Jessa's. The drag of Otto's palm on his thigh electrified him, but the finger sliding under his balls sent his heart into hyperdrive.

Otto kissed him, a smile playing on his lips. "Your speed," he murmured.

"O-okay."

Nudging Jessa's thighs apart, Otto teased his hole, that place nobody had ever touched. A mix of embarrassment, excitement, and curiosity racked him with shivers.

Otto nipped his chin, pulled his hand away, and opened one of the packets. "I want to see your face, but it will hurt less if you're on your hands and knees."

"Less?"

Shit, did his voice just squeak?

"At first. A little."

"Have you?..."

"Yes. A few times. I think you'll like it."

He nodded, his gaze fixed on Otto's eyes, pale in the dim light, but crinkled at the corners with a warm smile. All he had to do was hold onto—

"I want to see you."

Otto tipped his head, quiet for a moment, his gaze moving over Jessa's face. "I'd like that."

He lowered himself, kissing Jessa, while his hand snaked between Jessa's thighs again. His kiss was deep, a slow exploration that stole Jessa's breath. Closing his eyes, Jessa fell into the sensations, trembling as Otto's finger circled his hole, tantalizingly light, a feather touch. Jessa rolled his head back, gasping for breath. Mouth pressed to Jessa's neck, Otto sucked, and his finger breached Jessa's body. Shocked, Jessa held his breath again, as Otto's finger slid in deeper, waking a burning warmth inside him. He bit his lip, spots flashing in his eyes, memorizing the strangeness of that one finger sliding in and out, the burn going with it, flaring again as Otto's finger slipped back in.

"Breathe."

Jessa gasped. "That's..."

"Odd?"

"Hm." He nodded. "Odd."

"Not bad?"

"No." Was it... Good?

The burn deepened, and his hole protested Otto's second finger with a sharp stab of pain. He panted, and the pain spread, lost in the growing warmth. Jessa groaned and spread his legs wider. He melted into the bliss and the burning and the aching, the itch inside him strangely worse now. He wanted more. He squirmed and rocked. Otto curled his fingers and—

"Oh fuck." Pleasure exploded inside Jessa's ass and spread a warm luscious ache into his balls. His cock jerked and leaked on his belly. "Oh my God."

"Good, hm?"

"Oh, I... More of that."

He pulled his knees up, and Otto chuckled and hit that spot in him again. He arched, groans rolling out of his chest as Otto slid his fingers in and out, adding another and another until half his hand was inside Jessa's body. Jessa wanted to see that but halfway breaking his neck only got him a view of Otto's wrist. Maybe next time. Mirrors. Would there be a next time? Oh God, he wanted a next time.

He rocked and wriggled on the fingers inside him until suddenly they were gone. He jerked his head up. "What are you doing?"

"Getting ready to fuck you," Otto answered. He grinned now, eyes alight like water in the sun.

He opened another packet of lube. "No condoms," he said.

Jessa shook his head. "You don't have to worry. I'm half vampire. We're safe."

"I don't have anything, but I don't want to take a chance."

"You won't be. That's why I can drink from humans."

Otto nodded, solemn now. "This is a first for me."

Jessa smiled. "Me too."

He opened his arms, and Otto lowered into them, bracing his weight on an elbow, but pressing into him, enveloping him in warmth. Jessa hugged him, opening his mouth to him, sucking on the tongue that invaded him. He moaned into Otto's mouth and rocked his dick against Otto's hairy belly. *Oh, good... so good.* Sparks of friction lit up like fireworks behind his eyelids. His balls ached, urging him to thrust. His pleasure rolled out of him in a low humming sound.

He chased Otto's lips, but Otto drew away, his eyes, solemn now, locked on Jessa's. His heart galloped at the hard nudge of

Otto's dick pushing into his hole. He grabbed Otto's biceps, squeezing hard, panting with a panic that ebbed with the stretch of his ass, widening, letting Otto into him, changing him, wrecking him, reforming him, ruining him. Otto froze, face slack. Shock glazed his eyes. He groaned, as though chains bound him, and not the silken ribbon wrapping around Jessa's heart. But his heart sang—*You are mine. My fated.*

With a moan, he pulled Otto closer, and Otto rocked all the way in and whispered, "Holy fuck."

His body vibrated in Jessa's arms. Skin sticky, slippery, breath hot against Jessa's cheek. His lips skimmed Jessa's face, dick dragging out, sliding in, every delicious inch searing Jessa's insides with pleasure. A wicked ache. An insatiable itch.

"Oh God."

"Fuck, you feel good," Otto moaned.

His thrusts sped up, arms hooking under Jessa's legs and curling him into a ball.

A frenzied glow filled Otto's eyes. Jessa lurched underneath him, pummeled, dazed, his heart throbbing in time to the waves of pain and pleasure in his belly. His cock ached, his tip smearing precum on his skin. Otto dropped to his elbows and cupped Jessa's head, a kind of dazed alarm in his eyes. "Okay?... Okay?" he murmured.

"Want..."

"Yes."

"Want... you," Jessa whispered, panting each word.

Want you forever. Fated. As doomed as Qudim and Dawn. He'd never love Wen. Never forget this. But his thoughts burst apart. Otto's thrusts turned into raggedy jolts that jammed Jessa's cock through his grip. He jerked himself, his fingers sliding on damp skin. His lungs labored, and his eyes blurred.

Otto grunted and slammed him into the mattress, and Jessa spurted in wracking shudders.

His vision went white.

He rose into the whiteness, light as air, floating on clouds.

Kisses brought him back, warm and soft on his cheek. The bed sank as Otto fell beside him and wrapped him in his arms. Jessa was grateful. He didn't want to look into Otto's eyes and not see a reflection of the love surfacing in his. It rose from his heart with every beat.

"Sweet vamp," Otto murmured.

Jessa closed his eyes and fell asleep.

32

MAL THE TEACHER

THREE DAYS HAD PASSED since Otto dropped Jessa off at the castle. Three days of trying not to think of him and failing. Three days of trying to rationalize the ridiculous pitter-patter in his heart. He'd caught a virus. He was dehydrated. Or sober. Maybe a drink would cure him. But it for sure as fuck wasn't love. Otto refused to fall in love with a vampire. A drainer. They were murderers. Maisie's murderer.

He got into his car and started it with a roar.

But the memory of fingers closing around his heart the minute he'd sunk into Jessa's body still echoed inside him like a caress in his chest. He'd drowned in Jessa's frantic eyes. Was that old myth true? Were blood mates real?

God damned if he'd let Jessa bite him.

He backed out of his driveway and headed down his street. Lights glowed in the quiet houses, and there was no one on the streets.

Why hadn't Jessa connected with Isaac this way? Why fucking Otto? But no. It wasn't real. Glorious sex, yeah, but that was all it was. Skin on skin. Jessa's newness. The impossibly tight grip on Otto's dick and the searing heat. *Jesus.*

Otto's hands grew sweaty on his steering wheel.

Fuck, he wanted a drink. He licked salt off his lip. But getting a drink was a stupid idea. This case was going nowhere. It had been two months since Acalliona's murder. *How could you fall for him in only two months?*

It's fated.

Like hell. That was a myth. Even vampires scoffed at the idea.

He ground his teeth together as he made his way to the community college on the other side of Comity, got out, and climbed the stairs to the coffee shop where Mal was supposed to meet him. He bought a coffee and took a chair at a table in the corner of the room. He hadn't gone to college. Had Jessa? Who cared? The guy was a prince who lived in a castle and grew flowers for fun. He didn't remember the world he'd come from. This was his place. And he lacked for nothing.

Except for love.

He was never getting that from Wen.

Or you.

Otto took a swallow of his coffee, gaze on the door. He swallowed as it opened and Mal strode in. He blinked in surprise. Her hair was in a straight ponytail, unadorned. No micro mini. No spiked heels. No glitter or glam or blood red paint. She wore jeans, not too tight, a white button-down shirt, and sandals.

Going to the counter first, she got a cup of coffee, carried it over, and sat down. She wasn't wearing makeup either.

"What?" she asked.

Her voice was a bark though, all Mal.

Otto cleared his throat. "I almost didn't recognize you."

She smiled sweetly. "I have many talents."

He grunted a laugh and took another swallow of his coffee. It burned going down, and he winced. "I bet you do."

She cocked her head. "What can I do for you, Detective?"

"How's Jessa?"

"Moping."

"Why?"

She raised an eyebrow. "You rejected him, didn't you?"

"Hardly."

A stillness came over her face for a moment, and every hair on his body stood at attention. But then she bit her bottom lip, sighed, and said, "I see."

"That's not why I'm here."

"You did ask about him."

"I care about him. We're friends."

"Jessa is not your friend. You don't strike me as somebody who would lead him on."

"I didn't."

She set her coffee to the side and rested her forearms on the table. "I know we hover. I'm not angry. Grateful, really. Wen is Jessa's choice. Yes, Rune presented him. Arranged marriages are common. It made sense, but it was always Jessa's choice. I just think everybody should feel passion at least once in their life, so I'm grateful to you for that. Hurt him, though, in any fucking way, and I will peel your skin from your body piece by piece over a thousand fucking days."

She straightened and took a sip of her coffee.

"You teach with that mouth?"

Her laugh choked her. She coughed and swallowed, waving her fingers at her lips. "I guess I deserve that."

"I won't be in the picture for long, but I won't hurt him."

He doubted she was convinced. She gave a small shrug and said, "But that's not why you're here. I have fifteen minutes before class begins by the way."

"Tell me about the Letters of the Revelatory Passion."

She drew back, frowning slightly. "What's to tell? They're

just symbols like cuneiform in human culture. An early writing system."

"Only seven?"

"Well, at one point, there was a working language. Some of the history books mention nine letters because at one time there were nine families. Now, of course, there are seven, so one letter for each family."

"They show up in your art. On Jessa's necklace."

"True. Vampires are somewhat obsessed with their fall from grace. In human culture you were cast out of a garden. The Ellowyn believe we are descended from the fallen angels, thrown into the bowels of hell. In our case, literally the bowels of the earth."

She paused and glanced at the clock on the wall.

"And the letters symbolize that?"

"In a way. Our redemption, like the second coming for Christians, was promised to us. Over thousands of years of retelling, this redemption became a reward for our faith and patience. The letters symbolize qualities God desires from us. The reward," she shrugged. "Who knows about that? I haven't seen it."

"Any ideas what it might be?"

"Oh, there's the usual stockpile of gold theories. Or a treasure gathered from the riverbeds of Eden." She smiled. "Fancy cars. Trust funds."

"Any chance somebody would actually believe in it?"

"Probably. Have you heard of the Adini Treasure?"

He nodded. "Once."

"Somebody puts stock in it. Frankly, I think it's right up there with the Arc of the Covenant."

"Some people think that was found."

"Some people will believe anything." She pushed her chair back. "Now I have to go. Will you call for Jessa?"

"I don't know. I don't have any leads right now."

Mal stared at him with a strange mix of fondness and derision. "You're an idiot."

Gaping like the idiot she'd just called him, he sat there with his cold coffee and watched the place empty for the start of classes.

Was he?

Did he have the guts to take a chance?

After all these years, he wasn't entirely sure why he'd never tried to love somebody.

But his fluttering heart warned him away. Something would go wrong, and it wouldn't be him who paid.

33

ATTACKED

THE GARDEN on the corner of Comity House was walled off
from the rest of the property by a hedge and arranged in wedges
with a fountain at its center. Shrub roses, lavender, and
hydrangeas bloomed inside the boxwoods that formed the
wedges. Between the bricks that lined the walkways, wild lilac
grew, and stray pots held geraniums and vinca.

Jessa sat on a stone bench that gave him a view of the
fountain.

His ass didn't hurt anymore. He wriggled a little, trying to
wake the ache back up, but it had disappeared as completely as
Otto had. Waking up in the lodge without Otto beside him had
flooded him with shame. He'd gotten into the shower, and when
he'd reemerged, Otto was there with coffee and a smile, but the
feeling of abandonment still clung to him. It had colored his
mood and made him nervous and chattery the whole way home.

The next day Otto hadn't called, and now it was four days
later.

Maybe he'd feel better after he'd fed.

He sat with his eyes feeling heavy, waiting for Isaac, struggling to come up with a reason to contact Otto. Something he'd

discovered, something he remembered, but he ran into a wall. He didn't know what he was looking for. He wasn't any good at being a detective. His books filled his imagination but fell flat in real life. He wasn't Jackson Stork. He wasn't anybody's irresistible love interest either. Now he wasn't even who Wen had always thought he was.

Opening his sleepy eyes, he stretched his arms over his head, dropped them in his lap, and stared at the doors leading inside. The sun hit the glass and spread across it like a glaze. A shape moved on it like the image of somebody approaching from inside, and for a moment, Jessa thought it was Isaac. But then it swelled as large as the door.

Somebody behind him.

Shock ricocheted through Jessa's body. He jumped up and spun in confusion. Flowers leaped out at him in brilliant color. The sun was too bright and stabbed his eyes like a knife. He gasped until somebody grabbed him under the chin and jerked his head back. His feet left the ground as he kicked and clawed at the arm holding him. A grunt followed a hiss of pain, but it wasn't his. His pounding heart flooded his brain with the last of his oxygen, searing every sense with sharpness. The bastard choking him to death panted. Jessa dug his nails deeper into the arm in his grip and got another hiss. Kicking up and pushing into the body behind him, he slammed his heels backward. More grunts.

"Vile... crossling."

Even through the ringing in his ears, the venom came through.

Jessa twisted, almost slipping loose. His lungs swelled as he drew in a breath before the arm crushed his throat again.

A full vampire.

He'd always lose against a vampire.

Through a deepening fog, Otto's voice floated close and curled around him. *Wanna arm wrestle?*

Now a giddy giggle echoed in his head. Was he laughing about this? Wasn't he dying? His memory fixed on Otto's face, holding on, but the blackness thickened like pitch, drawing him down. Where was he going?

Celestine?

The grave?

No!

He thrashed, bombarded by memories of darkness and heat and airlessness and his mother's bloody face.

Not. This. Way.

His knees thudded onto the ground, and he fell on his hands, face smashing brick, nose in the fragrant violets.

"Jessa!"

His lungs heaved, and he flung himself onto his back. A tangle of shapes clashed above him.

Isaac hauled him up, and they stepped backward. Jessa gaped at the scene in front of him as Wen and the strange vampire fought. People poured out the back doors and ran toward them. The vampire shoved Wen backward and leaped over the box hedges. Wen staggered on the pebbled path, but Anya caught him, holding on until he stood steady again. "Dammit!"

Jessa was startled. Wen never swore.

Nor did he ever glare at Anya the way he was now. "How did he get in here?"

"I don't know," she said.

It wasn't her fault though, and Wen ran a hand down his face and said, "Of course not." He cupped the side of her head, fingers trailing through the white streak in her hair before he turned away and strode to Jessa and Isaac.

Jessa's legs shook and his chest burned. He held his shaky

hands up, and Wen took them. Cool and dry, but Wen had fought for him. Worry filled the dark eyes that now probed Jessa's.

"I couldn't get a good look at him in that getup. Do you have any idea who it was?"

"No." Jessa's voice burned like fire, and he pulled a hand free to clasp his throat.

"Let me see him."

Both Isaac and Wen turned. The house doctor approached, rested a hand on Jessa's shoulder, and said, "Come inside."

Jessa didn't want to go inside. It was dark in there. The sun fell warm, bright, and beautiful, and his shaky legs wouldn't support him without Wen. He'd be dead without Wen.

The touch of lips against his temple confused him. Wen nudged him, Isaac holding onto his arm, the yawning dark of the door swelling in his vision until it blocked the sun.

Mama...

She'd died in the dark. He knew that, but he'd never seen it before. The memory as hot and airless as though he'd been right there with her.

They were in the lounge now, following Dr. Cameron down a hall to the other end of the building. Jessa didn't like the doctor. He was as pretty as a Hollywood movie star but as cold as the vampires of myth. Isaac said he wasn't bad though. He took care of them. And that's why Isaac was late, Jessa remembered. He'd been getting his monthly exam.

"I'm okay," he said.

"Let's check anyway," said Wen, tightening his grip on Jessa's arm as though he feared Jessa might bolt in a post-attack panic.

"I don't—"

"Humor me," Wen murmured.

They turned a corner and headed toward a bright window.

The room they entered at the end of the hall was small with only a sofa, a few chairs, and a stack of books on a coffee table.

The doctor disappeared through a doorway.

Isaac glanced at Jessa, his face furrowing with worry. Jessa grimaced at him. "You don't have to stay."

"You still need to feed."

"Later," said Wen. "Sit."

Jessa dropped to the sofa and stared out the window on the parking lot. Wen motioned Isaac to the door with a jerk of his chin. "Wait for the police up front, please, and bring them back when they arrive."

Isaac went, and Dr. Cameron returned. "Take this, please."

He stood over Jessa with a glass of water and a pill on his palm, and no expression on his face. Maybe he hated drainers. Jessa took the pill.

His head pounded now, and the pill threatened to spew back out with all the bile in his belly, but he let the doctor feel his throat and check his heart, while his gaze tracked Wen's pacing on the carpet. Head down, hands on his hips. The bile surged again. Did Wen love him? Had Jessa misread him all this time?

"I'm okay," he rasped.

Wen stopped in the middle of his march across the floor and clasped the back of his neck. "You aren't safe."

"You got there in time, Wen. And it could have happened to anybody."

Wen let out a gusty laugh. "Apparently, you don't know what an assassin looks like."

Dr. Cameron straightened. "Are we in danger here?"

"No."

"I want to discuss this later," said the doctor. "In the meantime, your prince will recover." He turned his gaze on Jessa. "Get some rest."

Jessa glared at him, but he was already walking away.

Your prince. His old restlessness rose, but he bit it back. *You aren't Wen's prince.*

He cleared his sore throat. "An assassin?"

The word sounded ridiculous, and even Wen backed away from it now, waving a hand as though brushing it off. "He wore a mask. It just... threw me."

An image of the attacker rose in Jessa's mind. Of course, he was a vampire. His strength had been... too much.

A chill raced over Jessa's skin. He wanted to throw up. Comity House wasn't a bank. People robbed banks in the middle of the day. Or jewelry stores, but this... The guy had worn only black and a mask with slits for the eyes. A vampire. Strong and quick and not a robber. Wen was right the first time.

"Why me?"

"You were there."

True, he didn't usually sit outside by himself. Usually Isaac was with him or—

The minute Uriah's name entered Jessa's head, he appeared, headed over, dropped to a knee, and clasped Jessa's hands in his.

"Prince."

"I'm okay." He was tired of saying that. He was plain tired actually. "I just want to go home."

"Go," said Wen. "I'll bring Isaac to you."

"You'll be safe in the castle," said Uriah.

Wen nodded. "We'll get to the bottom of this soon and put it all behind us."

Uriah stood, waiting, and Jessa rose shakily. His unsteadiness came more from Wen's words and the meaning underneath them. What did Wen know about Jessa and Otto? His grip on Jessa's arm was gentle, his kiss on Jessa's cheek, light and honorable. But under his civilized façade was a vampire who'd fought off an assassin. Or a robber willing to kill. But he'd done it for Jessa.

And now they had to move on.

Wen wasn't waiting anymore.

And Jessa owed him.

34

WEN'S ULTIMATUM

WEN STEPPED INTO THE STUDY, and Rune closed the door and gestured to a chair by the hearth. Flames leaped in the massive fireplace, and shadows danced on the walls. Thank God, Jessa didn't have his brother's compulsion to live in a furnace. The room was thick with heat. Rune wore jeans without shoes and a shirt opened in front. After he sat, he ran his fingers through his unruly hair, picked up a glass of wine, and said, "Get yourself a drink."

Wen poured himself a fungali and took a sip, savoring the rich porcini flavor on his tongue. He topped off the glass and took his seat, gazing into the dark stare of the slouching Rune.

"What the fuck, Wen?"

A flare of fury turned Wen's eyes red, and his fangs itched to drop. But not in front of Rune. Power poured off the quiet body, and Wen clamped down on his emotions.

"I wonder the same, prince. Your cop is useless."

Rune chuckled. "My cop?"

"I want Jessa. I can take care of him."

"Wasn't Jessamine with you?"

"I put stock in Jones—"

"Who wasn't there. You were. What. The. Fuck. Happened?"

"I don't know. I was working upstairs. I heard a commotion outside and jumped down. A vampire was dragging Jessa away."

"And you didn't recognize him?"

"I didn't see him. He was covered."

"But male. You're sure?"

"Well—" Wen paused and let his mind drift back. The bell-clanging rush of adrenaline sped through his veins again. The swelling of his head. Vivid colors on the perimeter of the vampire. Black clothing and mask. Not a hint of skin. Rock hard blows, but slippery, wily. Wen hadn't been able to get a grip. He shook his head. "I think male."

He took a sip of his drink.

Rune stared with a sullen glower. "That donor Jessamine likes."

Was it a question? A statement.

"Isaac," Wen said.

"I want him brought here from now on. This is the second act of violence in Comity House."

"As soon as the murder is solved—"

"Maybe."

"Maybe what?"

God, Wen was going to roast to death. He fidgeted in the heat, sticky under his shirt. The air lay against his chest like a blanket of stone. He thought of rocks raining down and the roof of the earth cracking wide.

Rune's lips twisted, a scrunch of thoughtfulness narrowing his eyes. Stunningly beautiful. Not so Jessa, who had too much human in him for Wen's taste. Still...

A good match.

A necessary match.

"The threat to Comity House is thin. Ellowyn drink from

humans. Always have. We'd have no blood whores otherwise. No," Rune mused. "This is darker. And hidden. I won't risk Jessamine to an enemy I can't see."

"Hidden? What are you saying? I run a reputable establishment. This isn't about Comity House."

"No, I agree. Thin evidence, remember? Yet, two attacks have occurred on your grounds. If not the house itself, then someone in the house..." Rune got up with his empty glass and strode to the bar. He poured more wine, drank, and returned. "Too risky for Jessamine. I want Isaac brought here."

Wen sighed. "That's tedious."

Rune smiled and cocked his head. "Really, Wen?"

"Will you keep him locked up? Clearly your cop isn't up to the task."

"Your tone," Rune said, and though his voice was mild Wen went cold despite the heat.

"What if it's Isaac?"

Rune laughed, and his face became more impossibly beautiful. "Jessamine loves Isaac. I trust his opinions. Otherwise Wen, I would suspect you."

The heat evaporated with the shadows, and a breath of ice froze Wen to the marrow. Wen swallowed. "I am loyal to the Ellowyn."

"Only the Ellowyn?" Rune murmured.

"To you, my prince."

Rune smiled again and inclined his head. "It was good of you to visit, Wen."

Startled at the dismissal, Wen rose awkwardly and set down his glass. It wasn't until he was in his car, heat blasting, that he began to thaw.

35

CAVING IN

OTTO CLAMPED his head in his hands, elbows on sticky wood. Music banged in his ears. Unpeeling his eyelids from his dry eyes, he looked around.

A bar.

Dark and crowded. Not a dance bar, though a few couples stood plastered together in the open spaces between tables.

He had a glass in front of him, melted ice, no color to the liquid. He had no memory of drinking it, no memory of walking in here. Did he drive? Fuck, he had no idea.

The street looked dark through the windows, but people strolled by outside so it couldn't be late. He thought he might be hungry, but his stomach was on fire. Squinching his eyes half shut, he forced his memory backward until he was at home again, turning to gaze at his police scanner, freezing at the sound of Comity House.

His stomach turned, and he clamped a hand to his mouth, cramming his lips against his teeth. *Jessa.*

He hadn't been there for him. Exactly like he'd known he wouldn't be.

He swallowed the ice water in his glass, desperate for the taste of bourbon. He got nothing but a thin bitterness.

"You ready? Though I doubt it's gonna help."

He blinked at the woman standing on the other side of the counter with a bottle in her hand.

"I don't need help. Jus' that."

She smiled. "Tough guy."

She gave him a clean glass, fresh ice, and a good pour. A momentary gratitude softened him to her. "We've all had our hearts broken," she said and turned away, not expecting him to answer.

He picked up his glass in a shaky hand and clamped his other one around it too. The first swallow went down hot and sweet. Gazing around, he found nothing recognizable about the place. Where the hell was he? A sudden panic raced through him.

"Hey!" The bartender turned back. "What day is it?" he asked.

"Tuesday."

Fuck. He'd lost a day. A whole day.

The glass shook. He took another swallow to keep from losing his drink. By the time he got to the bottom he didn't much care what day it was. He swayed, slapping his hand down on the counter to brace himself.

"Enough." Somebody had a hand on his arm, squeezing gently. "Give me a name."

"A name?"

"A friend to come get you."

"I don' gotta friend." *Jessa.* No. No friends. No family. "I'm poison," he muttered.

"No, sweetheart. You're just drinking it."

He had another drink, but the sweetness of it turned his stomach. "Wha's this?"

"Sweet tea."

"Fuck for?" he muttered.

"Want coffee?"

"A drink."

"That is a drink. Time to sober up."

Too late. Past time.

He'd let his angel of a vampire down.

Wen was better for him. Wen had been there.

Otto got up, staggering down the hall to the bathroom. His bladder ached as though he hadn't emptied it in days. And his stomach knotted again. He splashed water on his face and shuddered at the cold. Acid rose into his throat. Somebody had choked Jessa in broad daylight for fuck's sake. Had he just been in the wrong place? Was it that easy? That explainable? The same set of meaningless actions that had sent Jessa on a flower hunt the same day Otto had been at the warehouse? And if Jessa hadn't been taking pictures...

It was fate.

Fated.

No. That was a silly, romantic story.

Otto gripped the edges of the sink, holding on with all his strength, his arms shaking, his head pounding and throbbing. No good. He was no good. And he needed a goddamn drink.

But when he went back into the hall he paused. He wasn't getting a drink here. He stared through the muggy bar and past the swaying dancers to the front door. Forget that. He turned and exited into a half-used parking lot.

Pale stars twinkled in the sky.

Holding onto the wall of the building he worked his way around to the street, hunting for his car.

The air was cool, the buildings familiar now. He was in a part of Comity once called Pittsburg. Hell was he doing here? He blinked, trying to focus and get his memory back. Jewelry and glass. He'd gotten some books from the library, but not much of it dealt with the Ellowyn. Had he found something? Not likely. Not one twinkle in the mass of clues lit his way. Jesus Christ. He was fucking lost. He shook his head and staggered.

"Hey, you okay?

"Fuck off."

"That's not nice. Slow down, okay? Let's talk."

Fucking hell.

He turned with a glare and found himself face to face with a cop. *Shit*. He patted at his pockets.

"Hands in the air. Where I can see 'em."

For fuck's sake. "I'ma cop."

"Sure you are. Why don't you lean up against the car here, and I'll take a look."

The cop had a hand near his holster, tab unsnapped, weight even on his legs. Otto smeared a hand down his T-shirt. Tan spots smudged the dingy white. "I gotta go," he said.

"Up. Against. The. Car."

Would the guy shoot him? Would it matter?

Fuck it.

He turned and ran. Surprisingly, he made it down the block and around the corner, but here the street was busier, more people on the sidewalks, dodging sideways, slowing him down. He bolted into the street and tires squealed. Somehow he found the other sidewalk and made it halfway across the parking lot of a strip mall before pain exploded in his leg, and he tumbled onto his hands and knees and fell flat on his stomach. A weight landed on top of him and his arms bent back. He groaned at the click of the cuffs and said, "Check my pocket. I tol' you I'm a cop."

"'Course you are."

The cop pulled him up. His stomach somersaulted, the contents spewing out onto the asphalt.

"You asshole," he muttered, retching from the stench.

"Lucky for you, you didn't do that in my car."

The cop walked him back the way they'd come. He found Otto's ID and rolled his eyes. "I'm still taking you in."

He shrugged, leaning painfully into the corner of the car, trying to control his stomach through every bump and turn. They put him in an empty cell, and he fell asleep on the cot. It was still dark when he awoke to the sound of the cell door sliding open. A face he didn't recognize peered in.

"C'mon. Get up. Your ride's here."

"I don't have a ride."

"Tell that to your prince."

His prince?

Otto stood and walked out into the night.

36

A MIDNIGHT SNACK

OTTO FROZE HALFWAY into the limo.

Rune smiled at him. "Hop in."

The other vampire, Uriah, stood behind him, holding onto the door. Otto grunted his surprise—he hadn't expected Jessa, let alone Rune—and slid onto the opposite seat. The door clomped shut behind him.

"Um... Thanks."

"Better me than Zev. Zev doesn't appreciate human antics."

Frankly, Zev had been a lot less scary than Rune, but Otto didn't argue. He rubbed his face and blew out a breath. "Well, thanks anyway."

"I wanted to talk away from the castle."

Away from Jessa, most likely. Well, that was fine by Otto. He cleared his throat and rubbed at those tan spots on his T-shirt. "What about?"

But Rune didn't answer. He swiveled on his seat and gazed through the partition. "Pull over for a minute. Check to see if we have a fresh shirt in the trunk."

Uriah said nothing, but the car eased to the side of the street.

Rune sat forward again. "We get in some nasty places. I usually keep an extra set of clothes."

"You?..."

"Draw maps."

"Right."

Rune smiled over white teeth. No fangs in sight right now, but Otto didn't trust the burn in the vampire's eyes. The car rocked as Uriah got out and slammed the door. A moment later the lid went up. "How do you get your jobs?" Otto asked.

"Usually the Council. Universities sometimes. Areas I surveyed only a few years ago have already changed. New valleys and lakes, higher mountains, diverted rivers. My people lived in the same cities for thousands of years. This is fascinating to me. What fascinates you, Otto Jones?"

Jessa.

"Justice."

Rune's smile broadened. "An idealist. Or a man with an agenda."

Somewhat sober now, Otto's eyes sharpened on Rune's face. "You don't believe in justice?"

"I'm counting on it."

Before Otto asked what Rune meant by that the door opened, and Uriah held out a shirt. It was a simple blue chambray, but it was clean and didn't stink. Otto yanked his T-shirt over his head and pulled on Rune's.

"Uriah," said Rune.

"Yes?"

"Find us a place to eat."

Otto's fingers froze on his buttons. "You don't—"

Rune waved a hand at him. "It's four in the morning. I need fuel too."

"You don't sleep during the day either?"

"Usually I do, but I have a job coming up, and I do what I do in the light."

"And your art?"

"At night. My heart is its truest self in the dark."

Otto laughed, the sound a low chuff. So was his. "I never liked vampires... until Jessa."

"Jessa is both human and vampire. Which do you like?"

He shook his head. "I don't know."

"Why did you reject him?"

Jesus. First Mal, now Rune. "Protective much?" he muttered.

"Enough you ought to worry," Rune said quietly.

Otto gritted his teeth in annoyance. Fucking vampires. He was drowning in them. Or just drowning.

"He's engaged, remember?"

"Not quite. Try better."

Now his fangs showed under his smiling lip.

"I've let down all the people I plan to."

Hearing those words reverberate in his head rocked him with a rush of dizziness. *It's the booze.* But it wasn't. He didn't know what kind of glib thing he'd meant to say, but it sure as hell wasn't the truth. Especially not a truth he did everything in his power never to look at.

He met Rune's eyes fixed on him in silence. Then Rune rocked his head with a thoughtful smile.

"A person can interpret that comment in several ways."

"I meant only one. Somebody attacked him." *On my fucking watch.*

"I know." Rune's voice fell into a lethal whisper, soft as a deadly mist. His lips were closed, but Otto knew those fangs had dropped again. Then he smiled. "You weren't with him. You couldn't stop it."

Reason annoyed him, dug under his skin like scabies. It

itched and ate at his nerves. He wasn't a kid who needed stroking. Fuck, not even his dad had ever tried to console him over anything. "I know what I'm doing."

"You'd better fucking know what you're doing better than this from here on. You slept with him. Sex is nothing to vampires. Love is on a par with Santa Claus. A cute story you wish was true. Jessa loves stories. They gave him hope when we all thought he was going to die. He lives in those romances of his, the tales of our father and Dawn." Rune laughed. "Eternal passion. Fated love. That is what Jessa lives for." Now Rune smiled, a laugh in his eyes. "Pity it's just a fantasy. I know he won't get it. I wouldn't have led him on."

"I was honest."

"Oh. That old bromide. Tell me truly you didn't know he was lying to himself." Otto didn't have a chance to answer before Rune went on, waving a hand in front of him. "We all do, of course. We pretend everything's normal while the floor rots out from under us. No point wallowing though. That means you. You feel sorry for yourself. Well, too bad. We all lost things in the war."

Otto somehow didn't burst into flames, though his body was hot with rage.

"And after," he squeezed through gritted teeth.

"Yes," Rune murmured. "And after."

A wash of light bled into the car as Uriah turned into the parking lot of a Denny's knockoff Otto had never been to before. Uriah shut off the engine and followed them inside though he took a seat at the counter while Otto and Rune continued to a booth. Only a few were occupied. The place was quiet, but Rune still chose a booth in back.

"I don't have any money," Otto murmured.

"I'm loaded," said Rune with a grin. "Besides, you work for me now."

"I do?"

"I can't lock Jessa up anymore. I picked Wen for him because I didn't have much of a choice. Marrying Jessa is an honor for the Wrythin family, and Wen can provide what Jessa needs. He's still royal, and he's below me. But you? You don't treat Jessa like a drainer. I want that for him, and I think he's safest with you."

"Is that my job? Watching out for Jessa?"

"And solving the murder."

A waitress with short black hair and giant silver hoop earrings that grazed her shoulders appeared with a pot of coffee and two cups hooked on her fingers. "You ready to order?"

"Mushroom burger," said Rune. "Lots of mushrooms."

"Regular burger for me," said Otto, pulling his cup to him.

"No cheese?"

"No. Wouldn't mind some coleslaw on it though."

"Comin' up."

The first swallow of coffee hit his gut like a cannonball but mellowed a moment later. "This murder makes no sense," he said, smothered by a wave of grief. Nothing lit up in him, none of the old wonder as clues tumbled into a picture only he could see.

"Maybe it was fortuitous," said Rune. "Wrong place, wrong time. Prey and predator."

"Acalliona had no reason to be in that field unless he was hooking up with somebody."

"So Acalliona was the predator and the prey got lucky."

Otto snorted. "The prey was human. Like my sister. A drainer killed her."

Rune gave him a long stare. Maybe he already knew, though Otto hadn't told Jessa yet. "She had no chance," Rune said. "To get away, I mean."

"I don't know."

But he did know. He'd missed any chance to save her the minute he'd let her walk away from him certain there'd be another chance to convince her to change her life.

"My father always told us we had hidden powers, but nothing saved us. I left Mal and Jessa and Dawn to go back into Celestine," said Rune. "I thought they were safe. By the time I got back, Dawn was dead and Jessa was injured. I believed Synelix was safe and it almost killed him. I let you humans tattoo him to keep the peace. I made the trade-offs I had to make."

Otto waited until the waitress set down their plates and refilled their coffee cups. His stomach knotted at the aromas of meat and mushrooms, and his fingers trembled. He ate a few fries while Rune bit into his burger.

When Rune swallowed, Otto asked, "Why isn't food enough for you?"

Rune squinted, a slightly perplexed look on his face as though the question didn't make sense to him. Maybe it didn't. Otto wasn't sure anybody knew the answer. "I don't know. What would happen if you only ate seeds? Wouldn't you die?"

"Not right away."

"Neither would we. We'd get sick first." He snagged a mushroom off his plate, turning it to and fro while smiling at it. "But we crave the blood of our other halves. Of you. We can't live without it. You can live without us, but we are stronger and harder to kill."

"My sister fought. I was in the academy when it happened. I should've quit, but I stayed in thinking I had a better chance of finding her killer."

"And now?"

Otto laughed. "I'm not in or out. Six a one, half a dozen of another. The guy who did it's still out there. Or died in a goddamn field."

"Brillen wasn't a drainer."

"Any vampire can drain a human."

Rune pushed his empty plate away and folded his arms on the table. "I broke with Qudim over the war for Jessa's sake. We had no home to return to. Our world is here. The Adi 'el Lumi want revenge, but the King wants peace at any cost."

Otto frowned. "Adi 'el Lumi?"

Rune smiled. "A sect lost in the fantasy of Ellowyn glory. They want to enslave you."

"Oh, nice. The good old days."

Rune laughed. "Qudim thought so. They revere him."

"Are they dangerous?"

Rune frowned for a moment, looking thoughtful. "Ideas are always dangerous. They scattered years ago. Hate never dies though. I admire your idea of justice. It has a touch of fanaticism to it." He leaned in against the table. "Solve your murder, Otto Jones. Keep Jessa safe. That is your job. Don't fail me."

Otto stared into the burn of Rune's eyes until Rune slid out of the booth and strode to the door.

37

OTTO'S SURPRISE

FUCK.

Jessa glared at the reflection in his bathroom mirror. Earrings and braids and smoky eyelids. He pouted into the glass. This wasn't a date. He hated his face anyway. Average-looking people never showed up on book covers. He wasn't exactly ugly, but he wasn't Rune or Mal either.

Otto had fucked him and disappeared.

Jessa leaned in and peered up close. His eyes weren't even a real color. Not black, not brown, not blue, not green. A mix like his hair. Mousy brown, dirty blond, brassy red.

You aren't going on a date.

He was working. This was a job. He and Otto. Whether Otto liked it or not.

So why are you made up?

He turned on the water, waited for it to warm, and scrubbed his face. After he dried it, he looked in the mirror again. He disappeared. So forgettable.

With a groan, he returned to his bedroom, slipped on his jacket, and headed to the front porch where he sat on the steps for five minutes before Otto's car appeared in the distance. He didn't move until the car swung in a half circle and stopped in front of him.

He got in and slammed the door.

"You don't have to do this."

He didn't even look at Otto. Fuck him. Fuck the burn in his nose and prick in his eyes. *I want him to like me. Fuck, fuck, fuck.*

"Jess."

"You can get any vampire to work with you."

The car idled, warm air puffing from the heater vents. A misty haze turned the day gray, and condensation formed inside the car.

"I don't want any vampire. I want you."

His stomach somersaulted, and a chill gripped him. *Want me for what?*

Maybe Otto was setting him up. The awful boyfriend who drove the heroine running to the real hero. *To Wen.*

Ultimately, it was Wen he'd return to.

"I can't help you. I get all my ideas from books."

"This isn't about the case. I have a surprise for you. I think you might like it."

Now Jessa looked sideways, the frown on his face setting in deeper. "Why?"

Otto's lips parted, but nothing emerged. He took a breath, and Jessa stared at the shadows under his eyes, the scruff on his jaw. Clean, but beat up looking.

"I'm trying to make up with you."

"Like a friend?"

"I want to be friends."

Not me. But he didn't say that. He merely nodded and rubbed his sweaty palms on his knees. "Why'd you stay away?"

"I have a lousy track record with people."

"Maybe because you stay away."

Otto snorted a laugh. "Maybe."

"I'm easy to please," Jessa murmured.

A slow smile formed on Otto's face. "A low bar might be a good thing for me."

Jessa shook his head. "That's sad."

"That's me."

"I thought you didn't like me." Just saying the words sent a knife through his chest again.

"I like you, Jess. I like you a lot. I want us to be friends."

Fuck friends. Except... Friends to lovers stories were Jessa's favorites. So... "We can be friends."

"Good."

Friends had sex, right? He hoped so. He buckled his seatbelt, and Otto shifted the car into gear.

"What's my surprise?"

"A surprise."

Jessa gusted a sigh, fogging the window beside him. The rain broke, falling in sprinkles and splats through the trees.

"Have you been working on the case?"

Otto shook his head. "We'll talk about it after your surprise."

By the time they got into Comity, the rain had stopped, and the sun shone on the shiny wet streets. They crossed town and drove into a busy retail area where curved streets branched off the main one like the fronds on a palm branch. Otto turned at a signal light, turned again into a parking garage, and found a spot on the second floor.

Jessa glanced around then hooked his hair behind his ears. "What's here?"

"Wait and see," Otto said.

He huffed but unbuckled and got out of the car. They followed a family downstairs and exited onto a short street between the garage and—*a movie theater!*

Jessa grabbed Otto's arm. "Are we going to a movie?"

"Is that okay?"

"Yes! Oh my God. I've never been to a movie. We have a movie room at home, but that's not the same. Can we get popcorn?"

"Anything you want," said Otto.

The pleased look on Otto's face made Jessa giddy, and he grabbed Otto's arm and yanked him across the street. "Which one are we going to see?"

Otto pointed to a poster under glass.

Titanic.

"It's a ship."

"Trust me," said Otto. "I think you're going to really like this."

Honestly, Jessa didn't care what movie they were going to see. He dragged Otto into the lobby and to the snack bar where Otto bought a tub of popcorn and two tall soft drinks. The popcorn was perfect—greasy and salty and delicious.

"I forgive you for everything," he whispered in the dark, and Otto burst out laughing. "Quiet," he added. "I don't want us to get kicked out."

Otto leaned over and whispered too, breath warm against Jessa's face. "I have a gun. We're safe."

Jessa snickered. He didn't feel twenty-three anymore. He felt fourteen... Or ten. The world was full of things he'd never done, and a surge of excitement raced through him as music blasted in his ears. By the end of the movie he was sniffling, and when Otto pressed his lips against his temple, Jessa leaned into him. Now the music was playing again, and people were getting out of their seats and making their way up the aisles.

Jessa sighed. "That was so sad."

"It's just a movie," Otto whispered.

"But it was so romantic."

What if Jessa did that? Loved somebody so much he'd die

for him. That wasn't exactly a happy ending. Nobody died in his romances. He had no experience with the idea and didn't particularly like it. Living for love was a lot more romantic. He was pretty sure it was harder too—and took forgiveness and kindness.

"Thank you for doing this."

"Oh, it's not over yet," said Otto. He stood and pulled Jessa to his feet. "How about pizza?"

Oh yeah. "Mushroom?"

Otto chuckled. "I like mushrooms."

Outside, the low sun lit the tops of the buildings and the clear sky shone like silver. They stopped at a Round Table and got in line. Jessa brushed Otto's hand with the backs of his fingers. "Order it to go," he murmured.

Otto gazed into his eyes, a playful smile teasing the corners of his lips. "Extra cheese with that?"

Jessa grinned. "Oh yeah."

He left Otto at the register and sat at a booth. A TV hung on the far wall, but nothing was on. A DVD player sat on a shelf underneath, so maybe they had movie nights too. A pool hall would be fun to go to. A sketchy place with dartboards and dangerous people. People like Otto. Who wore a gun under his jacket and was carrying two Cokes with him.

"Just for here," he said when he set the drinks down. "The pizza goes with us."

Jessa grinned again. "Good."

"Tomorrow, back to the case."

"What are we going to do?"

"I wish I could see how all of this was connected. You. Comity House. Jewelers. Mateo. Was he the witness, or did he just move on?" He turned his head again, frowning at Jessa. "Is Isaac lying?"

Jessa startled. "About Mateo? Why?"

"Maybe Mateo asked him to. Isaac told us where to go to see Mateo's family. Maybe he was leading us away."

Jessa squinched his eyes half shut, thinking back over his last times with Isaac. He shook his head. "They're not good friends."

"They wouldn't have to be."

"Okay. Mateo makes a deal with Brillen and meets with him. Brillen is murdered, and Mateo runs away. Or Mateo was in on the murder with someone else."

Otto shook his head. "Not from what I saw on the surveillance tape. If that was Mateo, he was running for his life. Maybe he was part of a robbery that got out of hand, but Acalliona wasn't robbed from the looks of him."

"Unless it was just one thing they took."

"Like what?"

"I don't know. Maybe he had something they wanted."

"Well, the obvious thing would be a jewel, but I can't see a jeweler wearing a piece of jewelry somebody would go to the trouble to steal. I don't know, I just see somebody like Acalliona being more cautious. So, was it something he wasn't supposed to have and was selling on the sly? And where does Mateo fit in?"

"Maybe Brillen didn't have it and was supposed to. Or maybe it was something he didn't even know he had. Mateo, if that was him, was just in the wrong place at the wrong time."

"Which would bring us back to the convention, and that means we're looking at someone attending the convention or a guest, which opens the pool of candidates to just about anybody."

"Would the hotel or the organizers have a list?"

"Both would. We interviewed a number of people right away. The problem is anybody can walk into a hotel. And in this case maybe they didn't even need to. They could have just waited for their moment."

"Vampires for sure. They weren't worried about Mateo."

"Wonder why they let him go though?" Otto frowned and turned his glass in a slow circle. "They... or whoever it was, let him go."

"Or something went wrong and gave him time to get away."

Otto took a swallow of his Coke, gaze going distant until he swallowed and set the cup down. "Yeah. Time. The first murder was two years ago and looks like a hate crime. Probably not connected, but if they are, the killers are in no hurry."

The plot to one of Jessa's romances popped into his head and he said, "I read a suspense story once where an ex-cop was protecting a victim of an attempted murder. She was perfectly innocent and had no idea who would want her dead, but the crime looked like an earlier murder. For most of the book they couldn't figure it out, not until they discovered there were other murders in between, and they realized it was—"

"A serial killer."

Jessa nodded. "That's right. A woman—"

"A woman serial killer?"

"Yes. She was killing people who checked out the book of a guy who'd rejected her. She'd killed him too, but it looked like an accident, so nobody guessed."

Otto smiled.

"You're laughing at me."

"I'm agreeing with you," said Otto. "I mean I don't think this is necessarily that, but you're right. The victims are the clue."

"The victims were drainers."

"And in the last two years only two drainers have been killed in this area. Ten years ago, somebody drained a... a human. Could be who we're looking for, though it's a stretch, I guess."

The distance had returned to Otto's eyes, tamping out the light this time. A shivery feeling crept over Jessa's skin.

Ten years ago. That meant...

A vampire who drained somebody ten years ago did it out of malice. Synelix had been on the market over eleven years. That meant it wasn't hunger that drove the killer. Unless...

He was a drainer.

Jessa pushed back against the booth as a drenching shame at being what he was washed over him. "A real drainer?"

Otto nodded. "And a cold-blooded murderer. Got away too."

"Were you on the case?"

Otto shook his head. "No. This was in Heritage. Not too far away."

"I don't get it. A drainer doesn't have to drain anyone for real blood."

Otto's eyes went dark. "I'm guessing he just felt like it."

"Could it be connected to our case?"

"I don't know. Maybe. The victim was a blood whore like Mateo."

"But Brillen wasn't a drainer. Maybe that first murderer wasn't either. Any vampire can drain a blood whore."

Otto didn't move, his gaze unfocused. Looking back through time? Back to the case that wasn't even his? Another wave of dread hit Jessa with a sick thump. Ten years ago, Otto's...

"Who was the victim?" he whispered.

Otto blinked and took a breath. "My sister."

The floor dropped away, and Jessa's stomach fell with it. He grabbed onto the edge of the table, and Otto grabbed his wrist, holding him still. Heat rose up his arm and spread into his chest.

Otto sighed and shook his head. "Lousy way to break it to you. That was a shitty time. My dad blamed Maisie for him giving up on life, but he'd checked out a long time before. Upwood Prosper, the detective who got Maisie's case, was and is a lazy fuck who let her killer go. A friend of hers saw her with a vamp that day. A drainer. Prosper claimed her friend was a druggie and refused to follow up. It was just too fucking ironic that questioning every last one of her friends was the whole extent of his efforts. It was laughable. They were unreliable for fuck's sake."

He sat back, his hand sliding free, but Jessa grabbed it. "That's a horrible story."

Otto smiled and squeezed his fingers. "Yours too, Jess. We all got a raw deal. I'm over feeling sorry for myself. Maisie wouldn't want that. She was full of life. You remind me of her."

"Really?"

"Yeah. The minute I saw you stuffing romances into your bag."

Shock drove Jessa back against the booth again. "You remember?"

"So do you."

"I wasn't sure."

Otto nodded. "Weird how life works."

Fated.

"Can I go home with you?"

Otto grinned. "Well, we're not eating the pizza here, babe."

Babe.

Jessa liked that. Liked the closeness to Otto. The sharing of their secrets. Even though a thread of darkness slipped inside him and wound its way into his heart. Something told him Maisie's murder wasn't as simple as a distant memory, and that buried secrets never stayed buried forever.

38

A BENDY BOY

THE AMBER EYES burned like fire.

Otto's nerves jangled like prey's in a dark wood in the moonlight when a branch snaps. Something ancient rose inside him, but he wasn't prey. He finished his water, skimmed his gaze over Jessa's half-finished beer, and took his plate to the counter.

"Pizza was good," said Jessa.

"Too many mushrooms."

"Ha. Funny."

He circled behind Jessa's chair and smiled at the vibration that hummed in the air. Otto imagined Jessa's breath coming short and fast, every hair on his body standing on end, waiting for Otto's attack.

Was that what it was like with vamps? Stalking their human prey in the night.

And humans...? Succumbing with no fear that anyone would see their submission?

Well, Otto was switching things up, feeling the pounding of Jessa's heart in his own chest, the fire of his burning breath.

He slid his fingers into Jessa's hair and pulled his head back, staring into hooded eyes.

He bent and Jessa reached for him, wrapping his arms around Otto's shoulders. Otto kissed him, drinking him in like nectar. Soft lips gave under his, opening. Moans met him, quiet at first, then loud and throaty. Jessa yanked himself up, still clinging to Otto's shoulders, and Otto backed him slowly across the room, kissing him the whole way.

His bedroom wasn't much of anything, gray with the seep of a distant streetlamp. A bed, a dresser, a decade of nothing. Nobody had made this place his home. But now it was a palace, his bed as soft as a cloud, made to catch Jessa's fall. He grunted, and Otto covered him, stroking him from belly to chest, rolling a nipple under thin cotton.

Jessa groaned and arched.

Opening his shirt, Otto sucked the flesh into his mouth, pulling until Jessa thrashed and gripped Otto's shorn head.

"No fair," Jessa muttered. "You don't have any hair to grab."

Otto chuckled against the firm, warm chest, then lifted his head. "Method to my madness."

The feathery caresses of Jessa's fingers over his short hair traveled down his spine and sent shivers all over him. He rolled his hips, and Jessa hissed and opened his legs.

Otto whispered, "Tell me, baby prince, all those nights you spent all alone, sweaty and aching, what were you dreaming of?"

Jessa made a strangled sound. "Um... dicks."

Otto chuckled.

Sweet thing.

"Imagine you're dreaming now."

"Oh... okay."

He popped the button on Jessa's jeans. "Are you naked?"

"Y-yes."

"Am I?"

"N-no."

Otto grinned. *Well, well.* His voice fell lower still, barely a whisper. "Tell me where you are."

"I'm on... on my bed. Your bed."

No hanging from the chandelier. No sex on the kitchen counters. No matter. He needed the light on, all that skin blushing pink, hot and tender and twitching at his touch.

He pulled off Jessa's shoes, jeans, and underwear, then turned on the overhead light. It poured down on the startled Jessa. Wide-eyed. Rash red on his chest and neck. He stared at Otto and pulled his legs up. Otto gripped his knees and pulled them apart, and Jessa's face softened like putty. But his legs kept tightening, trying to close again.

Letting him go for a moment, Otto turned and pulled the drapes open. Jessa gasped.

"Shy for a vampire," Otto mused. "You posed nude before."

Jessa huffed and tried to tug the comforter over him. "I wasn't having sex."

"You aren't having sex now. You're exposing yourself to me."

Jessa groaned. "I don't... I was just..."

"Fantasizing." He pulled the blanket away. "Did you play with yourself?"

A giggle struggled through the hands Jessa clamped over his face. Otto pulled them away. "Wish I'd been there."

"No."

"Feel this." He leaned over Jessa's naked body and rubbed him with his crotch. "You make me so fucking hard. You playing with yourself. All hot and sticky."

He circled his hips. Jessa rocked back and spread his legs wider. Slipping a hand between them, Otto rubbed Jessa's hot hole and gazed into Jessa's fluttering eyes before they rolled up in his head. "Did you play with this?"

Jessa whipped his head back and forth, and Otto bit his knee. "Why not?"

"You did."

"What did I do with it?"

Jessa shuddered, bit his lip, and let out a whimpering moan. "You looked at it."

"No," Otto whispered. "You spread yourself for me, did you? Let me check out your hole and decide if I wanted it?"

"Oh." Jessa rocked again, his dick sliding like hot steel across the strip of Otto's skin exposed under his shirt. "You... wanted it."

"You have a pretty hole."

"Yes."

"Sweet."

"Uh huh."

"Show me."

The blush on Jessa's chest and neck spread with the heat rising off his skin. A pink, splotchy, innocent, wanton sign. An urge to devour, to tear into the flesh below consumed Otto. He gasped at the shock of it, trying to catch his breath.

"Show me," he rasped again.

Jessa groaned, gripped his legs beneath his knees and curled up. His pink sac shrank around his balls. His dick hovered above his belly, dribbling a pearly string to his reddish treasure trail. His hair was sparse around his hole. Pink splotches marred his skin where his ass had lain on the mattress. So tender. Like the flowers that had fallen in his garden like snow.

Otto traced the inside of Jessa's thighs with his fingertips, his light touch sparking shudders the whole way. He reached Jessa's ass and probed between his cheeks. The soft hairs tickled him, the rough wrinkling drawing him like a treasure. He moaned in strange relief and fell to his knees beside the bed. This was —*Mine*. Though Jessa would never be. Though Otto was unworthy.

He buried his face in Jessa's ass. Flesh rose to meet him,

bucking against his mouth. He pulled away and tickled the insides of Jessa's cheeks with his tongue. The light red hairs glowed like gold, his marble-like skin glistening under the light.

But Otto drowned him in shadow again, teasing his rim and clamping down on his squirming hips.

Sweet skin filled his senses, floral, salty, a little soapy. He probed the center of Jessa's hole.

"Oh my God."

Otto raised his eyes. Jessa's rosy red balls contracted. He leaned up and swallowed one. A screech rent the air. "Fuck, fuck, fuck."

Otto dug his fingers in to keep the thrashing hips still and gently massaged Jessa's ball with the flat of his tongue.

Jessa moaned now, his fingers rubbing Otto's scalp.

Otto pulled off with a pop. Jessa braced on one elbow, his other hand still holding onto one leg, his face a weird twist of pain and pleasure. A brush of Otto's bristly chin against the tip of Jessa's dick sent him floundering back on the bed with a hiss.

Working his thumb against Jessa's hole, Otto murmured, "Did you like fucking yourself?"

"Um... I... wanted someone."

"You got off though?"

"Y-yes."

"You taste so good."

Jessa blinked at him, his mouth in a soft O shape. Sweat beaded his forehead and upper lip. Shiny, human teeth. "Thank... you."

"I want you to taste yourself," Otto murmured.

Jessa shuddered. "O... kay."

He grabbed his other leg again, and Otto scooted his knees underneath Jessa's back and eased his feet toward the wall. "Pull that pillow under your head and relax. I won't push."

Otto's heart beat with crazy lust.

After Jessa dragged the pillow under his head and bent his neck to face the dick looming toward his lips, he flicked a slightly queasy look at Otto.

"What?" Otto asked. "It's gorgeous."

Jessa's face twisted. "It's mine."

"You seriously never tried this?"

Jessa's eyes widened as Otto rolled him deeper into a ball. He grunted and stretched his neck. His cock was right there, hovering at his mouth. Nervous as he was, he was hard, twitching, his tip shiny with precum. Otto groaned. "Go on."

Jessa rolled his head back, face red, took a breath, and leaned forward again. His tongue snaked out and flicked his dick. With a gasp, he fell back on his pillow. "Oh God."

Scooting closer, Otto braced Jessa's sweaty back against his chest. His hot skin was slippery and the scent of his musk bloomed. "Was it good?"

"Not really."

"Why not?"

Jessa scrunched his forehead, face reddening again. "I didn't really feel it on my dick."

"Where'd you feel it?"

"My tongue."

"Put it in your mouth."

Only Jessa's weight held Otto's body in place. His head floated, his heart pounding at light speed. The picture of Jessa with his cock in his mouth took over Otto's thoughts. It gripped like any temptation. Overwhelming. Compulsive. Like a vampire's desire for blood.

"Go on." His voice fell to a whisper.

With a glazed look, Jessa curled his body and opened his mouth. A locomotive was barreling through Otto's chest. His ears rang with a high-pitched clang. Jessa stuck out his tongue, and Otto's lungs froze. *C'mon. You can do it.*

"Oh fuck," he muttered when Jessa gasped and grunted and... wrapped his lips around the crown of his cock.

Otto's head swam for three seconds before Jessa's head fell back on the pillow, and he panted, blinking at the ceiling.

"There's a reason," he gasped, "guys don't do this."

"They aren't bendy."

Otto leaned back, letting Jessa's legs sprawl across the bed.

"That was... like sucking your dick except... awkward. It's not like—"

"This?"

Otto stroked Jessa's cock, rolling his thumb over the tip. Arching, legs stretched and tight on either side of Otto's hips now, Jessa sighed and smiled at the ceiling.

"That," he murmured.

"This," Otto agreed, bending over Jessa's crotch and sucking his dick into his mouth. It leaked on his tongue. He stroked slick skin and slid down half way. Jessa rocked and Otto hummed. Jessa was honey sweet, like no one else in Otto's life. His heart slowed but beat hard. Music filled his head, a strange far away sound like an orchestra. Jessa's fingers, stroking at his head, lit him with warmth and fluttered across his scalp like feathers.

Fated.

He popped off, gaze running along the body before him. Muscle and bone, lean and long, with hard curves. His belly and pecs had a whisper of definition, the hair under his belly button as soft as down and damp with sweat. The eyes on Otto now were hot and serious and predatory.

"Fuck me," Jessa whispered.

Oh yeah.

Otto reared up and ripped his shirt off. He grinned as Jessa's lips parted and his chest rose and fell.

"Show me that hole."

A moment later they were back where they'd started before

Otto's strange fantasy took over. And it was strange, the sight of guys sucking themselves off firing his lust like molten lava in his balls. And Jessa, so innocent. So eager. So... Fresh. As though the Upheaval had never happened. As though vampires were only a myth. But if they were... No. No thinking of a world without Jessa when he lay right here on Otto's bed with his arms around his legs, thighs framing his cock and balls, glowing eyes at half-mast.

The baby prince.

With a shudder Otto kicked his pants and boxers off, grabbed his lube out of the table beside the bed and slicked his over-heated dick. The thing jumped in his hand, and his hips lurched. *Fuck.*

Jessa whined and wiggled.

"Not fair," Otto whispered.

"Put it in."

"You mean here?" Otto asked, shoving his finger up Jessa's ass.

A guttural groan fell from Jessa's lips. "Touch it."

Otto crooked his finger, found the spot, and stroked.

"Oh God." Jessa's eyes rolled, the tip of his tongue protruding as he panted.

Glorious.

Otto slicked up, tossed the lube, and sank into Jessa's body.

The tightening of thighs around his ribs crushed the air out of his lungs. "Ooooh." The low moan rolled out of him like a wave. Hot silky flesh surrounded his aching dick, squeezing and rippling around it.

He bent down and met Jessa's lips.

While his cock burned like an overworked piston, all the rest of him floated, drifting in Jessa's embrace. Pillowed by his lips, rocked by his arms, sustained by the energy burning in his core.

Jessa rocked, and Otto slammed into him. The delicious, blissful friction ripped him from his daze. He pulled most of the way out, Jessa's rim contracting, holding onto him. The vamp's face contorted. He snarled, fangs as sharp as ice picks glistening in his mouth. Otto plunged back in, fire consuming him. *Fuck.* So fast.

Jessa thrashed and bucked, whipping his dick in a frenzy.

"Let me see you come," Otto groaned.

The edge was there, Otto was tipping, but...

Scowling and grunting, Jessa threw his head from side to side, bucking to meet Otto's thrusts, slamming into him with reverberations of aching pleasure. Darkness seeped into the edge of Otto's vision. His chest burned.

"Oh... Oh..."

Jessa spasmed, clamping down, spilling sweet sour spunk all over his chest and belly, sending Otto spiraling skyward. He shot without a sound, locked in rigid pleasure, his balls tight, cock pulsing.

Moaning sounds teased the edges of Otto's consciousness before emptiness swallowed him, and he fell into a bottomless dark.

39

MURDER ONCE MORE

A BODY... a body...

At Comity House, but Otto said he didn't know whose it was.

The front door slammed. Jessa dragged on his pants and stepped into his shoes. Footsteps approached, and Otto appeared in the hall, shrugging into his coat, pulling it closed over the holster strapped to his shoulder. "Let's go."

Jessa's mouth went dry, but he nodded and followed Otto outside.

The street was quiet, only an edge of daylight seeping into the sky. Skeins of mist under the street lamps.

It was cool and Jessa shivered. Even summer was cool now though and it was only the end of May. He got into the car and braced his fingertips against the dash as Otto jerked the engine into gear and took off. He sped through the empty streets. The twinkle of distant lights was incongruously beautiful, until they abruptly winked out and the streets fell dark.

"Great," Otto muttered.

Jessa swallowed against the dryness in his throat. "Was it a burglary?"

"I don't know, Jess. I wish I could tell you. I think... You should probably stay in the car. Let me check it out first."

"I'm not brittle," Jessa bit out.

"I didn't say you were. Jessa, you know these people. I'm a cop. This is my job."

"Well, it's my job too right now. I can't sit in the car. What if it's..." *Wen or Isaac?*

"I don't know anything right now, only that Wen wasn't at the center or his family's house. Does he ever stay anywhere else?"

Anya's? "I don't think so."

Jessa's shoulder hit the door with the next turn. The lights flashed on again, and Comity House took shape up ahead. The car thudded over the entrance into the parking lot. Jessa unbuckled as the car squealed to a stop at the steps.

"Wait!"

Otto tried to grab him, but he bolted from his seat and rushed into the old lobby. Empty and dark. The glow from the skylight in the atrium drew him. The place was silent. Was anybody here? Was it a trap?

He rushed through the palms, following the twisty pathways in the ghostly light floating down from above.

Otto caught up to him at the stairs and spun him against his chest. Jessa relaxed for a moment, melting into the kiss Otto pressed to his temple. The cold that enveloped him when Otto pulled away froze him to the bone. Voices reached him, humming like chants.

Jessa followed Otto upstairs and down the hall. A light led them around a corner to a room Jessa had never been in before. Cavernous and deep. Luxurious swaths of fabric and furnishings. Tapestries on the floor and walls. All gold and blood red. Otto strode in, and Jessa stood alone in the doorway.

Nobody looked his way. His gaze darted from place to place, probing through the cops, seeking—

Anya.

She stood at a window, a silhouette against the coming day.

Strangers. Wandering. Milling around. Bending over a... body. Jessa stared in bleak horror. Was it Mateo? His hair was dark but his eyes were empty, and Jessa couldn't tell. A plastic sheet fell over his face, and Otto materialized from the crowd and headed Jessa's way.

Jessa gazed at him, searching his face. "Is it Mateo?"

Otto nodded and rested his warm palm on Jessa's arm, but a commotion at the door drew him away again. Two humans in white uniforms wheeled a gurney to the body. A square of gray plastic was folded on the mattress. A body bag. The humans shook it out and laid it on the floor, and Jessa fixated on it. A few quick, efficient movements later and the bag fell open. The humans uncovered Mateo, lifted him, and set him down again on the bag. A ripping sound followed the zipper from bottom to top. After settling Mateo on the gurney, they wheeled him away. Most of the cops followed.

"I don't care."

Jessa stepped farther into the room. Otto's glance flickered over, the anger on his face washing away. With most of the people gone, Jessa's line of sight shot straight to a couch with Isaac sitting on it. Jessa's knees weakened, relief making him dizzy. Otto took his arm. "Come sit. Listen to me though." His grip held Jessa back. "Wen's car is here, but he isn't anywhere in the building. Has he ever just walked off before?"

Jessa shook his head, looking at Anya still standing by the window, her lips pressed to her steepled fingers, the white streak in her hair otherworldly in the dim light.

"I don't think so."

Otto loosened his grip, and Jessa rushed to the couch where Isaac sat buried in a blanket, his chin against his chest.

Shaking.

Dr. Cameron stood behind him, a palm raised, but Jessa dropped to the cushion and wrapped Isaac in his arms anyway.

Above him, the doctor sighed. "I have no issue with the prince being here, but you have to wait. No questions until the boy calms down. I insist."

"Unless you outrank the King, I don't give a fuck what you insist on."

"The boy is hysterical."

"Your boss is missing, and another boy is dead."

"I can talk," said Isaac.

He shuddered, but his voice was strong. Jessa held him tight, his attention following Otto's stare. Several beds with red satin coverlets formed a half circle on the far side of the room. Otto turned and stared at Anya.

"Seems your boss wasn't as on the up and up as he said."

Anya dropped her hands, eyes narrowing. "This room is for comfort."

Otto snorted, yanked a coffee table in front of Isaac, sat down, and looked up at Dr. Cameron. "You can go."

"You can't—"

"And take Anya with you," he added.

Otto looked pale, tight lines on his face, and a deep crease down his forehead. Like somebody in pain. While Jessa... Jessa didn't feel anything. Otto met his gaze, then shifted it to Isaac.

Wen was missing. Was he dead? Was that why Otto didn't want to hold his stare?

Wen.

Would Jessa feel him die? They weren't really bonded though.

Isaac made a strange sound, half growl, half moan. "I can't believe this."

"What part?" asked Otto. "You were keeping shit from me, and this is what happened."

Isaac reared back, and Jessa held on.

"I didn't want this."

"It doesn't matter. You made a bad call, and now you need to talk to me."

"He's dead."

"What was he doing here, Isaac?"

Isaac's mouth opened and shut. He drew in a deep breath, exhaled, and said, "Money. I was going to give him some to get out of town." A weak laugh spilled from his lips. "God, how that sounds. Like they couldn't find him wherever he went anyway."

"Who is they?"

Isaac's eyes widened and fixed on Otto. He shook his head. "I don't know. Vampires, I guess."

"You've known all along it was Mateo with Brillen."

"No. Mateo wasn't with him," Isaac said. "He set him up with a friend who's still working as a blood whore."

Otto straightened. "What friend?"

Isaac stiffened, a flat look coming into his eyes, a cynical twitch to his lips. "I don't know. I didn't ask."

A muscle jumped in Otto's jaw, irritation flashing in his eyes. "Whatever you do know, tell me. Include everything tonight."

Jessa shook Isaac, who curled his shoulders, locking up on himself. "You have to. Something's happened to Wen. He wouldn't just leave."

Isaac shot him a startled stare. Well, why wouldn't he be surprised at Jessa's worry? Everybody knew Jessa and Wen weren't in love. But Jessa didn't want this. He'd never want this.

"I'm sorry, Jessa." After another breath, he looked back at

Otto. "I always thought some vampires got special privileges. I don't know if Mateo was a part of that or not. I don't think so. I think Mr. Acalliona got turned away because he was a stranger. Mateo said Mr. Acalliona contacted him, so he set him up with somebody else because he didn't take private jobs anymore. The next day Mateo was gone. I didn't know where he was the first time I talked to you."

"But he got in touch."

Isaac nodded. "I guess the other guy, the one with Mr. Acalliona, came and told Mateo what had happened. Mateo was scared that whoever killed Mr. Acalliona would come looking for him, maybe thinking he was the one at the scene."

"And you don't know who the friend was?"

"I think they just knew each other. Not really friends. Mateo hid out by himself for a while, but he ran out of money, so he snuck in here, and I hid him in my room. I have money saved." His chin quivered. "It was just for the night. I went to get us food and..." Tears started. "Somebody saw him come in, I guess. I didn't even get back to my room before somebody grabbed me and brought me here. Mateo... Mateo was on the floor. I tried to get him to wake up."

"Was he alive?"

"I... I think so. The vampire..." His voice trailed off.

"Can you describe him?"

"Big. Older, I think. A-A vampire. I don't know..."

"It's okay," Otto said. "Just keep talking. Get it out."

"I thought I was going to die. I couldn't move. I never saw... saw Mr. Wrythin come in, but then he was there, and he told the vampire no. That he had to go. That Comity House was Mr. Wrythin's, and he took care of us, and nobody was going to hurt us. They... they fought. I couldn't get to the door. I wanted to. I think the vampire did something to me."

The eyes he turned on Jessa flared with a kind of panic.

Jessa looked at Otto. Other than dimming in the gray light of dusk and dawn, vampires had no hidden powers, but Isaac had turned stiff again under Jessa's arm.

"Fear can do that," said Otto. "It wasn't your fault."

Isaac took Jessa's hand and squeezed it, and Jessa stared at the place their fingers linked as Isaac's words floated into his head. "I saw Mr. Wrythin lying on the floor, and the vampire coming at me. I think... think he was going to drain me. And I froze."

Wen's dead.

And Jessa had felt nothing. No sign at all. He wasn't sure what he felt now, but when Isaac said, "And then I saw the fog," he dropped Isaac's hand, his heart pounding blood into his head.

Otto went rigid then slowly leaned forward. "Fog?"

"In the room," Isaac said. "It... got the vampire. I can't explain it, but I felt somebody else in the fog. The other vampire disappeared into it. They fought, and I didn't do anything. I couldn't even run. The vampire got free somehow and jumped out the window."

Jessa glanced over his shoulder, baffled he hadn't noticed the cold air blowing in or the glitter of glass on the floor. Shards rimmed the open window space like vampire fangs.

"Who was in the fog?" Otto asked.

"I don't know," Isaac said, but his face had shuttered. "It blew away. There was nobody in it. I thought I'd dreamed it until I remembered Mateo. But this time... I knew he was dead. I guess I-I passed out. Anya woke me up and waited here with me."

"And Wen?"

"Was gone."

Dead.

And still Jessa felt nothing. Isaac rested his elbows on his knees and ran his hands through his hair, and Jessa stood and approached the window. The crack of glass ripped through him. There were no other cops in the room now. He might as well be alone. Even Otto's warmth behind him froze in the cold.

Otto squeezed his arms. "I'll find him."

"You won't. I don't feel him. All I feel is the fog." Though the day was clear. Gray deepening to blue. The sun visible, the mountains green and lush. "It follows me."

40

AFTERMATH

THE LITTLE ROOM looked bare without its books, though the plump cushy chair, the bed, the lamps, and the pictures on the wall remained. Even Isaac standing in the middle of the room with his bag draped over his shoulder looked out of place. He gazed around with a slightly frantic look, as though afraid he'd leave something behind and never be able to come back for it.

Otto leaned against the doorframe behind them. Finally, he straightened and said, "Let's go," and Jessa reached for Isaac's hand, surprised he didn't pull away. Giving him a tug, Jessa led him outside.

Fritt met them at the door of the castle, waiting inside the threshold where the shade fell.

They had many unused rooms, but Jessa took Isaac downstairs to the suite by Rune's studio. Isaac was quiet through the trek down the gloomy basement hall, but his eyes widened when Jessa opened the door on the light-filled rooms.

"You have your own door to the garden here and your own space. You don't have to worry about anything anymore."

Isaac gave him a wan smile. "I'm alone here?"

"Rune's studio is next door, but he's away right now. Make yourself comfortable. I'll find Bettina and get us something to eat, okay?"

"Sure."

Isaac's smile brightened, and Jessa headed for the kitchen. He paused in the receiving room and looked out the open front doors. Otto stood in the driveway, his satellite phone to his ear. Jessa hurried to the kitchen where Bettina was already cracking eggs.

"I hear you brought home a stray," she said.

"My friend."

Bettina looked over her shoulder and raised an eyebrow. "Nice ring to that."

It had a nice ring to Jessa too, but it also stabbed him through with guilt, and Bettina left her eggs and came over to him.

"Child." She cupped his face. "What is it?"

"Wen. I think..." *I know.* "Somebody was killed, and Wen is gone."

"Gone? You don't think Wen had anything to do with it?"

"I think Wen is dead, Bettina."

She stroked his cheek. "Do you feel it?"

"No. That's the worst part. I don't feel anything."

"That's not your fault. You aren't to blame. I don't approve of arranged marriages."

"Yours was arranged."

She rocked his face in her palms. "I am the exception. Go to your detective and tell him to come inside for breakfast."

Without another word, she went back to her eggs.

Jessa hurried outside just as Otto started the car. He flew down the steps and grabbed onto the handle of the back door. The car stopped, and he staggered forward a few steps before rounding back and climbing in.

"Get out," said Otto.

"I saw you on the phone. It's Wen, isn't it?"

"Jess."

Jessa's voice rose. "Isn't it?"

After feeling nothing about Wen before, a knot in his belly and balls told him everything. And it was his fault. He was to blame. That room with its crimson beds was evidence he'd known nothing about Wen.

Otto stepped on the gas, and Jessa buckled up.

"They found a body at Frenn's consignment store. It sounds like Wen."

What an idiot Jessa was. Otto's words hit him like a shockwave. Buffeting him and leaving him sick and dizzy.

You aren't to blame.

But he was. Bettina was wrong.

"You should stay, Jessa."

"Keep going."

"I am."

He let his head fall back and shut his eyes. Under the numbness in his chest, a dull pain throbbed in time to his heart.

"He wasn't who you thought he was, Jess."

Jessa kept his eyes closed. Wen wasn't bad either.

"I might be wrong," Otto said. "I hope so."

If Wen was alive...

Well, Jessa would marry him. Wen wasn't an obstacle to Jessa's happiness. He was using Jessa, but not maliciously. Rune had gone to Wen to arrange their marriage. Maybe Wen had dreamed of marrying Anya until Rune tempted him away. Jessa had never seen Wen as a whole person. He was a duty or a sacrifice. Not somebody with dreams and strange secrets. Wen wasn't Jessa's savior.

And neither was Otto.

Jessa didn't need anybody to take care of him. He had his jewelry business, and there were other donors besides Isaac.

He opened his eyes and looked at Otto.

"Was Solomon there?"

"I don't know a lot. Nobody's being held though, so I'd say no."

Wen had come for brunch with the family before Rune and Uriah had left for Rune's job a few days ago. He'd been his usual distant self, though he'd given Jessa's hand a quick squeeze. Now... To think that... That he was gone, just like that.

Jessa shoved his hands into his armpits.

"So they wanted Mateo and Mateo's dead. Now what?"

Otto turned at the bottom of the mountain and sped up. "Whoever killed Mateo wanted something. Either something he had or to keep something he had a secret."

"Like that room?"

"The killer already knew about it. It wasn't an accident he took Isaac and Mateo there. He wanted someplace private. Someplace to ask questions. Acalliona wasn't a drainer, but drainers are in every part of this. Stick close to me when we get there," Otto added, glancing sideways.

Jessa bit back on a laugh, but it escaped anyway. "You know I'm stronger than you right? My hero," he added.

Color rose in Otto's cheeks, but he flashed Jessa a grin. "The offer to arm wrestle's still open."

"I'd still win."

"You're supposed to let me win. I'm the hero."

I know.

A hero Jessa had to lose. This was the predictable complication in every damn romance, except this one didn't have a happy ending. Which made it real life actually and not a romance at all.

He didn't want to think about it anymore though, so he

closed his eyes again, and the rhythmic whistling of the tires on the pavement lulled him to sleep. Otto's hand brushing his hair off his face woke him up.

"I'll do this however you want," Otto said. "I can go in first and you can wait, or come in now."

"Now."

He owed Wen to be the one person in there who actually cared about him.

He got out of the car and waited for Otto, who showed his badge to the cop at the door. The place was a wreck of shattered glass and torn canvasses. The artwork, which had hung on cables, lay in shards. Holes gaped in the wall where the display cases had been ripped from their bolts. Jewelry littered the carpet like the detritus tossed by a wave.

"Damnit," Jessa muttered.

One of his necklaces hung from the skeletal frame of a broken display case.

"You the guys from Comity?"

A cop stood in a door in back.

"Yeah."

Otto stepped over the wreckage, and Jessa followed him, but when he reached the door, Otto turned back.

"Are you sure?"

"I have to."

But some force rose to push him back while he struggled to step into the other room. Otto went around him, the cop turning with him, and Jessa stood like a plaster cast. His limbs ached, stiff and brittle, as though all it would take to shatter him was one sharp tap. But the tap he got was like the weight of Celestine coming down on him.

Otto returned and blocked his view. "It's Wen."

"I know."

Closer to him in death than in life.

He patted Otto on the chest and pushed by. A human in a suit stood in a circle of cops in uniform, and a voice rose from somewhere near the floor. "... got interrupted before he could do much."

Otto went to join them, and Jessa let his gaze roam. Without seeing Wen, it was hard to make this real. The room he stood in was stuffed with tables and folding chairs and large enough to seat thirty. A whiteboard hung from a wall, and an accordion door to a studio like Rune's stood partway open. The floor was cement, and a large kiln stood in a corner of the room. Jessa let his gaze drift back to the cops.

"Were they—"

"Cuttin' 'im up?" somebody said. "Yeah, I think the plan was to burn 'im."

"God, what a stink that woulda been."

"How long since anyone's seen the owner," Otto asked.

"Yesterday. You think the owner's involved?"

"Gut feeling."

A prickly heat ran over Jessa's body and evaporated the air in his lungs. His head swelled, and voices boomed inside it.

Why... Why... Why Wen?

His body took him across the space, and he pushed his way into the huddle. "Why not let him go?"

Heads turned, and Jessa swayed, but Otto didn't touch him. He stared hard-eyed at Jessa and shook his head. "I don't know, Jess. It's a good question."

Jess.

Grown and strong. The son of a king. He gritted his teeth and looked away from the black holes in Wen's neck. "Isaac said he was unconscious, but somebody came back and got him. It makes no sense to do that."

"Makin' sure he didn't spill his guts about something probably," somebody said. "Though why they didn't just kill him there is kinda strange."

God, he hadn't known Wen at all.

Forcing himself not to look down again, Jessa turned away and wandered to the studio. The setup was functional and cold. Rune's space was stuffy and dark and hot and colorful. Here, nothing cluttered the space. No statues. No vases. No tubs of glass. Maybe somebody should burn it down. Let Wen go. He was a corpse. A clue on the floor. They didn't know him.

You didn't know him.

"Jess."

He swallowed. "I'm okay."

"Frenn had a safe. Whoever brought Wen here broke into it. The kid working here before doesn't know what was in the safe other than a few pieces of jewelry, and at least some of that jewelry is still there. So somebody took something but not the rest, or they got nothing, but either way they were looking for something."

"And they killed Wen. Why were they even at Comity House if this was just a robbery?"

"The answer is in whatever they took."

Jessa turned with a frown. "What if it was Solomon who brought Wen here?"

"I'm guessing he did and staged it to look like a robbery. Typical overboard shit, trashing the place like this. I'm betting there was something in that safe, something Frenn came back for, because he isn't the only one who wants it."

The fog.

"Wen was involved," Jessa murmured.

"Oh yeah. But I don't think he knew what he was up against."

"I didn't see any signs. Wen just seemed like... Wen."

"This isn't your fault."

You aren't to blame.

Was Wen? Or Isaac, for hiding Mateo? Or Mateo, for setting somebody up with a vampire masquerading as a drainer? How far back did this go?

He was a part of it without knowing how or why. And now—

"Jones." A cop from the outer room appeared. "A call just came in from King Dinallah. He wants you to return to Senera Castle right away. A car will pick you up and take you to him."

Otto frowned. "How the hell did he find out about this already?"

The cop shrugged.

"Spies everywhere," he said, and Jessa remembered his own adventure in spying when he'd skulked outside of Rune's study, listening in on Wen's complaints about Rune's agreement to let Jessa work with Otto. His excitement had deafened him to Wen's tone. He'd tuned it out and wrapped himself in a Jackson Stork fantasy. Everything had just fallen into place for him. But now, the memory of Wen's voice reverberated inside him. *I don't want that filthy human near him.* The sound had stretched thin and metallic. But it hadn't been the sound of greed, or a desire for jewels or precious art.

It had been the sound of hate.

41

CALLED TO THE MANOR

THE CLOUDS, gray edged and billowy white, chased the car. The gloom, tumbling across the sky, pissed Otto off, so far from the blistering summers he remembered when he'd burned his feet on the boiling sidewalks.

It was Zev he was really pissed at though. And Wen for getting himself killed. Not that Otto wanted competition from him, but Jessa was a prince. And a drainer. Not that that mattered, because that wasn't the only reason being with Jessa wouldn't work. Jessa was royal and a vampire. Otto was human and a cop. An ex-cop really, and one who sucked at his fucking job, because now two more people were dead. It was too much to ask Jessa to forgive. Wen might not have been the love of his life, but he'd still been ready to marry him. Wen being dead didn't make Jessa free.

He glanced sideways before he veered onto the exit to Comity. Jessa sat staring outside.

"I'm sorry, Jess."

"Me too. I didn't know him."

"Not your fault. People are fucking mysteries most of the time. It's hard to know what's in a person's heart."

He caught Jessa's frown before slowing at an intersection. A few raindrops splattered the windshield.

"Have you ever... been with somebody?" Jessa asked. "Lived with them?"

Otto shook his head. "Not my thing."

"Why isn't it?"

Because I'm obsessed. Bitter... Empty.

Being with somebody was about making plans and believing those plans would play out and you'd keep loving the same guy or girl, and you'd stand together when life ripped you bloody. But his mom and dad had fought nonstop, and after his mom died, his dad had sunk into the booze as though he'd had no idea how to get through the day without her anymore. And after Maisie's murder, Otto and his dad had found nothing to say to each other, because there'd been only Maisie between them, and that had been a bottomless pit Otto had known to steer clear of, and his dad probably had too. Somehow, when Otto wasn't looking, the space between them had filled his whole life.

"I just never really thought about it," he finally said.

As the road curved up the mountain, Jessa braced his hand on the dashboard and Otto noticed the nail polish again. It wasn't chipped yet. He must have put it on fresh when Otto took him to the movie. Where the heroine was betrothed to someone else, and the hero drowned.

Just like real fucking life.

Duty and responsibility, and if you tried to get away from it...

"You don't have to come with me to see Dinallah. You can stay and make arrangements for Wen. Mal could probably help you, I'm guessing."

"Wen has family. I should have married him. Now they're still where they were before. Marrying into my family was supposed to be a step up for them. I guess that's ruined too."

"Jess..." The flat tone of Jessa's voice got to him. "You need some time."

Jessa laughed. "I wonder who they'll find to marry me now. Who's going to run Comity House? And what's going to happen to the donors? Wen took care of them."

"We can figure it out."

"Wen's family will figure it out. I won't have anything to say."

"You have influence, Jessa."

"Not really. I still don't know why the King thought I could help. Wen didn't. And he didn't want me around you either."

Otto shot him a look. "What? How do you know that?"

"He said. Don't take it personally. He didn't like humans. I never saw that. I guess I wasn't looking."

How easy was it to hate? Otto had never thought twice about it. Vampires had murdered half the human population over an accident. One of them had murdered Maisie and stolen his dad's will to live.

And Otto... Otto was a shell. The only reason he'd rescued Jessa in the parking lot was because he hated bullies. That and not knowing Jessa was a vampire. And now? How the fuck was he supposed to give up everything that had gotten him this far?

Hate and revenge.

"You deserve somebody who loves you, Jess."

"I'm a drainer, Otto. I'll take whoever Rune finds for me."

"Well, for fuck's sake. Just live alone. It's better than a love-less marriage."

"I could've loved Wen."

"Is that what you're telling yourself now? I get it. People look a hell of a lot better when they're dead sometimes. They don't contradict you. They don't bitch at you. They don't pretend they're doing you a fucking favor when it's the other way around."

The waspish sound in his voice surprised him, welling from somewhere in his chest and chasing a strange chill through his body. What the fuck was that about? He had no idea. But he didn't have time to worry about it before he took the last turn to the castle.

"Think about whether you want to come with me."

Jessa frowned. "Gem Fest is in two days. We were going to that anyway."

Otto sighed and pulled up at the steps. *Right.* "I'm gonna go pack a few things then."

Jessa's leaning over and nuzzling Otto's face surprised the hell out of him. So was hearing him say, "You aren't to blame. Somebody wise told me that."

Before Otto had time to respond, Jessa climbed out of the car and darted up the steps.

Otto wanted to believe Jessa, but even if he weren't to blame for Wen, he'd never be free of Maisie.

He shifted the car back into gear. When Jessa disappeared inside, he drove away. Traffic was light, and he made it home in twenty minutes. His neighborhood looked desolate as cold wind blew bits of paper down the street. Otto grabbed a bag from his hall closet and stuffed it with a few clothes. On his way back down the hall, he reached for the closet door to close it but held onto its edge when his gaze flicked to the shoe box on the shelf. The cliché shoe box filled with cliché family photos. Well, not filled exactly.

Dropping his bag, Otto grabbed the box and pulled off the lid. It didn't take him long to shuffle through his few photos to find the last photo he had of Maisie, sitting on his couch, legs crossed, arms stretched across the top. Smiling at him. She wore her white dress with the giant red and yellow roses on it, bangles on her wrists, and her necklace. Whoever she'd been about to meet, she hadn't been afraid of him. Opening his bag, Otto stuffed the photo in a pocket inside and headed out.

42

INTERLUDE

BY THE TIME Otto returned to the castle, the car Dinallah had sent for them was idling by the front entrance. Jessa stood on the driveway with a bag slung over his shoulder, waiting for Otto. They got into the car and a few hours later arrived at the manor where another one of the King's butlers took them to a room lit by an array of candles and a fire in the fireplace. The bed was covered in puffy comforters, the air warm and spicy.

After a short and fitful sleep, Otto woke to light creeping in through a gap in the drapes. It was pale and clear and lit Jessa's profile with gold. Otto stared at the bumps on his skinny nose and the curve of his skinny upper lip. A parade of faces that had kept him company in bed marched through his memory. Nothing warmed him but the body beside him.

After a moment, he rolled away and went to the window. Their room overlooked a mountain range, dark in the early light, laced with thin mist in the hollows. *"It follows me."*

Twisting his head, Otto gazed back at the bed. Jessa's mouth was slightly parted. A wave of tenderness rushed over him at the sight. No reminder he was staring at a vampire worked to dim his emotions. The pointy little fangs had grown on him. The comical hisses.

With a sigh, Otto padded across the thick rugs and shut himself in the bathroom. By the time he'd showered and wrapped himself in a towel, Jessa sat naked on the side of the bed. Violet colored shadows smudged the skin under his eyes. His nipples were a fresh pink, highlighting the red in the hair between his legs. His soft penis lay against the cushion of his balls. Would Otto ever have that sweet flesh in his mouth again?

"I don't feel anything." Jessa's voice was dull, but fear wriggled like a living thing in the shadow of his eyes. "I'm glad I didn't love him though. That would be worse. I just accepted everything about him. I can't believe I got it all so wrong. I can't trust myself."

"Why not, Jess? You said yourself he did good things. People do bad things for a lot of reasons that don't make them bad people. We aren't one or the other. We're both, and sometimes the line between isn't all that easy to see. You do your best, and maybe Wen did too."

Jessa's gaze didn't waver, but it brimmed with doubt.

Approaching cautiously, Otto sat beside him, and Jessa's shoulder met his as the bed sank underneath them. The strands of his hair, tangled from sleep, slipped across Otto's skin like silk. His lips were dry from breathing through his mouth. Stray freckles grew darker in the growing light. Otto leaned in and Jessa met him. The kiss was soft and dry and sweet. Otto leaned away until his eyes focused on Jessa's. The russet of autumn leaves or wild honey.

Precious amber.

He leaned in again, and this time Jessa opened to him and sank back under Otto's weight. With a groan, Otto pressed him down into the soft sheets. He pushed deep into Jessa's hot mouth, shivering at the scrape of his fangs as they slipped out.

He grazed his palms over the soft skin and dragged his thumb along the inside of Jessa's hip. Jessa's shudder shook him, his breath hot on Otto's face as he yanked away and rolled his head on the covers. The arch of his back pushed his dick into the towel around Otto's waist. His voice roughened and croaked. "I can't... can't help it."

"Don't help," Otto whispered, silencing him with another kiss.

He rocked his hips, grinding into the space between Jessa's legs. The hiss Jessa let out had an edge of pain to it. But Otto kept on until Jessa bucked against him, and when he rose and peered into Jessa's eyes, they were glazed and senseless with lust. So pretty, the flush in his cheeks, the pearly shine of his fangs. The urge to touch overtook him and he slipped a finger into Jessa's mouth. The little vamp closed his lips and sucked. The look in his eyes turned voracious.

"You like that," Otto murmured.

His other hand had found Jessa's cock. He kept his grip loose, barely touching, slowly drawing up until he circled the hot wet head with his thumb. Jessa's mouth parted on another hiss. Otto pressed his finger against the tip of a fang and gasped as it pierced his flesh. Blood welled in a deep red ball. He stared in shock. Jessa moaned, his body as tight as a wire, thrumming with tension. Hunger fought with desire. Sweat beaded his upper lip and his eyes grew heavy. *Fuck.* It was beautiful. The raw desire. His tongue flicked out, searching for the ball of blood. Spellbound, Otto's gaze locked on his own hand as he extended it. Jessa panted, his eyes frantic now. He shook his head, whipped it back and forth until he flopped back on the pillow. He grabbed his cock and stroked it, lips still parted, tongue still visible.

Otto dropped to an elbow, pressing close. Jessa whimpered. "You want it," Otto said. "You fed though."

A guttural rasp emerged from Jessa's throat. "Yours."

A burning heat rose from Otto's chest into his head. His heart thundered, his flesh itchy, sticking, aching. "Only mine," he whispered.

"Yours."

Fated.

Not Wen's. Nobody else's. Not even Isaac's.

But if he did it? If he fed Jessa? Would he ever escape? Would he be like Dawn, Jessa's mother, an alien among a people never to be hers, forever exiled from her own world? Would he understand Maisie? Finally.

Jessa rolled his head again, catching gold and ruby strands on his sweaty cheeks. Otto tugged his towel off, swiped his finger on it, and dropped it on the floor. Moans rolled out of Jessa's mouth. "I got you," Otto whispered.

A thunderous roar filled Otto's head. A storm, a quake, rumbling louder and louder. His dick throbbed, reddish purple, jerking at the touch of the air. He ached to be in the vamp beneath him, buried in his sweet ass, a place so hot he'd melt in its embrace. *Mine.*

He spun away, gone only long enough to grab the lube from his bag.

The scent of arousal filled the air. Oddly floral and woodsy at the same time. Working his arms under Jessa's legs, he rolled him and stroked his dick between Jessa's ass cheeks. The soft rasp against his flesh soothed him and stilled the storm in his head. Jessa panted, but sense had come into his eyes again. He licked his lips. Otto bent down and kissed him. "In me," Jessa whispered. "Be in me."

"Yes."

He snapped the cap on the tube and drizzled lube onto Jessa's hole. A shudder shook the vampire when the liquid landed on his hot skin. Otto dropped the tube and rubbed around Jessa's hole with his thumb. His golden red hair glistened and his hole contracted. "You want," he murmured, rubbing harder until the little hole loosened and let Otto's thumb slide in.

"Want," Jessa agreed.

He swiveled his hips.

Otto stroked himself with his slick hand, pointed his dick between Jessa's cheeks, and pushed inside him.

Jessa's groan sent shivers down his spine.

Mine, mine...

But Jessa wasn't. Not in this world. Jessa was a vampire. Conquered and conqueror. But here—and now—Jessa gave way. His steely strength softened around Otto's cock, warm and welcoming. As Otto sank in, he slid across Jessa's gland and shuddered as hot flesh clenched around him. Jessa stroked Otto's arms and shoulders, dug in with his fingers, rolled his head back and whispered, "Oh fuck, oh fuck, oh fuck..."

The light in the room grew bright, the shadows gone. Jessa's skin was as luminous as marble, his eyes as dark as a twilit lake. Could he dim? Fade away, so all Otto had of him was sensation? Satin and steel and scorching heat? He thrust into a furnace, going faster and faster, kicking the flames into a conflagration. His heart ignited. Cries fell from Jessa's lips and swirled in his head with the roaring winds of fire. Lightning struck and raced down his spine. Jessa grunted, his nails digging into Otto's skin, body rigid, dragging at Otto's dick until Otto exploded, his climax swooping down like the rocks on Celestine City, burying him in darkness.

Mine...

43

A PISSED-OFF KING

AS HE HAD the last time he was here, the King defied Otto's expectations. Clad in jeans and a plain white T-shirt, he strode barefoot down the hall.

"Who was this dead human?"

The vamp turned his face away as he spoke but not before Otto caught a glimpse of despair in his eyes.

They passed portrait after portrait down a hall Otto would swear was longer than the house.

Zev had cooked their breakfast in a kitchen with white cupboards and a black and white checkered floor. No servants anywhere.

"It's just us," Zev had said. "My cousins are asleep."

Vampires hiding from the sun that had poured into the kitchen.

Before departing with Otto after breakfast, Zev had opened the back door and gestured Jessa outside. "My gardens. Enjoy."

Now they were talking about dead people. *Mateo.*

"I thought he witnessed Acalliona's murder," Otto said.

"Yet he didn't go to the police."

"No, but that's no surprise, not for a street kid."

"Kid? Do you mean that literally? How old was he?"

Otto shrugged. "About twenty."

Zev's relief was obvious. His face, whitewashed in the light streaming into the hall, warmed with color.

They reached a door, and Zev paused. "You thought he was a witness. What do you think now?"

"A friend of the witness."

Zev humphed. "We're talking about a human, right? A human who might know the identity of the murderer?"

"If he's still alive," Otto said. "The dead boy, Mateo, told another friend that the kid disappeared shortly after the murder. Mateo hid because he guessed he'd be suspected and only surfaced because he'd run out of money. His friend Isaac, Jessa's donor, was going to give him enough to disappear."

They turned a corner and entered a library. But instead of the grandeur Otto was expecting, the room was cozy and comfortable. A fire burned in the giant fireplace, and here too the windows stretched from floor to ceiling, but they were narrow and nestled between book shelves.

"Sit," said Zev, gesturing to the chairs in front of the fireplace. "Forgive the long walk. I think better here because it reminds me of home. The greatest library ever imagined was in Celestine City, you know. Carved out of rock crystal. Of course it was destroyed." He waved his hand. "I have reminders."

Otto had his picture of Maisie. His reminder of what he needed to do. As he sat, his gaze rose to the portrait over the mantle piece. Zev. The pose was strange and striking, nothing like the portraits in the hallway. His hair was loose, his elbow braced on something off the canvas, chin resting on his thumb, eyes glittering and blood hot. His shirt was red, and he wore a necklace like Jessa's. So human.

Otto met Zev's curious gaze. "This has more to do with your people than mine."

Zev smiled. "Sounds like you want to discontinue the investigation."

"Can I?"

"I'd prefer not."

"Why am I here?"

Zev's face went cold, his eyes like ice. "Why is a human and another vampire dead? Did you misunderstand what I wanted from you?"

Otto flared. "You expect me to stop a vampire?"

"Too many vampires wouldn't want to stop another vampire, Detective Jones. That's why I have you."

"You want to."

"I have nothing against humans." He waved his hand again, the ring that had once belonged to the Seneras winking in the light. "Not all of us do. It's the others I'm thinking of. I trust you. You have a promise to keep."

Those last words sank deep into Otto's chest and took up space. His lungs struggled. "You don't know anything about me."

"You aren't as transparent as you think. You were fired, you know? And you had multiple warnings. You've been on the downslide for a long time. You want what I want. It doesn't matter if we want it for different reasons." Zev leaned forward, elbow on his knee, thumb at his chin, mimicking the pose above. His thumb rubbed at his chin, rasping slightly. A slow smile lifted his lips and his eyes heated to melting again. "I have enemies. I brought a peace that offends my own people. Killing is nothing to them. Your sister. An innocent boy. We have suffered for thousands of years, paying for a crime none of us remember outside of myth. We fell into darkness, but the darkness that lurks now is deeper by far. It is a darkness of the soul. Who are the elusive murderers in my midst?"

A vision of fog came to Otto, and he clamped down on a shiver as his thoughts went to Jessa.

He reminded himself vampires didn't matter to him. This was about Maisie and the hatred in him of those who fed off others. At the bottom of it, nobody got away with murder if he had a say.

"You tell me," Otto said.

Zev glowered. "I hired you."

"You aren't paying me."

Zev grinned, his fangs sliding down, tattooed with an intricate design that looked like wings, but the tiny image was a blur that vanished as Zev's grin disappeared. "Consider your payment due on delivery."

"You're keeping something from me," Otto said.

Zev rested both elbows on his knees now, shoulders bent, no trace of humor on his face anymore. His eyes had darkened to something beyond black, to a lightless pit where Otto imagined his demons lay. "A human boy is dead. Two vampires. At a minimum. Why in God's name would I keep anything from you? Hate is a power that consumes everything in its path and bides its time in the dark if it has to. Things crawl out into the open when good people pay no attention. Why hate drainers? They feed on humans. We have always fed on humans and, yes, the evil among us have taken lives that weren't theirs to take. All the old stories are true." He flicked his hand in a quick wave. "We have lived off each other, Detective. And you have killed mine. The old, infants, buried in rubble. I have every right to rage, but of what use is it? I am the king of my kind. I could embrace a thousand years of war, and they would follow. I do not want war. You, me, too many others, we have all lost too much. Family, friends, lovers..." He faltered for a moment, or maybe it was the pause as he sat back in his chair that made it seem so. "Somebody wants to destroy what I have built. I want you to stop them. I don't want anybody else dead. I will drain you myself, Otto Jones, if you fail me in this."

For fuck's sake.

Otto gripped the arms of his chair, tightening his body. The heat in his face grew. "Don't fucking threaten me. It's not an incentive. I will do my job because it's not in me to let a murderer go free. Maybe it's payback for my sister too, maybe it's for Jessa, but I don't give up."

"I know," said Zev. "That's why I hired you."

Otto stood. "The necklace."

Zev frowned. "What?"

"The necklace in the picture. I noticed a couple in the portraits in the hall too, all with writing on the stones."

"It's a common design, like our tattoos or your scrimshaw."

"Jessa has one. So did my sister."

Zev looked taken aback at the mention of Maisie. His expression grew reflective for a moment before he pushed himself from his chair and glanced at the portrait. "The Revelatory letters are meaningful to us, ancient, but they're only symbolic. There's no actual value to them. They mark the qualities we must learn before our return to God's grace. They aren't even unique to us, but at one time an amulet of a precious stone with a particular letter belonged to each of the seven families. For my family, it is *Dilme*, the symbol for resurrection. But the importance has become diluted with time, and necklaces like this are everywhere."

"What happened to the real ones?"

"Lost, I guess." Zev shrugged. "Or maybe they were just a myth."

All the old stories are true.

Otto returned with Zev to the kitchen and stepped into the garden where Jessa stood gazing at the mist-shrouded trees.

44

A PRETTY POSTCARD

WAVES AS GRAY as granite crashed against slick black rocks, and lichen dripped from the cypress trees. Jessa hugged himself, standing coatless and barefoot on a path that led to a rocky cliffside.

"Hey." Arms closed around Jessa's shoulders, squeezing him tight. "What are you doing?"

"Looking. It's scary. Like the lakes underground. Black and bottomless."

Otto tightened his grip. "You remember that?"

The flash of memory startled him. Not that it was a bad memory, only that he didn't think he had any of Celestine. Yet, it was there. The memory of a still, black surface spreading into a darker dark.

"Maybe I remember. I don't know. Maybe I saw a picture. It scares me to think people might still be living down there."

"Why?"

"What kind of people would do that?"

Otto was silent, and Jessa thought maybe he wasn't going to answer.

"My dad was that kind of pissed. Not able or willing to get

over it." Otto's voice turned heavy, and when Jessa turned in his arms, he was frowning. "I guess that was me too."

"I'm not sure I hate my life," Jessa murmured. "I wouldn't be here with you. I wouldn't have my gardens or romances. If Celestine still stood, Rune would be king though, and I'd have my mom. I wish she had lived, but I don't hate my life. I'd be scared to go back."

Otto rubbed Jessa's face with his cheek. "You don't have to."

Of course not. Who would make him go back into the dark? But he was still afraid.

"Let's do something fun."

Otto nodded. "You got it."

The Cypress Inn, where they were staying now because it was closer to Gem Fest, offered shuttle rides into town where they explored the shops that lined both sides of a wharf. When the sun fell low, they headed back in the direction of a restaurant that overlooked the bay.

"Wait," said Otto. "I want to look in here."

The shop Otto stepped into was a small, snug square filled with crystal necklaces and sun-catchers hanging from the ceiling. A U-shaped display case took up the center of the floor, and posters and paintings hung on the wall.

A woman behind the counter by the door smiled at them. "Let me know if you need any help."

Jessa headed to the display case, but glanced back when Otto said, "Did you paint these?"

He stood by a rack of postcards.

"Not me," the woman said. "A local artist brings them in."

"Vamp?"

Jessa returned to Otto's side.

"Human," the woman said.

The postcard was painted in shades of brown and blue and white. A mountain against a blue sky. After a moment, Jessa noticed the clouds formed the shape of the letter for forgiveness. A strange vertical wisp cutting through a pair of clouds formed an undulating horizontal wave. *Weird.*

"What're the names of the mountain ranges around here? This isn't part of it, I don't think?"

The woman gave a perplexed frown and tapped her lips for a moment. "Well, the Santa Lucia and Gabilan, for sure, but I think... the San Benito is close, and the Diablo range is one, I believe."

Otto rapped the card against the fingers of his other hand then set it back in the rack. "Thanks," he said.

"Sure."

They returned to the cold outside.

"What was that about?" Jessa asked.

Otto chuckled. "I have no idea. The picture just caught my eye. I have a feeling it should matter, but I don't know why."

"That was our mountain, wasn't it?"

"It looked like it. A stylized version anyway."

A few minutes later, they were sitting by a wall of windows. The restaurant was dark, decorated with wood and red and black leather, but the light at the windows was bright and silver. It lit Otto's cheekbones but filled the hollows under his eyes with shadow.

"Tell me what you think is going on," Jessa said.

Otto's mouth twisted and he shook his head. "I should know, but I feel like I'm grasping at straws. Or postcards. The whole fake tattoo thing seems too far out there just to get some blood. Suppose Acalliona did think of himself as too good for a blood whore. So he went to some trouble to arrange luxury accommodations at home. But in a town he didn't know? A blood whore would just be so much easier."

"I know, but I told you. Some vampires despise blood whores even more than drainers. They wouldn't want to."

"But if they used them..."

Jessa thought about it. "They wouldn't like it."

"It might jack up their hatred even more," Otto mused, dropping his gaze to his menu.

Jessa stared down at his. The print blurred in the shadows. "Wen didn't like to read."

Otto glanced back up with another mix of smile and frown. "Me neither really."

It's a human pastime, Wen had said.

That wasn't true though. They'd had all kinds of books in Celestine, some with jewel-encrusted covers. Jessa had seen pictures of the library.

"I wonder if Wen hated me. Up until... you..." Otto's smile faded, his frown deepening. "Up until you," Jessa went on, "I never heard him say a word against humans. It shocked me, and I told myself that's not what he meant. I'm stuck on that room in Comity House and what Wen was doing because it doesn't fit with stealing jewelry if that's what's going on. Wen didn't need money or status."

"Not every piece of a puzzle has to fit. People are too crazy for that. Even vampire people. And money? Some people never have enough. And anyway, I still think it has something to do with drainers."

"Brillen was a fake."

"He wanted blood."

"And Wen helped."

"It looks like it."

Jessa swallowed. The idea Wen might have fed on human blood had never occurred to him. Bile flooded his mouth. He picked up his water glass and drank. "Maybe there was a whole group of people. I mean, with that... room."

"Like a conspiracy? And with Frenn our only link."

"Why bother going to Gem Fest then? He couldn't be so stupid as to show up there."

"We're here, and it's another rock to look under."

A last flare of light hit the window before the sun set, twinkling orange and pink and silver on the ocean waves.

Back at the inn, Otto lit a fire, and they went to bed to the light of the flames. The flicker of shadows reminded Jessa of the fire pits at home. Rune had wanted them because they reminded him of the ones in Celestine. As the room warmed, Jessa nestled into the arm Otto held him with and fell asleep until a dry scrape on the back of his neck roused him again. It was a kiss, but cold, and he squirmed away, pushing off the covers as the kiss pursued him. He sat up, staring blindly into the dark room.

"Otto?"

There was no reply, only the brush of a cold palm on his shoulder now. He jumped up and turned toward the touch.

"Jessa."

The voice was a dry rasp. As dry as the kiss.

"Wen?" The figure on the bed took shape now, gossamer as the strange fog that scared him and yet didn't. Wen's face had hollows where his eyes and mouth were supposed to be. "Aren't you—?"

"Hungry," Wen rasped. "Hungry."

Jessa shivered. Where was Otto? "Lemme... lemme turn on the light."

"No!"

Why doesn't Otto wake up?

Jessa's hand fell away from the lamp. He was half human and his eyesight wasn't as good as a true vampire's, but he moved away from the lamp, closer to the door.

"C'mere," Wen whispered.

Like hell.

"I'm sorry, Wen," Jessa whispered.

"You never loved me," Wen said. "You defiled yourself."

The prickly cold in the room froze his skin, but inside a ball of heat grew where his heart was. "I'm human, Wen."

"Human blood," Wen said, rising off the bed.

Jessa bolted for the door, but he tripped and fell and threw his hands toward a floor that dropped away beneath him. He fell and fell. Darkness swallowed him. He wasn't awake. He was dreaming. *You're just dreaming. You'll wake up.* But terror made his heart pound. Wen was a weight following him. The shine of hidden minerals and jewels encrusted in ancient walls loomed out of the dark. *Celestine!*

Claws grabbed him. Twisting, his gaze fell on long talonlike fingernails digging into his shoulder, gleaming like bone. He landed on the street of a destroyed city. The ceiling of the earth rose above him, a dome of gleaming white and gray rock. Boulders and rubble strewed the landscape, but a still-standing building drew his eyes. The rubies that encrusted the face of the Celestine Library with the Letters of the Revelatory Passion shone blood red.

Jessa stared, then Wen swooped in on him and there was nothing but bone left of his face. Gaping eye sockets. A black maw of a mouth. Tattooed fangs, carved and gleaming.

"Hungry."

Jessa screamed, struggling back as Wen shot forward, teeth coming for his throat.

Until—

The fog!

Soft and heavy and gray. It appeared out of nothing and drowned Wen in its folds. Jessa staggered back as the amorphous shape undulated, turning from slate to black to soft gray again.

Then it was gone, and all that was left was a pile of bones on the dark city street.

Jessa screamed again.

"Hey! Hey!"

He was back, buried under the covers, wrapped in Otto's arms. "Otto?"

"Shush."

Silver wisps of fog clung to the sliding glass doors and a faint warm glow came from the fireplace.

"You just had a nightmare," Otto murmured.

No.

Jessa had gone to Celestine City, a place he had no memories of. But even as he held onto the picture, it faded, though he knew he should remember. Something that wasn't the fog.

Though the fog was dangerous too.

He listened to Otto's slow breaths and stared into the dark. The shapes of empty windows formed in front of him, and glowing red eyes slowly surfaced.

Fallen angels?

Or black souls?

Or *worse*...

45

GEM FEST

GEM FEST SPRAWLED over a mile of property. This section of town, once wrecked in the Upheaval, had been reclaimed by the Ellowyn, and many of the old warehouses had been converted into artist and jewelry-making studios. For the next three days the streets were blocked off. Festivalgoers meandered the streets from place to place. Outdoor booths decorated the area with brightly colored fabrics, and umbrellas carried by sun-sensitive vampires dotted the crowds. The air was fragrant with the salty sea breeze, cooking food, and incense.

Coming from the direction of a square gray building near the main entrance to the grounds was a pair of vampires in a golf cart. The one not driving jumped from the vehicle when it stopped and rushed toward Jessa and Otto. Despite his haste and smile, no subservience rolled off him. The dip of his chin bringing his head down with it carried the weight of a being who knew his power.

Shifting beside him, Otto tilted his head. "Aren't you Zev's cousin?"

The vampire's smile broadened. "You remember. I'm flattered."

He offered his hand and, after a minuscule hesitation that maybe only Jessa caught, Otto shook it.

Now the vampire turned his smile on Jessa. "I am Moss and honored to be your host, Prince Senera. Are you an artist like Prince Rune?"

Jessa laughed. "I make jewelry. Costume jewelry. I have a co-op."

"You should show your work here next year and maybe coax a piece from the prince."

He nodded with a smile, but Rune never sold his pieces. He created in a frenzy and gave them away. "I'll ask."

"Good," said Moss. "Good. In the meantime, I'm at your disposal. Don't hesitate to ask for whatever you need. The golf cart here is for your use, and you, Detective Jones, are welcome here, but you will encounter surprise. We seldom admit humans. Anything you need, just ask. I'll be in my office for most of the day."

Taking the keys Moss held out, Jessa grinned at Otto, and they headed to the golf cart.

"I've never driven one of these."

Otto slid in cautiously. "Don't tip it over."

"Very funny."

It jerked when he first stepped on the gas, but then it ran as smoothly as any car. At the first corner though, he slowed down and said, "So where are we going?"

Otto took a brochure from a holder attached to the dash and opened it to a map on the back. "Well, Brillen worked with metal clay."

"Let me see."

Jessa leaned over, resting against Otto's shoulder. As he gazed at the map Otto's breath in his hair sent a shiver through him. "You're distracting me."

"Fair's fair," Otto muttered.

"Well... This... this word here." Otto nuzzled his neck, and a warm, drifty feeling filled Jessa's head.

"Hm..." murmured Otto. "What word?"

"*Falla*," he whispered. "It means... metal in Celes Ellowyn."

Otto drew back, and the warm air suddenly cooled. "Okay. Let's go there."

With a nod, Jessa shifted the cart into gear and pulled back onto the street. He drove slowly as he rolled through the crowds. Tents dotted a large lot, shading the tables and chairs underneath. Vampires gathered around, playing games. Balloons bobbed, attached to a helium tank.

A few minutes later, Jessa parked the cart alongside a grassy park where kids played on ladders and jungle gyms.

Otto bought a tub of calamari from a vampire who took his money with a suspicious glare, and Jessa popped one of the morsels into his mouth with a moan. "Um. That's so good."

"We'll check the auditoriums too," said Otto. "They're supposed to have presentations going on all day."

On foot now, they moved along with the flow of the crowd past booths displaying metal bracelets, rings, and goblets. Ceramic pottery in another. Oil paints, wood carving, bead jewelry, and an array of necklaces, earrings, bracelets, anklets, body chains, and rings at Falla's Follies. The Revelatory jewelry was too heavy for Jessa's taste, but his gaze strayed to the same body chain Otto was focused on. The Letters of the Revelatory Passion hung from the silver chain, all cloisonné, and flat and thin as parchment. Otto traced a finger under the chain, and it rippled like water.

After a moment, he drew back and ran his palm over his bristly scalp. "Jewelry, drainers, Solomon Frenn. Acalliona was related to the Nezzarams and Frenn was Abadi's lover. Frenn and Acalliona both dealt in jewelry and both knew or had met Wen. Frenn was suspected of killing a drainer, and Brillen was pretending to be one." The frustration on Otto's face grew. "I'm getting nothing."

"Come on," said Jessa. "You can't force it. Let's walk for a while. I love this weather."

"Feels good," Otto agreed.

The breeze had quickened, slapping loose banners, spreading the scents of incense and spicy food.

An auditorium as large as a hangar held the presentations. Inside, Jessa lost himself at a glassblowing exhibition where the artist created goblet after goblet in shimmery blue and green glass. Each one looked as translucent as the sea. Occasionally, he caught sight of Otto checking out the different exhibits. When the glass blower took a break, Jessa looked around again, but Otto was gone. A jolt of panic zapped his heart.

Silly.

But where was he?

The bigger vampires hid his view. He rose to his toes. For fuck's sake. Otto wouldn't leave him. Why did Jessa even think that?

Wen did.

Well, Wen was dead, that's why.

He hated you.

No, he didn't. Jessa was sure Wen didn't hate him. His dream... *was your guilty conscience.*

For not loving Wen. For loving Otto when—

Loving Otto?

You know you love him.

His heart squeezed, because how dumb was that? *This isn't a romance story. You aren't going to end up with the hero.*

Well, why not? Why did Jessa read those books unless he halfway believed them?

"Jess!"

He stopped, vampires bumping against him. A hand rose. *Otto.* He stood outside a black tent-like enclosure.

Jessa hurried over. "What's this?"

"Books. Come see."

Incense filled Jessa's senses, strong and spicy, and curls of smoke floated in the air. Shelving units stuffed with books stood against the fabric walls.

Jessa bent his head to look at the spines. Poetry and cookbooks. A few novels, but no romances. Children's books and a human bible.

Otto gestured to a glass curio cabinet in a corner. "Vampire, isn't it?"

Ellowyn cuneiform decorated the covers of the books inside, but they had to be replicas. Only special books had covers, and those were precious and only displayed in libraries.

Otto pointed at a black book with a picture of a vase in brilliant jewel tones on its cover. "I saw a vase like that at Frenn's. What does it mean?"

"Gloria Adi. Um... Adi is treasure and gloria is the honor or praise you give God." Jessa chewed on his lip. "This is switched though. The order of the words. Sometimes that matters. Usually it would be Gloria Adi because God always comes first. This is more like a treasure you get because of your honor to God."

"How religious are you people?"

"Like humans. Some a lot, and some not at all."

"I'm going to get it. You pay for it though. I doubt the guy selling it will talk to me."

The vampire didn't want to talk to Jessa either. "Why do you want it?"

Jessa went blank for a moment.

"It's a precious item," the guy added.

Annoyance kick-started Jessa's tongue. "It's not original. I like the cover. We have a vase like that at home. And besides, the cover degrades its value if it is an original."

The vampire's eyes narrowed. He was skinny but towered over both Jessa and Otto. "It's original."

"And degraded."

"A hundred bucks."

"A hundred bucks," Otto echoed. "Is the cure for cancer in there?"

A sneer twisted the vampire's face. "Like I care about cancer. It's out of print. It was put out by some masons that aren't even active anymore. You want it, a hundred bucks. You don't want it, get out."

Jessa paid, and Otto stuffed the book into his pocket.

Outside the tent flaps, Jessa said, "What now?"

"We eat. Then look around some more."

Otto slung an arm over his shoulder, and for a while, they were just a pair of guys enjoying a festival. The sun kept shining, and the breeze kept the day cool. They ate fish and chips at a picnic table and drank spiced iced tea and took the golf cart up and down the streets. By the time the sun fell low, and they'd returned the cart, a shuttle approached the gravel entrance. Light and shadow flashed on the windshield, black and eerily red like a pair of eyes. Jessa recoiled but got nowhere before the earth shook and threw him off his feet. He tumbled forward, and the shuttle swung sideways, flying straight at him. He hit the ground with a jolt, grinding his cheek into the gravel. A roar filled his ears, and the sky somersaulted. He flew backwards, stumbling into a hard wall with arms that wrapped around him and crushed the air out of his lungs.

"Jesus Christ," Otto whispered in his ear.

The shuttle stopped, its doors swinging open, and the

driver, a vampire, emerged and stared with eyes that... No. They didn't glow. God, he was seeing things that weren't there now.

The driver's eyes were dark and narrow in the sun.

Plain, everyday eyes.

.

46

EPIPHANY

THE ORDINARY SOUND of a running bath gave Otto comfort. A cupboard door clapped shut. Something clanked on the counter.

That quake had scared the hell out of him. Seeing Jessa go down had done crazy things to him. His heart had slammed against his chest with enough force to knock his air out. No sound had come from his mouth when he'd yelled, "Jess!"

But Jessa was okay.

What was Otto doing getting so wrapped up in the vamp. When this was over he'd go back to his life. Would he get his job back?

Taking a breath he tried to concentrate on that, his job, and opened his book, squirming back into his pile of pillows to get comfortable. He'd taken a shower, ignoring Jessa's attempts to coax him into the tub. He wanted to get to his book. Finding it was written in English was a surprise, but Jessa had said, "It's because it's not from one of our cities. It's new. Most computers are still only set up for humans, so we print in your languages."

"Which you all know," Otto had said with a strange bitterness, as though all of humanity had been the unsuspecting victim of a skeezy Peeping Tom for the past ten thousand years.

"We were always a part of your world. You just didn't look."

"You hid."

"You wanted us... dead," Jessa had whispered against his cheek before stepping into the bath.

Wanted. And hated. Or feared. The allure of the lost soul. When there'd been nothing left in the world to save, Otto's struggle had been over. He'd drowned it in whiskey, and his parched throat still ached to swallow the fuzzy emptiness the booze had brought. But there was still some light from somewhere in him. Something that didn't want to give up on Maisie, Brillen, Mateo... himself.

He settled back and began to read.

Adi Gloria, devoted followers of the first faith, unwavering adherents...

Otto skimmed the introductory passage and code of ethics. The Adi Gloria appealed to merchants of a particular style of jewelry called Guardian Reminders. All metal clay and gemstones.

A loud groan interrupted him. He raised his gaze and stared at the open bathroom door.

"This feels so good," Jessa called out. "Come and see."

"What are Guardian Reminders?"

"Revelatory jewelry, like the letters for the seven families, but for everyone."

"Costume jewelry?"

"Kind of."

With gems. But gems were abundant in the underworld. Otto continued reading. *Every true guardian has a unique position, no one above the other in placement. Always seek a circle of the Nine, continuous and unbroken, in the order of the true ascendancy.*

Nine? Weird.

So far, he'd found no mention of the vase on the cover. After a few more pages he came to a list of bylaws, grievances, meditations, and fees for the different levels of membership. Flipping back to the beginning, he reread the passage that still had no obvious relation to masons—*Every true guardian has a unique position.*

"I'm insulted."

Otto's gaze snapped up and locked on Jessa. His breath lodged in his throat. Jessa leaned against the doorframe, strands of wet hair clinging to his broad shoulders and chest. His position forced a gorgeous curve on his body as his waist dipped in and sloped back out into an angular hip. His dick dangled between his legs, rosy pink from his bath. Damn, he was hot. Otto tried to imagine him frail and sickly but came up blank. Jessa was strong. Stronger than Otto would ever be. Maybe in every way.

"Never," Otto murmured. *You are a treasure.* "I'd never insult you."

"You gave up a bath with me to read your pamphlet?"

"A hundred-dollar pamphlet, and you're still here."

"I could shun you."

Otto laughed. "I repent."

A smile brightened Jessa's face. Even from across the room his dimples flashed. With a slight grunt he pushed off the doorframe and came across the room. Otto swung his feet off the bed and cupped Jessa's hips. His skin was warm and smooth, his scent fresh and soapy. Under Otto's gaze, Jessa's dick twitched, and he bopped his hips. "Taste it."

Otto chuckled. "Well, aren't you bold."

Whatever happened to his shy, flower-loving baby prince?

He took in the expanse of fair, freckled skin to glowing eyes. That wasn't human. It scared Otto for a moment. The intensity in the gaze, the burning of emotions Otto knew to steer clear of.

Soon. Soon this would be over.

He leaned in, resting his lips against the skin under Jessa's belly button. That was all at first—feeling his skin contract, the muscles underneath tightening. He inhaled. Would he ever forget the sweet fragrance that was all Jessa? Flowers and spice and musk.

Oh God.

Just sex. *That's all.*

His life since Maisie's murder had led him here, and he was close to the killer. Murky images tickled his brain. He had to stay strong. Get justice. Revenge. Every fiber of his being burned for it. For Maisie. To make the drainers pay.

Otto lifted his gaze.

Jessa bit his lip, a slight frown furrowing his forehead.

Otto tugged on him, leaning back until they lay on the bed, Jessa on top of him. Slowly, a glassy lust replaced the worry that had come into Jessa's eyes.

Please don't let him say it.

"I love you," Jessa whispered.

"You can't."

"But I do." His voice was as soft as his breath.

Otto held his face, bringing him closer until their lips met. He breathed Jessa in, thumbs stroking his cheekbones, tongue teasing the seam of his lips. Jessa opened, surrounding Otto in his heat and sweetness. They ground their cocks together, rubbing against the cotton of Otto's briefs. Sparks of pleasure caught fire in Otto's belly. He pushed Jessa's head away, taking in the tips of his fangs that showed through his parted lips, his flushed cheeks, and hooded eyes. Otto nipped his bottom lip before rearing up and flipping Jessa onto his back. A startled look flashed in Jessa's eyes, but he smiled.

Otto kissed him again. Slowly. Exploring his mouth as though he'd never been there before, drinking in Jessa's moans, pressing down on the muscles bunching and straining beneath him. Jessa gasped as Otto broke the kiss and trailed his tongue down Jessa's body. His warmth radiated like the heat off a sun-baked rock. Steel muscles quivered. He scraped his teeth along Jessa's belly.

"Oh... fuck," Jessa muttered, bucking his hips.

Otto lifted his head. "Is that a hint?"

A growling sound rumbled out of Jessa's mouth. A command.

"In that case, my sweet prince..."

Otto slid his lips over the head of Jessa's cock. A sharp hiss and Jessa's hands clamping down on his scalp rewarded him. Sweet, salty musk filled his mouth. Closing his eyes, he suckled on the hot flesh, letting the sensations on his tongue and the fire in his dick wash over him. Jessa's whimpers followed him into the dark. Thought was gone. Flesh consumed him—hot and soft and hard. He clamped down on Jessa's hips, bone pressing into his palms, and slid his lips up and down, feeling a slight pulse against his tongue, Jessa's body pushing against his hold, but not too much. Steely muscles tightened and softened. Any control Otto thought he had was Jessa's gift to him.

"Oh... Oh... Stop."

Otto rose slowly, dragging his lips along the soft skin. A tiny spritz of precum sang on his taste buds.

He popped off, and Jessa gasped with a relieved-sounding laugh though his hips bucked anyway, chasing Otto's mouth.

"Oh God," Jessa panted.

"Ride me, baby."

"Yes... Yes, I want that."

Otto flipped onto his back again and shucked his briefs, kicking them somewhere across the room. The sight of Jessa swinging his leg over him burned into his brain in a way he hoped would never fade. His dick bobbed and his hole winked. The heat of his ass resting on Otto's crotch flowed like a wave through his body.

He groaned, and Jessa rolled his pelvis, leaning back with his palms on either side of Otto's legs. The position thrust his rigid dick out. A bead of precum quivered on the tip. Otto salivated, but he made no move toward it, only stroked Jessa's thighs.

The slip and slide of Jessa's crack across Otto's dick sparked through him like fireworks. He bit down on his lip, grunting at the sensations, absorbing Jessa's blissful face. His eyes were half-closed, his lips parted.

"Really want in you," Otto muttered.

A smile grew on Jessa's face, and he blinked, letting out a breathy laugh. "I can do that."

"Then do it," Otto growled, and Jessa scrambled off, dug the lube out of the bedside table and squirted some onto his fingers.

Without thinking Otto grabbed his wrist and said, "Turn around. I want to see."

He ducked at the sight of Jessa's foot flying toward his face, but it breezed by above his nose as Jessa swung around. Holding onto Jessa's hips, Otto eased him back toward his face.

"Fuck yourself."

Jessa grunted as he reached behind him and probed at his hole. "Too bad I'm not a twin."

"Oh, fuck yeah," Otto growled.

Jessa's fingers wriggled their way inside him. Otto stroked his balls and Jessa groaned. His dick jerked and a string of precum stretched to Otto's belly. Jessa's body pulsed with heat. Sweating, Otto lubed his own fingers and joined his with Jessa's. He tugged on Jessa's rim and bent forward to kiss his flushed perineum. The tendons in Jessa's legs shook, and a few seconds later, he pulled his fingers loose, dropped both elbows on the bed, and poked his ass closer to Otto's face. Otto pushed in deeper and nibbled around his hole.

Jessa gasped and bent down to lick at Otto's cock.

"Oh fuck."

Otto froze for a moment, shocked at the jolt of pleasure that hit him like a punch, rolling through him with a dull, achy throb. *Oh shit, shit, shit.*

Jessa worried the nerves under Otto's cockhead with the tip of his tongue. Otto stiffened, curled his fingers, and got a yelp as Jessa threw his head up and jammed himself backwards. Otto rubbed the little bump inside him again, back and forth.

"Sweet... sweet."

He nibbled a rosy cheek and licked through the rasp of soft, fine hairs.

"I think... I think I'm ready," Jessa moaned.

"Get on."

He swung around again, this time half-collapsing on Otto's chest before pushing back up. His hair clung to his face now, and his fangs emerged. Wild-eyed, he planted a foot on the mattress and lifted himself over Otto's cock, reaching down to guide the tip to his hole.

Otto's eyes rolled as Jessa sank.

Heat engulfed him. Life-generating heat. The heat of the sun or the earth's core.

He groaned, the sound dragging up from his aching balls. He dug his fingers into the sheets and held on. Jessa's muscles gripped him and tore another groan out of him. He squeezed his eyes shut.

"Look," Jessa whispered. "Look at me."

The lure of Jessa's voice dragged Otto's eyes back open. He was bendy and bewitching, a dark creature who hid his fangs. But Otto remembered when hordes of screaming vampires rent the bloody sunsets with their silhouettes. Night after night, hunting humans in the rubble. Otto's whole reason for being was to avenge Maisie's death against Jessa's own kind. Against Jessa. The last thing Otto wanted was this vision of ecstatic innocence. His purity of heart and wanton body. Otto concentrated on the bouncing cock and flexing thighs, his dick disappearing into the grasping heat between Jessa's cheeks.

But he stroked Jessa's ribs, running his palms to his chest where his heart pounded and his amulet flopped on his chest. The letter cut a jagged wound across the stone. *Hell. Remorra.* Remorse? Something stirred in Otto's brain, but he couldn't hold onto it. He cupped Jessa's face, feeling the heat of his breath on his wrist as Jessa twisted and buried his face in Otto's palm. A jolt ran up Otto's arm straight to his heart, a bolt that threw his lungs into a stutter.

Fated... love.

But, no. Not to a vampire. Not for a drainer. Not until everybody paid for Maisie, for the life he'd lost to hate.

"Jack yourself."

Jessa nodded. Sweat ran down his face, dripped from his chin. A smile fluttered on his lips, then he groaned as his hand closed around his dick, and he pumped it in a blur. Otto thrust, holding onto Jessa's waist, pushing himself in deeper and deeper. His thrusts grew shallow, and Jessa's pants turned into soft cries.

Otto gritted his teeth, growling "Come," and Jessa slammed himself down, clenched hard and spurted creamy ropes onto Otto's chest. The splash set him off, and a bolt of electricity swept down his spine. His vision whited, fire shooting out his dick.

Otto froze, locked like a stone.

In the dark behind his lids, he imagined Jessa's face twisted in a rictus of pain he had no hope of taking away. A moment later, Jessa's weight pushed him down into the mattress, and Otto wrapped him in his arms.

Hours later, he struggled awake to a pain in his shoulder.

Jessa's necklace.

It was jammed into him, smashed against his arm and Jessa's chest. The vamp lay on his side, arm stretched across Otto's body. The fire had burned down, and dark pressed against the sliding glass door. Otto stared outside until the trees took on shape against the black sky. The wisps of a dream floated away but left him anxious. He'd been dreaming of Maisie. Though nothing appeared in the dark, not even her ghost, she'd come to him. The clamorous presence in his brain was her trying to tell him something, but in the dull-eyed realm of consciousness, he was deaf and blind.

Cautiously, he slid out from under Jessa's arm. The vampire moaned and drew himself into a ball. After grabbing his book and an extra blanket off a chair, Otto eased open the sliding glass door and stepped outside.

The wind was still, the air soft and chilly. He lit a lantern on the table, wrapped himself up, and sat down, opening his book. Over the next hour he read through to the end before flipping through it page by page again. Amid the practical matters of rules, history, resources, and vision statement were snippets of vampire lore, religious dogma, and strange, out-of-place comments. He finally found reference to the vase, a sketch done in more detail than the picture on the cover. In a pale script underneath was the phrase *Order of Ascendancy in True Faith.* What order? What faith?

Leaning back against the chaise lounge Otto rubbed his shoulder, still marked from Jessa's necklace. Stars winked over the tops of the trees, fading quietly as day came on. He traced a ridge on his skin, letting his eyes close.

Come to me. A sign. Anything...

And as though summoned, Maisie floated in the dark toward him. She wore the dress she'd died in and her necklace, though the necklace had never been found and...

Another face followed hers and cold seeped into Otto's bones and froze his lungs. No, not... And yet...

His gut churned with... *Your instinct.* The instinct that had kept him in a job he hadn't deserved in a long time. The one that made sense of clues that made no sense.

Remorse. Remorra. The cuneiform symbol for the Seneras. *Hell.*

Otto understood hell. He'd been living in it.

And so had Rune.

He dug a finger into the ridge Jessa's necklace had made on his shoulder and stared blindly into the dark. When he'd bent over Brillen where he'd sprawled in the weeds, the dull tattoo had drawn him to it. Its image rose into his mind again—its broken edge and a scratch mark, like a fingernail or a... burn. Like the burn of a chain pulling off. The chain of a necklace. And now he was back in an all-night diner, Rune smiling a bitter smile at him from across the table. *"I went against my father..."*

How far would Otto's guilt over Maisie's death take him? How far would Rune's guilt take him?

Remorra.

"I admire your idea of justice. It has a touch of fanaticism."

The burning dark of Rune's eyes pierced him. He was a fallen king, and those weren't the eyes of someone who had accepted defeat. The necklaces were common, but what if some were real, and Rune collected them on his travels while he mapped the new earth. Was he searching for the source of the treasure too? Jessa's necklace might be Rune's way of hiding it in plain view. If it were real. But Maisie's must have been. She'd gotten herself killed by stealing it, and someone had stolen it back.

Rune.

But what about the Adi 'el Lumi? Otto had no doubt they wanted the treasure too. Was Rune a part of them? He must be, but so was Solomon, and Solomon hated drainers.

Otto stared into the dark as though all the pieces of the puzzle would align in front of him. But they swirled— disjointed, oddly shaped. Was he crazy? Dragging his theory out of thin air?

When he was a kid, before his mom got sick, his dad had spent months in the garage building a sailboat from scratch. Every time Otto joined him to watch all the pieces coming together, he'd asked, "What's this thing... what's that one?" and his dad would shrug. "I dunno." By the time he'd finished building, he'd had a pile of parts he had no idea what to do with. Otto's mom had refused to go sailing with him and wouldn't let Otto or Maisie go either.

Maybe that's what Otto was doing now. Trying to build something from scratch and coming up with too many pieces. Were they important and would the whole contraption fall apart without them?

Otto had fallen into a black lake that stretched into a misty distance. In front of him were Brillen, drainers, Solomon, the necklaces, the robbery at the shop, the attacks on Isaac and Jessa, the murders of Wen and Mateo. And what about the guy Mateo's uncle had told Otto about? The one who'd come looking for Mateo. Was he a piece? Or just a guy looking for a friend? Otto suspected he mattered, though only one ripple stirred the still lake, and only one face broke the surface.

Rune's. Rune was Brillen's killer.

Stripped of a crown. Qudim's avenger. Maybe he hadn't meant for Qudim's death and for the vampires to turn on

Qudim, as dead sick of fighting and blood as the humans had been. Dinallah had come into possession of the formulation for a synthetic blood and had used it to broker peace. But Qudim had fought on until a mob set loose by Rune chased him, and he leaped to his death into the rupture above Celestine City. As the murderer of a king, Rune paid for his crime with the dishonor of his family. Was he now avenging Qudim against those who had gone too far? He was Abadi's son, connected to Solomon Frenn through her. Connected to the Adi 'el Lumi? He had the means to collect the necklaces through his travels and he had motive.

What was the treasure to him?

Money. Power. *My father always told us we had hidden powers...*

Rune needed the necklaces because the letters somehow unlocked the chamber. *A circle of the Nine.* Originally, there were nine families, Mal had said. Maybe Rune knew that, maybe not. But if he did and didn't have all the necklaces yet, that would mean... More bodies.

Otto returned to the book, flipping pages until he found the passage, *"Always seek a circle of the Nine, continuous and unbroken, in the order of the true ascendancy... Apply the revelations, the prize of punishment suffered, to unlock the promised gift."*

The evil close to Zev was his old boyhood friend—the one he'd conquered and disgraced. The one who wanted revenge.

Otto's mind had tied itself into a knot when his gut went quiet, but all along the motive was simple. Greed, and revenge for ancient crimes.

Maisie.

Otto didn't want to believe Rune had killed her. Jesus, Otto liked him. Vampire or not, something about the guy drew him. His darkness and passion, things Otto understood, the things that had been his fall. And he was still falling and about to drag Jessa into the dark with him.

Fuck. How was he going to tell Jessa?

A piercing silver light lit the backs of the trees as the sun began to rise.

But if Jessa's necklace was real, as soon as Rune found the treasure he'd want it back. Was Jessa safe? Was Rune's love real or possessive?

And Otto's love?

Getting up, he slipped back inside, dropping the blanket back on the chair. As he approached the bed, Jessa rolled over and smiled at him. "Hey," he murmured sleepily.

Otto climbed over him, imagining himself like a dark cloud, suffocating everything light and bright and good. He buried his face in Jessa's neck and held on.

47

TRAIN WRECK

THE TRAIN THRUMMED on the tracks. Jessa jumped on, disappearing inside. Clambering after him, Otto pushed through a group of people jostling for seats and took his by the window facing Jessa.

His stomach lurched, but not from the vibrations underneath him. He tried to keep a normal face. Tried not to ruin Jessa's excitement. He was pressed to his window, watching the crowds outside.

He flashed his bright gaze at Otto. "I'm so glad we're taking the train."

Otto smiled weakly. Jessa's innocence left him with an oddly frail feeling. He wasn't up to it. Wasn't strong enough not to break Jessa's heart. The minute he told him...

All the joy in Jessa's life was an act of a different kind of faith than the Adi 'el Lumi knew. He'd fought back from death and struggled through years of sickness.

Rune cherished him. *Doesn't he?*

The crowd on the platform thinned, and the people in the car sat, and the train lurched. Jessa drew in a breath.

"You're going to be bored before you know it," Otto said.

"I don't get bored." Weird and matter-of-fact. Jessa smiled. "It's beautiful outside."

It was. Thin silver and plum-colored clouds bounced back shadow and light. A few minutes after the train chugged ahead, eucalyptus trees surrounded them. Jessa settled into his seat, head tipped back, eyeing Otto from under his lids. A smile played on his lips.

"Something's going on," he murmured.

"Like what?"

"You tell me. I can see you thinking." His smile broadened. "I have a feeling I don't want to know what you're thinking about. You look sad. Is it about us?"

Otto worked his tongue over his teeth, buying time. Jessa wasn't usually blunt. Otto had a feeling he'd often been told things weren't going to go well for him and had grown tired of it. He'd defied it instead. But this... This was the ruin of his family.

"I'm not sad."

Jessa was quiet for a moment while he looked outside again. It was dark under the trees and the shade of the leaves flashed across the glass. He touched the window with a fingertip, then dropped his hand and faced forward again. "Are we eating on the train?"

"We'll be home before lunch. Are you hungry?"

"I need to feed soon."

A shiver of desire he didn't want to think about ran through Otto. "We'll be home in a couple hours."

"Is it about us?" Jessa said again.

Otto bit back a groan. "I have to bring Brillen's killer to justice, Jessa. That's my job."

"Making us about that is a lie. I felt you change."

"What?"

"This morning. You felt different to me."

"Letting murderers go free just isn't something I can do. I've given years of my life to hunting this one down."

Jessa frowned. "What are you talking about? Maisie? You really think this is the same killer?"

The words left his mouth, quiet and heavy. "I know it is. I think I've always known. Jessa—" But now his voice failed.

The train rocked, and Jessa gripped the seat on either side of him. "Tell me what's going on."

"I read the book. I think there are messages in it about the treasure."

"The Adini Treasure? It isn't real. At least not anymore."

Otto shook his head, letting his gaze rest on the shape of the necklace under Jessa's shirt. "The Letters of the Revelatory Passion unlock it."

"Where is it?"

"I don't know. I think the Adi 'el Lumi are trying to find and locate the keys."

"The keys?"

"In the necklaces." He nodded at Jessa's chest. "The letters are the key."

Jessa laughed, a hand to his chest. "But these are nothing. Reproductions."

"The real ones exist. I think that one is real."

Jessa tugged his out. Shook his head. "Rune gave—"

He stopped, and horror dawned the moment he understood. His head moved to the side. Back again. He shook it harder, pushing back into his seat as if to get as far away from Otto as possible. "You can't take the easy way out just because solving this is hard. Or because you want to break it off with me. Just because Rune was at our father's side, or because he bowed to Zev for my sake... You think he'd kill people out of... Out of what? Revenge? To get rich? And do what? Go where? No vampire would accept him."

"The Adi 'el Lumi would. They want power back. For vampires."

"They'd kill me."

"Not if that was Rune's price."

"For power? For riches? To save my life again?"

Otto sat forward, and Jessa scrunched back further. "Guilt and shame are terrible things to live with," Otto said softly.

Jessa's face hardened and seemed to age twenty years. "Rune is honorable. Zev honors him."

"Zev bought him."

"With my life," Jessa said bitterly.

"Your family was brought low."

"We are still royal."

"Listen to me. Throw a stone and you'll hit a vampire connected to the jewelry or art trade. I got distracted by that. Brillen was a sleaze. He preyed on humans by pretending to be a drainer. He knew what he was doing when he went to Wen, but Wen didn't know him and turned him away. So Brillen hooked up with a blood whore. Maybe he didn't mean to drain him. That would bring too much attention. But he was followed and killed for the necklace he wore."

"What necklace?"

Otto's imagination had taken a massive leap, but he was sure of himself now. "He had a scratch on his neck. It seemed like something he might have gotten in a struggle. Now it makes sense he got it when the killer ripped the necklace off of him."

"You're guessing."

"The blood whore got away. We thought it was Mateo, Isaac's friend. And, at first, it just seemed like a coincidence Isaac was in the kitchen during the first robbery at Comity House, but I don't think it was. They wanted information and thought Isaac would have it."

"They? They came after me. Who are you talking about?"

"I think it's possible Rune is with the Adi 'el Lumi. Maybe you were just a distraction too. You weren't hurt. Wen was there to protect you."

"So Wen was working with them too. A conspiracy now?"

Otto's lips twitched with a smile. "It is a conspiracy, so yes, it sounds outrageous, but listen and it all fits together. They finally got to Mateo. I'm guessing they'd been watching the center. Wen got in the way. I think he was on the periphery, a hanger-on. He didn't know enough, but he wanted status. He would've been easy to manipulate. They took Wen's body and—"

"Left it at Solomon's."

"I doubt that was the plan. I think taking him was an attempt to muddy the waters, otherwise there was no reason to, they could've killed him and left him there. I think Solomon was interrupted—either by the clerk coming in or something else. I think they planned to dump the body somewhere that would lead the investigation in the wrong direction. For years Rune has been searching for the treasure. He has the perfect job for it. And maybe while he's been doing his job he's been collecting the real necklaces. For some reason he gave you one."

"I told you why. I was sick. I... I liked it."

Otto nodded. "And you would keep it safe for him. I don't know how much time we have before he's ready to make his move. I wouldn't be surprised if he knows how close I am."

Jessa laughed. "This is crazy. Rune is working. He doesn't know anything about this. He blows glass in his spare time. Or sculpts. Or paints. I know Rune didn't do this. I know it, Otto."

"How, Jessa?"

"In my heart." His face twisted. "In my heart. Where I also know you're too afraid to love me." He got up.

"Jessa."

"No, I—"

He tilted.

And suddenly Otto flew across the train and crashed into the ceiling. Screams and screeches of metal rent the air. Otto rolled with the motion of the train. Glass shattered. The edge of a seat careened toward him, and a burst of light flashed in his eyes, and everything suddenly went dark.

48

BROKEN TIES

OH GOD.

A high-pitched keen tore through Jessa's head. It ricocheted inside with a jangling sound of its own. Groaning, he clenched his hands into fists. Dirt and gravel ground into his knuckles.

He was outside.

Heat baked into his back and pierced an eye with its glow. The sun. He peeled his eyelids partway back. He lay on an expanse of gravel. Bodies littered his field of vision. Some were moving, but others...

He swallowed.

A few people were carrying the injured away on blankets and coats while other people crawled out of giant blocks of metal. What were those? He frowned, trying to remember how he had gotten here.

Somebody touched him, a woman hurrying by, glancing over her shoulder at him. "Okay?"

He nodded.

The sun on his back seeped into the gravel all around him, and the desire to sleep dragged at him like a weight. He didn't want to think about—

What?

A shriek rent the air. "Heeelp!"

Blinking rapidly, Jessa pushed at the ground, got to his feet, and swayed. Somebody waved an arm from inside one of the metal boxes. "Heeelp!"

The box was silver blue. Other, similar boxes lay in disarray across the open field.

"Heeelp!"

Jessa headed toward the voice. A couple sat on the ground, a woman dabbing at a man's bloody face with the hem of her shirt.

"Are you okay?" Jessa asked.

She gave him a bewildered gaze. "I think so."

"What happened?" he asked.

Her mouth opened, and for a moment nothing emerged. "An earthquake," she answered tentatively, as though maybe it had been something else.

"Oh."

Jessa staggered on. He helped somebody else off the ground and went on toward the nearest box.

Train.

It was a train. He'd been on a train. With—

"Otto!"

He started to run toward the mass of cars strewn pell mell across the weeds.

"Heeelp!"

The car with the waving arm was on the opposite side of the tracks with a few others. Staggering over, Jessa dragged himself onto the side of the car, now the roof. A woman stood inside, holding onto the edge of the broken window with a bloody palm. He recoiled as she fixed a cold, flat stare on his, until a second later panic filled her eyes and she whispered, "Oh my God. Please help us."

She released the broken window, reaching for him.

Jessa trembled, a wave of dizziness breaking over him. The blood scent drowned him and stole his air. It wasn't Isaac's scent or the sweet spice he'd detected under Otto's skin, but his teeth ached, protruding past his incisors, reminding him of his hunger.

"Please," said the woman again.

Then she ducked back inside, and Jessa followed her, slid over the edge of the window like an idiot, and yelped when the glass cut into his skin.

The woman spun back, but he waved her off. "I'm okay."

She turned away, crawling over the broken seats, leading Jessa to the far end of the car. When his gaze fell on the guy lying there, he wanted to cry. He'd been impaled by the leg of one of the seats and nailed to the floor.

"Can you get it off him?" the woman asked.

Jessa worked numb lips. He wasn't sure how much time passed before he made words. "I-I... I have to get help."

The woman grabbed his arm. "No. You can't go. That's what the others said, but nobody's come back. You can't leave us."

Oh God.

He wanted to cry again. The pounding in his head sounded like thunder.

Go. Find Otto.

The order rolled through him like a gentle wave. He guessed it was his own voice, but he wasn't sure. It didn't sound like his.

He retreated, bringing the woman with him. "We can't get it off him by ourselves. We need help."

"You help. Don't go."

"I promise." He let his fangs drop, and she took a step back. "I promise on my family's honor, I won't leave you. I promise."

She squeezed her hands together and clasped them under

her chin. The shine in her eyes made them look like rocks. He shuddered and staggered again, catching himself on one of the seats before he scrambled from the car.

Now some of the people on the ground had shirts and blankets over them. Somebody running toward the biggest collection of cars knocked into him. He spun at the impact but followed.

"Otto! Otto!"

His call joined a dozen others. He stopped at a small crowd and helped a few passengers clamber from another part of the train. After they stumbled off, he slipped between the couplings of another pair of cars and froze as the ground rumbled underneath him. Screams rang out. Somebody sobbed nearby. But then the ground stilled again. On a road below, two vehicles roared out of the trees, and a few seconds later, the occupants tumbled out and rushed to the wreckage.

Where was Otto?

Jessa turned away. Purple-slate clouds piled on the horizon. A wisp of fog floated through the trembling eucalyptus. Jessa shivered in the growing coolness and headed back the way he'd come.

Somebody pointed down the hillside, and the others carried the injured. Jessa swept his gaze across the activity but didn't see Otto. His heart sped, and bile soured his stomach. All of a sudden he was afraid to look at the bodies on the ground. *Please don't be Otto. Please don't be Otto.*

The woman's voice rang in his head again—*Don't leave us*—and he began to run.

The clouds winked out the sun, and shadows raced across the field. At the car where the woman waited he looked back again and spotted him. *Otto!*

He opened his mouth.

Jessa.

He spun around. "Rune?"

But there was nobody there. He glanced back, but this time he'd lost Otto in the crowd. A laugh rang inside the car, giddy, almost shrill. Startled, heart trip-hammering again, Jessa climbed on top of the car and peered in through the broken window.

Rune stood in back, smiling faintly at him. And beside him... The guy. Standing on his two feet now. He wore a T-shirt smeared a garish black with blood. The woman—his mother?—stood with her hand on his shoulder. He was blond. Golden even in the darkness. Short, as though trying to tame its curls. Healthy and whole.

The woman fixed her stare on him and laughed again. "It looked so awful. So much worse than it turned out to be."

Jessa made a move to jump down, but Rune shook his head, looked at the woman and the guy and said, "What are your names?"

The woman spoke. "I'm Louise Lytton. This is Emek."

Rune's smile widened. "Perhaps we will meet again."

Then he walked away.

"Rune," Jessa said. "I don't—you aren't supposed to be here."

"I was on my way home. I sent Uriah on ahead of me."

Jessa slid back down the car, and Rune followed, catching Jessa's wrist as he started down the embankment.

"I saw Otto," Jessa said.

"Wait. Remember Emek's name and tell Zev."

Jessa frowned, chilled under the sunless sky now, Otto's voice floating in his head. *It's Rune, Jessa.*

But that was a lie he'd never believe.

"Rune, I—"

But now Louise and Emek jumped down from the top of

the car beside them, Louise's stare fixed on them, a small smile on her lips. Inexplicably, Rune hissed, lifted his hand and brought it near Jessa's face, lowering it slowly, shadow following his fingers until darkness covered Jessa's eyes, and he fell.

49

GEARING UP FOR A FIGHT

THE CLOUDS LOOMED OMINOUSLY, the air tangy with electricity.

Otto ran through the shadows flying across the field, coming to a stop at the last car and looking back again.

Otto!

Goddamnit. "Jess!" The voice was loud in Otto's head, but it wasn't coming from nearby. Otto had caught a glimpse of him between the cars, but now he was gone. More trucks and cars arrived at the edge of the field. Otto plowed back down the hillside.

One of the cars had a light bar on it.

When he spotted the uniform, he pulled out his badge and showed it to a gray-haired woman in a small group of civilians. "I need a car."

Her eyebrows rose. "Well, you can't have mine. How about a truck? You can take my nephew's."

A young guy nearby glanced over and frowned but tossed him his keys. Otto caught them, and the guy pointed to a beat-up blue Ford.

"Thanks."

"That's a loaner!" the gray-haired cop yelled after him.

He waved as he ran over the clumpy ground. A minute later he was on the road. Otto wasn't much of a believer in fate, but right now all he had to go on was the image of a mountain on a postcard, and the hope Rune was going home to whatever treasure was buried there.

50

BACK AT THE CASTLE

MAL LET GO of the doorframe and looked across the kitchen. Bettina held her hands in front of the cupboards as though she planned to catch them if they flew off the wall.

"For God's sake, Betts. Next time get under the table."

"Says the woman standing inside a sliding glass door."

True. She glowered. "You might show me some respect."

The older vamp guffawed. "Earn it."

"Jesus," Mal muttered. "I'm checking on the others."

The temblor this time had packed a punch though it hadn't lasted long. Mal glanced back at the wall of clouds that had driven her inside. Her gaze fell on the water lapping against the edges of the fountain on the veranda.

"Find out the epicenter for me if you can."

Bettina's dark eyes turned sharp. "Is everything alright?"

Was it? Rune was hundreds of miles away. Jessa closer. "I'm sure it is," she said.

But her skin prickled with uncomfortable heat. She met Fritt in the hallway leading to the receiving room.

He halted in front of her. "Malia."

She gritted her teeth and forced a smile that probably made her look like a skeleton. "I was just coming to check on you."

"I'm fine. So are Hod and Elssa. I was on my way to see to our guest."

"I'll do that. Will you call Dinallah Manor and bring me news of Jessa."

"Of course. I'm sure he's fine. You would sense it otherwise."

That was the problem. She sensed nothing from Jessa. But Rune... Why was he close?

She forced her teeth apart and flashed her fangs. "I'm over protective."

"We have been telling you that for years."

Mouth hanging open, she watched the old bastard march past her. *Jesus.*

A few minutes later, she crossed the receiving room to a door hidden behind one of the tapestries and headed downstairs. It was quiet in the hall, but the door to Isaac's suite was open. So was Rune's.

"Isaac?"

"In here."

She followed the sound of his voice into Rune's study. He crouched on the floor, gathering papers. His moppy hair flopped over his eyes, and he swiped his arm across his forehead, brushing his bangs away.

"I heard a crash." He motioned with a twist of his head behind him.

"Oh fuck," Mal muttered.

The red and gold figure had shattered on the floor. She made a quick perusal of the room. Other than stray paper and rolled plans, it looked to be the only casualty.

Rune.

Nothing. He had cut her off. They were too close and had

been since childhood for her not to sense him. The hot prickle cooled into a chill, but of course. It was cold in here. Even Isaac shivered.

"Are you okay?" she asked.

He glanced up. "Yeah."

She gathered a couple of Rune's maps and set them on the table. Isaac joined her a moment later, the quizzical look on his face registering distantly. She didn't move, and his gaze followed hers to a knife stuck through the map in the middle of the table.

"I'm assuming you didn't do that," she said quietly.

"No. It's a map of Comity."

The surrounding city was, but the knife stuck out of a spot on the far side of the mountain.

She leaned closer. "Black Diamond mines," she murmured.

"What's there?" Isaac asked.

"Nothing. The mines have been dead for a hundred years." *What are you doing, brother?* "Come on," she said. "Let's go upstairs. It's time for lunch."

She strode out, the door closing behind her a moment later. Isaac trailed behind her. Bettina set a plate of sandwiches, marinated mushrooms, and a fruit bowl for Isaac on the table. As they sat, Fritt came in from the veranda and set the phone on the counter.

"Another earthquake struck down the coast this morning. Jessa and his detective left for home on the train an hour before. Another train was on route in the opposite direction. They were close to each other. One of those trains derailed, but there's no news yet on which one."

Isaac gasped. "Jessa."

Mal met Fritt's stare. The cold that had been gripping her slowly unfroze. Fritt swiveled to glance behind him. There on the veranda stood Uriah.

Mal got up. Uriah entered and dipped his chin.

"Where is Rune?" she asked.

Uriah shook his head. "We were returning home. When I awoke this morning, he was gone."

Mal struggled with a wave of dizziness that swept over her. A chair clattered, scraping the floor, and Isaac clutched her arm. "Jessa?" he whispered, his voice thick, clogging his throat.

She shook her head and glanced at Fritt again.

"I will go to the accident site," he said. "The King has also sent a contingent, but there are other casualties they will need to attend to."

"I don't think you'll find Jessa," Mal said. "Look for the detective." Fritt cocked his head with a frown but nodded. "And you, Uriah. Stay here in case I'm wrong and Jessa and Otto return." She straightened and brushed Isaac's hair off his forehead. "Don't worry," she murmured. "I'm fine. Eat your lunch and I'll be back soon."

"Where are you going?"

Isaac followed her.

"To check on things at the college."

"That's a lie."

She spun, and he stopped, keeping a distance.

"Smart boy. I want you to stay here. Jessa hasn't fed in several days."

She watched Isaac consider that. "He's gone longer," he said. "A lot longer."

"Not under stress. I won't be long. I just need to check on something."

"I can help."

"You can help by staying here."

She left him in the hall and hurried to her room, changing out of her dress into a pair of jeans and walking shoes.

When she returned downstairs, the entryway was empty, but when she pulled one of the cars onto the driveway, a glance in her rearview mirror revealed Isaac standing in the open doorway.

"Goddamn little bastard," she muttered. "Better stay where he is."

The trees and shadows and hills blurred as she flew on the road into Comity. Slate-colored clouds released a few raindrops.

She cut around the mountain on the city streets, maneuvering around the base to the other side.

You better not hurt him, Rune.

It sickened her thinking that. Would he? Rune had given up everything for Jessa. Destroyed their father. Ruined their family. It had meant nothing to Mal. War was the common denominator of their existence since the fall of both angels and humans. It was the unbreakable, banal thread through all of their history, and she was happy to see it finally snap. She'd wanted to teach a new history, relish life and freedom, fall in love one day. But Rune... Rune was a vampire in the darkest and truest sense. Passionate and haunted, driven and vengeful.

Would he hurt Jessa? Half human. Half of the creatures who'd destroyed Celestine City and murdered Abadi and Dawn?

Rune!

Go back.

No!

She wailed it. Because he was here, and it had been him all along. Had he murdered the drainer, Wen, and the whore?

Rune, please. It's not too late.

He laughed, and a shutter crashed shut in her mind, darkening her thoughts.

The raindrops quickened, falling faster.

She pulled in front of the car beside her and drove off the highway, turning toward the mountain. By the time she reached the mines, the rain fell steadily. There was no sign of Rune. She shut off the engine and clenched the steering wheel in her fists, then removed a flashlight from the glove box and got out.

Hills surrounded her. Lush green with tall grasses and the white and yellow of summer flowers. She hurried away from the parking lot, her breath loud in her ears, and climbed a hill to one of the old portals. The iron gates drew her on. They stood wide open. She wouldn't put it past Rune to open up the entrance here and enter through another one. But it didn't matter because the whole complex was connected, and all but the oldest shafts had been renovated before Rune's job had taken him away, and he had no more time to spend here.

She had no fear of the dark, but light shone inside. She slowed up, stopped, and took a breath. *Light.* The electricity had been restored.

"Rune," she whispered. "What have you done?"

There was no following him in secret. Clenching her hands into fists, she ran into a cavernous space still filled with equipment and memorabilia from the old mining days. Pipes and cables snaked on the floor and overhead. The weight of the rock pressing down woke her memories of Celestine. Woke her vampire instincts. Her fangs dropped, and her skin tingled. *Rune?* Was he close?

She ran until she reached a flight of stairs and went deeper into the tunnels. Wood beams lined the sand-colored walls as though holding them up. She stopped at the top of another flight of stairs.

"Rune!"

Nothing.

Except...

She whirled.

Vampire!

Looming without a sound, not human at all. And not Rune. She glimpsed an older face, handsome, cruel, and fearless.

"Who are you?" she gasped.

"The light bearer," he answered.

She spun and staggered. The vampire grabbed her, his hand in her hair, yanking her head back. He swept her off her feet. The rock ceiling spiraled over her head and she flew, pinwheeling her arms. She landed on the railing at the bottom of the stairs and rolled off onto the floor. Pain exploded. She gasped, eyes wide open on a gaping hole above her. It sank deep into the rock, blue black, peaceful dark.

Run!

Rune.

The vampire thundered down the stairs.

She staggered up, stumbling, bent double. Warmth filled her. The walls swayed, leaning in and out. Something sharp hit her in the back, and the floor flew up at her. She hit it and flipped over, the swell of pain washing away in a strange heat. Wasn't death cold?

Blurry-eyed, she looked at the vampire crouched above her. A whooshing sound grew in her ears. It was her blood, she thought. But it was slowing. She was dying, but confused. Maybe something had broken inside her.

"Too bad," said the vampire, stroking his finger against her cheek, but his words sounded like laughter.

As her vision drew in, sorrow and fear filled the darkness. She'd never fall in love now. She'd failed Jessa. She wanted to cry, but not now. Not here. Seneras didn't weep. They laid waste. Nothing changed in this world, not even in her. She was vampire, and Rune's roar thundering behind rock filled her with a dark glee.

51

IN THE DARK

THE HOWL ROCKED through Jessa like a bomb. Like Celestine City raining down, drawing him out of the deep dark. The light, dull as it was, pierced his eyes like knives. A flashlight beam ricocheted off a wall as his legs crumbled and he dipped out of Rune's arms and dropped onto his side, slowly focusing on Mal's eyes and outstretched hand. His heart pounded agonizingly fast, but his body was frozen around it. Pain burned through him.

Solomon.

The vamp stood behind her, slightly crouched as though braced against the force of a thunderous roar. It bounced off the walls in booming waves. *Rune.*

Jessa stared, shocked, the burn inside him freezing in a chill.

Rune glowed, a sullen reddish smolder, brightening, expanding, sizzling from the tips of his fingers. Solomon backed away, raising his own hands. The red bolts shot from Rune's fingertips, but arced upwards as the ground rose and shifted and dropped beneath them. The force of the aftershock rolled Jessa against the far wall. A roar filled his ears, shuddering like thunder. There was nothing to grab onto. He rolled again, this time against Rune, who fell over him then scrambled back up.

"Rune," he whispered.

Fingers brushed against his face, and his strength seeped away.

When his eyes opened again, he was alone, lying on his side. The lights didn't work here, and a cone-shaped glow from a lantern spread up the wall in front of him. Strange shapes oozed out of the black rock—all golden orange like the lantern light, all dripping like fossilized syrup. He rolled his eyes, casting a look above him. Mist spread across the rock wall, thinning, thickening, laying flat, receding.

Then, inexplicably Rune was back, kneeling down and lifting him up. He grunted and staggered under Jessa's weight, his breath heavy.

"The cave-in cut Mal off. I couldn't get through, but we'll find another tunnel and come in from the other side. I can feel her. It's okay."

It took a long time. Or maybe it was only moments before Jessa got his voice to work again. "Why?"

Rune shifted Jessa's weight. "I put you to sleep because I couldn't leave you. I didn't trust that woman on the train. I thought you were in danger, so I brought you with me. I don't want you to fight me either, and I know you will. A long time ago, I found a tunnel in Celestine that I didn't have time to explore, but I never forgot it. I was young enough and romantic enough to think it led to the treasure."

"Crazy..."

Jessa's tongue was thick, words trapped in his head. But it didn't matter. Rune went on talking.

"Qudim was a... a strong ruler. But in love. Deeply. Passionately. A royal. I defied him. I would do it again. Who is wrong? The one who preys on another for thousands of years? Or the one who stumbles onto a victory? And the Upheaval... That was no victory. Still... We were tossed to the bottom of the heap. Our family, once above the Dinallahs, forever disgraced. Qudim was insane with grief. That is our legacy. Passion. Obsession. The others... They act only out of greed. Vile hate. I won't let them get the treasure. It is for us. For our redemption."

Jessa recoiled. Or he wanted to. Maybe he managed to withdraw a little because Rune's arm tightened around him.

"Mu-murder."

Rune flashed him a look, the whites of his eyes gleaming in the near dark. He shook his head, hurt crossing his face. "No, brother. Not murder."

52

IT'S WHAT FRIENDS DO

MAL'S CAR was in the long strip of parking lot and the only one there, but Isaac had lived long enough on the streets he'd learned to trust nothing, so he swung the car away and drove back to one of the thicker clumps of trees. It wasn't great cover, but it was better than nothing.

He got out of the car and staggered like a drunk. The horizon tipped like a teeter-totter, back and forth. Wrapping his arms around a tree, he clung to it until it stopped.

Leaves showered to the ground.

After a few minutes he pushed off but only made it halfway to the mine entrance before he ducked down into the grass as a figure in a cap and heavy jacket emerged from the mine and came down the road at a run. The guy threw a glance over his shoulder, then fled through the weeds. It took only a minute before he disappeared into the trees.

Isaac hurried on now. At the entrance to the mine, he tucked the flashlight he'd brought with him from the castle into the back of his jeans and—

A hand clamped down on his shoulder.

"Wait a—"

"Fuck!" Isaac lurched forward and swung around in a panic, flashlight raised before he brought it down with a swipe. "Jesus Christ."

"What the hell are you doing here?" asked Otto.

"I followed Mal."

"Mal? What is this, a family reunion?"

"Vampire-style."

Otto snorted. "Funny. Wait here."

"Like hell. You're hurt anyway."

Tiny bandages held together a cut near Otto's hairline and a purple bruise bloomed around them.

"It's nothing. Rune is here."

Isaac tried to hold back his shiver at the tingle of electricity that ran through him.

"Why?"

"He has Jessa with him. He's after something. A treasure of some kind. I think he thinks he can get to it through the mines. People have died for it, so I don't want you here. Go on home." Otto slid by him. "Do you have a car?"

"One of the Senera's. I hid it. Somebody ran out of here a few minutes ago."

Otto pinned him with a stare. "What did they look like?"

"Vampire. Bigger than most. Scared though from the look of him. What if it caved in in there?"

"It probably has. More reason for you to stay out here."

"I'm not a kid. I've been through worse, an' I ain't goin'."

Otto's jaw bunched, but then he only said, "Stay out of my way," before he advanced through the portal door.

Glowering at his back, Isaac followed him. His heartbeat slowed at the sight of a brightly lit cavern off the corridor. Otto detoured inside where a dome-shaped ceiling towered above them.

"What are you doing?" Isaac asked.

Otto tapped a display case attached to the wall. "It's a map."

Isaac rubbed his arms in the cold. He wanted to turn tail and run, but something was pulling him on. A whispery tug that had him trailing Otto back into the main corridor. A caress like the one that wrapped around him at night and clung to his skin during the day. A presence. It permeated every stone in the castle and lingered in his memory from the day Mateo was killed. It was the same presence that had been in the fog, and Isaac wasn't afraid of it. He longed for it with every remembered feeling of comfort and safety he'd once known before the Upheaval had stolen everything from him.

It was good. And he was sure it was Rune.

They turned into a tunnel that was panel-lined like somebody's living room. The cold deepened here, and Isaac shivered. And then Otto was running. Movement drew Isaac's eye to a figure on the ground. "Mal!"

He raced after Otto, who dropped to a knee when he came near her and bent over her. Isaac landed against Otto's back and fell beside him. Blood came from Mal's mouth, staining her fangs. Her beautiful face was colorless, slack, but her eyes burned.

"Let go," she murmured. "Can't... stay."

Otto stroked her hair back. "Let go?"

"Rune," she whispered. "Let me... go."

Blood seeped underneath her. Tears flooded Isaac's eyes, and he took her hand. "Don't die."

A smile pulled at her lips. "Sound like... Rune. I hear him."

"What happened?" Otto asked.

"Vampire. Hit me. I fell... on something. I can... can feel it. Rune... is with Jessa. The ceiling... fell."

"Is Jessa okay?"

She squinted and shook her head, fingers tightening on Isaac's hand. "Rune... charmed him."

"I thought that was a myth," Otto said.

Like teleportation, thought Isaac. Like turning into a fog and—

Feed her.

Isaac's back snapped straighter. Otto stared at him.

"Go on. Get Jessa," Isaac said. "I can take care of Mal."

Otto gaped. "How?"

"I'll feed her."

"You can't. Not with an injury like this."

"I won't... stop," Mal whispered.

The voice came again. *Good boy. Don't be afraid.*

"Go," Isaac said, pushing at Otto. "That other vamp that ran off. We have to hurry before he comes back with help."

As though he hadn't thought of that Otto's face blanched in the dim light. He looked down. "Mal."

"Go," she whispered.

After another few seconds, Otto jumped to his feet, snatched the flashlight still sticking out of the back of Isaac's jeans, and hurried for the ladder.

Isaac returned his attention to Mal. She grimaced, forcing a smile.

"I told you to stay."

"I ignored you," Isaac said.

Slowly, he bent, his gaze on the rock wall, his heart fluttering in a panic. How much blood until he died? But the voice whispered in his head, the same voice that stole into his dreams at night, the voice in the fog, the voice his heart told him was Rune's.

Trust me.

"Trust yourself," he whispered, right before pain shattered his brain.

53

ON HIS WAY

THE EARTH ROCKED AGAIN. Daylight beckoned him, but
Otto detoured to the map in the display case and dragged his
fingertip over the glass to the next nearest entrance. Hurrying
on, he dashed back out into the dim daylight.

Adrenaline drove him, pumping through his veins like fire,
pushing away his worry over Isaac and Mal. He had to get to
Rune.

A thin strip of cracked, forgotten pavement appeared in the
weeds. He ran until he reached another gate in a cage around
another entrance. The metal lock on the gate hung on a rusty
hinge. He dragged the gate open and snapped on Isaac's flashlight. The shaft in front of him angled down into a dark that
swallowed the beam of his light. He took a breath and
plunged in.

Now he hunted Rune, tracking him into the guts of the
earth like the vampire from hell he was. No dark was dark
enough to stop him. Jessa was his.

Mine!

Fated.

His Jessa. His light and joy in the utter darkness that had

been his life for so long. It was fitting the battle should happen here, underground and in the suffocating dark.

Only Jessa breathed life into him now.

His flashlight led the way. When he came to a split, he headed back the way he had come. When he hit a dead end, he reversed and crawled through an opening in the wall. Soon he ran toward the sounds—solid, thumping echoes.

His light revealed a figure in front of him.

Rune ignored him. His shirt was off, sweat beaded on his tattooed skin. Otto slowed, mesmerized by the intricately lettered design on his back. The Letters of the Revelatory Passion.

When only a few yards separated them, Rune turned and hissed. His fangs glistened, his eyes burning. But he followed the hiss with a laugh. "Damn earthquakes. All your fucking fault," he muttered.

"Get away."

Jessa lay on his side beside the wall of rock Rune had just dug through. Cool air wafted into the corridor.

"There is no treasure, Rune."

"You're wrong. An earthquake a few years ago opened a fissure that drops down into a cave in Celestine. When it happened, I stopped the renovations as a precaution and later on pretended I'd lost interest in starting them up again. I was too busy, I said, but I wasn't too busy to explore. I know where the treasure is now. You should have brought a gun. It's all that'll stop me."

"I'll stop you."

A grin split the beautiful face in front of him. Once, before the darkness had entered him, Rune must have been as light as Jessa, and the flash of understanding that hit Otto at that thought seared him with a cold fire. He was no better than Rune. He'd brought on his own fall too.

"Give up, Rune. It's over."

"You don't know what *it* is, human. It's my duty. My destiny."

"No." That was a whisper. Jessa's.

Rune stooped, but his gaze hung on Otto's. "I don't want to hurt you."

"I can't let you go," Otto said. "You're a murderer."

Rune's smile was slow and sad. "A killer, yes, but not a murderer."

"Brillen was garbage, but you don't pick who lives and dies."

"That wasn't murder. I stopped a murder, and the victim got away. You don't know what you think you know."

"Turn around and put your hands on the wall."

Rune laughed and—*flew*.

He soared, arms swooping like wings, and Otto staggered back, trying to twist away. Rune landed on his feet with a smile. "You can't win against me."

"I already have."

Shock flashed in Rune's eyes, darkening to anger. He lashed out, slamming his forearm across Otto's face. It knocked him against the wall, and he fell onto his knees. His ears rang, and a booming sound filled his head. Rune reached for him, and Otto lunged. His momentum pushed them both crashing into the rock wall. Otto wrapped himself around Rune, but Rune twisted, and his slippery skin slid out of Otto's grip.

Scrambling sideways, Otto crouched over Jessa and grabbed him under his shoulders. Jessa's arms flopped as he tried to lift them and hug Otto back.

"Go," Jessa whispered. "Rune won't—"

Otto soared on a crash course with the ceiling before Rune tossed him back onto the ground. Otto's air blasted out of his lungs. His throat seized and strangled him. Rune grabbed his shirt and yanked him up.

"You can tell Zev to leave me."

Otto gasped. "You. Are—"

"Cursed but free," Rune said with a smile.

"Under. Arrest."

Rune laughed and tightened his grip on Otto's collar, choking him again. "Will you pursue me to the ends of the earth as one of your great poets suggested? Are you such a tortured soul, Detective?"

"Committed," he gasped.

Rune's face twisted with some strange pain. "To whom?"

"My sister."

"Laudable, but you must lose today. Not me." Rune twisted his grip on Otto's shirt and dots began to dance in Otto's eyes. He took a chance that Rune didn't know about the circle of the Nine. His lungs heaved, and the sound that burst out of his mouth grated like broken rock. "You don't... have... all... the necklaces."

Rune's grip tightened, and Otto's ears rang. The whoosh of air rushing back into his lungs lit him with fire. Rune's lips pressed close to his face. "What are you talking about?"

Otto dragged in another raspy breath. "Nine... nine necklaces."

His roaring blood deafened him until Rune chuckled. "What necklaces?"

Otto gasped. "You don't... have them... all."

"I don't have any, and you have nothing."

The darkness flooded back, the pain flaring to life in his lungs. Otto knew he struggled, kicking. Then the earth shook again, and he tumbled downward. He hit his head and light burst, flashing like a strobe. Rune was fighting with something on his back. He howled in pain and surprise and twisted like a dervish right as the light winked out and darkness descended.

54

A DRAINER WITH BALLS

JESSA SANK his fangs into Rune's neck. The fingers that grabbed the back of his shoulders dug in like pounding nails. The pain wracked his shaky body for only an instant before lassitude slipped over him. His limbs went slack and warm. His jaws relaxed, and Rune twisted and wrapped an arm around his waist, holding him up.

No anger. The rage fire in Rune's eyes had gone out. He smiled. "Silly boy. So be it."

Jessa fell, landing on something warm and solid. A heart beat under his ear, suddenly quickening. *Otto's.*

Otto sat up, bringing Jessa with him. Jessa rolled to his knees, grit seeping back into his body. Otto stood, and Jessa followed him. But Rune was already halfway through the hole he'd ripped from the wall. He pulled a silk bag on a string from around his neck and shook his head when Otto took a step forward.

"No," Rune said. "We are too alike, you and I. But I am lost. You? Live and pick a new fight." He dropped the bag on the ground. "Those are the necklaces. Give them to Zev and don't follow me."

"Stop," Jessa said. "Don't go. I know you didn't hurt anybody. I know you."

"You were born of love. I was not." He shifted his gaze to Otto again. "I wasn't the only one hunting the necklaces. Your sister died over one. Her murderer is dead too. I'm sorry I wasn't in time to save her."

Otto swayed, and Jessa grabbed him.

"*Geli'feth*, brother."

Dumbstruck, fumbling in his mind for the meaning of the old Celes word, Jessa said nothing. And then Rune was gone, vanished in a mist that disappeared behind the wall. Otto darted forward, but there was nothing there anymore besides the bag on the ground. He scooped it up, and Jessa remembered.

Goodbye...

55

OTTO'S NEW JOB

"YOU WANT me to work for you?"

Otto ignored the champagne glass in Zev's fingers as he waited for an answer. Not that he liked champagne. He didn't, but the desire for a drink still crept up on him. He took a swig of the fizzy apple juice Mal had bought for her *I'm-not-dead* party as she called it. Vampires survived grave injuries, but she'd almost bled out by the time Isaac fed her. She'd gotten lucky, and now she was celebrating, and Otto was sipping apple juice from a bottomless supply because she'd bought cases of the stuff as though she anticipated he'd be at every family function until the end of time.

Zev sipped the champagne then set it on the wall that surrounded the veranda. "Come. Walk with me."

Scowling, Otto obeyed. The bastard was a king, after all.

"Some people would consider a job offer from me an honor," Zev added.

"You threatened to drain me."

"Well... a sometimes effective means to an end. What would you do anyway?" asked Zev. "Work for the police? Do you want that?"

Did he?

Was he the same person who'd started this investigation? He'd been hunting his sister's killer and now?

"Probably not."

Zev took them onto a gravel path alongside the castle. Lights lit the way and twinkled in the trees. The air was balmy, like the summers he remembered from childhood. *Miss you, Maisie.*

Laughter followed them, mixed with the clomp of car doors outside as people continued to arrive. Behind them trailed several vampires, Uriah among them, conscripted to Zev's bodyguards.

"Well," said Zev. "I'm offering you work, you know. I trust you."

Otto shot him a startled stare. "Why?"

"You are honorable," said Zev. A grin flickered on his face. "Volatile, but honorable. You honored your sister's memory. Honor matters more than loyalty. If you want loyalty, get a German Shepherd, I always say."

Otto laughed, the sound and the feeling of it in his chest, surprising him.

"I'll remember that."

Now the grin stayed on Zev's face. "Consider my sense of humor a perk."

The path took them alongside the front porch and busy driveway. From where she stood at the top of the steps, Mal turned to gaze at them. Fritt stood at her back, dipping his chin to their guests and gesturing to the front door. Mal wore another red dress that barely covered her ass and black spiked heels. Her hair hung in the same profusion of braids she'd done Jessa's in for the night. The gloss on her lips gleamed red from across the distance. She lifted her chin and flashed a smile at him.

"A bit of a contradiction, that one," Zev said.

Otto would never have imagined he'd have any fondness for her. "Who knew she'd have a heart."

Something like sadness crossed Zev's face. "We all have."

Did he mean Rune? Well, they had been boyhood friends, hadn't they?

"Do you want me to find him? Rune? Is that why you need a private detective?" Otto asked.

Zev was quiet for a moment. The crunch of their footsteps on the gravel grew louder as they put the house behind them.

"I want you to find a human actually, though I will have many other tasks for you to do."

"What human?"

"We'll have time later for that. Will you or won't you?"

"You never asked me for an accounting of the investigation, you know?"

Zev shrugged. "You solved the murder. It was what I asked you to do."

"I solved something. I'm just not sure it was a murder. But you knew that all along."

"I didn't actually."

"You didn't tell me everything you knew. You didn't tell me Rune was involved."

"I didn't know he was. I only suspected. I couldn't tell you how he fit in."

"What's your relationship with him?"

Zev's face softened, his look of tenderness visible even in the dark. "We were friends once. Before the war. Before Qudim's fall. I have no idea what he's doing."

"I won't call you a liar, King Dinallah."

"That's advisable. We don't always know what we think we do."

"Somebody always knows something," Otto said. "And I know Rune's in the middle of this. I just don't know how. Jessa says Rune promised he'd never leave him, so that means he's still around, but Jessa's a romantic. People are dead and Rune's hand has been in most of it. He killed Acalliona."

"You still aren't saying murder," Zev commented.

"Somebody else was there. Somebody who got away. My gut tells me Rune stopped Brillen from killing him, whoever he was. Okay. Good. But why was he there?"

"I don't know."

"Me neither, and I don't like that. He had seven necklaces, and he gave them up."

"For you to give to me, so I could give them back to the families."

"There are two more necklaces."

"According to you."

"Rune is on the loose and looking for them. The Adi 'el Lumi killed Mateo, thinking Mateo was the blood whore with Brillen. Brillen is dead, probably by Rune's hand, and the blood whore got away. The drainer who killed my sister is dead too, her necklace stolen by Rune when he killed her murderer for it, I'm guessing. Wen was supplying the Adi 'el Lumi with human blood and got caught in the crosshairs. Maybe he knew something, or maybe he was just expendable. My guess is that Solomon Frenn knocked him off and took his body to confuse things. I'm also pretty sure Frenn had one of the necklaces at his shop and Rune got it after trashing the place looking for it. For a while, I thought Rune was connected to the Adi 'el Lumi, but now I don't, though I think Frenn is, and both him and his cronies and Rune are after the last two necklaces. Now here's the curious thing. The Adi 'el Lumi most likely plan to take Rune down to get the necklaces they think he has. But Rune... He gave them up. Why? Now he's looking for two necklaces that won't get him the treasure without the first seven. That's the thing that isn't making any sense to me."

"I guess that's a mystery for another time."

Otto smiled into Zev's amused eyes. "Is it though?"

Zev shrugged. "I trust you'll solve that mystery too. Just be patient. I'll have work for you in the meantime. If you agree to work for me, that is."

Otto took a breath, smelling oak and jasmine. Blew it out again. "Yeah, okay. I'll work for you."

"Good."

"What about the first necklaces?" Otto asked.

"Baubles," said Zev. "And the mines are too unstable now, anyway."

Otto had lost the bag in another quake. All his energy had focused on getting Jessa and Isaac and Mal out in time. A crack in the earth had raked across the valley and water, gushing from a hidden aquifer, had raged through it, snapping trees in its wake and filling another valley below.

"And the treasure?"

Zev chuckled. "Your theory of the crime was interesting, but the treasure is a myth. I told you. The Adi 'el Lumi perpetuate it because it serves their purposes, that's all."

"What is it?"

Zev's lips twisted. "I told you, it doesn't exist."

"I changed my mind about calling you a liar, King Dinallah."

"And you are a disrespectful employee, private detective Jones."

"The start of a wonderful relationship," Otto commented.

Zev grinned. "I agree."

56

MINE

THE NIP in the air was welcome after the early warmth. It was after midnight, but the celebration went on.

Jessa found Otto in the kitchen, sitting glumly, while Bettina and the temporary help arranged food and drink on the platters the servers took to the guests.

"Chicken. You can't hide in here."

"Yet, I am," grumbled Otto.

His glare was a smile to Jessa. He met it with a real smile. Though Rune wasn't here, he had gotten away, and Jessa was sure he was close. For days, he and Isaac had pieced the broken statue in Rune's studio back together, Jessa remembering enough about glass to meld the pieces into one. It looked bent and battered, but Jessa kept it in his room, anchored to the wall.

"Have you seen Isaac?" he asked.

Otto shook his head. "Not since before the party."

"Hiding, I guess."

"Smart kid."

Jessa took Otto's apple juice away, set it on the counter, and snatched Otto's hand. "I know a better place to hide."

He flipped his hair back and pulled Otto onto the veranda and down the steps.

"Where are we going?" Otto asked.

He was slow, slowing Jessa down, but he didn't resist. They went under the trees in the miniature orchard, the air sweet with fallen fruit.

Jessa fell back into the arm Otto slung around him. "You look beautiful tonight," Otto said.

Jessa sighed a laugh. "Mal's handiwork."

"No," Otto said.

He was taller than Otto tonight in the heels Mal put on him, and he wobbled on the rocky path. But soon they exited the shelter of the trees and headed for the moonlit greenhouse.

Inside, Jessa kicked off his shoes. "Look."

He hit a switch by the door and the center panels in the ceiling slid apart. The stars glittered, and moonbeams slanted through the dark air.

"Pretty," Otto said, but he stared right into Jessa's eyes.

Jessa leaned in and cupped Otto's face, thumbs at the corners of his mouth. His blood-red nails looked black in the dark, but Otto's pale eyes shone like the starlight.

"After the train wreck," Otto whispered, "I sometimes think I'm only dreaming you."

Jessa touched his lips to Otto's and leaned away again. "We don't always lose, Otto. Sometimes we win. I wish Rune had remembered that. Our father told us that we had powers, but the only real power is love. I love you, Otto. And I'm right here."

He turned his lips into the palm Otto cupped his face with and let Otto pull him closer. "I won't ever leave you again, baby prince. You are my fated love and the one I pick. Mine," he whispered, swallowing the whimper Jessa let out.

Love.

He had not thought he'd ever hear it, but Otto said it again. "I love you, Jess."

He pushed into Otto's embrace, meeting teeth and tongue, letting Otto bring him slowly down until he lay on the warm earth, surrounded by the fragrance of flowers and the light of the stars.

"I can see you," Otto whispered.

Tiny lights lined the inside of the greenhouse and joined with the stars and the moon to paint the world in shades of gray like the granite that once lined Celestine City.

Sitting on his heels, Otto pulled off his shirt, and then stuffed it under Jessa's head. Though stronger than Otto, Jessa loved Otto's chivalrous gestures. His words seldom conveyed his emotions, so it was his actions Jessa counted on.

He trembled as Otto's hands slipped under his shirt, gliding over the body chain he'd secretly bought at the jewelry festival. The push of Otto's thumbs against his nipples sucked Jessa's breath away, and he arched, hissing as his cock brushed against Otto's thigh. He grabbed Otto's ass, dragging him down, grinding against him.

"Hungry boy."

"Yessss."

His fangs broke through, and he let his mouth fall open. Otto consumed him, and Jessa burned. He wrapped Otto in his arms and legs, but he was parched, thirst mad and starved. Cold touched his skin, and his nipples ached. Vaguely, he was aware of Otto rising above him, pulling his clothes off. He spread his legs, his dick molten metal against his belly, arms wide. The fire raced under his skin, burning bright everywhere Otto touched him.

"Mine. All mine," Otto whispered, trailing each word with a kiss.

Jessa panted and arched his neck, feeling the scrape of Otto's teeth. What if...

"Bite me."

The nip was sharp zinging pain, but it wasn't—"Feed!"

Otto swiped a tongue along Jessa's jaw and bit his bottom lip. "I can't. I'd hurt you. My teeth aren't right."

"Bite me." His voice thickened and rumbled. "Please." Otto cupped his head, his hands solid and firm and strong. Jessa melted, a laugh tickling his tongue. "I want you."

"You have me," Otto said. "You're my light, Jess. Go ahead and feed."

The words floated in Jessa's head, dreamlike and impossible. He remembered the welling drop of blood Otto had withheld from him. The hypnotic scent that pulsed in Otto's veins inches from his teeth, whooshing like a constant wind in the trees.

And now...

"Fated," Otto said. "Forever."

Because even love begged the breath of life. A breath that escaped Jessa's lips in a soft sibilance. "Yesss."

Sitting up, Otto reached back for his pants with a grin. "Always prepared," he said as he rummaged through his pockets.

"You brought Band-Aids?"

Otto barked a laugh. "Brat."

"Baby prince."

"Yes," Otto agreed.

Jessa pulled his knees to his chest and shuddered at the touch of Otto's fingers. The slide inside brought a sharp burn with it. Jessa pulled air between his teeth. Goosebumps erupted on his skin. The touch on his gland sent shocks of pleasure through him, and he grabbed his dick, squeezing it in his fist.

"Oh fuck." *So good.*

He rocked on Otto's fingers, the bop-bop-bop on his gland tearing groans out of him. "Now. Now. I can't hold off."

A shocking emptiness followed his words, seconds before the push of Otto's dick split him open, bathed him in heat and stuffed him to bursting. He held still, absorbing the pain, its sharpness rolling away in a languid throb. He stroked his dick, rolling it into his fist.

"There you go," Otto murmured.

"Good," he said.

"Oh yeah."

Otto slung his arms under Jessa's knees, rolling him tight, stabbing deep into his belly. He nipped Jessa's lips between kisses.

"Like it?" Otto asked.

"Fuck yeah." His voice squeaked.

Otto grinned. "Gonna buy you a big fat dildo and watch you fuck yourself."

Jessa wasn't exactly sure why the thought of Jessa fucking and sucking himself was so enticing to Otto, but his dick jerked at the idea too. *Weird.*

"Faster."

Otto pumped his hips, jarring Jessa's body with thrust after thrust. He bent low, his pants hot against Jessa's cheek.

"Bite... bite," he grunted. "Bite, you gorgeous vamp."

And Jessa reared as though Otto had called on the Ellowyn in him. His fangs erupted to their full length in a split second of agony, and he sank them into Otto's neck. Blood poured into his mouth. Rich as the earth. Sharp with metal. Sweet like the moldering of leaves. The taste and aroma swirled like a fog, smothering him, pushing him down in the dark. He clutched Otto's shoulders and struggled to pull himself into the light, panicking as the blood pooled in his belly, weighing him down.

But suddenly he gasped, and the blood turned to sugar in

his mouth. Exhilaration sang in his veins. Otto's hoots of joy filled his ears.

"Fuck, yeah, my goddamn vampire!"

He laughed, warbling as Otto pounded him harder and harder. His ass burned, his balls full and achy, about to burst. He whipped his dick, blind to everything but the stars and the wisps of mist across the moon and the dig of Otto's fingers in his hips as he pulled Jessa's ass hard against his crotch, buried deep inside him.

Otto's climax shook through Jessa's body, and a fire as hot as the core of the earth shot out of his dick in blissful spurts.

Otto fell on him, and Jessa clutched him closer, the beat of Otto's heart the sound of his own.

LOOKING FOR HIS

A LINE of light spread on the horizon, and Isaac rolled off the picnic table at the first rest stop he'd come to outside of Comity. After washing up in the bathroom, he trudged along the highway a few minutes later. Mateo had told him the name of the whore with Brillen and where he'd run, and that's where Isaac was going. He was probably a fool to leave the people who cared for him, but Jessa didn't need him anymore, and he doubted Rune would ever return—and Rune was waiting for him.

Calling him.

THE SECOND BLOOM

THE SUN WAS HIGH, shining down on the quiet yard. Birds sang, and a breeze carried the scents of the garden onto the veranda. Jessa was half asleep on a chaise lounge under an umbrella. Otto sat beside him, staring at the blue surface of the pool.

A dragonfly hovered above the water, lifted, and motored off.

August.

Only five months since Otto had stood here with that putz Prosper at his side, staring derisively at a freckled crossling.

He touched his throat. His skin tickled, and the touch of his fingers awakened Jessa's scent in his nostrils. Stretching over the arm of the chair, he stroked along one of Jessa's red-tipped fingers and watched the smile form on his face.

"You're the high prince now."

The smile faded. Jessa opened an eye and tilted his head. "Mal is higher. I'm yours."

Otto smiled. "You can be anything you want, Jess."

"Yours," Jessa said, turning his head away again and closing his eyes.

Mine.

Otto drank his lemonade, wishing it had bourbon in it, but not wishing it enough to go get any. He watched the faint ripple on the water's surface and enjoyed the heat of the pavement baking into his heels.

Somewhere in the mountain that loomed beyond the garden was a treasure worth killing for. An obsession that had endured ten thousand years.

It meant nothing to Otto.

He turned to gaze at Jessa's face again. Perspiration beaded on the side of his nose. His hair was tangled from his braids, his nail polish chipped in places. Otto's blossom. He wanted to go searching for his flower that afternoon. *It blooms twice, he said. Early spring and late summer.*

Maybe this was Otto's second bloom. And his last.

"I love you," he murmured, watching the return of Jessa's smile.

"I love you too."

Love was the only worthy obsession anyway.

Looking back across the quiet pool, Otto watched the fog slide out of the trees and disappear in the sunlight.

ABOUT THE AUTHOR

So... About me. I've never run a marathon or scaled Mt. Everest. I've never scuba dived or sky dived. I've surfed though. That was fun. I have six tattoos, and I really love ink. I also love all plants. Zinnias are one of my favorite flowers. If you've never see a zinnia, look it up. Very pretty. It's an old-timey plant but super easy to grow. Anyway, the big thing I do is write m/m erotic romance. But as much as I love romance and sex, I really love going deep into the dark with my characters. What are their wounds? How can I peel them raw and drag them into the light? This leads to some fairly dark stories sometimes, but even the dark ones come with humor. I think the contradictions in people are ripe for hilarious scene setups. I need humor and light in my life, otherwise, I go into some pretty dark places myself. I live with only one cat now—I once had thirteen. That was crazy. I take up most of the things I research for my characters—photography, tarot, and jewelry making for example. I even bought a recorder once because Ori from *Jesus Kid* played one. I love that part of my job. I also love to walk and lift weights. I'm not a big fan of yoga—just throwing that out there. So far, all of my characters embody something of me, and all of my characters have given me something of them. But no matter what the struggle is from book to book, love always wins out. I'm strong on plot, strong on character, stronger on love. You can count on happily ever after from me every time. I write my stories to open hearts and uplift spirits. Love matters. It counts. And it's for everyone. Peace.

Made in the USA
Middletown, DE
07 July 2019